Dear Reader:

Shattered Souls: how many of them do you know? In the majority of my books, I include backstory of the characters' lives because I am a huge believer that what happens to us in our childhood is a direct indicator of how our lives will turn out. In this wonderful novel, Dywane D. Birch does a magnificent job of getting that point across.

Shattered Souls tells the story of four friends who are bonded by unconditional love and repressed childhood memories that creep back into their lives to haunt them, control them and, unfortunately, remind them of the hurt and pain they were forced to endure at the hands of people they trusted. It is a candid and flavorful novel that addresses the aftereffects of abuse, neglect and abandonment in a thought-provoking, page-turner that will not only make you laugh, cry and scream out loud but keep you hanging on for more.

I have been a huge fan of Dywane D. Birch since I first read the self-published version of this book years ago. In one of my acknowledgments I commented that publishers were crazy for not re-releasing it because it should have sold hundreds of thousands of copies by then. I am delighted to actually be the publisher given the opportunity to announce this prolific author to the world. Dywane was also a contributor to *Breaking the Cycle*, the 2006 NAACP Image Award Winner for Outstanding Fiction.

Thanks for your support of this novel and all the other Strebor titles.

Stay Blessed,

Zane

Publisher
Strebor Books International
www.streborbooks.com

ZANE PRESENTS

SHATTERED SOULS

2007
Gladys—
Peace, love & many blessings
Enjoy the journey!

Soulfully
Jane B

ZANE PRESENTS

SHATTERED SOULS

DYWANE D. BIRCH

SBI

STREBOR BOOKS

NEW YORK LONDON TORONTO SYDNEY

Strebor Books
P.O. Box 6505
Largo, MD 20792
http://www.streborbooks.com

ISBN-13 978-1-59309-110-1 .
ISBN-10   1-59309-110-9
LCCN 2006938903

Cover design: © www.mariondesigns.com

First Strebor Books trade paperback edition May 2007

10 9 8 7 6 5 4 3 2 1

Manufactured in the United States of America

For information regarding special discounts for bulk purchases,
please contact Simon & Schuster Special Sales at 1-800-456-6798
or business@simonandschuster.com

DEDICATION

In memory of all the children whose souls have been shattered
by abuse, neglect and/or abandonment… And to the men and women
who still carry the hurt and pain of their childhoods.

ACKNOWLEDGEMENTS

Wow! Six years after the initial self-published release of *Shattered Souls*, three subsequent novels and publication in two anthologies, and this journey still seems surreal. I truly know I would not be where I am today if it weren't for the Almighty Father who has guided my steps. I am humbly grateful for His grace and mercy. Despite whatever obstacles that have been placed before me, He has blessed me with a gift, and has allowed me to touch the lives of others through the power of words. I thank Him for the wonderful people He has placed in my life, people who have made a lasting impression, leaving their prints in my sand.

So, with sincere gratitude, I would like to acknowledge the following people for touching my life, whether for a season or a lifetime:

My mother, Alice, for being the glue that has kept me together when I have felt like falling apart;

My siblings, Melissa, Jason and Yolanda;

My nieces and nephews, Mykeeya, Carissa, Daniel, Danieya, Faakhira, Na'eemah, Aanisah, Quaadir, Zhaakira, Damonte, and Antiniyah;

My grandparents, Mrs. Roberta Reevey and the late Rev. Kingdom J. Reevey;

My extended family, Aunt Mary, Aunt El, Uncle Ronnie (I miss you immensely!), Mychele, Denise, Michael, Tamiko, Pam, Pat, and Duane;

My sister in heart & spirit, Val-Val;

My special friends, Cynthia Manning, Rodney & Cynthia Fisher, Lonjeté Garland, Trena Parks-Bradley, and Tradawn Parks;

My other "moms," Ms. Vernetta Williams and Ms. Etta Caldwell;

My literary friends, Danita Carter (congrats on the new book! We still need to get together soon to celebrate), Anna J, Nakea Murray, Cashana Seals, and Tiffany;

My wonderful agent, Sara Camilli, for her patience;

Zane, for being my biggest supporter and fan from the beginning;

Lonnie & Joyce Railey, Leslie Taylor, Stacy Foster, Lorie Stroble, Yasmin Allen, Angela Coleman, and Derek Overton;

Tru Books/Café and the rest of my Hartford, CT family for always showing me love;

The Book Clubs, Ujima-Nia Book and Social Club (NJ), Deep in Thought (NJ), Illuminations (NJ), Imani Book Club (AL), Ebony Expressions (DE), In the Company of My Sisters (DE), As the Page Turns/Jonestry Book Club (PA), Club Mimosa (PA), Sistahs by the Shore Reading Circle (NJ), Sacred Thoughts Book Club (NJ), Minds in Motion (MD), S.T.A.R. Book Club (PA), P.E.A.R.L Book Club (NJ), Shades of Soul (NJ), Just Between Sisters (NJ), Literary Voices (NJ), Sisters in Spirit (VA), Circle of Friends VIII (NC), and the many others, for supporting my literary endeavors, and embracing an unknown with open hearts and minds;

To all the readers, and my "special" fans, for always spreading the word, embracing me as one of your favorite authors, and sharing words of encouragement. It is because of you that I remain inspired to write—thank you!

And finally, to the one who has made this journey worthwhile, my partner in crime, Collen Dixon. I can't fathom this voyage without you by my side. Thank you!

Indy, Tee, Britton and Chyna are extensions of me. They have become more than characters who are friends in my head, they have taken up space in my heart and have become family—people I have cried for, cheered for, and continue to hope for. Hopefully, they touch you as well in some way, no matter how big or small. With that said, fasten your seatbelts and enjoy the ride.

Soulfully,

Dywane D. Birch
Email: bshatteredsouls@cs.com

BRITTON: **LIFE**

DAMN, LIFE IS GOOD. Here I am sitting out on my terrace in the nude, listening to a Tracy Chapman CD, drinking lemonade, and taking in the most mesmerizing view of sparkling turquoise water. Right at this moment, I feel blessed and I'm thankful. I give thanks for my life—I am debt-free, stress-free, and carefree. No one believed me when I said I was packing my bags and leaving the States. But I knew, from the first time I set foot on this island four years ago, that this would become my home. Was it a difficult choice to make? No doubt. But it was something I needed to do for me. See, I am a firm believer that no one else can live your life for you. And your life shouldn't be consumed with trying to satisfy everyone else all the time. There comes a time when you have to make choices for yourself and live accordingly. And now that I've had time to reflect and to become more in tune with what my needs are, I have finally come to realize that there is a big difference between making a living and having a life. I got tired of just going through the motions. I got tired of living among the walking dead. And I was damn sure tired of putting other people's needs before my own. I knew that if I didn't make changes in my life, I would have fallen into a deep pit of depression. And I was afraid of being haunted by the "would've-could've-should've" syndrome. So, for once, I threw caution to the winds and said, "Fuck what others think or feel." I worked three jobs to save enough money to live here comfortably. I paid off all my bills, sold my town house and car, rented out my condo, and placed all my valuables in storage. Then I made sure I had access to enough emergency cash just in case things got crazy, cut up all my credit cards except for my platinum American Express, and bought a first-class ticket to the Dominican Republic. So here I am, living on one of the most beautiful tropical islands in the world, with peace of mind.

Now, don't get me wrong. I'm not saying life has always been kind to me, because it hasn't. And it damn sure isn't perfect. Trust me, I have survived my share of personal storms. Some with more wind and rain than others. But I've weathered them. From light drizzle to hurricanes, I've endured the beatings of cold droplets and heavy gales. I am convinced it was a higher power that gave me the mental and physical strength to pick myself up, brush myself off, and press on. Although the skies have cleared for now, I know lightning and thunder can still strike at any time. That's why I try my best to take nothing for granted. At this point in my life, I am better prepared, with experience and well-taught lessons, to pay closer attention to life's storm warnings. Basically, I've made a conscious choice to keep dead weight and negativity out of my life. For good!

I think the hardest part of packing up and moving was knowing I wouldn't be able to spend much time with my friends and family. When I told my mother I was moving, I thought she'd flip, but she didn't. She hugged me and said, "Good. Just make sure you have enough room for me because I'm going to need a place to stay when I come down for vacation." Then she smiled and said, "I love you very much and I just want you to be happy, so if this move makes you happy then I'm happy. You deserve it." My eyes were heavy, but I didn't let any tears surface as we embraced. I knew then I'd miss her more than I'd thought. It seems like mothers always know the right things to say at the right time.

Now, my sister, on the other hand, felt it was her duty to let me know exactly what she felt about it: "The Dominican Republic? Isn't that one of the poorest countries? Why in the world would you move there? Boy, every time I turn around, you're running off somewhere. I don't know why you gotta keep moving around. Don't you know you can't run away all your life? And what do you plan on doing down there?" My sister is four years older than me and can be overbearing and too opinionated. So, of course, when I told her I planned on doing *nothing*, I thought she was going to blow a gasket. "You mean to tell me, as hard as it is to find a good job, you are giving up a good-paying job to lay around on some beach?! Sometimes I just don't understand you. You're not going to be able to live off your savings forever." I love this girl dearly, but I wish she'd try harder to just be my big sister instead of my mother.

Yes, I gave up my full-time job as a school psychologist, a job that I'd had to struggle to keep because of all the political crap that goes on within school districts. They had a problem with me not conforming to their rules and with being too vocal. I guess I was a bit too rebellious for them. Well, I had a bigger problem with them. Anytime I had a fifteen- or sixteen-year-old in front of me who read and wrote on a third- or fourth-grade level, I wanted to know what the hell was going on. How in the hell do you just pass a child from grade to grade without ensuring that kid has mastered every task on or above grade level? Each time I had a fifteen-year-old still in the eighth grade, I wanted to know what alternative support was being offered. And what would really set me off was the school's audacity in allowing students to graduate without being properly armed educationally to survive in this world. Come on now, if children can't read or write, then that means they can't fill out an application. So how do you expect them to become self-sufficient? As far as I was concerned, someone in the school system failed those children and I wanted schools to be held accountable. I really couldn't get with the concept of just throwing students out of school or classifying them "emotionally disturbed" just because they were disruptive. Yes, there are some youth who really do have significant emotional problems, but many disruptive behaviors in the classroom are due to teachers failing to properly educate and prepare our youth for the next grade level. It just seemed like no one was *really* interested in trying to understand that maybe some kids disrupt the class because it is the only way they know how to avoid being embarrassed by the limitations we have imposed on them.

So, when we fail our youth, what do we do? We expel them. Bottom line, it just seems much easier to throw these children out of school or classify them as requiring special education than to deal with the real cause of the problems. And because many parents don't know that legally, most schools can't just drop students from their rolls—they can't suspend or expel them without providing an alternative learning environment—I would inform parents of this and challenge teachers and school officials on it, and remind them of their responsibility to properly educate our youth. So, in a nutshell, my presence in the school system wasn't welcomed with open arms. But, hey, I never cared about being liked as long as I was respected. And respect is what I got, regardless.

I also gave up my cushy part-time job as an adjunct professor teaching psychology. But that still doesn't explain why my sister should concern herself with my job security. After all, I do have marketable skills, and I'm confident that I'll have no problem getting a job when I decide to move back.

Anyway, a part of me knew what she was *really* getting at. She thinks I moved because I was running away from commitment or another failed relationship. I'll admit that when I was younger, I did use moving from place to place as an avoidance mechanism. It was my way of trying to control my feelings and ensuring I didn't get hurt. But this was different. I moved as a means of letting go. True, I pulled out of a relationship. But I didn't run off or move on because of it. I moved because I needed to be alone. I needed a sabbatical year, or two, to collect my thoughts without interruptions. I needed space to sort through my own emotional baggage, far away from family and friends. Okay, so maybe moving here was going to the extreme but sometimes I am an extremist. I'm either hot or cold. In or out. Sometimes downright impulsive. There is just no in-between with me.

To be honest with you, I could sing the blues all day and all night about some of my impulsive behaviors and failed relationships. But why bother? It's not like I can change what's already happened. As far as I'm concerned, the past is a chapter in my life I don't wish to revisit. I am living for this second. Hoping to live for another minute. Another hour. Another day.

Nothing in life is guaranteed, so I am living for the moment. I'm just hopeful that I will continue to awake to another day, and I'm thankful when I do.

Whenever I call home to get the 411 on what's happening in the States, I get hit with the 911. Someone has either been robbed, killed, raped, beaten, or all of the above. It's really a damn shame. The U.S. is *supposed* to be one of the most advanced technological forces to be reckoned with, and it can't even properly protect its citizens. Makes you wonder what the country's priorities really are. Hell, that's probably one of the reasons I never felt connected there. Never pledged allegiance to the flag. For what? I've always questioned the U.S.'s allegiance to its people's struggles. I'm not necessarily referring to the individual struggles of being African American. Although that *is* a key issue. I'm talking about the struggles within our families. Within our communities. Within each race. Well, one thing's for sure: As long as there is no justice, there will never be peace.

I will say this: Living here has definitely given me a whole new attitude about life and the things we take for granted. Like family and *true* friends. I think sometimes we get so caught up in the hustle and bustle of just trying to survive that we tend not to tell the ones who mean the most to us how important they really are to us. I know in the past I was guilty of that, on more than one occasion. Family for me consists of my mother, my sister, and my nieces. My extended family? *Puhleeeeze*. Let's just say I don't play 'em too close. I know I can't control who I'm related to, but I can sure control how I relate to them. As far as friends go, and I mean *real* friends, I have only three—Damascus, Indy, and Chyna. That's my clique for life.

Damascus, who goes by the name Tee, is the first and only male I can honestly say I've embraced as a soul brother. Even though we've had our disagreements and a couple of fistfights, we've still been able to keep it real with each other. I've admired his strength in being able to come out on top despite having no one positive in his life to guide him. On the surface, he comes across like a self-absorbed ruffian from the 'hood who's only concerned with his own self-indulgences, but I know better. Hell, we were roommates for three years, and one thing's for sure: You never really get to know a person until you live with him. So all that slick shit he talks...let's just say I know what's underneath the steel armor. Still, he is probably one of the most conceited and sex-crazed brothas I know. I've always believed his mother meant to name him Narcissus. I swear, he is stuck in that stage of development in which his body is the object of his own erotic interest. I've always teased him about falling in love with himself the first time he saw his reflection in the mirror.

But I'll give him his props; he is a smooth-looking brotha, and a lot of females are big on him. I've just always had a problem with the way he measures manhood.

Indy gets the award for having the most attitude and I love it. I like the fact that she calls it like she sees it, and she's not afraid of challenges or taking risks. She doesn't care what comes out of her mouth; if she feels it, she says it. She tells you from the gate what her expectations are, and if you can't flow with it, then she just moves on without blinking an eye. I tell her that that's not always a healthy way of handling things, but she says, "Boyfriend, please. It's my way or the highway. Besides, how you gonna give me advice you don't live by?" Anyway, aside from being angry with almost every man in the world, she is a very successful businesswoman who will not settle for anything less than the finer things in life. In layman's terms, she's material-istic as hell. But then again, people say that about me.

There's a rawness about her that is exciting and provocative and men *love* it. There's also this kinkiness about her that seems to drive men crazy, figu-ratively and literally. I've warned her to be careful because that could be dangerous. She has this remarkable way with words that just cracks me up. You have to hear some of the things that come out of her mouth to under-stand what I mean. Nevertheless, despite her sometimes sharp tongue, she is a very sweet person as long as you don't cross her. If you take her kindness for a weakness or try to play her, *watch out!* And when she says she's gonna do something, that's what she means. Trust me, she's a woman of her word.

Out of everyone, Indy is my road dog. Back in the eighties when we were away at college we used to travel back and forth, by car or plane, between Virginia and New York just to get our weekend workout in at The Paradise Garage, Nells, The Tunnel, you name it. Oh, and I can't forget about Club Zanzibar out in Jersey. We used to tear those spots up. We'd carry our back-packs filled with bottled water, baby powder to make the floor slippery, and a facecloth and towel to wash and dry off the sweat. We'd change into our dancing gear, move toward whoever was generating the most energy, then find a nice corner to spin until daybreak. We took road trips to the Aggie-Fest in North Cacky-Lackey, the Freak-Nic in Atlanta, and the Greek Picnic in Philly (then on to the Belmar Beach in Jersey the next day). And no summer would be complete without the annual Labor Day weekend in Virginia Beach. That's where we first met and clicked. The summer of 1983.

Now, Chyna is what many brothas would refer to as a "dime-piece." She's gorgeous. She's flawless. She's just one classy, sophisticated woman who carries herself like a lady at all times. I don't think I can ever recall her cursing or saying anything negative about anyone. Imagine a young Lena Horne with green eyes and long, sandy brown hair that flows past her butt. She's the only one of the three of us who's married and she has four children—one daughter and three sons. Her husband, whom none of us can stand, is a successful businessman who has given her every material thing imaginable; yet there's always been something missing. We—no, let me speak for myself— *I* don't like him because I've always felt like he treats Chyna as if she were his trophy. If you met him you'd understand what I'm saying. Granted, he has a great physique, but that face…Aaaagh. Let's just say he has the body of Hercules and the face of Magilla Gorilla. Outside of that, I just don't feel he appreciates her the way she should be appreciated, nor has he encouraged her to do anything other than be dependent on him. So I consider her knocked up and locked up by a man who likes being in full control of her. But I do give her a lot of credit, and I'm proud of her. Even though she was a young teenage mother and wife, she still didn't let that hinder her from completing her undergraduate studies and then going on to grad school to obtain two master's degrees. It's too bad she's done nothing with them. She chose to be a full-time mother and wife instead, for which I commend her. Having a home filled with love is something she's always wanted. Well, she has a gorgeous home in pristine suburbia; I just wonder how much love her husband has been able to fill it with.

The four of us are different yet so much alike. We come from different backgrounds, but our struggles…let's just say we've been able to look to one another for support, encouragement, and understanding. That's probably why our friendship has survived for fifteen years. Now, I'll be the first to admit, Indy's mouth has sometimes created tension among us, probably because she says what she feels. But she says what needs to be said out of concern—

nothing more, nothing less. In any event, there's mutual respect among us, and nothing any one of us says to the other would or could put a wedge between us. Hell, our friendship has been sealed with tears, laughter, and *unconditional* love. Besides, I know all their secrets.

I'm sure one of the reasons I love being in the Dominican Republic is because there is a sense of family and community. The community *is* your family. An outsider who has gained their *confianza* will be embraced as family. Believe me, it's not something easily gained. Personally, I like the fact that trust is highly valued here. It's too bad it's not the same way back home. Maybe the world would be a better place to live if it was. There just seems to be a lot of phoniness at home. I have never been able to get with the superficial people and smiling faces who'll stab you in the back with the same hand they extend to you. There's always some type of hidden agenda. That's cool, but I'm not the one. And I'm definitely not with all the negative energy they generate. I only wish we could embrace one another for who we are instead of for what we have. Perhaps a pot of peace and happiness would be found on the other side of that rainbow of madness we slide across.

Here, life is sweet and simple. There's not that sense of urgency that you experience back home. Everyone is so laid-back and friendly. I have to admit, I've had to make some adjustments in my attitude and get used to not having many of the expensive luxuries I thought I could never live without like my 325i convertible, the fifty-two-inch-screen TV I hardly turned on, and the convenience of buses and subways. It really took me a while to get used to riding a moped to and fro. I haven't got up the nerve to upgrade to a motor-cycle yet. But I'd rather do that than ride in a passenger van that carries people and animals together. I tried that once and threw up from the thick July heat, the smell of sweaty bodies, and the odor of funky farm animals.

I also had to get used to the fact that here, friends and relationships are more important than work or being on time for appointments. Sometimes I laugh trying to imagine waltzing or whistling into work forty minutes late because I was talking to a friend. Ha. Not in Jersey. Friendships and family are definitely not priorities there. The one thing I still struggle with is the fact that privacy is unimportant here more so in the rural areas. Now, I don't mind company from time to time, but this popping in and out is not my cup of tea. Here, doors are kept open and it is considered strange to close them and not accept visitors anytime, day or night. Whether invited or not, guests will be offered something to drink and asked to stay if mealtime is near. Hell, back home, if you came to my spot unannounced, I wouldn't let you in. And if you continued banging on my door or ringing my doorbell, I might just throw a mixture of bleach and shit down on you. But I'm changing. Slowly.

Well, I don't know about you, but I'm gonna finish listening to my Tracy Chapman CD, finish reading this book by Ernest Gaines, *A Lesson Before Dying*, then pack my luggage. In two days, I'm off on a seven-day Carnival cruise. Yes, this is truly the life. And I have to agree with Tracy Chapman: "Heaven's here on earth."

At 5:00 a.m. I was up pacing the oak wood floor in my bedroom. I couldn't sleep. My mind raced with thoughts of the character in that book I read last night. The book was deep. I really hate it when a book can stir up feelings in me. I felt angry, sad, and happy all in one reading. I think what touched me the most was his diary to the teacher. I honestly had tears in my eyes and for a minute, I almost allowed them to flow. Almost. But I opted to run. I ran two miles in the sand along the water's edge. The wet sand felt good under my feet, and when the cool water pulled back into the ocean, I could feel myself being gently pulled in too. I ran fast and hard against the ocean's soft morning breeze. I needed to outrun my thoughts before they caught up with me before the tears I felt for the character in that book overwhelmed me. So I ran and ran and ran until it hurt. Until I could think of nothing else except getting home and back to bed.

Before I even got through the door, the phone rang, and I knew it could be only one of five people calling. But I guessed it was my sister because she's the only one who calls me all hours of the day and night. She seems to think that because I don't have to get up to go to work every morning there are no time restrictions on when she should call.

"Good morning, snookems," I said while glancing over at the round wood clock hanging over the door. Six-thirty a.m. This better be good.

"Hey, Brit," she said in a sullen tone. "You're up awful early. What are you doing?"

"I was just sitting here waiting for you to call," I said sarcastically. "What's wrong?"

"It's Daddy. And before you go off, just listen to me, okay?"

I asked her to hold on, lit two sandalwood incense sticks, pulled off my wet clothes, sat on a wooden barstool, then took two deep breaths and picked up the phone. "I'm listening."

"Daddy's real sick and he really wants to see you. He knows you won't call him or accept any calls from him, but he wants to talk to you."

"About what? I have nothing to talk about and I'm not interested in seeing him."

"My God, Brit," she said with annoyance. "Can't you just let go of whatever it is that's been eating away at you? Our father is dying, and the least you can do is give him a chance. I don't know what you think he's done to you or hasn't done for you, but he's tried to be there for you. You've always pushed him away."

"Look, we've gone over this a thousand times already. I don't have any ill feelings toward him. I just have no use for him. I let go a long time ago. Now, I'm sorry to hear about his health but I can't feel something I—"

"No one is asking you to *feel* anything," she snapped. "All I'm asking is that you, for once, stop being so damn selfish. Just go see him or at least call him. Please. He's our father and he needs you. You owe him a chance."

He needs me? Ha! That's a laugh. What the fuck was he doing when I needed him? She acts like I should embrace him with open arms because he's on his deathbed. That's not my problem.

"I don't owe him shit! You know what? I'm really not feeling this right now. So let's either change the subject or hang up. Better yet, if you feel the need to mention him to me every time you call here, then I'd rather you not call me at all. I'm glad you have a relationship with him. I respect that. So why can't you try to respect the fact that I don't want one with him? Never have, never will."

She sucked her teeth, then took a deep breath. "Brit, you've never tried. He's your father. Just give him a chance before it's too late. Can you at least do that? Brit, don't you understand life can't always be about you? People make mistakes, and just because they don't measure up to how you think they should be or should've been doesn't mean they can't change. You need to get off your high horse and stop being so stubborn. You act like you're so damn perfect."

I let silence fall between us for what seemed like minutes before I went off on her. She was really trying to get on my last nerve. It's a good thing I don't smoke 'cause I would have killed for a pack of Newports right about then. I knew what I needed: air. This wench was suffocating me with this shit. I walked over to the patio, pulled open the double oakwood doors, and leaned against the frame.

The reddish-orange sun had finally risen to its spot in the sky. The blue Atlantic Ocean rolled calmly up against the white sand. I could see a young couple holding hands while they walked along the beach. She stole a kiss, then ran off with him chasing behind her. Although they couldn't see me, I could see smiles on their faces. It was picture-perfect.

"Perfect! Amira, get over yourself. There's nothing perfect about me, and I don't come off like I think there is. So what the hell are you talking about? You call here like you know what's best for me. I'm thirty-five fucking years old and I don't need you telling me what to do. I live by my own rules, and rule number one is: I will do what the fuck I want. Rule number two: Don't call my fucking house telling me what I need to do. I love you very much but you have plucked my last fucking nerve."

Click. She hung up on me. She calls me, works my nerves, then hangs up on me. I really didn't mean to snap on her but I asked her to drop it. But no. She just wanted to keep flapping her jaws. I'll call her later to apologize, maybe. She acts like I'm supposed to fulfill his last wish or something. Why should I? He didn't fulfill mine. So what if he didn't know what my wishes were? He should have asked. And so what if I pushed him away? I was only a child, and he should have been there for me, regardless. No parent should let a child dictate to them how they should react or respond to their children. Parents have a responsibility to love and protect their children as best they can. His best was not even trying. So, as far as I'm concerned, he gave up on me. He failed me as a father and I won't forgive him for that.

After I took a twenty-minute shower, I ate a fruit salad, put on my Oleta

Adams CD, opened the glass balcony door, then lay across my unmade full-size bed. I drifted off to Oleta singing "Get Here." When the phone rang, I jumped. I glared over at the clock on my dresser. I had slept for four hours. I contemplated whether or not I should answer it, then picked up on the eleventh ring. "Hello."

"Okay, you dirty-birdy. Are you ready for round two?" It was my sister. "I don't appreciate how you went off on me this morning. But I'm ready for your ass now," she said, ready to attack. "I've had my coffee and a good fuck; now it's on, boy." Her voice was stern. I burst out laughing as I imagined her standing with her hand on her hip and her finger in my face looking and smelling real raunchy after "a good fuck."

"What the fuck is so funny? Don't make me have to fly down there and curse your ass out then fly back home."

I sat up on the edge of the bed and stared out the window. "Oh, girl. Kiss my behind. I'm sorry for screaming on you. But sometimes you don't know when to just drop shit. If I go see that man, let me do it on my terms. If I don't, then it's on me. Let me be the one to live with whatever decision I make. Please just respect that."

"Brit, my childhood was affected by him as well. But that was years ago. He's tried over and over to make up for his mistakes. No one is asking you to have a relationship with him. Just listen to what he has to say. That's all. Please think about it, okay?"

Again, I became silent. I walked out onto the balcony, leaned against the railing, then closed my eyes real tight. When I opened them, I spotted a man and a little boy building a sandcastle on the beach. The man hugged the little boy, then kissed him on his forehead. I answered, "I'll think about it."

"Promise?"

I sighed heavily. "Yes, Amira, I promise."

"Good. Now, guess what?" she asked, then answered before I could guess. "I'm pregnant."

Pregnant? Her house is already overpopulated, and she's excited about bringing in another mouth to feed. "Damn, girl. Seems like every other year you're spitting another baby out that cooch." I laughed. "Don't you think eight crumb snatchers are enough?"

"Nope. I already told Wil we are going to keep trying until I have a boy. But he says he's gonna have a vasectomy."

"Well, good for him. That's probably the smartest thing he's said. For his sake, I hope it is a boy," I said, sounding sympathetic. "Maybe he just doesn't have any extra Y chromosomes to pump out."

"Well, I'm not consenting to no damn vasectomy, so he better start drinking a whole lotta protein shakes."

I shook my head. That poor man. I don't know how in the world he puts up with her. All she does is sit at home and have babies while he works two jobs just to make ends meet. She loves to argue, but he lets her fuss, which she hates because homegirl likes to rumble. He never raises his voice or his hands to her. But when he puts his foot down, she changes from a lioness to a kitten. Yep, she really lucked out when she married him. I don't think anyone expected them to stay together this long. She was a feisty city girl and he was a laid-back country boy who was ten years older than her. Twenty years later, they're still going strong. I don't care how many hours of the day he works; he always has time for his girls, including my sister. And on his days off, he watches the youngest girls so my sister can have some free time for herself. My nieces are lucky to have a father like him.

"So, Brit, when you gonna settle down and have some kids? Your nieces would love to have some little cousins, and I'd like a few nieces and nephews of my own to spoil rotten."

I snapped out of my daze, then walked back into my bedroom and stood in front of the floor-length mirror. I ran my fingers through my thick braids.

"Excuse me? Girl, you musta lost your mind. Never. I am *never* having kids, and I'm as settled as I'm gonna be. I'll leave the baby-making for you and Wil."

I've already been there, done that, and I don't want to go there again. Yes, I was married. A long time ago. My family thought I had gone mad. Of course, my sister had the most to say. "Boy, you're too damn young. …You should get to know her better before you run off getting married. …What in the world is your rush?" Telling them my intended bride was four months pregnant nearly shifted the earth's axis. "Pregnant?" My sister's eyes almost popped out of their sockets. "How in the world are you gonna support a baby and stay in school? I know you don't think you're gonna drop out.

...It's probably not even yours. ...Girls will try to trap a man in a minute, especially if they think he's a good catch. ...And you're fine as hell, got good hair, and she sees success written all over you." I was flattered by my sister's concern, but my mind was made up.

I was barely nineteen, a sophomore at Howard University, and still living off my father's child support. So what? I was in love and there was nothing anyone could say or do to change my mind. My mother just shook her head and said, "This is not the kind of life I wanted for you. But it's your life, so you're gonna do what you want. I just wish you'd wait until after the baby's born." I could hear the disappointment in her voice as she tried to sort through my earlier rambling about how I didn't want *my* baby born without being married. I saw the hurt in her eyes, but like she said, it was my life.

Celeste was three years older than me, a junior studying English and communications, and already had a five-year-old daughter, whom her parents were raising. Apparently, she had peeped me way before I even knew she existed. We were in a few writing classes and electives together, but I didn't notice her much because I was too busy setting my sights on another Howard cutie. Sad to say, I was a sucker for a gorgeous girl with pretty hair, and H.U. was notorious for having some of the finest women on any campus. Celeste was definitely one of them. She was walnut brown, with wavy brown hair that she wore in an asymmetrical bob. She had beautiful brown eyes and the body of a young Tina Turner. She was the sophisticated, prissy type, the type I always fell for. You know, the type who always has her head in the air. It's sometimes hard to tell if it's out of conceit or just confidence, but for her, it was definitely both. Her makeup was always done to perfection, her hair and nails were always on point, and she always rocked a designer pocketbook and wore expensive shoes. A sista pumping a nice handbag and rocking a sweet pair of matching pumps always got bonus points with me. However, I didn't particularly care for her at first glance because she had a snottiness about her that I couldn't digest. She came off like her shit didn't stink, and if it did, nobody would care because it was *all* about her. I guess she had reason to think that way since a lot of brothas sweated her and gassed her head up to no end. Besides, the snobs were usually the ones who liked to get their freak on the most. But I wasn't one for sweating no one's child, no matter how fine she was.

Anyway, to get to the point, I let Celeste talk me into going back to her place after a Kappa Alpha Psi formal. As soon as we stepped into her sparsely furnished studio apartment, she seduced me. Well, actually, I'm not sure if she seduced me or if I just gave myself to her. We both were feeling no pain from the countless shots of Hennessy we took to the head. From that night on, it was nonstop sex. At her place, my place, in the backseat of my bronze Eldorado, in the dark at Rock Creek Park. Anytime, anyplace…we sexed it out.

So there I was, many orgasms later, standing at the altar in a beige double-breasted suit, nervously waiting to take a girl I'd known less than a year as my bride. Any uncertainties I'd had faded with the sound of the organ playing "Here Comes the Bride" as I watched the mother of my child wobble down the aisle, eight months' pregnant, with the twinkle of stars in her eyes and the most illuminating glow I'd ever seen. I was determined to love her "till death do us part." We said our I do's and pledged our love in the presence of a few friends and family at a small chapel in Maryland. The first and only thing my sister said to her was, "If you try to dog my brother out, I'm gonna whup your ass." My mother embraced her halfheartedly but was able to say an almost sincere "Welcome to the family." That's when it hit me: *I am nineteen, married, and about to become a father. What the hell am I doing?*

Life was full of twists. Everything was happening so fast. Before I could really think it through, it was too late. The damage was already done, and the honeymoon was over as quickly as the flip of a light switch. Reality set in. I had to juggle going to school fulltime, working fulltime, being a husband fulltime, and mentally preparing myself to become a dad fulltime, something I wasn't prepared to be. Not at nineteen. But I was *in love*.

Then, during the still of the night, I was awakened by loud screams coming from the bathroom. "Pleeeeeeeease God, stop these pains!" It was two-thirty a.m. I leaped out of our full-size bed to find my wife huddled in a corner between the tub and the sink with her arms folded around her swollen belly. She was sobbing and rocking, rocking and sobbing. My heart jumped in my throat; beads of sweat lined my forehead, then slid down the bridge of my nose and down the sides of my face. The seven minutes it took for the ambulance to respond to my 911 call seemed like an eternity. We were having a baby.

After fifteen hours of labor, I could see the crown of my baby's head. It was then that I felt the most wonderful feeling I ever dreamed possible. A life I helped create was about to emerge into the world. I silently prayed to God to give me the strength to be a good father. The doctor coached Celeste on when to push. First came the head. The doctor gently held it. Then came the shoulders. "It's a boy!" the doctor announced a few moments later as he placed his hands under my baby's head and back, then slowly pulled the rest of his body out. Our eyes lit up with joy when we saw our beautiful baby. I kissed Celeste, then smiled. I felt this rush of energy go through my body as I repeated, "It's a boy! It's a boy!"

But our baby wasn't breathing. There were codes sounding and doctors yelling, "Stat," and nurses scurrying around and Celeste screaming, "What's wrong with my baby? Don't let anything happen to my baby." And then there was me. Standing there in a fog. Seeing everything but hearing nothing. People's lips were moving, but I couldn't make out their words. The only thing I heard was, "I'm sorry, Mr. Landers, there was nothing we could do." I had gone from elation to devastation in a matter of seconds. My son was stillborn.

"You still think about your son, huh?" Amira paused, then sighed. "He woulda been almost sixteen."

"Yep," I said solemnly. "Sometimes I wonder what he'd be like if he were alive. I wonder what type of father I would have been." I paused, trying to keep from choking up. "I don't want to go through that kind of experience again. Never. You know, Amira, I never told you this, but the whole time Celeste was pregnant, I asked God to please let me have a pretty baby with good hair. I just took for granted he would be born alive and healthy. I've felt so guilty."

There was a moment of silence between us. "You would have been a great daddy. It's not your fault. Everything happens for a reason. That doesn't mean it'll happen again. I love you," she said, then kissed me through the phone.

I did the same. "I love you too, sis. Thanks."

"For what?"

"For always being in my corner. I really do miss you."

"Hey, that's what big sisters are for. I miss you too. Well, I gotta go. Don't be such a stranger. Keep your promise and give Mom a call before she starts bugging. Your nieces say hello."

"Give 'em all big hugs for me and tell my brother-in-law I said he's in my prayers. I'll keep my promise."

We hung up. My smile was replaced with a frown as I slowly walked back out to the balcony. It's moments like this when I wish I were back home. I could really indulge my addiction right about now. I guess being here has forced me to stay strong and not fall prey to my weakness.

Yes, I'm an addict who's been in recovery for almost three years. Moving here has helped my treatment. Lord knows I'd be hell on wheels right now if there were a Bloomingdale's or Saks. Hell, I'd even settle for a Macy's. That's right, I am a shop-a-holic. Oh, don't tell me…you thought I was a drug addict, huh? No. Not the kid. I think anyone who falls prey to drugs is extremely weak. I've seen too many people waste away from drugs. In fact, drugs are what destroyed my marriage.

A few months after we buried our son, I was offered a job as a bill collector for a small finance company in Norfolk. We both agreed a change of scenery would do us good. So we moved, transferred to Norfolk State for the fall semester and hoped for the best. Well, not only did the scenery change, so did Celeste. She started hanging out late, sometimes not coming home for two or three days. Stopped going to school. Stopped taking care of her self. Stopped caring. For one year after our son's death, I chased behind her from crack house to crack house trying to keep her off that shit. I know she was hurting. I was hurting too. But I couldn't keep coming home to shit missing out of the house or having money stolen out of my wallet while I was asleep. It's not like I didn't see the signs. When I found the small bag of baking soda in her pocketbook, she told me, "I use that to brush my teeth." Well, I guess she used the tablespoon with the burnt bottom as her toothbrush. When I found razors with white residue on them, a mirror with powdered residue on it, a bottle of cigarette ashes, cigarette lighters and makeshift pipes that had aluminum foil with tiny pinholes wrapped around them, I had to face the fact that I was sleeping with a basehead.

By the time I finally realized I couldn't keep trying to save someone who didn't want to be saved, I was already on academic probation and had been fired from my job. It became clear to me that she loved the streets and the drugs more than she loved me—or herself. And I damn sure knew it was time to bounce when I found out she was out tricking for product. I loved her. Seeing what she had become was just too much for me. I watched one of the finest girls on Howard's campus become one of the living dead. I thought I could love her enough for the both of us. Boy, was I wrong. I found out the hard way. But when you're in love, you see only what you want to see.

Since that time, my anthem has been that song "It Takes a Fool to Learn that Love Don't Love Nobody," which is why all of my relationships have been tenuous. I'll have a fling here and a fling there but nothing more than that. My heart has been under new management with a sign that reads Love Don't Live Here Anymore. Period.

Between my sister and that book, I don't know which to blame for my sullen mood. I'm so glad my cruise is tomorrow. Seven days of rest and relaxation is just what I need. I'm not gonna stress myself. Tonight, I'm gonna light every candle—I have about fifty—in this joint, listen to Curtis Mayfield's *New World Order*, and just chill. I'm not letting nothing or no one disrupt my groove.

2

INDERA: **MACK DIVA**

I HATE MEN. Well, not all men. And maybe *hate* is too extreme a word. But I definitely dislike them. Okay, okay…I dislike some men. And I know *all* men aren't bad. But the ones who are—I can't stand. As far as I'm concerned, they are here on earth strictly to get on a woman's last nerve. Men are usually the cause of most women turning into cold, nasty b's. And at the core of every woman's scorn usually lies a man.

I definitely hate—excuse me, dislike—the world for its double-standard attitude. Please tell me why it is that when a man sleeps around with as many women as he wants, he's a playa, the mack. It's cool because it's a dick thing, right? But when a woman does it, she's a low-down, trifling, dirty, stank ho. A trick, right? Well, let me break it down to ya: I don't care what you call me. I am none of the above and I gets mine. Hello. I don't playa hate. I regulate and congratulate. In a phrase, I'm doin' me. So, for all you men out there who wanna lie and mistreat women and for all you men who wanna cheat on your women, do your thang. If you wanna kick it with me, it's fine by me. Just know, it ain't gonna be no free ride. If you wanna play, you gotta pay. Make no mistake.

Sorry, ladies. Yes, I'm sayin' I'll sleep with your man. Nothin' personal, but any man who is willing to cheat on you is no damn good, and there must be a price to pay for betraying your trust and destroying your home. Wait a minute. Don't cut your eyes at me like I'm the cause of your home being wrecked. I'm a man-checker, not a home-wrecker. Don't get it twisted. As far as I'm concerned, a real man won't act on, or even entertain, the idea to cheat on you because he's committed to you and to his convictions to love you and only you. Real men don't run out on their families to be with another woman because their family is their priority. Real men stand their ground in the presence of temptation because they are emotionally, physically, mentally, and spiritually focused. So, if you're lucky enough to have a real man, then I guess you have nothing to worry about, now do you?

Oh, I'm sorry. Here I am dishing you my business and—hold up. Am I sensing attitude from some of you? Don't go there, okay? I am not interested in your man. I don't even go after men. They press me, okay? If I know a man is involved, I pays him nooch, but if he insists on cheesin' in my grill, then I'm gonna drain his ass. Simple as that.

Wait another minute. Did I just hear someone call me out my name? Oh, but I'm sure you're thinking it. Well, let me tell you like this: Before you start passing judgment on me, I suggest you take a look in the mirror. Because some of you have no room to try to come for me, okay? You know who you are—the ones who will throw up their legs in a victory V for free, then get left with nothin' but a swollen, stretched-out crotch and a stepped-on heart. Why? Because you confuse sex with love, and you think that if a man sleeps with you, he loves you. Honey, please. He is using you. And what about those of you who look for love in all the wrong places and faces because you'd rather have a piece of a man than no man at all. Why? Because you're afraid to be without a man. A man makes you feel like a whole, complete woman. Get over yourself. Oh, and what about those of you who are so desperate to have a man that you're willing to do anything to keep him. You'll move him in, you'll feed him, clothe him, put money in his pocket, let him lie around the house all day and ride around in your car all night while you work like a dog tryin' to support his ass. You'll accept his abusive behavior and his cheating ways because you don't think you deserve better. You think over time you can change him. Girlfriend, please. A man won't change unless he wants to change.

And let us not talk about those of you who will ride up and down on trains and buses to visit a man in prison. You'll stampede in the visiting halls like cattle to get to the nearest corner to hike up your skirt, to slob down his knob, or to pull drugs out your ass…all in the name of love, right? Then, on your way out, you got the nerve to try to be ghetto-fabulous smelling like a wet skunk with greasy lips. And then there are those of you who will spend your whole welfare check lacin' your man in the latest Timbs and Air Max flavas while you parade around in your Lerner and Dots fashions looking like a circus clown. And while he's stylin' and profilin', it's usually with another woman. Must I go on? Yes, yes, yes. I don't want *anyone* to feel left out. You wanna get fierce, I'll show you fierce, *okay?!*

So now I wanna give a shout-out to all the fatal attractions out there. You know who you are. The ones who will stalk a man to try to keep him. You'll slash his tires, put sugar in his tank, break into his house to cut up his clothes or him. You'll throw a brick through his window, you'll make your presence known any way, any how. You'll crank call his ass to no end and even harass his wife or significant other. All in the name of "love." Bitch, please. Your ass is *crazy!* And, you, Miss Night Prowler. You'll drive around all night tryin' to spot his ride, then sit outside until sunrise to see who he comes out with. You'll creep and crawl around corners and trash cans like a cat on crack, duck and roll between trees and bushes like some G.I. Jane, or shimmy-shimmy-coco-pop your way up fire escapes and balconies just to catch him knockin' someone else's back out. But then, even after you've seen it with your own eyes, you'll still let him talk your dress up and your drawers down. Ain't that much good dick in the world. Your ass is just dumb. And, you, Miss Inspector Gadget. Don't think I forgot about you. You'll drive yourself crazy checking his pockets and wallet for phone numbers. You'll check his collar for lipstick stains, you'll look in his underwear for sex crust, and then your nasty ass will even sniff and lick around his balls and dick for any leftover love drip. Now, you's one sick bitch, okay?

Then there are the groupies and jock-chasers. That's right, the traveling "ho, ho, hos" and away you go. You'll spend your last dime to slut around the world in search of a hip-hop or NBA star. You'll suck and fuck anyone with celebrity status just because you're a dumb, desperate, broke-ass trick looking for a treat. Oh, then there's Miss Cyberspace. You Internet and chat-room tramps are downright triflin'. Your insecure asses will sit in front of a computer screen for hours clicking through ads in search of love and will run off with the first nut who responds to your pitiful cry for attention. Get a life!

And, last but not least, the other woman. Miss Lonely on Holidays. Now, *you* are just pathetic. Girlfriend, where do you expect him to be on Christmas? With his family. Where do you think he's gonna be on New Year's Eve? Somewhere ringing in the New Year with his family. And what about Thanksgiving, Valentine's Day, Mother's Day, Memorial Day, Independence Day, and all the other traditional holidays? That's right, with *his* family. Now, he might be able to squeeze you in on April Fool's Day. Because that *is* what you are. One big-ass fool.

So, as I was sayin' before I was rudely sidetracked…I haven't even formally introduced myself. Since we'll probably be spending quite a bit of time with each other, I think it's only right that you know whom you're chillin' with. But first, I wanna apologize if I've offended anyone. I don't like giving fever, and I'm not down with the phoniness. So, if you got a problem with me, either come correct or bounce. Otherwise, try to get to know me first before you twist your face up. Ain't nothin' fake about me. I likes to keep it real so if you can roll with that, then it's all peace.

Anyway, if you'd like, you can call me Indera or Indy. Just don't call me out my name unless you add "miss" in front of it. Although I am Brooklyn born, I was bred within the confines of a Connecticut boarding school for most of my life. I guess with the exception of the three years I attended public school, it was a rewarding experience for me. That's if you want to call spending your time with a bunch of snotty, rich, white girls rewarding, and being the token "well-to-do" black girl an experience. In any case, my elite boarding school was where I felt accepted—even if there was a tuition attached to it. Ah, forget this crap. See now, messing around with you, I started digressing. And I know you really don't want me to go into my trick bag. So, movin' on.

Anyway, I have to count my blessings. At thirty-six, God and gravity have been good to me. I can still go braless without my breasts dropping to my knees, and my round, plump rump is still tight, right, and bubblicious. Well, okay, with the help of exercise and a low-fat, no-meat diet, I am able to maintain this hourglass shape. Some say I favor Me'shell Ndegeocello. Don't get me wrong, she's fly and all, but I can't see it. Others say I have the raunchiness of Grace Jones. Perhaps. Now she's one fierce diva. I'm definitely feelin' her, so I have no problem putting a little "Grace in your face."

And if I've given you the impression that I've been sorta liberal in the sex department, well, hey, I like to get my freak on. Men do it. Besides, when a sista like me got it goin' on from the top of her head to the bottom of her feet, it's only natural for men to wanna be all up in my space. But despite the number of men I've had, my love snatch can still grip a Tic Tac. Okay, okay, a Jolly Rancher.

Before we go any further, let me clear the air about a few things. First, I am by no means some around-the-way chickenhead nor am I some thirsty gold digger. And I'm damn sure no slouch. Financially, my thing is tight. Between my inheritance and smart investments, I am set for life. I am the proud owner of Weaves and Wonders, one of the most successful nail, hair, and body salons in the tri-state area. So, on the real, I don't need a man to do jack for me. Oh, I need to pause. My phone's ringing. Excuse me for one minute.

"Hello."

"What's up, sexy?" a smooth voice asked.

"Tee?"

"Yo, where you been, girl? I've been tryna reach you all morning."

"Boy, don't be checkin' for me like you my man."

"Yeah, a'ight. Don't front," he said, then blew a kiss in the phone. "You know the score."

"Fuck you."

"I've been tryin,' but you're scared of this."

"Whatever. So what's up?"

"Yo, check it, I wanna scoop you up today."

"Uh-huh. For what?"

"I miss you, Boo. Can't a brotha just wanna chill with his girl?"

I smiled. "Yeah, yeah, yeah. Hugs and kisses to you, too. Pick me up at the shop around six. And don't call me your damn boo. I hate that shit."

"I'll be there. And you betta not have me out there waiting all damn night. You got that?"

"You'll wait for as long as I make you wait, boy."

He laughed. "Yeah, a'ight, you heard what I said. Hey, yo?"

"What?"

"You still my boo." *Click.*

He makes me sick. Oh, I guess you wanna know who that was. It was Tee. No, he's not one of my men. We've been friends since college. Yes, I am a college-educated sista. A 1984 graduate of Hampton Institute. Oh, excuse me, Hampton University. Actually, I started out at Spelman like my mother but...

Anyway, we met at a Sigma-Zeta formal in Newport News, Virginia. I was dressed to kill in my green velvet, scoop-neck, Bill Blass cocktail dress with a cut-out back. My hair was pulled up in a French twist with little Shirley Temple curls cascading down my face, and I wore my mother's two-carat diamond earrings and matching choker. You woulda thought I was going to the Soul Train Music Awards. Well, from the moment my two sorors and I stepped out of my '81 forest-green Benz, we were turning heads. Brothas were like, "Damn, baby, what's your name...Yo, can I get those digits, sexy?" So, of course, I asked this one brotha who was standing in back of me, "What you drivin'?" As soon as he said he was riding with his boy in a blue Pacer, I looked him up and down, smiled, and said, "You're outta your league." Then we heard someone say, "Man, fuck them high-post bitches." My sorors and I turned in the direction of those words, and there he stood with two of his boys. Tee had on a tan single-breasted tweed suit and Pierre Cardin shoes and a tan Kangol tropic cap. The other two had on nondescript blue polyester suits and Florsheim shoes. *Country*, I thought to myself. Anyway, the three of us asked in unison, "Excuse me?" The light-skinned brotha with the Donnies Super Curl shag and round glasses said, "You heard me."

"You betta watch your mouth before I put my knuckles in your lip," I said, and handed my soror my gold-beaded clutch purse.

"You ain't gonna do shit, but if you keep talkin' shit, I'm gonna slap my dick in your lip," he said in a Southern slur.

Smack! Pop! Pow! That dumb-ass should've seen it coming when I got up in his face. I slapped his glasses off his face, then punched him dead square in his mouth. My two sorors jumped in and started punching and kicking him. We worked that fucker over. His boys were laughing and teasing, "Damn, James, you got your ass whupped by three fine sistas." The poor fool got up looking all dazed with his busted, bloody lip and scary curl.

"The next time you disrespect me I'm gonna piss in your mouth, you country-ass bitch," I said as my girls and I high-fived one another. The crowd laughed and clapped as we collected ourselves and strutted into the dance like *Three the Hard Way* to the sounds of "She's a Bad Mama Jama."

So for the rest of the night, my girls and I turned the party out. The sounds of *Blu-Phi, Eee-i-kee, Oooo-Oooop, Skeeeeee-Weeeeee, O-6,* etcetera, etcetera, echoed over the jammin' beats. Anyway, sometime toward the end of the ball, when they started playing all the jams—Barbara Mason's "Another Man," Jean Carne's "Love Don't Love Nobody," and Teddy Pendergrass's "Love TKO"—Tee walked over to me, grabbed my hand, and said, "Let's dance." Before I could say "Hell no," he had me in his arms, grinding deep into me to Luther Vandross's "Forever, for Always, for Love." The smell of his Kouros cologne pulled me closer into him. He had big strong hands, a muscular back, and, Lawd have mercy, a third leg that throbbed against the inner part of my thigh.

"Where you from?" he asked in my ear. For a minute, I thought he was going to stick his tongue in it.

"Brooklyn, and if you stick your tongue in my ear, I will slap the shit out of you."

He smiled. "That's nice," he said, and held me tighter in his arms.

No, you gettin' your hands off my ass and not tryin' to squeeze me to death would be nice, I wanted to snap. "Do you mind loosening up your grip and pullin' your dick from outta my thigh? I don't give out free nuts; it's bad enough I'm giving you a bump-and-grind blue-light special," I said, rolling my eyes.

When the lights came on, I got a chance to get a good look at him. You know how it is when you're at a party or club getting your groove on with a brotha you think might have it goin' on, but as soon as the lights come on, he looks like something from out of fright night? Well, not Tee. He was tall and deliciously dark. He had a wide nose, big brown eyes, and full lips that were wet and inviting. His smile revealed nice, white teeth and two dimples set deep in his cheeks. He sported a faded beard and short stay sof 'fro that was neatly cut. Okay, he was fine and sexy and had dick for days but he was also cocky and arrogant.

"So what's up with the digits?" he asked as he walked me to my car.

"What you drivin'?" I asked, then smiled when he pointed to a navy blue 318i parked two cars away. "Sorry, but I don't give out my number."

"Then let me get a kiss," he said, licking his lips and showing off the print of his thickness. "You know you want some of this."

"Nigga, get a grip," I said, closing my door in his face. My girls burst out laughing.

Now, I'm gonna keep it real with you. That night I was almost tempted, but I'm glad I didn't. That brotha is a whore. He's been through more women than cars through the Lincoln and Holland Tunnels. And like I said, the brotha is fine and he knows it. He's six-three, two hundred and ten solid pounds of sexy, chiseled man. Girl, he's almost every woman's dream: deep, dark, and delicious. Now, I'm not one to gossip, but from what I've been told, he's like biting into a box of Godiva chocolates, then waiting for the creamy treat to cling to your tonsils. Gag me, why don't you?

Anyway, back to me clearing the air. Where was I? Oh, yeah. I was saying I don't need a man to give me jack. And I'm damn sure not looking for love.

Make no mistake, there is no emotional connection for me. It's about sex, money, and control. You see, I can fuck their brains out, run their pockets, and send 'em home to their wives or girls, drained. And one thing I've learned: If you have good pussy, you can get almost *anything* out of a man. I'm not saying all men, but definitely some men. Those are the ones I take to the cleaners. Why? Because they are pathetic, confused little fools who think they are getting over on all women. Well, maybe some, but not this sista. Hell, most of the time I don't even have to fuck 'em. Usually, all I have to do is lay back, spread my legs, slap on the whipped cream, and let 'em eat this pussy out strawberry shortcake-style. Once they get a taste of this sweet treat, it's on; I have 'em hooked and wrapped. Then, when they've decided to pack up and walk out on their loved ones, I cancel them out like a bad check. *Poof!* Be gone! Just like that. I close 'em out and move on. Please. Because he says he wants to be with me doesn't mean he's gonna be with only me. Bottom line: Once a cheater, always a cheater. What I look like, some fool? Now, be careful how you answer that. I don't wanna read anyone.

Don't get me wrong. I do have a certain set of rules I always live by. Rule number one: No glove, no love. Any man who won't put on a latex wrap before slidin' up in me gets nada. Raw dawg is out.

Rule number two: No money, no honey. Money and expensive trinkets are what moisten my panty liner. So a broke man is a no-can-stroke man. I don't do charity sex and layaway pussy is out.

Rule number three: No place, no face. I am not layin' no man up in my spot. Papa can be a rolling stone but he *ain't* layin' his dick in my home. End of discussion.

Rule number four: No licky-licky, no sticky-sticky. If you can't eat this pussy right, you definitely out the box. Point blank: If you can't work the lips, you can't stroke the hips. And I *will* shut you *down*.

In addition to my little rules I have certain standards from which I will not deviate. First, he must be at least thirty—mentally and chronologically. I damn sure don't want no fifteen-year-old boy in a forty-year-old man's body or a thirty-year-old man boppin' around like he's still eighteen. I left the playground a long time ago.

Second, he must have at least a six-figure salary. Now, I'll work a brotha who's not packin' six figures, but he betta be well connected and have some political or corporate power. Whatever he does, it betta be a legit j.o.b. A brother pushing drugs is out. I don't want no Big Willy wanna-be tryna free his little whale in my sea of love. And I certainly don't want no feds runnin' through my spot seizin' and freezin' shit.

Third, he can't be fat. I don't want no piglet trying to oink-oink his porkroll in my nookie, suffocating me with his flab, or knocking me upside the head with one of his big-ass titties. I'm sure you can get more bounce to the ounce, but I'm just not down for two tons of fun. I have no time tryna roll some nigga's stomach up to get at his dick. Please.

And, last but not least, a suite—in the Waldorf, the Ritz, or the Plaza—is the only place I'll give up this love funk. A lady with class deserves a nut in style. Hold up. I think I better check my voice mail for messages. Excuse me for a minute.

There's four messages from Tee—he wants to see me tonight. Well, you already know that. There's one from Gordon. He'll be in the city next week and wants to spend the weekend with me. I might. He's a short, stocky brotha with a nice body and sexy smile. I met him at the Shark Bar a few months ago. He's single and lives somewhere out in Jersey. He looks as sexy as he sounds. But he has a lotta game with him, and he ain't tryna spend his dough. He definitely got his thang goin' on, though. I ain't givin' up the sex, but we can hang, maybe. Oh, and there's two messages from silly-ass Nick. Now, he's one of them weak-ass brothas I was talking about. I think I betta save these. This brotha is really off the meat rack. Listen: "Indy, why the fuck you send that shit to my wife? That was some real foul shit. Word on my dead daughter, you got yours comin', you crazy bitch." *Beep. Beep.* "What the fuck is on your mind? I've been good to your ass, and you turn around and dog me out. You got my wife beefin' with me. You definitely got it comin.'" Well, I guess you wanna know what that's all about.

Check it. I met Nick Simms about two years ago in D.C. while I was in Maryland visiting my sista-friend, Chyna, and her family. Chyna is married, has four beautiful children, and a fierce home. Girlfriend has money for days, okay? Well, it's her husband's, but who cares.

We met at a Norfolk State step show in, like, '81. I, along with a few other sorors, had driven up from Spelman for their homecoming activities. Well, when Chyna and the rest of my NSU sorors came out to step, she was front and center, throwing down. And, of course, they won first place. After the show, we exchanged numbers and we've been like sisters ever since.

Anyway, I talked homegirl into going to that club D.C. Live. So off we go, sharp as tacks. She sported a conservative mint-green Chanel pantsuit with matching pumps. Girlfriend was *ova*, okay? Now, Chyna is one fly diva. She always looks like she stepped off the cover of *Vogue* with her smooth, creamy skin and emerald green eyes. From a distance, you'd think she was a white girl because of her fair complexion, but when you get up close, you can tell she's a sista with those hourglass hips and that basketball booty.

Anyway, I was fly as hell in my black V-neck Versace minidress and matching black mule heels. Girl, that dress hung off the shoulders and clung to every inch of this body. And I was iced out from my two-carat emerald and diamond earrings to my five-carat matching tennis bracelet and anklet. We were *fierce!* As soon as we walked in the door, the brothas were all in the grill piece. Now, Chyna, as fly as she is, was tryna act all shy and shit at first. But I said, "Girlfriend, we did not come out to be wallflowers, so you betta act like you know and work this crowd." After a few Rémys, she loosened up some, but she still wasn't havin' no man up in her face or space. She'd hold up her ring finger, flash her ten-carat diamond, then say, "I'm married and I'm not interested." I, on the other hand, would look the brotha up and down from head to toe. If his gear was official and his footwear was on point, I'd give a friendly smile and put an extra shake in my ass. Unfortunately, I had to blast a brotha for steppin' up in my grill, then placin' his damn hand on the small of my back while he tried to get his mack on. Wrong move, okay? And he had the nerve to rock a leather suit with a cowboy hat and lizard-skin cowboy boots. I was a split second from tossing my drink in his face, but I tried to yank his damn arm outta its socket instead. "Listen, country," I snapped. "You betta back the hell up outta my space before I do-si-do your ass across this floor." Please. Who the hell did that rhinestone cowboy think I was? If you wanna talk, cool, but don't put your damn hand on the small of my back. Betta yet, don't put your hands on me at all. Anyway, the place wasn't all what people hyped it up to be, and I was ready to go once I heard that go-go music. It's definitely a D.C. thang.

I peeped a few sistas clockin' my work. "Nice dress" and "Girl, you workin' that dress" were some of their comments. One sista had the nerve to ask me if my dress was DKNY. *No she didn't!* Didn't she know DKNY was for broke bitches like her who couldn't afford the Donna Karan line? And, on top of that, she didn't even have her designers right. I smiled, "No, dear, it's Versace. Don't get it twisted." Country-ass. Anyway, I couldn't say the same for most of them. However, I will say, those girls from D.C. and Maryland will keep their hair laid. There may be a whole lotta fashion violations goin' on, but those wig pieces are always on point.

So, around one-thirty, Chyna and I were heading toward the door when this mahogany-colored brotha with a pug nose, big lips, and round Gucci-framed glasses stopped in front of me. Chyna, of course, being the lady she is, politely excused him and kept walking toward the door. I, to the contrary, put my hand on my hip, twisted my face up, put my finger in his face, and told him, "Get the fuck out my way!" He stood there smiling and looking all stupid.

"Damn, sexy, is that any way to talk to an admirer?" he asked while grabbing my finger.

"Do you know me?" I asked, snatching my finger out of his hand and glancing over at his Rolex. Now, I've seen fake Rolies but not in stainless steel.

"Sure I do. You're the woman in my dreams."

"Brotha, please. Not with that tired-ass line. Now get out of my face." Instead of the brotha just going about his business, he took it upon himself to walk alongside me. I hate to admit it, but he was kinda cute in a strange way. Almost like one of those little Pekinese dogs. At first glance, they're ugly as hell, but then they get cuter as you continue to look at them. So here was this little Pekinese look-alike rockin' a brown Laurentino suit, Ferragamo shoes, a chunky platinum bezel rope around the neck, and pushin' a Lamborghini Jeep.

I dropped him my pager number and that's all she wrote. He paged me every day, leaving cute little sweet nothings on the voice mail. I finally returned his call after two months of playing him like an old sweater, and we started dating. He'd drive up to New York to wine and dine me. When he told me he was married, I told him from the gate I didn't think cheating on his wife would be wise. For the record, I *always* try to give these cheatin'-ass men a chance to think about what they're saying and doing before they get into something they'll regret later. But, like so many others, he insisted.

"Look, what my wife doesn't know won't hurt her. I know how to keep shit on the low. I really dig you so let's leave my wife outta this."

"So what you want? Some side-dish pussy to tide you over when you and wifey ain't getting along? Well, there's a price for this pussy, and I don't think you're gonna be able to afford having me as your little mistress."

"Like I said, my wife ain't got nothing to do with what you and I are doing. Anything you want, baby, it's yours. Here, this is for you." He smiled and handed me a long slim box neatly wrapped in silver foiled paper. "It's just a little something to show you what I think about you."

I tore off the paper, opened up the Tiffany & Co. box, and smiled. It was a twenty-four-karat gold necklace with a cross filled with clear, sparkling white diamonds. We went back to his hotel suite and I gargled down his big, hairy balls. No, no. I only suck dick on special occasions. Like, when you buy me a full-length mink or give me an all-expenses-paid trip to Europe. Anyway, I sucked his balls, jerked him off, and then let him stick his pencil dick in my chocolate furnace. I gave it to him analiciously. From that moment on, the brotha was strung. He would always surprise me with expensive gifts. And although he liked "momma's ass gravy," he wanted to slide up in this hairy love slot. But I made it very clear: "You wanna stick it, you gotta lick it." I'd squat over his face and rub my fat pussy lips over his mouth, but he insisted that he only ate his wife's. *For now,* I said to myself. Hell, he'd try to suck the shit out of my ass but wouldn't eat my pussy. Go figure.

Then, about two months later, he called saying he was in the city, was horny as hell, and was "ready to tear the pussy up." *Humph, we'll see,* I thought. So I showered, gave the cooch a Summer's Eve rinse although I was already springtime fresh and shimmied into a gray Armani slip dress. I packed my Louis Vuitton overnight bag and grabbed a three-pack box of Zulu condoms—*oops! I forgot they weren't made with him in mind.* So I snatched the Trojans instead, and filled my satchel with my sex gadgets. I peeled around Grand Army Plaza to Flatbush Avenue and across the Brooklyn Bridge into Manhattan with a quickness. I decided that if he was going to eat me out and knock these suga walls the way he bragged, then it would be the night that I showed him how I really like to get my freak on. I planned to turn his world upside-down, especially when he mentioned he'd bought me the eight-thousand-dollar Louis Vuitton trunk I'd wanted. Girlfriend came prepared with whipped cream, blindfolds, French ticklers, vibrators, and a strap-on dildo. I was gonna give Mr. Simms the workout of his life.

Anyway, I get to suite 602 and he opens the door. The room was lit up with candles, the sounds of WBLS's "Quiet Storm" were coming from the stereo, Dom was chilling on ice, and there he stood in a burgundy silk kimono and matching boxers. The mood was definitely sexy. He grabbed me and kissed me with force and passion. While his tongue told me he missed me, he slid his hand under my dress and started massaging my clitoris. Then, with his other hand, he massaged and stroked my breasts through my dress until my nipples got as hard as rocks. My hand found its way to the opening in his boxers. *When God was giving out meat, he definitely forgot to put some on this bone*, I thought as I stroked his long, skinny sex. He pulled my dress up over my head and threw it in the corner. Then he picked me up, carried me into the bedroom, and laid me on the bed. He walked back out into the living room and returned with two crystal flutes filled with champagne. Our glasses clinked to his "Here's to a night you'll never forget" promise. We took a few sips. Then he fed me fresh pineapple, grapes, strawberries, and cheese. He placed a few chips of ice in his mouth and started kissing on my neck, nibbling on my earlobes, making wet puddles in the center of my chest, then lapping them around my breasts. He slowly kissed down to the center of my stomach. He kissed the inside of my right thigh, then sucked the toes on my right foot. Then he sucked the toes on my left foot, and kissed and licked the inside of my left thigh. I opened my legs wider. My mind sang, *Oh, yes… eat this pussy. Eat this pussy. Oh, please don't tease me. Stick your tongue in me. Oh, yes… work this pussy, work this pussy*, as he kissed my love canal. Girl, my pussy was jumpin' for some action since it hadn't been stroked in months. Finally, he mounts his mouth over my lips and…

"Ooooh, baby, damn you taste good. …Mmmm-mmm, you got some good, juicy pussy, baby." The way this fool was gnawing and gnashing at my clit, I thought for sure he was going to bite it off. I was too through.

"Uh-uh. Get up and get out," I said as I pushed his head from between my thighs. "Where the fuck you think you at, McDonald's?"

"What's wrong, baby?' he asked with his lips wet and his eyes as big as silver dollars. "You got me horny as hell."

"*Whaat?!* Chewin' on my pussy like it's an Egg McMuffin. I think not. I think you betta take your non-pussy-eatin' ass home to your wife, and while you're at it, go rub some Miracle-Gro on that skinny-ass dick."

"You trippin', right? Why you gotta take it there?"

"Take it there? Brotha, please. My clit has more meat on it than that," I said, pointing at his stiff Slim Jim. "You get me all heated up and shit, and you can't even eat pussy right. Nigga, please."

"Indy, baby, tell me how you want it. Show me. I'll make it right for you, c'mon, baby."

"Look, this is not 'Pee-Wee's Playhouse,' okay? I don't have time to teach no grown-ass man how to eat pussy. Your country-ass wife shoulda been schoolin' your simple ass," I said as I pulled my travel companion out of my satchel. "Now, this is what a dick is supposed to look like. Okay, Nicholas?"

To make a long story short, I wound up having to slap his face; he packed his shit and bounced his blue balls back home to his wife. But the poor soul left in such a huff that he forgot his wallet. Now, I could have taken the eighteen hundred dollars in cash he had but, since the asshole was nice enough to leave me in his suite, I opted to use his American Express instead.

"Hello, room service? This is suite six-oh-two. Please send up three bottles of Cristal and a tray of chocolate-covered strawberries." I figured I'd drink one bottle and save the other two for another occasion. Then I called 1-800-FLOWERS. "Hello, I'd like to send one hundred yellow roses to Mrs. Nicholas Simms. ...Yes, send them to 1110 Sixteenth Street, Northeast, Washington, D.C. Oh, and sign it 'Love, Dickless Nicholas.'" Hell, the least I could do was express my sympathy for her loving a man with a toothpick dick.

Don't misunderstand me. The size of a man's penis doesn't matter. It's the size of his cash flow that counts. And, of course, the motion of the ocean. Whatever! But when you tryna serve a bitch like me, you gotta come correct. Yes, I called myself a bitch. I'm very much aware of Webster's definition—a female dog. Well, I am a female. And I'm a female who will dog the hell out of a cheatin', lyin'-ass man. Now, Indy's definition of a bitch is a strong, confident, aggressive woman who knows what she wants, who won't settle for less than what she wants, and who won't take no shit from any man. None, nada, nooch.

Bottom line: I don't care if you got a big dick, small dick, long dick, skinny dick, short dick, or no dick. You betta know what you're doin' with what you got 'cause if you don't, I'm gonna blow your spot up. See, I ain't gonna gas a nigga's head up when his sex is sloppy, and faking orgasms is out. I know there are a lot of sistas who have no problem faking the funk in the bedroom, but my thing is, why bother? It's a waste of time and energy.

Anyway, now he's heated because I pulled his card. Oh, well...

Oh, shit. Look at the time! It's 2:30 p.m. I've been rambling on all morning. I gotta get down to the shop to check on my crew. Later.

3

DAMASCUS: **STROKIN'**

HMMM… *HMMM…HMMM…DAMN*, I thought when I woke up this morning, hard as a brick to the sounds of a warm, wet mouth slurping down this bozack. I didn't even open my eyes to look under the covers. I just folded my arms behind my head and let those big red lips glide down the length of my joint. I couldn't remember her name but I remembered the number of times she stuck fives, tens, and twenties in my G-string. And I remembered that big, cotton-soft ass that gobbled me up inch by inch. *Yeah, she'll definitely get a double star by her name*, my mind said as she gulped down the thick load I shot down her throat.

Yo, this dancing shit really pulls in the pussy. Word. Check it: For the past two years, I've been performing with Daddy Long Stroke Productions, an all-male dance revue owned by two hispanic sistas from Long Island. And, dig, these honeys are sweet crazy but will not give up any play. They are strictly about the business, and if your ass can't work the crowd, then your ass is history. There's about fifteen to twenty black and hispanic brothas who hold it down with three major requirements: body, dick, and rhythm. Most of the time, we are on the road making special appearances at all the latest hot spots up and down the East Coast. It's cool and all but I'm really thinking about bouncin' to do the solo thing. Over the past year, I've been performing at private parties when I'm not on the road. Yo, the private parties are where you can really get your freak on; the money's good and with tips I kill 'em. When you got a strong back, big arms, a chiseled chest, rock-hard abs, and huge hairy cow balls attached to an eleven-inch, thick, black, veiny horse dick, you become real popular with the ladies. They all want a piece of "T-Bone." Yeah, that's my stage name. But my peoples call me Tee.

Anyway, check it. The chick sucking my nuts hired me and my boy Hammer to dance at her cousin's bridal shower last night at Club Elite over in Brooklyn's Sheepshead Bay section. The club itself is pretty slick. It's a three-floor joint owned by a couple of Russian cats. The first floor has a real laid-back, candlelit, piano bar atmosphere. The second floor is a huge dance floor with wall-to-wall mirrors and huge go-go cages atop massive speakers. Suspended disco glitter balls spin nonstop to the thumpin' underground sounds of techno and house. The third floor is a long hallway divided into three lounge areas with TV monitors running X-rated flicks. Farther down is another hallway that leads to three large rooms reserved for private parties, each with its own full-service bar. The Blue Room is where forty or more women sat around seven large round tables last night, drinking, eating, and patiently waiting for the show to begin.

My man Hammer came out doing his thing in a black tux, bow tie, and no shirt. "Moments in Love" by the Art of Noise was pumping. The lights dimmed, he slowly unzipped his pants to reveal his pubic hairs, he flexed a few muscles here and there, then bent over, grabbed the cuffs of his pant legs, and yanked upward when Stevie Wonder's "All I Do" came on. His pants snapped off, and there he stood in a mesh Tarzan piece. The place roared with yells and screams from women of all shapes and sizes between the ages of eighteen and eighty. "Take it off...damn, he's packin'." He dropped down and started doing one-arm push-ups and deep thrusting and grinding motions with his hips. That's when I stepped up to the plate.

The DJ slid the beats into a Mr. Fingers piece, "Dead End Alley." I came out in a pair of blue Timbs, a blue Polo baseball cap, an oversized white Polo tank top that revealed my left pierced nipple, and a Blue Polo bath wrap. The muscles in my chest and shoulders shined from a mixture of baby oil and coconut oil. I free-styled for a quick minute, flexed the arm and calf muscles, did a few kicks and hip thrusts, a few spins and gyrating bends, then ripped open my tank top. I threw my arms over my head, flexed my washboard abs, and let the muscles in my chest bounce to the beat of the music.

Slowly, the beats took control. "Victim of Loving You" by Colonel Abrams, "Catacombs" by Krimp, "Zulu" by Circle Children, "Love & Happiness" by River Ocean. I snapped open my towel, threw it into the crowd, and stood wearing nothing but a black leather G-string with a low-cut dick sheath. The five elderly women at the table in front of me fumbled for their eyeglasses. "Lawd have mercy. …. Well, now. …. Oh, sweet Jesus," they said in unison.

My boy and I did our tabletop dances, shaking and grinding our bodies on eager, tongue-wagging women letting their hungry hands wander up and down our bodies. I loved watching their eyes and mouths pop open when they stuck their hands down in my pouch and felt my dick or when I pulled out my big, hairy balls. Yo, they bugged the fuck out when they realized I had my shit pierced. The more they drank, the more they wanted to see and feel. The atmosphere was definitely in freak mode. Yo, we lay back on tables and let 'em just do it. Man, listen. We just let 'em.

Finally, I opened my eyes, allowed my mind to savor the intense pleasure of popping that morning nut, then looked down to see the owner of the mouth. *Damn…Damn…Damn.* Another ugly troll giving good head. Once again, I'd let my dick talk me into bringing home another dick-thirsty beast. This time Godzilla's sister.

Now, I've laid a lot of chicks who were busted in the face but had bangin' bodies. But this ball gargler was the ooooogliest. Yo, fuck that two-star shit for suckin' dick; her ass gets a cover story on *Wild Life* magazine.

"Look, Tasha—"

"Tasha?! My name ain't no damn Tasha. It's Precious."

Precious? Now that's a lie. Oh yeah, Tasha's the chick from the other night. I met her at WaWa's, and after talking to her for half an hour, I got her to come home with me. It took me twenty minutes to get her to drop her drawers and then it was on. I tore that young ass up.

"Okay, Precious. Look, it's been real. The sex was good, but you gots ta get ta steppin'. Word up!" I jumped out of my king-size platform waterbed, pulled on my boxers, and stepped on three dirty condoms. *Damn*, I thought as I shook my head. I walked over to the window, pulled back the brown and orange-striped curtains, and opened the window. The cool morning air quickly attacked the smell of sweaty sex.

"Well, can I at least shower before I go?"

Hell no. Your ugly ass has got to go. "My shower is broke and my water is shut off," I lied while I handed her her 44D red lace bra. And, yes, her bra straps were clean. I picked up her red lace bikini-cut panties and tossed them over to her after I checked the crotch for crust. I exhaled when she passed the inspection. Last night I forgot to check. I mean, even though her snatch-box smelled clean when I pulled my two long fingers out of her, I still like to check. There ain't nothing worse than a chick offering you pussy that's been covered by a pair of dirty drawers. Yo, that shit bugs me the fuck out. Word up.

I stood in the middle of the bedroom, grabbed the thick brown carpet under my feet with my toes, and stared at her while she gathered her clothes. She sat back on the edge of the bed, leaned back on her forearms, and spread open her legs just enough to give me a peek at her big, wet hole. I lit a spliff, took four long pulls to the head, then exhaled slowly. *Damn...Damn... Damn.* "Look, don't sit there lookin' crazy and shit. Get your shit on and let's go," I said.

"Damn, why you acting like you tryna get rid of me?" Now she really looked pathetic with her fucked-up weave and alligator teeth. Her dark skin was almost purple, and she had the nerve to have on blue contacts.

Because I am. "Naw, baby, it's just that I gotta pick my sister up at the airport. Her flight'll be here in forty-five minutes. I'll drop you off at Penn Station and call you later," I lied, then turned my head when she walked over to me and tried to kiss me on the lips. Damn. Every time I lay down this pipe, some chick is tryna squeeze something extra. "Sorry, baby, I ain't wit' the lip-smackin'," I said as I pulled my dick out of my green striped boxers. "But you can suck this dick again."

She dropped to her knees and took me in her warm mouth. I grabbed the back of her head and slowly pushed in and out. "Yeah, you like this big dick, huh?" Her eyes fluttered yes. She rubbed her pussy with her left hand and used her right hand to rub my balls as she bobbed her head back and forth. The head of my dick hit the back of her throat. "Suck my balls," I ordered.

She obliged. She slurped and gargled me until I let loose a thick load of white cream that splattered in her face, around her mouth, down her chin, and over her breasts.

I grabbed a towel and wiped myself off, then threw on a pair of Polo overalls, snatched up my gray and red Air Maxes, and pulled my red fitted FUBU cap tight over my forehead. Then I put on a pair of my darkest shades. Looking at her hurt my eyes, and I damn sure didn't want to be seen with her lampin' in my ride. It's a good thing I tinted the windows out. "Yo, let's roll."

The digital clock on the dashboard read 7:58 when I sped down the driveway and headed north on Route 9. I cut my eyes over at my gruesome companion as she shifted her funky ass around in my beige leather seat. *Damn, you ugly*, I thought. But she damn sure didn't look that bad in the dark and from behind. That's how I usually like to get mine off. From the rear, especially when their grill is wrecked. She sported a gold hoop nose ring in her right nostril and her extra-large lips looked inflated with helium. Her jaws were slightly sunken in, probably from years of cock-sucking. And when she pulled her horsehair back, I noticed she had three small titties on her left ear. I let my gaze rove down to the center of her chest. The word *Nautica* on her gray cotton pullover stretched across her breasts. Yo, I ain't gonna front… My meat felt good between those knockers. I think I busted at least four nuts in her face.

I ran my tongue around the inside of my mouth, over the film on my teeth. *Damn, my breath is kicking.* I popped two Altoids mints in my mouth and pressed play on the CD remote. "Oooh, that's my girl," she said while she swayed to Phyllis Hyman's "I Refuse to Be Lonely." "That's a damn shame what she did to herself. It just goes to show you that people with money and talent can still be miserable. No amount of money can take away a person's hurt and pain, and it definitely doesn't guarantee you happiness."

I nodded, then changed the track selection. I didn't feel like getting into any psychodrama. "Oh, shit, is that Ten City?" she asked when "Goin' Up in Smoke" came on. "That's my group…Heeeey," she chimed while snapping her fingers and swaying her arms. "Hey, now."

Great. Dick Breath is gonna sing every track. I flipped the radar on and watched the speedometer jump to eighty. "Here, have a mint," I said. She declined. "No, you *really* need a mint."

"So what you tryna say, my breath is kickin'?" she asked defensively.

Damn, do I need to spell it out for this dragon? "Yeah, your breath is bangin,' so either take a mint or shut the fuck up the rest of the ride."

She glared at me, sucked her teeth, then snatched the tin box and took three. "You don't have to get all shitty with me," she said, then shifted her body closer toward the door and stared out the window.

Her breath smells like shit and musty dick hairs, and she gets vexed 'cause I offer her a mint. I really wanted to blast her ass, but I decided to make nice. "So did you enjoy the show last night?"

"It was a'ight," she said, talking at me into the window. "You did your thang."

Tell me something I don't already know. Hell, I know my thang is goin' on. Women just throw me the pussy after they see my work. Most of 'em try to slide me the digits on a folded napkin, matchbook, or piece of paper. Shit, like I said, having a nice body and a fat swipe definitely has its advantages. But there can also be some disadvantages. Yo, there ain't nothing more dangerous than being in a room half naked with a bunch of drunk, horny women. They get aggressive.

Man, I had this one chick pull my shit so damn hard, I thought she was gonna run off with it. "It's real," she yelled to her friends. You damn straight it's real. Now, I could understand her suspicions, 'cause I know a few brothas who stuff their shit. But I holds it down in the meat department, so ain't nothing fake about it. This shit right here is all beef, baby.

Another time, I had these two women grab the strings of my mesh thong and literally snatch it off. I just kept doin' my thing without missing a beat. By the end of the night, I had both of them begging to take me home. Did I do 'em? You damn right; I tore that pussy up. Yo, even the meekest, quietest girl will get on some rah-rah shit after a couple of Stolis. They start grabbing and tugging at the goods, and before you know it, they're straddled across your lap dancing. But, for some reason, it's always the ugly ones that will do—and will let you do—almost anything you want.

Like this cum-face sitting next to me. Last night, she jumped up out of her seat, got all up on me, and started rump-shakin' her juicy ass. After she stuck her hand down in my leather pouch, she locked her arms around my neck and started grinding her pelvis into me. I placed my big hands on her thick hips and pulled her into me to let her feel the length of my dick against her thigh, then she jumped up and locked her legs around my waist. So I slid my arms up under the backs of her legs, palmed her ass nice and tight with my hands, and bounced her up and down on my knot. I let her slide down to her knees, and then I hung my left leg over her shoulder and started grinding and shakin' my meat in her face. I slapped my rod across her mouth a couple of times and then she just got buck on me. She pulled and grabbed at my balls and started kissing 'em. Her mouth got so watery, she grabbed my shit outta my hand and started sucking it. The heat from her mouth told me she wanted me to knock her back out. Word up. And the crazy part is, her girls were cheering her on. Yo, women in the nineties are definitely going for theirs.

The clock read 8:43 when I pulled up in front of Newark Penn Station. "Be safe," I said, driving off before she could close the door. I shook my head. But on the strength, she had some bangin' sex. The ugly ones usually do.

As I headed home on Route 9, I turned the radio to 97.1 to hear some "blazin' hip-hop and R&B." Ed Lover was interviewing some porn star turned sexologist who was basically saying that if you wanna stay ahead of the game, then you should purchase her *How to Be a Better Lover* material. She offered a money-back guarantee. I laughed. Either you can fuck or you can't. It's as simple as that. Yo, don't get me wrong, that shit is cool if you're married or got a main girl, but if you just tryna pop a nut, what's the point? Kissin' and eatin' pussy is out. Me stickin' this dick to 'em or lettin' 'em suck me off is pleasure enough. You can save the extras.

I lit another spliff, hit the remote for the CD player, and turned up the volume. 2Pac's "Unconditional Love" blared from my Bose speakers. "Now, that was one deep brother," I mumbled. I wondered if there were such a thing as unconditional love. Hell, what's love got to do with anything? Life is always full of conditions. And it's damn sure not always full of love. Then came "I Ain't Mad at Cha." Before I allowed my mind to drift any further, I flipped open my Motorola and called Indy. Her line was busy. Knowing her funny-style ass, she had the phone off the hook. So I paged her and left her a message on her voice mail. "Hey, sexy. This is Tee. Give me a call when you get a chance. I wanna see ya. Peace." Now, that's one shorty I'd like to slide up in, with her fine ass. Yo, baby got back! Word up.

I flipped on the radar and hit eighty again. The only thing on my mind at that moment was getting home to wash the funk off my body and jumping back in bed. I didn't get home last night until two in the morning and didn't get to sleep until about five thanks to what's-her-face. I thought about my little ep this morning. Yo, word up, that sista should really be on the Discovery Channel. Let me stop. She knows how to ride a dick, and that's what really matters. I don't know who in the hell had the idea to have that damn party on a Thursday night. Now I gotta be caught up in all this damn rush-hour traffic. To make matters worse, I hit every red light on Route 9 and one lane was closed due to construction. I can never understand why the hell they don't repair the roads at night. Wouldn't that be the most logical thing to do? Hell no! They wait until rush hour. Needless to say, a thirty-five-minute ride turned into an hour and fifteen minutes because of some biddy driving like she was heading a funeral procession. Dumb ass.

By the time I turned onto Crescent Lane heading toward my housing development, I had tried reaching Indy three more times, and each time her line was still busy. I left three more messages indicating I wanted to see her.

For some reason, I was just really feelin' her. I hadn't seen her in a couple of months because of the road trips and shit, and I've seen her even less since I moved out to Jersey. Yo, Indy is real cool people. Even though she can be stone cold funny style and will check a nigga with a quickness, I dig her 'cause she keeps it real. Ain't nothin' fake about her, and she's always on point with a nigga. And the sista stays laced in all the butters.

But on the real to real, I'm really big on her. Yo, ever since I peeped her in that *Jet* swimsuit issue in '81, I've been tryna knock it down. She looked sexy as hell in that two-piece crochet joint. You know, the funny thing is, I still got that *Jet* centerfold of her tucked in a scrapbook. It was the January issue, and it read: "Endearing Indera (34-22-38) of Brooklyn, N.Y., is a student at

Spelman College majoring in economics and business administration. She hopes to one day own her own business...Among her many diversions are men, money, and fashion." Now, here we are seventeen years later, and she's still not havin' it. I mean, damn, it ain't like my game ain't tight 'cause I definitely holds it down. I stay dipped in the flyest shit, I push a sweet-ass whip, and my pockets stay fat. But she won't give a nigga like me no kinda rhythm. She'll give me excuses like, "I can't because we're friends. I wouldn't want one night of pleasure to ruin what we have as friends." She just can't understand that I'm a friend in need and a little bump-and-grind will only enhance our friendship. Sometimes, she'll hit me with "You're not my type." But when I really push up on her, she snaps, "Boy, get the fuck outta my face! You don't have any respect for women." I'd like to know where she got that from. Hell, I respect her. And I respect any other woman who respects herself. As far as I'm concerned, any woman who plays herself is a chickenhead, and how you gonna expect me to respect a chickenhead? Besides, the women who've been in and out of my life have never been worthy of any respect. And it's damn sure not like any of them expected it.

As soon as I turned onto Olive Lane, I spotted a metallic gray Prelude with fresh rims parked in my driveway. *Now, who the fuck is this?* The minute I pulled up behind it, the driver's side door opened and out stepped a string bean-thin girl with a big happy-to-see-ya grin on her face. It was Tasha. The one thing I hate is an unannounced or uninvited guest popping over. That shit is grounds for a verbal lashing.

"Yo, what the fuck you doin' here?" I asked, irritated.

Her grin dropped. "The other night you told me to come by today around nine-thirty."

Yeah, I told your dumb ass to come by at nine-thirty but not in the fucking a.m., "Damn, girl. I meant nine-thirty tonight."

"Oh. Well, if I've caught you at a bad time, I'll just come back later," she said while walking back toward her car. I peeped she didn't have on a bra because her breasts bounced for joy under her black sheer blouse. So, of course, my mind wandered, and I wanted to know what she had on under the matching black sheer skirt that hung to her ankles.

"Hold up," I said. "Since you're here, you might as well come inside and make yourself useful."

She put her hands on her hips and twisted her face up. "Excuse me? Make myself useful how?"

Now, there she goes tryna play the role knowing damn well her ass came by for some dick. "Like cooking me something to eat, cleaning the house, and then takin' *it* to the head," I said, looking down at my lump.

"What the hell I look like—one of the Merry Maids?"

"No, more like the clean-up woman." I smiled. She didn't.

Needless to say, by the time I finished my shit, shower, and shave, she had the downstairs of the house spotless. It smelled lemon fresh. Lemon Pine-Sol, lemon SoftScrub, and lemon Pledge. The week's worth of dishes stacked in the sink were washed, the kitchen floor was swept and mopped, and the stove and countertops shined. The living- and dining-room floors were vacuumed, all the furniture was dust-free, and the cobwebs that had hung on the lighting fixtures over the dining-room and kitchen tables were gone.

Damn, girl. I need you around more often, I thought as I leaned against the doorway of the kitchen with my arms folded, wearing nothing but a white towel, watching her begin her next task: cooking me a hot meal. When she bent over to get a pan out of the bottom cabinet, I snuck up behind her and grabbed her by the waist. She jumped.

"Damn, you scared me. Don't be sneaking up behind me like that," she said, smacking my hands off and trying to break free. "I thought you said you were hungry."

I dropped my towel and squeezed the base of my semi-hard dick with my left hand. "I am," I said, pressing myself against her flat ass and cupping her breasts and massaging her nipples.

She placed her hands over mine and tilted her head back so I could kiss the right side of her long neck. I removed my right hand from her right breast and slowly pulled up her skirt. When I felt nothing but skin, I smiled. *I knew it, no drawers*. I let go of her, picked up my towel, and said, "I'll be downstairs shooting pool. Let me know when it's time to eat."

My stomach growled when the smell of turkey sausage floated through the vents. It dawned on me that I hadn't eaten since around noon yesterday. Before the bridal party last night, I drank two banana protein shakes but hadn't eaten anything else. "I hope this chick can cook," I muttered out loud. I shot about two games of pool, then turned on the VCR to finish watching that movie *The Game* with Michael Douglas on the forty-six-inch wide-screen. Yo, that piece was the bomb. I tried Indy again. When I finally got through, I just told her I wanted to hang out later on. Of course, she wanted to know what we were gonna do. She's always so damn suspicious. So the plan is for me to scoop her up around six at her shop. I'm not sure what we'll get into, but if it's left up to me…well, you already know the score.

Tasha came down the stairs carrying a large tray with two plates. One had five neatly stacked banana pancakes on it with melted butter running down the sides; the other had six turkey sausage links, two eggs over easy, cheese grits, and two slices of wheat toast. She sat on the far end of the long brown leather sofa and watched me throw down. Word is bond! The girl did her thing-thing. I cleaned the plates, licked my fingers, and washed it all down with a tall glass of orange juice. I smiled. I really hadn't noticed how attractive she was. She had an oval face with a narrow nose, thin lips, and big brown eyes. Her brown skin was clear and smooth. She reminded me of Joni Sledge of the group Sister Sledge.

"What's so funny?" she asked.

"Nothing. I got my grub on, and now I'm ready to get my fuck on. So what's up?"

She leaned back on the sofa, crossed her legs, then said, "You tell me."

I shifted my body around to face her with my left leg across the sofa, rested my back against its arm, let my size-fourteen foot rub her thigh, then opened my towel. "This is what's up," I said, looking down at my hard dick. "So stop tryna front. You know you came over for this big dick."

She stood up, lifted her shirt over her head, slipped out of her skirt, then laid her naked body against the cool leather. She stared at my meat for a moment—I guess wondering how she'd get her small mouth to open wide enough to get more than the head in—then kissed and licked it like a chocolate Tootsie Roll pop. After she grazed my dick with her teeth for the third time, I decided dick-sucking wasn't one of her specialties. But I could tell by the way she rubbed between her legs that she was ready for the meat. I pulled her up toward me. When she crawled up over me, I could feel her hairy bush along the shaft of my thick dick. After she put the rubber on me (I know you didn't think I was gonna fuck her raw), I grabbed her by her thin hips and lifted her up so I could penetrate. She eased down on my throbbing head and slowly moved up and down until she was ready to take it all in. Once she was loosened up, I swung my legs around with her straddled across my lap, pulled her legs up over my shoulders, then stood up. She was light as a feather. At first, I was afraid I might rip her in two but she took it like a champ. One thing's for sure: Thin girls are definitely deeper than you might think. So I tightened up my grip and slammed in and out of her.

"Oh, yes, baby," she screamed. "Fuck me…harder."

"You like this dick? You want all this dick?"

"Yes…hmm. Oh, yes, baby…fuuuuuck meeeeee…harder…Oh, your dick is so big, baby. Hmm…hmm…oh, yes…It feels soooo good, baby… hmm… you make my pussy so wet…"

She arched her back, threw her head back, and dug her nails into my skin. Then her body started shaking like she was going into convulsions. I knew that was my cue to really give it to her. I slapped her narrow ass until it turned red and dug my dick deep in her with fast, heavy thrusts. A few strokes later, I grunted, "I'mmmm coooommmming," then filled the zulu with a hot sticky walnut.

The clock on the VCR read 1:30. It was time for her to go. Her "clean-up" was done.

The minute Tasha's fast ass jetted, I jumped back in the shower, jerked my shit off, then hopped in bed. I had my belly full, had popped a good nut, and was ready to nod hard. But the minute I closed my eyes, the damn phone rang.

"Yeah?" I asked, agitated.

"Hi, Tee," a soft, sexy voice said. "This is Crystal. Did I catch you at a bad time?"

I rubbed my stomach, then let my hand rest on my dick. "I'm in bed. What's up?"

"Well, I was hoping we could get together today. Maybe have a milkshake or *something*," she said, then paused. "But, since you're in bed, maybe some other time."

I'm tired as hell and she wants to play fuckin' games. "Let's just get to the point and stop wasting my damn time," I snapped. "It's two-forty and I gotta be in the city by six. So if you want some dick, then you need to come get it now." I rubbed my hairy balls, then waited for her dumb ass to respond.

"Damn, why you getting all amped?" she asked. "I just wanted to spend a few hours with you today."

"'Cause I don't have time for playin' games. If you want some dick, say you want some dick. If you wanna fuck, say it. You wanna see me? Cool. I got an hour's worth of dick to give you, so what's up?"

She got all quiet and shit, then sighed. "An hour, that's it?"

"Fuck it, then," I said. "Keep your ass home."

"I'll be right over."

I smiled. "The door is unlocked. Come in and be ready to assume the position."

Yo, this chick is kinda beat in the face. She looks like a cross-eyed frog but she's got a soft ass, a wet, creamy pussy, and she sucks dick like she's nursing. We met about three months ago after one of my shows. For about two months, she came to every strip show and would slip a crisp hundred in my G-string. Yo, Frog Face would spend her man's cash to rub my dick and let me grind her until her panties dripped, then go home all heated up and shit. Then one night while I was grinding up on her, she whispered real loud in my ear over the music, "I want to spend the night with you." I brought her home, knocked her back out, and her ass has been strung ever since. So, for the last three months, she's been creepin' on her man.

It was 3:05 when I heard the front door open, then close. When Crystal entered the bedroom, she had her clothes off and was wearing a big-ass grin. I threw the brown quilt off me, spread my legs wide open, then waited for her dick-thirsty ass to take me in her mouth.

"Hmm, don't you look sexy," she said while licking her lips. "I've missed you."

"You know the score," I said, then rested my arms under my head. "You have fifty-five minutes. So there's no need for chitchat."

She climbed up on the bed, kissed and licked my balls, tongued the underside of my dick, then wrapped both of her hands around the base. With slow movements, she slid her hands up and down as her big red lips encircled me. When my dick stretched in her mouth and hit the back of her throat, she locked her lips around the head like a pit bull, then swirled her tongue over it. She positioned her body for me to slip three of my thick fingers in her wet pussy. I buried them in her fast and hard, then rubbed the outer edges of her hairy pussy as she bobbed her head up and down.

"You ready for it?" I asked.

"Uh-huh," she said in between deep, heavy moans. "Yes, baby, give it to me."

She unlocked her lips from my dick, put the latex on, then rolled over on her back. I threw her legs up against her shoulders, then rubbed and slapped my heavy dick between her swollen pussy lips. The minute they flared open, I slid my long thickness deep inside her, then banged her up with fast, deep strokes until her hot pussy swished and sucked and slurped my dick. She moaned, then screamed in my fuckin' ear, "It hurts so good…oh, baby! It hurts so fuckin' good!"

When I felt my nuts swelling and my dick twitching, I pulled out of her. She jumped up, snatched the condom off, and took me back in her mouth. I closed my eyes and let the vibrations in her throat beat against the head of my dick until I pumped a thick creamy shake down her throat. The white cream filled her mouth, overflowed out the corners, and down the sides of my dick.

"Don't waste my shit," I said. She swallowed all she could, then licked my dick and balls clean. I smiled and said, "That's right, good to the last drop."

At 4:00 p.m. with the crust from her shake around her mouth, I put her ass out, then fell asleep sticky and exhausted, with the smell of sex in the room.

4

INDERA: **HAVEN'T YOU HEARD**

I T WAS A LITTLE AFTER 4:00 when I finally arrived at the salon. The place was packed with women patiently waiting to have their hairpieces laid. From micro-braids to dreads, from snatch-backs to upsweeps, from bobbed cuts to French rolls from facials to full-body wraps to waxes and massages—Weaves and Wonders caters to the needs of women and men of all races. Creating wonders is the one thing we take pride in. What has made us stand out from most salons is that we offer complimentary services, including manicures and pedicures. For our on-the-go mothers, we offer complimentary child care. For the sista who works the swing shift or likes to do a little hip-shaking, we offer midnight service by appointment. And for our shut-ins, we provide in-home services. With all these amenities, there's no reason for any sista to walk around, hop around, roll around, or lay around looking broke down and busted.

The success of Weaves and Wonders is partly due to the skills of my staff. I have a total of twenty-five employees from the child care workers to the shampoo girls, who are devoted to keeping every customer happy. After all, customer satisfaction is the name of the money-making game. I won't tolerate anything less than service with a smile. Now, I only feel it's right to acknowledge some of my key players. Truthfully, I wish I could say that there weren't personality clashes or attitudes that I have to deal with, but I'd be lying. Bottom line: As long as it doesn't get in the way of their work performance, I will try to tolerate almost anything.

First, there's my gender-bender sista, Alex, a.k.a. Alexi. This Miss Honey is a Spanish version of RuPaul without the wig. She rocks a platinum blonde Cleopatra cut, stands six feet two, and has hips, tits, and ass that put many *real* women to shame. She's tall, graceful, and fierce. And she can work the hell out of a pair of shears. Precision is her middle name. Not only is she my number one stylist, but she brings in the most customers. So you know she's alright with me. Well, at least she used to be. Lately, she's been acting real shady. She strolls in when she wants and sometimes just doesn't show up at all, then she has the nerve to give fever when you ask her about it. Lord knows I don't wanna have to square off on her.

Next, there's Mya. Mya has a pretty face and keeps her makeup and hair in place, but she's a bit on the chunky side. I don't know why someone from her past led her to believe she's a size twelve when she's really a twenty-four. But homegirl insists on wearing Lycra bodysuits and six-inch stilettos. Humph. It's like watching a whale on stilts. But, hey, who am I to judge? She can stitch and glue a weave with her eyes closed and weaves bring in the money. Every bald-headed child and their mama want what they'll never grow on their own: extra hair. So, as long as she keeps the cash flowin' in, she can wear a thong and gladiator heels for all I care. On second thought, uh-uh.

Then, there's my number one braid technician, Eva, otherwise known as White Chocolate. Glamour girl is ova, okay? She's a mixture of Christie Brinkley and Heather Locklear with a splash of ghetto princess in her blood. Now, between you and me, homegirl struggles with a severe identity crisis. Last week she rocked cornrows and this week it's an Angela Davis Afro wig. Go figure. Anyway, for a white girl, she can braid wonders around the tightest, nappiest scalp. And she loves *a lotta* chocolate in her milk. Need I say more?

My masseurs—Justice, Sharky, Bullet, and Lenny—are four gorgeous caramel, dark-chocolate, cinnamon, and honey-coated (in that order) hunks who have the hands to melt any body like butter. And just for reference, they supposedly have dick for days. Not that I've had any. Uh-uh. Don't start, okay? There's one thing I don't do and that is fuck the help. Don't get it twisted. Anyway, they've tightened up a few customers and you know how women like to talk. However, I think it's downright tacky and goes against my policy of not screwing the customers. All four of them have been served notice: If any of the hoes they've dicked down come up in my shop with drama, they'll be fired on the spot.

Oh, and over on the far right are my shampoo girls—Asia, Tiffany, and Monae. And the two divas over there in the back are my hand and feet technicians, Sharon and Stephanie. These two girls can make the rustiest, crustiest feet feel as soft as a baby's bottom. Well, maybe not that soft, but soft enough to keep you from stepping on glass or walking across hot coals. And, let me tell you, there's a whole lotta sistas out there walking around with some nasty feet. I just shake my head. How you gonna be fierce with crocodile feet?

Like all the other hair salons, Weaves and Wonders is a gossip mill. Underneath the hum of hair dryers and through the sizzle of curling irons, you can always count on someone dishing out someone else's filth. Sometimes it's worse than watching Ricki Lake. Other times it's like being on *Forgive or Forget*. Someone is always eager to confess their sins and beg for forgiveness. Every now and then, someone tries to go Jerry Springer up in here, but I am not havin' that shit. You will be kindly asked to leave or security will toss your ass out. One thing's for sure: When you go into the business of doing hair, you also take on the role of a human service technician. You become every lonely, lost, and confused soul's therapist, counselor, social worker, and healer of sin, and the list goes on. But it sure pays to be nice. Most customers will leave you a chunky tip just for listening to their trials and tribulations.

As soon as I walked through the door today and looked through the sliding glass window, I could tell Alexi and Mya were at it again. Alexi was finger-snapping and swinging her hair from side to side while Mya shook her double-D breasts and sashayed up and down the aisle. The regulars get a kick out of the two of them battling for points. I swear, one of these days somebody's gonna get hurt. The two of them can't stand each other—partly because Alexi stole one of Mya's many boyfriends, then Mya turned around and slept with one of her pieces. Just like scavengers.

"See Miss Thing, look at me and look at you. I *am* a real woman—something you can never be," Mya snapped.

"Well, that's not what your man said when he was licking my insides. See…

catch it! Every time you suck him, you sucking me, okay? You beached whale. You wish you could have a body like this," Alexi said while showing off her shape. "Remember one thing, Miss Freddie the Fish. You betta stay in your place before I erase you, then replace you."

I jumped in. "Alright, girls. Let's get back to work."

"Well, you betta keep Orca in her cage. She's got one more time to try it on my time, then it's on. I'm getting real tired of Humpty-Dumpty tryna get fierce. It's not my fault she can't keep a man," Alexi said, giving two snaps with a twist of the wrist. I swear, sometimes she's so full of theatrics. Then again, this *is* the Village.

"I don't care how many operations you have or how many estrogen pills you pop, you can never be a woman," Mya said. "Stop taking the pills and let's see how fierce you are then, Madame Lurch. And, for the record, *your man* liked this fish, okay?"

"Alexi and Mya,' I said. "I want to see the both of you in my office."

They both excused themselves from their customers, rolled their eyes at each other, then shuffled one behind the other down the long hallway that leads into my green-carpeted office. I sat on my cherrywood desk and waited for Mya to close the door. Mya sat on the green leather sofa and crossed her legs. Alexi stood with her hands on her hips.

"I hope you're gonna make this quick 'cause I have clients waiting," she said with an attitude.

I could tell this was going to be one of those days. I slowly counted to ten, then said, "Well, Alexi, what seems to be the problem?"

"The problem is all these fish in here trying it on my time, especially this tuna," she said, pointing at Mya.

Mya laughed. "She's pissed off 'cause this fish fucked her man—not once, not twice, but three times—and she can't stand it. Please. She did it to me on more than one occasion."

I shook my head. "You mean to tell me the two of you are still fighting over a man who doesn't want either of you? Both of you are ridiculous with this mess, especially when it's on business time."

"Who you calling ridiculous, Miss Indy?" Alexi asked.

"I didn't stutter. I *said*, you two are ridiculous. I told ya'll before that I will not have this mess in my shop, and I've asked both of you to not carry on with this foolishness in front of the customers. Now I'm telling both of you whores to knock it off. This is a place of business, not some comedy show."

"Whores?!" Alexi snarled. "Now I know you not tryin' it, Miss Indy."

"Excuse me. I'm still talking. Make no mistake: There's only one queen bee in this hive, okay? Now, like I said, I'm sick of you whores bickering back and forth."

Alexi glowered at me with her hands on her hips, which told me she was going to try to read me for points. Mya shifted back in her seat.

"I guess you *would* be the expert on whores since you use your pussy like a racetrack, okay, Miss Indy Five Hundred? Don't come for me." She snapped her finger at me three times.

Did she just say I use my pussy as a racetrack? I know this tramp's not talking after all the back-alley dick-sucking she's done. And don't get me started on the number of men she's had to pay to fuck her, or buy crack for just to suck his crusty dick. "Excuse me?" I asked.

Finger snap. "No, dear, there's no excuse for you. The only whore in this camp is you, so don't get the game fucked up." Finger snap. "Just because we cool don't mean you can come out your face any kinda way. See, I don't care whose nest this is, Miss Thing," she said, then stamped her foot. "I keep the coins flowin' in here, so you betta recognize."

All of a sudden I felt a nerve pop. "Mya, please excuse us for a moment. And lock the door on your way out." I took off my earrings.

"C'mon now, Indy, there's no need to get all bent out of shape," Mya said as she jumped up from her seat. "You know how Alexi and I get. I can't stand the heifer and she can't stand me. As long as he—I mean, she—stays out of my space, I'll stay out of hers."

Alexi stepped out of her size 13 black Kenneth Cole sling-backs and pulled her hair back. Then the door swung open. It was Eva. "There's a woman in the lobby yelling for you to come speak with her. I told her you were busy but she insists on seeing you…now."

"We'll be right out," I said, then cut my eyes over at Alexi. "You and I will finish this discussion later."

"Anytime you ready," she said. "Just make sure you come correct."

I can see I'm going to have to whup that ass before the day ends. This fifty-foot bitch is really getting grand. "Be careful what you wish for, dear."

I walked toward the front of the shop while Alexi and Mya apologized to their customers for making them wait for twenty minutes. There stood a short, stocky woman with a red head rag tied around her hair. She was fussing with Eva about our no-walk-in policy.

"What do you mean, you don't take walk-ins? I need someone to see me today. There's no way I can go another day with my head looking the way it does."

"Eva, thanks. I'll handle it. Hi, I'm Indy," I said, then extended my hand. "How can I help you?"

"You can help me by getting me the owner. I'm not leaving here until someone does my hair," Ragtop said. "I heard you people know how to do some hair, and I need mine done today. I don't care what the cost."

"Well, I am the owner. Now, what is the crisis?" I asked, still not understanding the urgency.

"This is the crisis," she said, pulling off her head rag. "Do you see what that motherfucka did to me?"

Everyone in the shop stopped what they were doing. All eyes popped open. Homegirl's hair was chopped up, with big chunks of hair cut out. It looked like the work of a blind Edward Scissorhands.

"Oh my. Let me see what I can do." I flipped through the appointment book and noticed Alexi's 5:30 had cancelled. I pressed the intercom. "Alexi, please come out to the reception area."

I could see her roll her eyes up in her head, then she leaned over and whispered something into her customer's ear. As she helped the lady get under the hair dryer, they giggled. Alexi then swished her padded ass extra hard toward me. "You rang?" she said sarcastically.

I kept my cool and smiled. "Alexi, dear, can you fit this young lady into your schedule? I see your next appointment cancelled."

She shook her head at the lady's butchered hair, then said, "This is Weaves and Wonders, not the Magic Shop. C'mon in the back and let me see what I can do."

"Thanks," Ragtop said. "I really appreciate this."

"You're in good hands," I said. "If Alexi can't do it, nobody can."

Alexi pursed her lips. "Humph. Come, chile, let's get this show on the road. Now, tell me, what in the world happened to you?"

I stood in the middle of the reception area and watched them walk toward Alexi's workstation. *I'ma fuck that bitch up real good*, I thought. Then I put the *Essence, Ebony, Source, Vogue, Cosmopolitan, GQ,* and *Vibe* magazines back in their places on the wall rack. I watered the huge fern hanging in front of the window, wiped down the huge leaves of my philodendron, and pulled the dead leaves off of the two peace lilies that sat on the two marble end tables. I lined up the ten green leather chairs so that they'd go around the wall in a straight line, then stared out of the window.

Across the street, there were two white security officers standing in front of the Kenneth Cole store, talking to a young black woman and gesturing for her to come back into the shop. I could tell she was going off on them. Serves them right. They probably thought she lifted some shit from the store. I smiled when, after she dumped open her leather backpack in the middle of the sidewalk, they realized they had made a mistake. I'm sure they tried to apologize, but the sista gave them the finger. Bastards! They're always so quick to assume we tryna rip 'em off. Hell, I can remember a few times being in Nordstrom over in Jersey, and security followed me around like I was a criminal. One time I had to tell the undercover agent, who really wasn't all that undercover, "Instead of watching me like I'm some crook, you shoulda been poppin' the white chick who just walked outta here with three Ralph Lauren pieces." They looked real stupid. Then there was the time I flipped the script on their dumb asses when I started ducking and hiding between clothes racks, then popped out on 'em like *gotcha!* Then, to really fuck with 'em, I started following 'em around the store. I had their asses spooked.

I walked back over to the reception desk, flipped through the stack of mail left in the incoming mail basket. Bills, bills, and more bills, a few advertisements and brochures, then I came across a letter from Brit. I ripped it open and smiled a big Kool-Aid smile when a picture of him standing on the beach in front of a coconut tree fell out. *Damn, he looks good,* I thought. I couldn't get over how long his braids had gotten. When he said he wasn't cutting his hair in the Dominican Republic, he wasn't kidding. A white Scrunchie was holding up a bunch of braids on top of his head while the rest of his thick braids hung past his ears. He looked sexy as hell with his copper red tan. That boy knows he has some beautiful skin; it's shiny and smooth. It looked like he'd been working out. His chest and shoulders looked broader and his arms seemed more muscular and defined, but knowing Brit, the last thing he'd be doing is lifting weights or working out. And those beautiful track legs? Mmm, mmm, mmm. He's just lucky enough to have that natural thang going on. All the boy has on is a white tank top, torn faded Gap jean shorts, and white Air Max sneakers and he looks good as hell. He's just too sexy.

I realized how much I've missed him. Of all my friends, Brit's the one I can talk to about anything, and he's always accepted me for who I am. I think that's what friendship is really about. Acceptance. And I don't have to worry about him pressin' me to fuck. I can't understand why most men think you gotta fuck 'em in order to be their friend. That shit really pisses me off. But Brit's not like most men. He's sensitive and really in tune with women. I mean, how many men can tell when you've put on a different shade of makeup or have on a new perfume? How many men know when you need to be hugged or notice when you're sad, even though there's a smile on your face?

Brit notices things like that. He knows when to just listen, and that's why I love him so much. No, not love like *in love*, but like a brother. He's a really gentle and passionate man. I can't understand why he has so many problems in relationships. It's not like he can't throw down in the bedroom. I mean, the brotha makes love like a woman. Ooooops! Damn it. You weren't supposed to know that. And if you tell him I told you, I'll deny it. Damn it. Okay, I slept with him once—so what? Okay, three times. Hell, it was good. Okay, yes, I also slept with a woman. Okay, a few women. But that was years ago, back when we were in college. Wait a minute, I'm still strictly dickly, okay? I just had my taste of the other side a few times. Big deal! Hey, don't knock it unless you've tried it. Besides, I know for a fact that there are a lot of women who fantasize about being with another woman. And I'm sure a few of you have rubbed your insides or licked your own nipples wondering what it'd be like with another woman between your legs. So don't try to act all uppity and shit. There's a little freak in all of us. I just happened to live it out.

I snapped out of my trance when I heard laughter coming from the girls' workstations. I glanced at my watch; it was ten minutes to six. I decided to call Brit. I reached over the counter and grabbed the phone. I needed to hear his voice but I got his answering machine. I left a message. *Knowing him, he's probably lying on the beach.* I smiled, then grabbed all of the mail and headed back toward my office. Eva was just finishing up her client's box braids, Mya was curling the ends of her client's shoulder-length weave, and Miss Alexi had cut Ragtop's hair down even and was using her comb to smooth gel across her head for finger waves. Sharon was finishing up her last pedicure, and there were four women under the dryer.

Ragtop was telling the girls how she had gone to a bridal shower and didn't get home until five in the morning. She said her husband chopped her hair up because she came home pissy drunk and called him another man's name when she crawled on top of him to make love. She laughed it off, saying one of the dancers had gotten her so hot, she wanted to give him some right there.

"Girl, my girlfriend's daughter hired these dancers for her niece's surprise shower last night and I'm telling you, they were just too fine. They really turned the party out. Hell, after rubbing up on all that body, the only thing I could do was go home and screw my husband's brains out and wish it were one of them. And, girl, the one with his thing pierced was just too much."

"You know, when I was down in Virginia three weeks ago, I went to a strip show, and there was this guy there who had his pierced too," Box Braids said. "That brotha had body and enough meat to feed all the women in Africa."

"Girl, that sounds like my kinda man," Weave Wearer said. "Was he hang-ing?"

"Like a horse," Box Braids said. "I like it big but not that big. That's too much meat for me."

"Oh, please. The bigger the better," Ragtop said. "As fine as both of those men were, I'm sure they both went home with some horny soul. Shit, if I wasn't married, I'd have gone home with one of 'em."

"Uh-huh…I wish I coulda been a fly on that wall. That's how I like my men—large and in charge," Mya chimed in.

"Yeah, 'cause anything less is like feeding a whale a Tic Tac," Alexi snickered.

Mya rolled her eyes. "Whatever, Priscilla, Queen of the Desert."

"Is he a tall, dark-skinned brotha with a bald head and a tribal band tattooed around his arm?" Crusty Feet asked. "With a pretty smile and dimples?"

Box Braids and Ragtop said in unison, "That's him." They laughed, then went on to describe the rest of the dancing entourage. But it was clear that Tee was their favorite. They went on and on about his chiseled body, his pierced nipple, the way he wagged his long, fat tongue, the way he moved his hips and licked his lips. They even shared how some chick licked his bald head and how another spent over a hundred dollars giving him tips. And they seemed really fascinated with his big, pierced dick.

"I think his name is T-Bone," Box Braids offered. "And he's one sexy hunk of dark chocolate."

Alexi purred like a tigress in heat, then said, "Well, now. Alright for T-Bone. I'll take mine well done with a little steak sauce, please." They all laughed. I didn't.

I'll have to admit my ears did snap to attention when I heard Tee's dick was pierced. I wasn't surprised to hear he was packing since he has all the signs: big feet, full lips, wide nose, big hands, and slightly bowed legs. Besides, I've seen his imprint in more than one pair of pants, even when he wears them oversized. But to hear he was pierced…humph. I'm not even going there.

Knowing Tee's nasty ass, he probably did take some tramp home. Now, I don't know why a sista gotta play herself like that. How you gonna go to a show, then go home with one of the dancers? I bet you it was the sista who put out the most tips who got the pleasure of being slayed. Like I said, I'm all for getting your nut off, but, damn, try to have a little class about yourself. Proper etiquette is to never spend *your* coins for a piece of dick and to never give it up on the first date. Give it up after a few dates and after a few gifts.

I shut my door, then straightened up my office before heading out to meet Tee. I placed all the papers that were scattered on my desk in one neat pile, changed the garbage bag in my trash can, then locked all the business checks and receipts in the safe. I put my eighteen-karat-gold hoop earrings back in, then went into my private bathroom to freshen up. I washed my face with a Neutrogena facial wash, put on a fresh coat of eyeliner, then dabbed some

Chanel No. 5 on my wrists and behind both ears. Just as I was about to lotion my hands, the phone rang. It was my private line.

"Hello."

"Hey, baby," a deep, dreamy voice said. "Did you get the roses and gifts I sent?"

I twisted my face up and rolled my eyes. It was Teddy. "Well, hello there," I said, trying to sound sexy and shit. "The roses were lovely and the gifts are beautiful." Three weeks ago, he sent me a dozen red and white roses. Two weeks ago, he sent me two-carat diamond earrings, and last week, he sent me the matching tennis bracelet.

"Just because," he said. Cheap bastard! I stopped wearing two-carat bracelets years ago.

"That was so sweet of you," I said as I sat on the edge of my desk.

"Well, baby, you know how I feel about you. I've been thinking about you a lot. I miss you."

Yeah, right, I thought. *The only thing you miss is this sweet pussy.* "Oh, Teddy, I've been thinking about you, too." I smiled to myself, then thought, *Yeah, I've been thinking how stupid your ass is.*

"Indy, I think it's time we take this to another level," he said in a delicious whisper. "I can't keep going on like this. I don't know what you're doing to me, baby, but I've got a love jones for you."

Another level? Please, the only level he's going to is sea level, with that big sperm whale head of his. Can't keep going on like this? Humph, sounds like he's ready to *hang it up*. "Oh really?" I said. "Well, where would you like to take this?"

"Baby, I'm ready to leave my wife."

"Leave your wife to go where?" I asked while I rubbed lotion on my hands.

"I'm ready to make a life with you. I think—"

"Wait a minute, Dr. Love. Don't think too hard," I snapped. "'Cause I ain't feelin' you like that. I mean, you know how to eat a mean piece of pussy and all, but that's all you know how to do."

"What's that supposed to mean?" he asked, sounding like a sad puppy. "I thought—"

"Listen," I said, standing up to put my hand on my hip. "That lazy-ass dick of yours is not something I want in my bed every night. So the only thing you should be thinking about is staying with your wife."

"So what are you saying? It's over between us if I leave my wife?"

"Listen up, hot lips," I said, getting really agitated. "You cheated on your wife. Now, what the fuck would I look like tryna make it happen with you? Now, if you wanna put those big, juicy lips on this pussy again, you're more than welcome to have a midnight snack, but anything other than that, I think not!"

There was a moment of silence, then he snapped. "What the fuck! You come into my life, fuck my head all up, and now it's over? Just like that? Nah, fuck that. Ain't shit over until I say it is."

"You sound really stupid," I said while laughing. "This party is over, so get over it."

"I don't think you heard what I just said. I *said* ain't shit over until I say it is."

"Lick my ass, psycho," I snapped, then hung up and unplugged the phone. *Tomorrow I'll have that number changed*, I thought. And since he wants to try to work my nerves, I'll have to send his wife a little snippet of how he likes to take it up the ass. That's right. I have his ass on videotape with me wearing a harness and a strap-on dildo knocking his back out. It's titled *Teddy Takes it in the Ass.* If he really pushes it, I'll send a copy to his J.O.B. *Now fuck with me if you want*, I thought, adding a mental finger-snap.

I grabbed the beige blazer to my Anna Sui pantsuit, slipped on my beige Anna Sui pumps, snatched up my Louis Vuitton, and headed for the door. It was 6:30 p.m. I walked through the shop saying nothing to anyone. *Make no mistake, I'm gonna get you next, bitch*, I said to myself when I caught Alexi peeping me out of the corner of her eye.

Tee was double-parked in front of the building, looking fly as hell behind the wheel of his tinted-out cranberry Ranger. Of course, he just had to be talking through the passenger side window to two average-looking sistas pushing a black Rover. The sista on the driver's side got out her freshly waxed whip and handed him a piece of paper. When she smiled, I thought she was doing a commercial for NYNEX. She had wires all across her grill.

Apparently, homegirl wasn't up on clear braces. And she damn sure wasn't up on fashion violations. How you gonna rock white slacks and white boots after Labor Day? I peeped her tags. Detroit. *It figures. Those Midwest hoes ain't up on shit,* I thought. I excused her away from the door, then got in. The truck smelled of fresh leather and Alfred Sung cologne. He smiled.

"What up, sexy?"

"You." I smiled. I looked at the two sistas parked next to me, then, with the press of a button, rolled the window up.

5

CHYNA: EVERYTHING MUST CHANGE

I GUESS IF YOU'RE AN OUTSIDER LOOKING IN, you'd think I was one of the luckiest women around. You'd probably even expect me to be happy. Hell, most women would kill to be in my shoes. I have a husband who owns four funeral parlors, four beautiful children, a home worth over nine hundred fifty thousand dollars, three expensive luxury vehicles, and a closet full of designer clothes and shoes—from Versace, Gucci, and Donna Karan to Issey Miyake. Then there's the climate-controlled vault filled with mink, coyote, beaver, fox, and any other hairy animal from stoles to floor lengths. You name it, I've got it. Oh, and let's not forget the wall safe full of expensive jewelry: diamonds, rubies, emeralds, and pearls, to name a few. Let's see, what else? Oh, yeah. The summer home in the Bahamas and one on Martha's Vineyard. So, I guess, if happiness were measured by financial status and material goods, then I'd be the happiest woman alive.

Well…let me be the first to tell you, everything that glitters isn't always gold. I am by no means happy. As a matter of fact, I haven't been happy in years. Not in this marriage anyway. Don't get me wrong, I love my husband very much, but not in the same way I did five years ago. I've changed. I don't think I've outgrown him but somewhere along the way the flame in our marriage blew out. Perhaps he's outgrown me. Perhaps he's fallen out of love with me. Perhaps my routine life, or my fantasy that people who fall in love stay in love, chased him away.

I am thirty-six years old and have been with one man my entire life—my husband. I'm not saying there's anything wrong with that, but I think it would have been nice if I would have done a little sampling first. As much as it hurts, I've suspected he's been doing a little sampling here and there. I might play dumb and I might be naive about certain things, but I'm no fool. I've just never confronted him on it, not yet. I've just swept it under the carpet and wrapped my life around raising our children. I don't blame him completely.

In many ways, I kind of pushed him away. Gradually, I shut him out sexually and emotionally.

I stopped sleeping in the nude or wearing any of Victoria's sexy secrets. Then I conveniently had a headache if and when he wanted to get sexual. Whenever I was feeling generous, I'd let him roll on top of me while I lay there like a dead fish. Every now and again, if I felt like stroking his ego, I might grunt like it felt good or even dig my nails in his back as if I were having the most fulfilling orgasm ever. But the truth is, it hasn't felt good in years. Five years, to be exact. I can't remember the last time I had an orgasm other than a self-induced one.

So, for the last two years, I haven't been responsive to any of his needs. I understand everyone has needs, and if they aren't being met at home, you eventually look outside of the home for fulfillment. I accepted that notion the day I packed his things up and moved them and him into the bedroom adjoining our master bedroom. Would you like to know what his response was? "Where's my toothbrush and electric razor?" The nerve of him. He didn't even have the decency to put up a fight—not that I should have expected it, but I had hoped he would.

A part of me really misses the early days when we had nothing but each other. We were determined to stay together and build a life together. There's a long history between us that I'm not ready to give up, not completely. To be honest, I'm not sure if I'm prepared to not have him in my life. Maybe that's one reason why I've held on to what little relationship we have left. I'm not ready to let go. When we speak to each other, it's in a tone that's distant and noncommittal. It's not bitter, just businesslike. In my heart, I know I don't want to continue with our life the way things are. Yet I've done nothing to try to salvage what's left of our marriage. I am going to have to make some major decisions and he'll have to make some choices as well.

Regardless of the outcome, a part of me will always have a special place in my heart for him. Always. Maybe, subconsciously, I've given up on our marriage prematurely. But it seems like he's thrown in the towel too. As far as I'm concerned, he gave up way before I did, when he cheated on me. Why haven't I said anything? Because for years I maintained the attitude that he can do what he wants as long as he takes care of me and our children, and the one thing he's always been is a good provider. So I silently dismissed his infidelity.

Of course, Indy thinks I'm crazy for not confronting him. She thinks I shouldn't let him get away with it. No one said I was going to let him get away with anything. I just haven't felt that it's something I'm ready to address yet. She thinks he will keep doing it because I allow it. Maybe she's right. But some things are easier said than done. And Indy, whom I love dearly, doesn't know the first thing about commitment—or even relationships, for that matter.

She recently said to me, "Girl, I don't know why you just don't get it out in the open. Enough is enough. And if he tries to lie, just slap the shit out of him and take him for everything he's worth. The one thing I can't stand is a cheating-ass man."

"I know, girl. I'm just not sure if I'm ready to deal with the truth."

"The truth?! Girlfriend, please. You saw the truth with your own eyes. What else do you need? And you know my motto: Once a cheater, always a cheater. I say throw his ass out and make him pay for his infidelity. Girl, his dipstick may be dripping something lethal. Ain't no telling what kind of package those hoes he's running around with have."

"Throw him out? Indy, this is as much his home as it is mine. I threw him out of our bedroom and closed up the sex shop a long time ago, so I don't care who he's sticking his dipstick in," I said, even though I did care. "Besides, I don't think he's running around with *hoes*, as you say. I don't even think he's sleeping with anyone right now."

"Oh, yeah? Well, ain't no man gonna go two years without sex. And I doubt he's just beating his meat. Humph. As much time as he spends down at those funeral homes, he's probably a necrophiliac. Girl, please. You can't tell me he hasn't looked in one of those corpses' pussies. I've got the scoop on a few morticians who are into some real kinky shit."

"Oh, Indy." I shuddered. "Do you have to be so morbid? This is my husband you're talking about."

"Well, let's say, for argument's sake, he isn't fucking around on you *now*. The fact of the matter is, he still cheated on you and you haven't said one damn thing to him about it. Humph. Girl, I don't know how you do it. Better you than me, 'cause Lord knows I'd really hurt him. Well, what do you plan to do if he decides he wants to leave you?"

Leave me? I had never considered that. My heart became heavy as I took a slow, deep breath. "I don't know. I haven't really thought about it. But I know I'm not leaving my home so he can move some little hussy in. I'd burn it down first."

Even though I said that, I knew I really didn't mean it. There was no way I'd ever go to the extreme of burning down my home just to keep him from moving another woman in. Besides, I believed in my heart that Ryan would never be that low. But, then again, I didn't think he'd ever cheat on me.

She laughed. "Well, alrighty then. So how are the kids? I got the pictures you sent. Girl, your boys are fine as hell." She chuckled. "It's a good thing I don't like my men young, 'cause I'd have to do all three of 'em."

"Indy, you're too much. Everyone's fine. Jayson's graduating from Pace next year—"

"Girl, you've got to be kidding. How old is he now?"

"He's twenty-one. Ryan is stationed in Japan. Kayin is a sophomore at Morehouse—"

"Now, that's what I'm talking about. Thirty-six and all the kids are already grown and out of the house." She laughed. "You betta work. And what in the world is up with Miss Sarina? I can't get over how much she's changed in one year."

"Sarina is still getting on my last nerve. I really don't know what I'm gonna do with that child. Last week, she came home with her eyebrow and lip pierced and she's dyed her hair strawberry red."

"You know teenagers these days," Indy replied. "They're really big on shock value."

I stared at Sarina's eighth-grade graduation picture sitting on the fireplace mantel. She wore bangs with a thick ponytail and had the face of an angel. Then I glanced over at her ninth- and tenth-grade pictures. In ninth grade, her hair was burgundy with gold streaks and her nose was pierced. In tenth, it was platinum blonde and shaved close on one side.

"Well, nothing she does shocks me anymore. Sometimes I really think she just does things to try to provoke me. I don't know where she gets her temperament from."

"From her Aunt Indy, of course. Miss Thing is almost as fierce as me."

"Well, Miss Thing is going to be shipped off to Utah or Wyoming to one of those farms for incorrigible teens if she doesn't get it together real soon. I don't know how much more I can take of her fresh behind."

"Well, what does Ryan say about all this?"

"Nothing," I said, feeling defeated. "Ryan doesn't know half of what Sarina gets into."

"That's a damn shame," she said with disgust. "Well, does he even ask?"

"He used to, but I never bother him with any of this."

"Girl, please. His ass lives in that house, too. Why the hell should you have to go through the ordeal of managing an out-of-control teenager by yourself?" She paused for a moment, then tsk-tsked me. "That child walks all over you. Maybe he needs to step up to the plate and be a fuckin' father for a change instead of a businessman."

"Indy, it's not all his fault," I said defensively. "I chose to keep things from him, but now it's gotten out of control."

"Well, he still makes me sick. He should know what the hell is going on under his own damn roof whether you tell him or not. He should make it his business to want to know. Speaking of that Grape Ape, where is he?"

"Indy, I wish you wouldn't call him names. I'm not sure where he is. Why do you ask?"

"Humph. No particular reason," she answered.

We both were silent for a moment or so. I'm sure she was thinking what I was already feeling. Helpless and hopeless.

"Maybe the two of you have outgrown each other," she said. "Hell, the two of you have been together since you were kids. Sometimes people grow apart. It doesn't mean they don't still love each other."

"Indy, I always thought we'd be happy with each other forever and grow old together, not grow apart."

"Chyna, just remember you have to create your own happiness. Your marriage can't do it nor can your kids. It has to come from within. Don't sit at home waiting for it to come bouncing through the door. Go out there and get it, girl. I love you."

"I love you too. I'll give you a call one day next week. Take care."

Indy was right. Ryan and I have been together since we were kids, and the reality is, we were too darn young to get so involved. But, as the saying goes, childhood ignorance is childhood bliss. I was fourteen and he was seventeen when we first started dating. I got pregnant when I was fifteen, married at eighteen, and had my fourth (and last) child by the time I was nineteen. Consequently, neither of us was psychologically or emotionally prepared to assume the adult roles and responsibilities that go along with having babies or being married. But his parents and my aunt Chanty made it very clear: "Since the two of you want to keep having babies, then the two of you will get married." Interestingly, every time I was pregnant, my aunt knew before it was confirmed. And after she *told* me I was pregnant the first time, she said, "I'll take care of you, but that little nappy-headed boy you let knock you up will take care of this baby. You can screw out of both sides of your pant legs if you want, but you *will* finish high school and you *will* go to college." That was the end of the discussion. My aunt was a firm believer that a mind was a terrible thing to waste and that you were nothing without an education.

She marched me over to his house, introduced herself to his parents, and said, "My niece is pregnant by your son, and I expect him to do right by her. If not, I will cut off his balls." Then my aunt lectured me to death while Ryan's father took the razor strap to his behind.

I used to think I would never have become a teenage mother or wife if I wasn't forced to live with my aunt in Norfolk. But the truth of the matter is, no matter where I would have been, I was bound to get pregnant. Because I was like so many of the young girls today—in search of love and wanting desperately to fill a void in my life. Ryan Littles did just that. Although he wasn't the most attractive boy who pursued me, he had the prettiest dark skin

I'd ever seen. He was black. Blueberry black, to be exact. I was mesmerized by the richness of his skin color. He was beautiful to me, and during a time in my life when I felt like the ugliest thing alive, he made me feel like the most beautiful girl in the world. He was well built for his age and was one of the most popular boys at Booker T. Washington High School. He was a senior track and football star who had been offered academic and athletic scholarships to Notre Dame, Northwestern, Morehouse, and Tuskegee. But, as per Mr. Littles, "Because of your parental responsibilities, you will work and attend school close to home." Mr. Littles was a tall, tight-haired, dark-skinned man from the old school who spoke in a deep baritone voice. You either did what you were told, or you were beaten until you bled to death. He believed in hard work and would "whup a lazy fool silly." Mr. Littles had only a fifth-grade education, but he made sure his seven boys finished high school and went on to college. Whether you wanted to or not, everyone in the Littles household went to school. There was no room for back talk. So Ryan chose Old Dominion University and worked full-time at Montgomery Ward.

At sixteen, I led the graduating class of 1978 as valedictorian, with an eleven-month-old son, Jayson, and eight months' pregnant with my second child. Back then being pregnant was like wearing the scarlet letter. Adults looked down on you, and your peers constantly ridiculed you. Well, that meant nothing to my aunt. She'd say, "You will go to school and you will hold your head up and keep up your grades." When Mr. Burton, the school principal, and a few other school officials protested against me giving the valedictorian speech—"Given her condition, it would not be in good taste or in the best interest of this school for her to address the student body or their families. We don't want to give the message that we promote unwed teenage pregnancy. She can participate in the graduation but..."—my aunt demanded a school hearing, named several girls who had been pregnant in school in the past, then threatened to sue them for discrimination. She even went as far as to threaten to "disclose the skeletons in your closet, Mr. Burton." To this day, I'm not sure what she had on him, but they all soon realized Aunt Chanty wasn't a force to be reckoned with.

By mid-June, I had given birth to our second son, Ryan Jr., and I was enrolled at Norfolk State by August. During the day, my aunt and Mrs. Littles took turns caring for the boys while Ryan and I juggled classes and parenthood. I have to say, if it weren't for my aunt and my in-laws, I don't know what kind of life we would have had. I am so thankful we had their support, guidance, and encouragement to finish our education and to make something out of our lives. True, our families were not pleased when I gave birth to our third son, Kayin. But they *still* made it very clear: "You will finish your schooling." It was something we both did. Ryan graduated in five years with a degree in biology and was accepted into Howard's pre-med program, but that was short-lived when he decided he wanted to be a mortician. So, off he went to the School of Mortuary Science while I stayed in Norfolk with our family.

In three and a half years, I graduated summa cum laude with a degree in psychology. In between those years of studying and being a mother, my aunt encouraged me to participate in extracurricular activities. So I pledged a sorority, and let me tell you, pledging for eight weeks and being a mother of two children was no walk in the park. No one gave me any sympathy. But, I stuck it out, and crossed the burning sands.

Anyway, over the last several years, our marriage has basically become a means of convenience for both of us. It's for appearance's sake. At any social event, you will see us smiling and holding hands like the ideal married couple. It's been torture trying to keep up this farce. For the sake of the children too, we pretend everything is okay. It's always been important to me that my kids have two parents under the same roof. Well, I'm not sure if that's done more harm than good, because I've basically done all the child-rearing by myself. Not that I'm complaining. It just would have been nice to have Ryan's help from time to time instead of having to be supermom all of the time. From orthodontist and pediatric appointments to soccer games, from piano and dance lessons to karate and Tae Kwon Do tournaments, from Cub Scouts and Brownies to sleepovers and private summer camps, my monthly calendar was always filled with appointments and activities for the kids.

I've stood by Ryan, I've struggled with him, I've endured with him—out of love. I married him and had his children—out of love. Anything he's ever wanted to do, I've supported him and encouraged him. I'm really proud of his accomplishments as a self-made businessman. I guess he was right when he said, "The more guns and drugs we have in our communities, the more bodies we'll have to bury. And the more bodies there are, the more money we'll have." To this day, I still have a problem with people making money off the dead. Why in the world should it cost anyone an arm and a leg to rest in peace? But, like he says, "It pays the bills."

I'll admit he's had more business than I ever imagined. He's gone from a tiny one-room parlor to four plush, finely decorated funeral homes in different locations throughout Maryland, and now he's looking to open his fifth in downtown D.C. I just wish it wasn't at the expense of some family's tragic loss.

I know Ryan's made sacrifices to ensure we've had the best of everything. But being able to provide for people financially doesn't mean you're giving them the best of anything. What about providing a little affection and support? What about some quality time with your family? What about being around to instill a little discipline? I made it my business to tend to the emotional needs of our children, out of love and my responsibility as a parent. I'm sure I overcompensated sometimes because he was hardly around. I don't know why I'm bringing all this up now. It's really a moot point. The boys are grown up, and the only one left to raise is our seventeen-year-old daughter, Sarina. And believe you me, I am counting down the days. Last week, my daughter made it very clear she lives by her own rules.

"Sarina," I said, looking at my watch. It was 3:00 a.m. "Your curfew is one o'clock. I've asked you not to come home at all hours of the night."

"Well," she said snottily, "if you were in bed, you wouldn't know what time I came home. But, *noooo*, you'd rather spend your life spying on me."

"Sarina, why do you insist on talking to me like I'm one of your girlfriends? I'm up because I worry about you. I can't sleep until I know you're home and safe."

She rolled her eyes so dramatically, I thought she was going to crack her eyelids. "Well, don't blame me because you can't get to sleep. Maybe you should try taking a bottle of sleeping pills. I don't need you worrying about me. I can take care of myself."

I remained calm as always, bit my bottom lip, then shook my head. "Sarina, you're my daughter. I worry about you because I love you."

"No," she snapped. "You worry about me 'cause you're always in my damn business. I'm almost eighteen, so you might as well let me do what I want. I'ma do it anyway."

"Listen, Miss Smarty-Pants," I snapped back, then quickly regained my composure. "Almost is not good enough. *Until* you're eighteen you are my responsibility and what you do *is* my business."

"Get a life!" she said, then marched up the stairs. "Muthafuckas are always tryna shit on me."

I wanted to get up and slap the taste buds out of her mouth but decided against it. I just watched her stomp up to her room and slam her door. I couldn't believe she used that tone with me, or that filthy slang in this house. I sat at the kitchen table, held my face in my hands, cried heavy tears, then stared at the calendar. *Two hundred and eighty-two more days*, I said to myself. In just ten more months, I am going to throw her the biggest party ever, then pack her bags and put her out. I love my baby dearly, but she has been my *worst* nightmare. I'd rather raise fifty boys than one girl. Trust me.

Then what? The kids will be gone, and there'll be nothing else to occupy my time. I guess I could go back to work. But where? Doing what? Five years ago, I worked part-time as a therapist for children and families in crisis. Although I liked getting out of the house, I wasn't happy being there. There was always one crisis after another, and it was mentally draining. I guess I could work on my doctorate since I've always enjoyed going to school and learning. I don't know what I'm going to do with myself. I mean, in between going to Howard to complete my master's degrees in social work and counseling psychology, the last fifteen years of my life have been devoted to providing a structured home environment for my children. Tending to the needs of my children has been my priority so I failed to consider my own. I never really gave any thought to what I'd do when the kids grew up and went out on their own. One thing's for sure: I don't want to become one of those busybody mothers who meddle in their adult children's lives because she doesn't have a life of her own.

And what's really scary is, if Ryan decides to walk out on me, I'll have nothing but what he's given me. Sure, I've saved some money, but not enough to maintain my lifestyle. Indy has always said, "Girl, get your own shit. This way, if your man decides to bounce, you can still do *you* without stressin' over how you'll survive." I never thought I'd have to even consider that as a possibility. Maybe it's not. Maybe I'm stressing myself about nothing. But what if I'm not? I've heard stories of successful men leaving their wives to fend for themselves after they've decided it was time to move on with their lives. Well, I'm not going to worry. Even if Ryan decides to move out, I am *still* his wife and the mother of his children. He'd still have to pay the bills and maintain my upkeep, right? There's no way I could continue living in this house on my savings. Lord knows I don't want to be another Bernadine in *Waiting to Exhale*.

It was after one in the morning when I heard Ryan close his bedroom door. I decided to take Indy's advice and confront him. If for nothing else, I needed some type of closure to this madness. I slipped on the red-and-black striped silk robe he had given me last Christmas, pulled my hair back from my face, and stood at his door—the one that connects to what was once our bedroom. Then I took two deep breaths. After I thought over what I would say, I tapped lightly on the mahogany door just enough to not be heard if he was sleeping. A part of me hoped he wouldn't respond.

"Yeah?" he asked with annoyance.

I placed my ear to the door. I could hear faint sounds of someone moaning. My heart jumped in my throat. "It's me. Can I come in? We need to talk." The whispery moans stopped, then I heard the muffled sound of his size-ten feet dragging across the thick gray carpet. The lock clicked. The door abruptly opened about six inches wide, then I heard him walking away. I came in and caught a glimpse of his nude backside as he climbed back into bed.

"Is there something wrong with the kids?" he asked while he propped two king-size pillows behind his back. It dawned on me that I hadn't seen him in over a month. Generally, he leaves the house at the crack of dawn and usually doesn't get home until after I'm sound asleep. Aside from calling me from time to time to discuss errands he needs me to run or to tell me about some extended mortician's conference he'd be attending, we haven't spoken in over a week.

"No. There's nothing wrong with the kids," I said, looking around the room. It was filthy. Suits were off hangers, dirty clothes were strewn across the floor. *Oh no, he doesn't have his wet towels thrown over my favorite oak rocking chair.* I walked closer and stood at the foot of the bed. "We need to talk about us."

He folded his huge arms across his hairy chest. His chest and arms were still well defined and cut. "What about us?"

I shifted my weight from one foot to the other, bit my bottom lip, then asked, "Are you having an affair?"

"Am I having a what? Affair? Where'd you get that crazy idea?"

"Well, are you?"

"Look, I should be asking you that question. You're the one who kicked me out of our bed. You're the one who stopped tending to my needs. So, if I am, why should it matter to you?"

"Ryan, I moved you out of our room because I felt we needed space, not because I was cheating on you. So don't try to twist this around. And, if you really want to know, the reason I moved you out of our bed is because I saw you at the Georgetown Golf Club—"

"So you wait two years to confront me? C'mon, that's the biggest bunch of bull I've ever heard. I don't know who's putting things in your head but—"

"So are you admitting that you cheated on me?"

"I'm not admitting anything. But, if I did, you have only yourself to blame. Anytime I wanted to make love to you or hold you, you'd have some lame excuse or you'd just act like it was something you *had* to do. Like your heart wasn't in it. So, if I did cheat on you, I probably wouldn't have if you had been a little more accommodating in the bedroom."

"Well, you could have moved your things back in. You could have questioned me. Hell, you could have acted like it mattered to you."

He shifted himself in his bed, then stared at the mute TV screen. *The nerve of him to start watching TV while I'm standing here,* I thought. He glanced at me.

"Look, you wanted space from me, so I've given it to you. You wanted to shut me out, so I'm out. But don't act like this is all my fault."

"I never said it was all your fault. Ryan, will you please tell me what I've ever done in this marriage besides love you? Nothing. And you don't even have the decency to be honest with me about something I already know."

"You shut me out of your life," he said in a tone tinged with sadness.

"Ryan, I did the only thing I knew how to do. What would you have liked me to do?"

"Nothing!" he snapped, then lowered his tone. "Look, do me a favor; get out of *my* bedroom. I'm tired. I have to get up in less than five hours, and I have a three-hour drive for a business meeting. If you haven't forgotten, I do have a business to run."

I felt my blood pressure go up a notch and a pulse in my brain throb. I inhaled deeply and prayed that I wouldn't lose my temper. The gall of him to tell me to get out of *his* bedroom and then make snide remarks about being accommodating and having a business to run. I should accommodate his behind straight to divorce court for adultery.

"You still haven't answered my question," I said, walking over to face him eye to eye.

"You figure it out. Now, please, get out and lock the door behind you."

He turned the TV off, reached over toward the nightstand, then pressed the base of the brass lamp. It was dark. That felt like a yes to me.

DAMASCUS: **R.E.S.P.E.C.T.**

A S SOON AS INDY GOT IN MY TRUCK AND ROLLED THE WINDOW UP on those sistas, I knew she was in one of her funny-style moods. Anyone who knows Indy knows that when she's in one of her moods, there's bound to be shit attached to it.

"I don't know why you waste your time with them outdated sistas," she said.

"Outdated? Girl, check this out. Pussy is pussy. Whether it's outdated or updated, it's still pussy. As long as it's clean, I don't care what the date is on it."

She tsked. "Typical."

"What's typical?"

"Your response. But, then again, it's coming from the biggest tramp around."

"Yo, I know you ain't talkin'. 'Cause you's a superfreak."

"It takes one to know one, so I'll take that as a compliment." We laughed.

Indy pressed the CD button, then turned up the stereo volume when Chaka Khan's "Eye to Eye" came on. She stared out the window and let her thoughts drift. Mine followed behind. The silence was broken when she noticed we were on Amsterdam Avenue. She turned the volume down.

"I know you're not going to the Shark Bar on a Friday night. Don't you know that place is probably packed with the after-work crowd?"

"Indy, chill," I said. "I got this, a'ight, boo?" I knew calling her Boo would get her going. Sometimes I just like to agitate her.

"Didn't I tell you not to call me your fucking boo?"

I smiled. "Yo, what I tell you about your mouth? I'll call you what I want, you got that, boo?"

"Oh, I can see you really want to get on my last fucking nerve, huh, Damascus?"

"A'ight, a'ight. You made your point." She knew I hated being called by my birth name, though not for any particular reason. I just preferred being called Tee.

She smiled her sexy smile, then said, "So, Tee, how was the show last night?"

"It was a'ight. How'd you hear about it?"

"Oh, news travels," she said. "Heard you made a lot of tips."

"Yeah, I did a'ight."

"Humph. I bet you did."

"Hey, when you're good, you're good. And I'm damn good at what I do. Yo, you should come check me out one night."

"Thanks but no thanks. You know how I feel about strip shows." Indy believes anyone who takes their clothes off for money in front of a crowd of strangers is insecure. She sees it as the only way they can feel good about themselves.

"Yeah, well, it's easy money and it pays the bills."

"And so does sleeping with the customers."

I let that slick remark slide and changed the subject. "Yo, when's the last time you heard from Brit?"

"Actually, I got a letter from him today. He told me to let you know he sends a shout-out."

"Word. I thought he forgot about a nigga, the way he just bounced off the scene. With his funny-style ass." She handed me the pictures he sent. "I see pretty boy is still doing his thing. Fly as ever."

"Now, you know, as vain as his ass is, he'd have it no other way," she said. "One thing's for sure: I miss the hell out of him."

I'll have to admit, a part of me misses him as well. I really hated to see him bounce. He's always been the one brotha I could count on to check a nigga like me when I was out of step. He'd constantly get on my ass when I didn't handle shit that needed to be handled. Like the time our lights got turned off because I forgot to pay the bill. Sometimes he'd vex the hell out of me with some of his ways. One time he locked up all the knobs and burners to our stove because I left it dirty. I came home hungry as hell and was gonna have one of my shorties hook me up a quick one until she came walking out of the kitchen, looking at me like I had two heads or something.

"Tee," she said, "how would you like me to fry this chicken?"

I looked at her like she was a real dumb-ass, then snapped, "On the stove, where else?"

"Well, smart-ass," she snapped back. "Why don't you come show me what stove you use."

"Girl, go on and cook my food. I'm too damn hungry to be playin' games," I said while I got up to walk into the kitchen. At first, I thought I was buggin' or something. But all the knobs and shit were missing. "Well, just bake the shit then," I said, vexed.

She clicked her tongue. "The racks are missing, too."

Man, listen…I was heated. It was like four in the morning, I was hungry as hell, and everything was closed. I ran up to Brit's room, swung the door open, ready to black on him, and his ass was gone. He'd left a note on the refrigerator: *Tee, I'm in New York with Indy. You'll have to order out because the kitchen has been shut down until further notice.*

But on the strength, he's always been cool people. What I've missed most is our deep raps. Sometimes we'd sit up for hours just talkin' about life. Yo, that brotha can really get deep on you. And I liked that. I've been through and seen a lot of shit, and he's the one cat I can honestly say I trust. He's the first brotha I've ever been able to be honest with about *everything*. Yo, I got mad love for him.

I smiled. "Let's go down and check his ass out. You down?"

"Hell yeah. You paying, right?"

"Yeah. I'll spot you, but you know what that—"

"Fuck that," she snapped. "I'll pay my own way." I laughed.

The Shark Bar was packed with people sitting at the bar or standing, waiting to be seated. We walked up to the hostess. I gave her my name, and we were seated in a corner booth at once.

"Oh, I see you made reservations," Indy said. "That was presumptuous of you. Now, suppose I didn't want to eat here?"

"Then I'd give you something else to eat." I smiled, then looked down in my lap.

"Boy, don't flatter yourself," she said. "Why does everything always have to be of a sexual nature with you?"

"I can't help it. I'm sexual by nature."

"Well, tonight, Mr. Sexual, you betta control your nature."

While we waited for the waitress to take our order, Indy gave me the low-down on her drama at the shop. I burst out laughing when she told me Alexi said her pussy was like a racetrack.

"Yo, she lit you up with that," I said, still laughing.

She chuckled. "Yeah, she got that off; but I got a little trick for her smart ass. Trust me. Everything woulda been cool had she not tried to grandstand on me. But she crossed the line. No bitch gets slick on my time and thinks she's gonna slide."

"Yo, Indy, just chill. Sometimes you gotta know when to let shit go."

"Oh, I'm gonna let go, alright. After I finger-snap her ass across the floor."

"Yeah, a'ight. With all those hormones she's taking, she's probably strong as hell," I said. "So when she beats your ass, don't come cryin' to Big Daddy."

"Big Daddy? Boy, please. I am not beat."

Indy then told me all the things the women in her shop said about me. I played the remarks off. Yeah, I'm proud of my body. I constantly hear, and have been told, how women brag about my body. But the truth is, the way she repeated their comments made me uncomfortable. She made it sound dirty and degrading.

I paused. Finally I said, "Oh yeah?"

She nodded her head, then stared at me.

I asked, "What?"

She was silent for a few moments, then shook her head.

Again I asked, "What?"

"Sounds like you and your pierced dick are really getting around. I guess a big dick is a hot commodity, huh?"

She said that like I was a piece of beef or something. I smiled through my uneasiness, then said, "You tell me. You like it big, don't you?"

"I don't care about dick size as long as a man knows how to use what he has. But I *will* blast his ass if he's lazy with it. Personally, I feel women who are stuck on the size of a man's dick have small minds and extra-large pussies." We both laughed.

When the waitress came over, Indy ordered blackened catfish, baked macaroni, greens, and two soul rolls. I ordered fried catfish, baked macaroni, string beans, a side dish of Buffalo wings, mozzarella sticks, and their bangin' peach cobbler. Indy smiled and shook her head.

"Damn, boy. You greedy as hell."

"Yo, I'm a growing boy," I said, rubbing my abs.

"Yeah, you're a boy, alright, but I don't know how much more growing you're gonna do."

I grabbed her left hand, then lightly rubbed my middle finger across her palm. "Oh, I'm growing, trust me." I licked my lips. "Long and strong."

She snatched her hand back. "You're so damn nasty."

I changed the subject. "Damn, you look good," I said, smiling and checking out her chunky diamond earrings, tennis bracelet, and the black pearl and diamond ring on her soft hand. "I see you still shinin'." Yo, word is bond; she looked sweet as hell. Those sexy-ass eyes of hers can make a nigga lose his fuckin' mind, know what I'm sayin'? And her smile...man, listen, she knows how to make a nigga weak. Damn, I just wanna...never mind, I was just feelin' her.

"Look who's talkin'," she said while pointing at the weight around my neck and wrist. "I see you're doin' your thing."

I smiled, then shifted gears again. "So what's been up with you?"

"Nothin' much. I'm chillin'. Nothin' major. Just tryna do me."

"I heard that," I said, then stared at her. I leaned back in my seat and folded my arms across my chest. "You still fuckin' married men?"

She twisted her lips up, then raised her eyebrows. And, with the flip of a switch, her attitude changed. "Not at the moment. Damn. You asked that like I'm some kinda trick or something."

"Nah, I'm not sayin' that. I was just asking." I watched her while she buttered a wheat roll. "Don't you think it's time you leave them niggas alone?"

Her tone was low. "They should be leaving me alone," she snapped as she bit into her bread. "I don't step to a brotha and say, 'By the way, if you're married and wanna cheat on your wife, I'll fuck you.' You act like *I* go after *them*. I could give two shits and a flying fuck about some sorry-ass married man."

"Then why even fuck with 'em?"

"The same reason you strip and sleep with every piece of ass that comes your way. Simple as that."

"It's not as simple as that. I strip for a living—"

"And you fuck for a living," she said. "So how does that make you any different from me? Especially when you've slept with married women yourself. Yeah, I've knocked a few married men off, so what? They wanted to play, so they paid."

"Check this," I said, trying to keep my cool. "I don't fuck for a living. Pussy doesn't pay my bills, it keeps my dick wet. And what makes me different from you is that I fuck for sport. You fuck for revenge. Don't get the game twisted."

"Revenge?" she repeated, buttering another roll. "Ain't nothing vengeful about draining the shit out of a cheatin'-ass man. If he respected his commitment, there would be no need for me to shut his cheatin' ass down."

I smiled. "Indy, sometimes you have a real warped sense of thinking. You're too damn fly to keep playing yourself."

"Playing myself?" Her jaws tightened and her tone became harsh. "How the fuck you figure?"

"Hold up. First, calm down. Second, don't talk to me with your teeth clenched. And third, just hear me out. Now, check it. If you expect men to give you shit in order to dick you down, then you're playing yourself. Whether you go after them or not, the fact that you know they're married should make you wanna send them on their way. But you don't. Then you try to justify your actions by saying men who cheat are no good. Well, neither are the women who cheat with 'em."

She rolled her eyes. "Whatever! I don't care what you or anyone else says. I'm not letting any man just fuck me for free. I don't care who he is, married or single. It doesn't matter. You want this pussy, it's gonna cost you."

"That sounds to me like a woman who fucks for a living too. Technically, I guess that makes you a prostitute with a high price tag."

"First of all, you know I handles mine without a man doing shit for me. Second of all, I am no fucking prostitute—"

"Okay then, a call girl."

"Kiss my ass, boy. I don't trick to pay the bills or to make a living."

"Okay, gold digger."

"Gold digger? Brotha, please. I am far from some fucking gold digger. I holds it down lovely on my own, and you know that. Don't *you* get the game twisted. I don't know how many times I gotta say this; I don't press men, they press me. If I choose to fuck them, it's on my terms, not theirs. I expect a nigga to have his pockets correct before he steps to me. I'm accustomed to having nothing but the best, and I'm not gonna settle for anything less— especially from some brotha who wants to slide up in this sweet pussy."

My dick got hard when she said that. "Oh, excuse me, Miss High Maintenance. I forgot you were born with a silver spoon in your mouth."

"If you wanna call it that. What can a broke-ass man do for me? Nothing. I'm not gonna be one of those women out here who gets used up or fucked over by some street straggler who's broke down and beat down."

"Just because a brotha doesn't have the financial means to offer you the things *you* can get on your own doesn't mean he can't treat you right."

"Fuck that. Like I always say: A broke man is a no-can-stroke man. So all that shit you talkin' I ain't tryna hear."

I shook my head. "I know what you need. You need a nigga with a strong back to beat that pussy up real good. That's what you need. A good fuck into reality." I laughed, but her face tightened.

Once again, I'd struck a nerve. Yo, she's real sexy when she gets heated. "You know what?" she snapped. "If we weren't in public, I'd slap the shit out of you. What you *need* to do is start respecting women. Something your mother shoulda been teaching your smart ass."

"Yo, don't talk to me about respect. What *you* need to do is start respecting women. Maybe if you did, you wouldn't be sleeping around with their husbands."

"Lick my ass," she growled, then excused herself to go to the bathroom as the waitress returned with our food. I watched her step, then smiled. Her pants were hugging the hell out of those hips.

I knew I had pissed her off, but fuck it. I know she likes to get her fuck on; and I'm cool with that. Yo, keepin' it real with you, there's really no difference between us. So I damn sure can't knock her for it. But all that crazy shit she's talkin' makes no sense to me. Granted, if a brotha is dumb enough to spend his money on a piece of ass, then she should spend his dumb ass. With all the free pussy out here, there's no way in the world I'm payin' to pop a nut. But, hey, there's some niggas out here who will and I know there are a lot of women out here who'll pay a man for a ride on his dick. I'm living proof of that. But I don't demand it or expect it. Of course, I don't turn it down either.

Shit. She knocks me like it's my fault that women just throw me the ass and I'm always down to catch it. Hell, I'm a man with a high sex drive. I like the feel of poppin' a nut. Fuckin' or suckin', it makes no difference to me. Fuck it. I don't care if it's in your mouth, in your ass, or in your pussy; a nut's a nut. Simple as that. The truth is, most of the time, I knock their backs out just for the hell of it, not because I'm feelin' 'em. Hell, most of 'em I don't even like. All it is to me is pussy—an opening attached to nameless and faceless bodies. And none of 'em get respect; as I said, none of them ever require it. All they've ever wanted from me was this long, black dick. It's been that way since I was a kid.

I guess it's kind of fucked up. But, hey, life is what it is. I've been fuckin' women since I was nine years old, and women have been playin' with and suckin' this dick since I was about seven. It felt good, so there couldn't have been anything wrong with it, right? Brit says I was abused. Yo, fuck that. Ain't shit abusive about an older woman givin' a young cat some pussy. They wanted a young, stiff dick and that's what I gave 'em. So what if they were old enough to be my mother? I see it as havin' been trained to fuck to get what I wanted and needed out of life. If I wanted food to eat, I'd fuck for it. If I needed clean clothes, I fucked for it. If I wanted a new pair of sneakers, I had to fuck for it. When I was fourteen and homeless, I fucked to have a warm place to sleep. This big dick paid for my room and board. Sleepin' on park benches or in abandoned buildings and subways ain't no fuckin' joke. So when I got older and saw how women respond to a young, strapping buck, I learned to fuck to get whatever I wanted. I had to fuck for survival. So women have shaped and molded me to be who I am.

As far as dancing goes, yeah, the pussy is in abundance, but it's not something I want to do the rest of my life. She acts like I enjoy being talked about by women like I'm some household appliance. She has no idea that there are times when I really can't stand being grabbed, rubbed, or touched by some strange woman. I hate the way their hands feel. I hate the way they beg and moan in my ear. Sometimes I just close my eyes and block out everything around me. I go through the motions because it's what they expect from me as a man. Fuck it. It's what they've always expected.

While I waited for Indy to return, I thought about some of the things Brit has said to me over the years and felt this funny kind of feeling. I can't explain it, but it was like a tightness in my chest. For some reason, he's always felt it his duty to challenge me.

"Tee, it sounds to me like you need to redefine your definition of manhood, because if you think having a big dick and a nice body makes you a man, then you are in for a rude awakening. Having a dick makes you a male, not a man. The size of your dick is just one characteristic of being a male; it's not what makes you a man. Being rugged and thuggish may make you appear manly, but it doesn't make you a man. If placing value on the length and the width of your dick and the number of times you use it is how you define who you are, then I'm afraid you will always be a boy in search of something you're not mentally prepared for. Maybe you put so much emphasis on your sexual conquests because you're insecure. No one can expect you to respect them unless you respect yourself first."

I never told him this, but sometimes I would lie awake at night thinking about some of the things he'd say to me. Sometimes I still do. What he fails to understand is that it has been women who've put a value on the length and width of my dick. It has been women who have defined who I am based on how I'm hung. I haven't been the one preoccupied with the size of my dick or how well I use it, women have. So what does that say about them? Still, we all have our reasons for what we do in life, right?

By the time Indy came back to her seat, our food had cooled. She cut her eyes at me, then flagged down our waitress. I smiled.

"Hi, is everything okay over here?" the waitress asked.

"I'd like to get a fresh drink," Indy said, handing her her untouched cranberry juice.

"Oh, is there something wrong with this one?" she asked while taking it.

"How should I know," Indy replied rudely. "I haven't drunk any. Just bring me a fresh drink and I want it in another glass, please."

The waitress looked at me, then back at Indy, who was staring her down. "I'll be right back with your drink," she said with a smile. I shook my head, but I knew that if I said anything, it would have been her cue to light my ass up. Although I knew she wouldn't turn it up too much in public, I figured I'd better just leave well enough alone.

While we ate, our conversation was light. I didn't want to beef, so I did my best to talk about anything and everything other than about the previous subject. It seemed safer that way, even though my thoughts were still there. We discussed our plans to go down to D.R. to check out Brit in December and to Maryland for Chyna's son's graduation party next June. We joked about Chyna being thirty-six with three adult sons and a daughter who is always full of surprises.

"Yo, Sarina sounds like a handful," I said while looking at the flicks Indy had brought of Chyna and her children. I couldn't help thinking what a sweet dime piece Chyna was. That cat Ryan had her bagged. I tried to figure out how the ugliest men in the world can pull the flyest honeys. It just always seems to happen that way, or vice versa. 'Cause I've seen a couple of mooseheads with some real sharp cats on their arms as well.

"Yeah, Chyna can't do a thing with her." Although Indy smiled, her attitude was as sharp as a knife. "I don't care how many kids you have, there's always one out the bunch who is going to give you a run for your money."

We stared at each other for a moment, then I asked, "Do you think you'll ever have kids?"

She placed her elbows on the red tablecloth, then rested her chin on her fists. "I don't know," she replied. "If I met a man who was sincere and could respect his commitment to me, then maybe." She became quiet. For a moment, I thought I saw a hint of sadness in her eyes, but she quickly dismissed her statement. "Hell no! I'm not fuckin' my shape up." On that note, I paid our bill and we headed toward the door.

I dropped Indy back off in front of her shop about nine-thirty. We were silent for the entire ride. Before she got out, I grabbed her by the arm and said, "Just remember, women aren't the only ones who get hurt or let down. There are a lot of good men out here who are committed to their families and to their mates. And there are a lot of men who can become good men and be committed if there's a strong woman behind them who's committed to standing by them. Sometimes the good men are the ones who get walked over or dismissed, but you don't hear them bashing all women the way you women bash all men."

She looked at me, then smiled. "Tee, I know there are good men out here. I just haven't met one."

"Well, maybe you haven't given yourself a chance because you're too busy being bitter."

"I'll keep that in mind. Thanks for dinner, asshole."

I smiled. "Good night, boo." She backhanded me in the chest, then quickly got out of the truck.

"You make me sick," she said, then slammed the door behind her. I watched her swish her way into her shop. She flipped me the finger. I smiled, tooted my horn, then headed toward the Holland Tunnel.

On the way home, I sparked up an L, then took a long pull. *Pspffffhhhh.* I held it in. It was smooth. *Psphhh.* The smoke filled my lungs, then found its way through my nostrils. Yo, *psphhp*, this is some good shit. I exhaled as the chronic fogged up my dark-tinted windows. *Psssspfffffffhhhh.* I thought, *After fuckin' with Indy's crazy ass, a good hit is what I need.* Once the blunt was a roach, I tossed it out the window, then blazed up another. I checked the voice mail on my pager. There were two messages from Tasha, one from Tracey, and another from Trisha. I decided to return the call from Trisha.

She picked up on the first ring. "Hello."

"Yo, what up? This is Tee."

"Hey, Tee. I wanted to know if you felt like chillin' tonight."

"What'd you have in mind?"

"*You,*" she said in a low, sexy moan.

"Word. I tell you what, I'm on my way home. Meet me at my spot around ten-thirty. And wear that little thing I like. Yo, I'ma tear that ass up." I ended the call, took another long pull, then blared 97.1 on the stereo to block out the cloudy images of the women who had shaped my life.

When I pulled into my driveway, Trisha was waiting. She stepped out of her black Maxima wearing a black trench coat and black heels. I pressed the remote for the garage door, then led the way inside. We walked through the kitchen into the dining room, then stood in the middle of the living room. I dimmed the lights, walked over to the sofa, then sat back with my legs wide open. Without saying a word, she opened her trench and let it fall to her feet.

She licked her lips and rubbed between her legs. "So you wanna tear this pussy up, huh?" she asked as she walked toward me in a crotchless fishnet bodysuit.

I smiled and pulled out my dick.

"You missed this, huh?" I asked.

She replied by dropping to her knees and taking me in her mouth. I lay back, rested my head on the sofa, then closed my eyes. The more dick she took in her mouth, the more my mind wandered. The harder she sucked, the further back my thoughts went. Yo, that chronic had my ass drifting through darkness. I've smoked a lot of trees in my day, but I've never felt this bent. Yo, fuck that, this shit was laced with some kinda PCP. A whole lotta ill shit started racing around in my head. I wanted Trisha to make my forehead cave in. I wanted her to suck my dick hard enough to suck out my thoughts. But she couldn't.

I heard the squeak of a door, then the faint sounds of someone whispering my name. The room was cold, but I could feel the warmth of someone's lips against mine. Warm hands slowly moved up and down my body, rubbing and grabbing me. My body tensed, then relaxed. Soft breathing became heavy panting when my dick was unleashed from my G.I. Joe pajama bottoms then sat on. Something hot and wet buried my dick. "Be a good little boy and make me feel good" echoed in my head. I tried to shake the thoughts and the sounds out of my head, but the harder Trisha sucked, the thicker my thoughts got. I felt fingernails dig into my shoulders while my dick was being pounced on. It felt good. I closed my eyes tight. Then a door slammed. There was yelling and screaming. Suddenly I felt the heavy blows of fists against my face and head. I was being kicked and beaten by a man who blamed me for his wife crawling into my bed.

Suddenly, everything became dark. The smell of mold and mildew suffocated me. The sound of chains rattled in my head. I heard another door slam, then the click of a lock. I opened and closed my eyes, realizing I had no sense of time. The days and nights seemed to collide together. Then sharp pains and angry growls from the pit of my stomach made me weak until I passed out. Beaten and chained, I had been locked in a basement and starved for five days because my bed, that of an eight-year-old boy, was invaded by my foster mother.

I closed my eyes tighter. It was foggy. Scattered images kept invading my mind—of a woman on her knees, in a darkened stairwell, sucking the dick of a young drug dealer. I could tell she'd once been a pretty woman who had let alcohol and drugs control her mind and erode her body. Her teeth were rotted and her hair was matted under a dirty head rag. The young dealer face-fucked her and slapped her in the back of the head until he exploded in her mouth.

I squeezed my closed eyes tighter, trying to erase the picture that kept fighting its way through the fog, but it kept attacking me. I tried to run from it, but it kept following me. I tried to concentrate on the sounds of the mouth around my dick, but with every slurp and every moan, the picture was still there. Then another image crept up. I heard gunshots, then saw a half-naked woman lying in a pool of blood in a stairwell with three bullet holes in her forehead. I tried to shake the vision out of my head, but it just kept grabbing me.

All at once, a strange feeling swelled inside of me as the blurry vision came into sharp focus in my mind. My eyes snapped open and my dick went limp.

I jumped up. "Yo, get the fuck out," I yelled. "Get your shit and get the fuck out my house."

I could see Trisha's fright and confusion. "What's wrong? What happened?"

"Nothing. I just want your nasty ass out of my fucking house."

"What?! Yo, you're one fucked-up brotha," she screamed as she snatched up her clothes and ran out the way she came in. I heard the garage door slam.

For the first time in my adult life, I cried. Heavy tears. Tears I hoped would drown out the images of a woman who spent her life on the welfare roll, selling her food stamps, abusing her body, and sucking dick for drugs. Tears I hoped would rinse away the blood of a woman who lost her soul to the streets. Tears I hoped would ease the agony of a woman who was raped and killed. Tears I hoped would drown out feelings of loss and abandonment in the life of a six-year-old boy.

For the first time in my adult life, I stood in the middle of nowhere, bruised and alone with images of my mother.

BRITTON: **CAUGHT UP**

THE FIRST THING I DID WHEN I GOT HOME was check my messages. There were about twelve. Now, I can be home and get one, maybe two calls, but I go away for one week and there are twelve—excluding the three callers that hung up on the machine. I fast-forwarded all of the unimportant ones, stopping to hear the others:

"Hey, sexy, this is Indy. Give me a call when you get a chance. You know what? I'm really hatin' you right about now. I got your pictures today; you look too damn fine. You betta work, boy! By the way, did you get the package I sent? I know how unreliable the mail system is down there. Call me soon. I miss you. Hugs and kisses."

"Hello, stranger. This is Chyna. When you get a chance, give me a call. I really need one of our sessions. I miss you. Love ya."

"Brit, where the hell are you? This is your sister. I've been tryna reach you all week. Call me A.S.A.P.!"

"Yo, Brit. What up, son? You don't know how to call a nigga, huh? Yo, I'ma blast your funny-style ass when I get up with you. Word up. Listen, Indy and I wanna shoot down for a little fun in the sun. Yo, we need to talk. Peace."

"Britton Landers, why haven't I heard from you? You know I like to hear from my number one son at least twice a month. It's almost a month since I've heard from you. Don't get down there and get jazzy. Call me the minute you get this. I love you."

I smiled. I have to say, I was happy to hear from my five favorite people in this world. I called Tee back first. The tone of his voice told me he needed a brotherly heart-to-heart. After five rings, I heard his "Hello," very dry and melancholy.

"Tee, what's up, boy?"

His voice perked up. "Yo, this betta be my nigga calling."

"That it is. So when you coming?"

"Yo, I can be on the next thing smokin', but I don't know about Indy and her crazy ass. We talked about coming in December, but now we beefin' so that cancels that," he said, then filled me in on their conversation.

"Well, she needed to hear it. I keep telling her to chill, but she's so damn hardheaded. I really believe what goes around comes around. I just hope she's prepared to handle whatever happens. But you know Indy; she's always right."

"Fuck it," he said. "Yo, where the hell you been? What, you don't love a nigga no more?"

"Come on now, you know better than that. I've just been chillin'. Actually, I just got back from vacation."

"Vacation?! Yo, how the hell you gonna take a vacation from a vacation? You just doin' it up, huh, kid?"

"I wish. I'm broke as hell down here."

He laughed. "Yeah, a'ight. You know I know betta."

"Do me a favor. Call Indy on three-way so I can see what's up with her."

"Damn," he said. "I'm really not feelin' her smart ass right now."

"Come on, now," I said, trying to sound really broken down. "You know I can't afford to make long-distance calls. Just don't say anything."

He sighed. "Yeah, a'ight. Hold on."

When he clicked the phone line over, I wondered what was on my boy's mind. Over the years, he and I have been able to talk about almost anything. I could tell he needed to talk to me today more than ever. While I waited for him to click back over, I grabbed my mail off my suitcase, walked upstairs to my bedroom, went out onto the balcony, then flipped through the stack of envelopes. There was a letter from Chyna, one from my attorney, and one with a return address from Germany. My heart jumped in my chest, but before I could focus on what I was feeling, Tee came back on the line.

"Yo, B, you there?" he asked while the third line rang. "I hope her ass doesn't say anything slick."

"Hello," she said in a voice as sweet as honey.

"What up, girl? It's your Caribbean road dog."

She screamed. "Boy, where the hell you been with your fly ass?"

"I just got back from a cruise."

"Boy, I'm too through with you. I've called you mad times. Did you get the sneakers I sent?"

"I know. I got your messages. And, yes, I got the sneakers. Thanks," I said, then blew her kisses through the phone. "So I hear you and Tee are coming down to see me."

Her honey-sweet voice turned to hot Bajan pepper sauce. "I am not fuckin' with him. He pissed me off something *fierce*. He's lucky I didn't slap his damn face off."

I played dumb. "So what did he do or say this time?" I asked, knowing damn well she was gonna burn my ear to no end. Which is just what she did. She gave me the Indy version of what happened, claiming that "just out of the blue" he asked her if she was still sleeping with married men, then called her a prostitute and told her she needed someone to "rough fuck" her, which she considered disrespectful and degrading. As to be expected, Indy was in rare form.

"Can you believe him? Ooooh, I just wanna take a metal spatula and whip the piss out of him. I just wanna slap him upside that bald, muscle head of his." Tee burst out laughing.

"Who's that laughing?" Indy asked.

"Now, boo, is that any way to talk about Big Daddy?" he asked, confident that she was gonna black.

"Brit, I know you don't have me on fuckin' three-way with—"

"Indy, chill out," I said, cutting her off. "I just wanna know if the two of you are coming down."

"I'll be down. And when I come, it's gonna be a classic club weekend, okay?! But I'm not going anywhere with that crude, nasty, skunk-ass. I'll call you when I know when."

"Yeah, yeah, yeah," Tee said. "Don't worry about it, sticky drawers. You still my boo."

Well, if gas and a match weren't cause for an explosion, I knew this would be. I could feel the heat and flames coming through the phone lines.

"Lick my ass, motherfucker! And, until you know how to talk to me, don't call my motherfuckin' house!" *Click*.

"Tee, you still there?"

"Yeah, I'm here. Yo, her ass is crazy. I told you she was buggin', right?"

I laughed. "Yep, she's still mad."

"She'll get over it. If not, fuck it," he said, then let silence come between us.

"Yo, Tee, is there something wrong?"

"Nah, man. I'm just thinking. Yo, check it out. I'm gonna be down in Miami Beach for a show on Friday. When I'm done, I'm gonna jet down there for a minute, is that peace?"

I smiled. "Sounds like a plan to me. What about Indy?"

"Fuck her! I'm flyin' solo. So, check it, it's Puerto Plata International, right?"

"Right."

"Okay. I'll snatch a cab to Sosua, right?"

"Yep. It's about five, maybe ten minutes away," I said. "And, Tee, when you're ready to talk about what's really on your mind I'm here for you. You know that, don't you?"

He was quiet for a moment, then said, "Yo, I gotta go. I'll see ya sometime on Sunday."

We hung up. I thought about Tee's and Indy's beef. If I had been the one having that conversation with her, she would have taken it in stride. We would have really gotten down and dirty about it, then laughed it off. But Tee? Oooh-wee, she is on the warpath with him. And when Indy is on the warpath, she shows no mercy. I recalled her outburst and laughed out loud. The two of them are always at each other's throats about something. They both, for some strange reason, like to provoke each other. Their love/hate relationship is too much for me. Actually, it's downright sickening. I shook my head. For a split second, I suffered a moment of insanity as I tried to imagine the two of them together, intimately. It made me think of that movie *Species II*. Two nasty, sex-crazed creatures in heat. It made me hysterical.

Then I remembered the letter, and my posture and mood changed. Tension coiled around my neck and the veins in my forehead throbbed fast and hard. I massaged both of my temples in slow circular motions, pressing the tips of my fingers in firmly. I leaned back on the balcony railing, grabbed the back of my neck with my left hand, rolled my head around twice, then stretched my neck from side to side. Closing my eyes, I tilted my head back, took a deep breath, held it in for ten seconds, then slowly exhaled. I repeated, sucking in the ocean's warm breeze, then blowing it out three more times before I went over to rip open the contents of the envelope from Germany.

I picked up the letter off the wicker and glass table, stared at it, then sat down in the wicker chair. I held it in my sweaty hands while I stared out into the Atlantic Ocean. For some reason, its crystal blue water always has a very calming effect on me. If only I knew how to swim. Isn't that crazy? Here I am, surrounded by miles and miles of beautiful beach, and I can't swim a lick. I'm thousands of miles away from home, and no matter how far I go, the past still has a way of finding me.

I opened the envelope and pulled out a one-page letter and a first-class, round-trip ticket to Nuremberg. I studied the way the date was written, in military form in the top left corner of the crisp white stationery. Suddenly I was six again.

My trance was broken by the sound of the phone ringing. I let the answering machine pick up but then ran into the bedroom to answer when I heard my mother's voice. "Hi, Mom!" I said, falling across my unmade bed.

"Britton?" she asked. "Well, hello to you too. I have been worried sick about you. Is everything okay down there?"

"Yes, Mom. Everything's fine. I was just getting ready to call you," I lied.

"Then what took you so long? Don't try to get jazzy with me, young man."

I laughed. "Mom, you know I wouldn't get jazzy with you. I just got back from a cruise."

"Humph. Well, you could have still called your mother. After all, you *are* my favorite son."

"Mom, I'm your only son," I replied with a smile.

"Then you better act like it, mister, and not have me worrying."

I apologized for not calling sooner or letting her know I was going to be away, even though I didn't think I needed to since I *am* grown and living on my own. But I understood her concern. I told her all about the ports of call—

Puerto Rico, St. Thomas, St. Lucia, Guadeloupe, and Grenada. She, in turn, told me about her new job working as a senior counselor at a battered women's shelter in Jersey City.

"Mom, have I told you lately how proud I am of you?"

My mother has always been my greatest inspiration. When I was a little boy, the way she wore her hair and makeup made me think she was a movie star. She always had this charm and grace about her. When I was around four years old, I saw Dorothy Dandridge playing in *Carmen Jones*, and I really thought it was my mother. That's who she looked like to me. To this day, she is the most beautiful woman in the world to me. And I'm grateful for the genetic blessings she's passed on to me. With the exception of the black mole on my left cheek, which comes from my father, you can tell she spit me out. From my hair and clear skin to my big, round, brown eyes and long eyelashes, I am definitely my mother's child. She's a reddish-tinted, caramel-colored woman of Cherokee, African American, and Irish descent who used to wear her shoulder-length hair in a French roll. Now that she's older, she wears it "short and sassy with a splash of gray," as she would say. Over the years, her hourglass shape has evolved into a more full-figured look, but, hey, she's sixty-two and still "da bomb."

Yes, I'm proud of her. This is a woman who dropped out of school in the eleventh grade, got married at eighteen, then left her husband after fifteen years. She became a single mother of two young children, and not once did she accept public assistance. Not once did she bring men around us. If she dated, we didn't know about it. If she drank or smoked, we never knew it. She worked as a seamstress during the day and went to adult school at night until she received her High School diploma. Then she enrolled at Jersey City State College, where she earned her bachelor's degree in social work. This is a woman who had no marketable skills and was told by my father she'd never be able to make it on her own because she had no education, no skills and two children. She was told no man would ever want her. Ha! She has a career now and is happily married to a man who loves her, unconditionally. Yep, Mr. Jay loves her in a way that makes her eyes twinkle when he walks into a room or when she talks about him. When he smiles at her or calls her name, her face lights up like the Christmas tree in Rockefeller Center. Having the opportunity to see her that happy is priceless.

"As a matter of fact, you haven't. But I already knew that," she said, and I could tell she was beaming. "I'm proud of you, too. Now, when are you coming home?"

"Mom, I really don't know." I sighed. "Right now, I'm content here. Why don't you come here to spend some time with me?"

"Well, maybe, once I get settled in my new position," she said, then changed the subject. "Amira told me she spoke to you last week. Have you called your father yet?"

I knew this was coming. Amira is always running her damn mouth. Like I said, she's always in my damn business. "No, not yet," I said. I stared at the letter in my hand for a moment, then asked, "Mom, how did you find it in your heart to forgive him?"

"Once I got tired of holding on to the past, I just let it go. I didn't have time to waste obsessing over something I could never change. I had to make changes for myself and within myself. Baby, it's okay to hurt, but if you hold on to it, you never get better. It will just eat away at you. I didn't want him to have that kind of control over my life. So I prayed and prayed until God gave me the strength to let go. Once I did, I was able to forgive him. I'll never forget. But I don't dwell on it because I've moved on with my life."

"Well, I've moved on with mine too."

"Honey, you may have moved on, but you've taken all the baggage with you. So where have you really gone with all that weight on your shoulders? It's just been dragging you down. Your father is not a well man. I don't want you to ever have any regrets. He has always tried to reach out to you. To make it up to you. But you were steadfast in your decision to not have anything to do with him. And, boy, you know I know how stubborn you can be." She laughed. "Where in the world you got that, I'll never know. Anyway, I just told him to let you be."

"Well, he should have kept trying."

"And what purpose would that have served? You have always been cold to him. Not rude, just short. He'd send you cards, money, and gifts, and you'd send them back or never open them. He'd send for you and your sister, and you'd refuse to go. You made it clear you didn't want him in your life. He made it clear that he didn't want me to force you to be a part of his. So he thought if he gave you your space, you'd eventually come around."

"So what does he want from me now?"

"I don't know. You'll have to ask him that," she answered. "Maybe he wants one last chance to see the man you've become. Your sister and I have always kept him abreast of your accomplishments."

I knew Amira would blab my business, but I didn't think my mom would. So I asked her, "Why?" And she said because he was *still* my father and that he took care of me whether I had wanted him to or not. Every month he'd sent child support, paid our medical bills, and made sure she had enough money to keep a roof over our heads. He bought our school clothes and paid for my education and my first car.

She asked, "How else would I have been able to afford all of those things on minimum wage? Well, baby, I gotta run. Just remember, whatever you do in life or whatever decisions you make, I will always love you. And as long as you are down there in that foreign country, I want to hear from you at least twice a month. Just because you're a grown man, don't think I can't still put a strap to your behind."

I laughed a real hearty laugh. "Mom, you're too much. I love you, too. You will always be my number one lady. I'll call you soon, I promise. Tell, Mr. Jay I said hi."

After we hung up, I stayed stretched out on the bed for about an hour and thought about what my mother had said. Hearing her voice made me feel warm inside and made me realize just how much I've missed her. I'm not sure why I didn't tell her about the letter, but I suspect she already knew about it. Mothers always seem to have a way of knowing more than you'd like them to. I leaned up on my elbows, opened up the letter, and began to read.

Dear Britton,

I don't know exactly where or how to begin. It feels like I let guilt put a lifetime of distance and space between us. Something I never wanted to happen. Something I did because of my own uncertainties as to what I did to you for you to not want me in your life. Whatever it is, I respect that it's something that has impacted the course of our relationship. And, for that, I am truly sorry.

I am sorry for failing you as a father. Regardless of what you wanted, I should have been there through your stages of development. I regret missing out on the best part of your formative years. I should have been there to assist in the parental process of shaping, molding, and preparing you for manhood. But I failed you and, for that too, I am truly sorry.

I've heard you've turned out to be a very responsible and productive man. Through pictures your mother and sister have sent over the years, I have watched you grow and turn into a fine man. Your mother did a wonderful job of raising you. I knew she would. She's just a remarkable woman.

Hearing of your accomplishments and successes, instead of being a part of them, hurts. Knowing that I failed you hurts. It's a pain that never goes away. I had a responsibility to you as a parent, and I let my own feelings of rejection negate my obligations to you as a father. The price for my negligence has been not being able to call you "son" because it's a right I haven't earned. That also hurts.

I'm sure you are aware of my deteriorating health. The doctors aren't sure how much longer I have left. But I'm holding on in hopes that you will allow me the chance to see the man you've become. I don't want to close my eyes for good without seeing the fruits of your mother's love and labor. I don't want to leave here not knowing what I did to push you away from me or not having the chance to apologize to you. I want to be able to tell you in person how proud I am of you and, most importantly, that I love you.

I have enclosed a roundtrip ticket in hopes that you'll find it in your heart to give me an opportunity to embrace you. I look forward to seeing you.

With all that is in me,
Your father

He included his phone number at the bottom. I rolled over on my back, neatly folded the letter, then laid it across my chest. With my arms behind my head, I stared up at the ceiling fan that slowly turned. With each revolution, I counted: one, one thousand, two, one thousand, three, one thousand. …I closed my eyes to the blood on the walls and the cries for help. The sounds of heavy fists against soft flesh echoed in my mind. Bruises and black eyes stained my memory of a beautiful woman. With the steady turning of the fan, warm tears slowly rolled out of the corners of my eyes as I said a silent prayer for every woman in this world who is beaten every twelve minutes by a husband or a boyfriend.

In the blink of an eye, it was 8:00 a.m. Sunday morning. I jumped out of bed when it dawned on me that in a matter of hours, Tee would be at my door. I noticed there was sand in my bed and in my hair. Fuck! My head throbbed from the six shots of tequila I'd had down at the Oxy-Dos (a multimillion-dollar disco that opened up on the edge of town about two years ago) last night. I'm not a drinker; as a matter of fact, I haven't had a drink in years, but last night I just needed to unwind. My body ached from dancing so hard. I hadn't been out dancing since I moved here a year ago. The place has several dance floors and the beats pump. I mean, it's not The Shelter or The Tunnel, but the place was packed with vacationers, and for a Caribbean island, you can get a good workout which was what I needed to sweat out my tension. From the merengue to free styling, I let loose. I dragged myself to the bathroom to relieve myself, then washed my hands and face. I needed to clean this place up. I went downstairs, threw about ten CD's into the JVC player, and pressed random on the remote. Terry Ellis's soulful voice danced through the villa. I went back upstairs and tackled the guestroom first, then my bedroom. I opened the windows to air out enclosed emptiness, replaced the old linen with crisp white sheets and white goose down comforters. I dusted the furniture, then mopped up the oak floors with Murphy's oil soap. I moved from room to room with the rhythm of each track selection. Jomanda met me in my bedroom. The Brand New Heavies entertained me in the kitchen. Arrested Development dropped their knowledge as I scrubbed down the bathroom. In an hour, the place was spotless. I stood in the middle of my airy living room and smiled. The room was impressive, with huge tropical plants. African masks and paintings lined freshly painted white walls. With the exception of a white sofa, a love seat, and a white marble coffee table, nothing inhabited the room's spaciousness, which made it feel more like an art gallery than a living room. The open patio door let in the morning breeze off the Atlantic, stirring a light scent from the sandalwood candles situated throughout the room.

After I ate breakfast and did the dishes, I went upstairs to shower. In my bedroom, I took off my checkered boxers, then stared at myself in the full-length mirror. I grabbed the small bulge of fat around my waist and thought, *This is not fly.* So I decided to do one hundred crunches but stopped at thirty when it started to hurt. I stood up and looked at myself again, hoping those thirty would have made a difference. They didn't. That's when I noticed bright red bruises along the center of my chest. There were strawberry patches on both sides of my neck. "What the fuck?!" I yelled. They were round bruises, the kind caused by heavy sucking in the heat of the moment. You got it, passion marks, or hickeys.

Now, the only way I could have gotten those love bites was from the girl I met down at the club last night. We made love. No, correction—She was a stranger; strangers don't make love. We had sex. Last night on the beach, I had unprotected sex with a nameless woman. Maybe she told me her name, but I don't remember. I do remember her saying she was from New York. Uptown? I think she said around the 174th Street area. She was sexy and she spoke English. Clear. Concise. Complete. She was a beautiful, warm body who was willing to let me release a load of backed-up tension. I could blame it on the tequila, but I wasn't really intoxicated. I could blame it on depression, but I wasn't depressed. Sad, maybe, but not depressed. Impulse? That's what it was, impulsiveness. Fuck! I know better. With AIDS being the leading killer of African American men aged twenty-five to forty-four and the second-leading killer of African American women in the same age group, we both should have known better. It's too damn risky to be living risqué. Fuck!

I had seen her earlier that afternoon down at the beach. Believe me, she was a dime piece. She was just sweet crazy. She had emerged from the crystal blue water wearing a sheer black one-piece bathing suit that V-lined to her navel and clung to her honey-colored skin. I, like many others, was mesmerized by her flawless beauty. Yet, she seemed oblivious to all the eyes that followed her as she strolled across the hot white sand toward her friends. Beads of water slid down her petite frame, then quickly evaporated in the whistle of the warm wind. I know, I know. It sounds like something out of a movie. But I'm telling you it happened exactly this way. Make no mistake, the Dominican Republic has no shortage of beautiful women, but she was the most striking I've seen. From afar, she looked like Pocahontas, with thick, curly black hair that was wavy at the roots and neatly pulled back into a ponytail. She had shiny black eyebrows that neatly arched over big, brown, dreamy bedroom eyes. She was just out-and-out sexy. I have always been a sucker for a gorgeous girl. Sade, that's who she reminded me of. I love me some Sade.

So when I saw her on the dance floor with the same group of women I'd seen her with at the beach, I decided to ask her to dance. I had studied her movements for about six songs before I approached her. Her body swayed smoothly with the music and I liked the way she gyrated her hips. Our movements were in sync and we worked up an energetic sweat.

After a few hours of dancing together, she asked me if I felt like going out-side to get some air. So we walked through town, past the small plaza of shops, until we reached the narrow road that leads down to the beach. During the day, the road is lined on both sides with a variety of stands selling Haitian paintings and other tourist souvenirs. But at night it's perfectly still and charmingly native. We both took off our shoes and walked along the shore-line, eventually reaching a small, secluded section of the beach reserved for lovers. The moon was full, the sky was bright with twinkling stars, and the ocean whispered soft music. We sat on the sand and let the cool breeze dance against our bodies. My thoughts drifted back home to the comforts of family and friends. I'm not sure what her thoughts were, but my reverie was soon interrupted by the sound of her gentle voice.

"A penny for your thoughts," she said.

"Oh, I was just thinking about life and the transitions we go through to get to where we need to be. It's an evolutionary process that never seems to have any rhyme or reason."

"I hear that. So, do you have any idea where you need or want to be in life?"

I thought about that for a moment, then looked into her eyes. "Yeah," I said. "At peace."

"Do you think you'll get there?"

"I hope so. And you? Where do you want to be in life?"

"Emotionally free," she said. "I need to be free from loving people who are emotionally controlling and no good for me. For some reason, I always end up with my heart thrown in my face."

We talked for hours as if we had known each other for years. She told me she was visiting her grandmother in Santiago, which was about two hours away, and that she'd be here for another six weeks. She said that every year, her mother and her two aunts fly over to spend the summer here. She told me how her family lived between Santiago and New York, then joked about how people who live part-time in the Dominican Republic are called "Dominican Yorks." I shared with her my reasons for temporarily relocating here. We laughed at the fact that I spoke very little Spanish and really had no investment in learning. She offered to teach me, but I declined. She listened and nodded as if she understood what it meant to just up and leave everything and everyone behind without ever looking back. She confided in me her need to get away and start a new life without someone else being the focus of it. I understood that feeling.

"Are you married?" she asked.

I sighed quietly. "No," I said after a while. "Divorced." Okay, I lied. My wife and I never legally divorced. I just divorced myself from her mentally and emotionally. Besides, I haven't seen or heard from her in over fifteen years, so as far as I'm concerned, I'm divorced. "What about you?" I asked.

"Sorta, kinda," she said while she dug her neatly polished toes deep in the cool white sand. "I'm married but not in the traditional sense. Actually, I'm separated."

"Oh, you were shacking?"

She laughed. "No. I'm a lesbian."

"Oh," I said, trying not to sound surprised. She was a beautiful woman who I'm sure was hounded daily by men. I just wouldn't have thought it. I smiled in return.

"What's it like?"

"What?"

"Being with a woman." I said, as if I had never experienced the wonderful pleasures of being with one myself.

She pulled her knees up to her chest, wrapped her arms around her legs, then rested her chin on her knees. She stared off into the ocean, pondering the question.

"It's more emotional. More intense than being with a man. Men are more physical. Women tend to be more sensitive to your needs because they have the same needs. Most men don't know the first thing about making love to a woman. They think that making love begins and ends with an ejaculation and that the definition of *foreplay* is kissing while penetrating or having their dick sucked."

I smiled again. "Have you ever been with a man?"

"Yeah, I've had my share. But they always seemed to have another agenda. Playing games and lying aren't part of my M.O. Besides, most of the men I dated confused good sex with having a big dick. And what's worse, they don't know what being sexual versus sensual means. There's a big difference between the two." She blushed. "I can't believe I'm sitting here telling you all this."

"Sometimes talking to a stranger is easier. You never have to worry about them telling your secrets to people you know. Besides, what's the likelihood of us running into each other again?"

"You never know. This is a small world."

We continued to talk until the wee hours of the morning. I told her about my failed marriage and my choice not to become romantically involved again. To just stay to myself. She seemed to understand my need to vibe alone. I even shared with her the fact that I hadn't been sexually involved with anyone in almost a year. Now, talk about disclosing to a stranger.

"So when do you think you'll move back to the States?" she asked.

"I'm not sure. Soon. I'm starting to miss my family and friends. But for right now, my life is here."

"Alone?"

"Yes, alone but not lonely," I said. "I'm finally learning about me. And in my process of self-discovery, I'm learning to love me. I no longer need anyone to validate who I am as a person or a man."

"Amen to that," she said. "You know, sometimes I can be surrounded by people and still feel lonely. Loneliness is a terrible feeling."

"I can't imagine a beautiful woman like you being lonely."

"Well, I am. People just assume...trust me, being beautiful isn't always a beautiful thing."

Her comment made me think back to when I was very self-conscious about my looks because of the constant pretty boy remarks I had heard growing up. It made me remember when I used to pray that one day I'd wake up ugly. But hearing her talk made me appreciate the fact that beauty really comes from within.

We both stared at each other and smiled. We seemed to be on the same wavelength about many things, and there was a lot of energy flowing between us. Positive energy. Sexual energy. The kind of energy that makes your heart do somersaults. Then something came over me. I don't know, maybe it was the smell of her coconut-scented oil or the fact that my hormones were going through some type of lunar spasm. It literally felt like my nuts were going to rip from the seams. They felt tight and heavy. And I dare not tell you about the hardness that throbbed against my thigh. Hell, this celibacy thing had gotten the best of me. It had worn me out. I am human and I have needs. And on this particular night, I needed more than the stroke of my own hand, or the feel of that stupid molded vagina I paid a hundred and fifty dollars for, or the Oriental blow-up doll I have tucked in my storage trunk. What can I say? The last year has been hands-free, missionary loving powered by two double-A batteries. I needed to feel the warmth of a woman next to me. I needed to taste the sweetness of a woman. I needed her.

She jumped up and started pulling off her clothes, then ran toward the water. "Let's go for a swim," she yelled over her shoulder. Her bare butterball rump had a nice, firm bounce as she jumped into the waves.

"I can't swim," I yelled back. I watched her swim under the water, then resurface out of nowhere. She treaded around for a while, then swam toward me. I smiled at her.

"Come on, take your clothes off and get in. The water's great."

Skinny-dip? I don't think so. If I drown, there's no way I want my body found naked. But she kept yelling for me to join her. When I kept refusing, she yelled out, "Whatcha scared of?"

"Nothing," I said. I looked to see if anyone else was around before I started stripping. I pulled off my T-shirt, then my shorts, then my boxers. I took a deep breath, held my little gut in, then walked toward her and the big blue ocean. As I walked, I could feel her eyes scanning my body. With the exception of my little paunch, I thanked God my body was still on point. I stepped in but immediately jumped back.

"Hell no! It's too cold."

"Come on in, scaredy-cat. It's great once you get used to it."

Her body glistened under the moon and stars as she walked toward me. She grabbed me by the hands and pulled me in. My body tensed. I felt my nuts retract. My nipples hardened and my dick shrank. As soon as she got my whole body in deep enough for her liking—the water rose to just below our chins—she started splashing me. Before you knew it, we went from a water fight to tickling each other to staring into each other's eyes to kissing.

No tongue. Just light, gentle kisses. The warmth of her lips warmed me inside. The water around us lost its chill. Her lips were soft and full. I pulled her in closer to me, kissed her neck, then nibbled on her earlobes. Then suddenly my knees gave out. Before I could catch my balance, my head and body were under the water. I tried to stand, but I kept losing my ground. It felt like I had been under for minutes before she reached down and pulled me up like it was no big deal. I coughed, gagged, and gasped for air as she escorted me back to shore. She pulled out a red towel she had in her straw beach bag.

"Here, sit on this. Are you okay?"

I coughed, then held my chest. "Yeah, I'm alright. I told you I couldn't swim."

She laughed. "You're so silly. All you had to do was stand up." She laughed so hard, she was holding her sides. I didn't see anything funny.

"I could have drowned out there with my ass sunny-side up," I said with an attitude.

She continued laughing. "You weren't going to drown. You should have seen how you looked." She wrapped her arms around me, then kissed me on the cheek. "How's that?"

"Better," I said, then pulled her back onto the towel with me. We lay face-to-face, cuddling and kissing. I could feel myself coming alive, inside and out. My erection pounded across my stomach as she greeted me with her tongue. Before either of us knew it, I rolled on top of her, kissed her forehead, her nose, her lips, her chin, and softly sucked on her neck. She tried to stop me, but I continued.

I licked down the middle of her chest, then moved toward her left breast. I sucked, licked, and blew on her chocolate-drop nipple. Then over to her right breast and nipple. I left a trail of wet warm kisses down to her navel until I reached her neatly shaved middle. She parted her legs as I kissed the inside of her thighs. I kissed her softness. The smell of her excitement was intoxicating. There it was, mmmmmm…that fleshy piece swollen with lust. I kissed it, sucked it, and slowly licked the creamy moisture that dripped from the juicy lips between her legs. I looked up. Her eyes were closed, head tilted deep in the sand, her back arched. Then came the moans. The groans. I slid my index and middle fingers inside her warm moistness and used my thumb to tease her small erection. We kissed. Tongues danced and danced with passion as she stroked my manhood. Her soft hands played a symphony with each stroke. Teasing it. Our breathing became heavy. She grabbed my hand and slowly sucked the juices from her love off my fingers. We kissed some more. Finally, I buried myself deep inside her tightness. It was warm and wet. It was a feeling I had forgotten felt so good. She gripped my manhood with every stroke—long strokes, short strokes, deep strokes, fast strokes, slow strokes—until all of my aloneness melted inside of her. Until all of her loneliness dripped along the shaft of my member. After our bodies erupted three more times, we kissed and stole a quiet moment under the twinkle of stars, never saying a word.

8

DAMASCUS:
BROTHAS GONNA WORK IT OUT

Y O, I WOKE UP THIS AFTERNOON FEELING GOOD AS HELL, or more like relieved. It was, like, eighty-five degrees. Bright skies and not muggy. Back in Jersey it was sixty-eight and raining. Today was definitely a beach day. Besides, I felt like peepin' some of the honeys. Word is bond! This is the place to be. There are some fine-ass pieces on this island. Word up. But I'ma just chill for a minute. Like I told Brit last night, I'm really gonna try to abstain. Of course, he got a kick out of hearing that. He just laughed. The way he looked at me told me he found it hard to believe. I couldn't blame him. After all, I've been the type of brotha who could bed down four or five women in one night and still be charged up for more.

"Excuse me?" he asked.

"Yo, I think I need some time to get my thoughts and shit in order," I said. "You know, take some time to chill out. Dig what I'm sayin'?"

"Did I just hear the pussy hound, the man who lives and breathes sex, say he's going on a sex-free diet?"

I laughed. "Maybe. Don't get me wrong, I'ma still be on pussy patrol but just not as often."

"Alright. So when's the last time you had some?"

"Yo, I haven't had any since last Friday."

"Nah, let me rephrase that. When's the last time you popped a nut?"

I grinned. "A'ight, the other night. Shit, I let this chick down in Miami give me head."

"I rest my case," he said.

"Damn. You can't expect me to go cold turkey. Not fuckin' in over a week is a big step for me."

We laughed, then the conversation changed to our days at Norfolk State. He took me back in no particular order. We drifted to the good ole days. And I laughed, hard.

"Hey, you remember when we had that townhouse in Virginia Beach?"

"Man, how could I ever forget that. You used to bitch constantly about the weed and the freaks."

"Oh, you mean your nightly sextravaganzas? What was the schedule? Oh yeah, Sunday was 'Yeah, baby, take this big dick' night; Monday was 'C'mon, open that pussy up…you know you want it' night; Tuesday was 'Stop, Damascus, you're hurting me' night; Wednesday was 'Oh, God, please take it out' night; Thursday was 'Let me fuck you in the ass' night; and Friday was cock-sucking night."

"Yo, you off the hook. C'mon now, I wasn't that bad."

"Bullshit," he said. "You'd call up two vixens to come over to suck you off, then say, 'One mouth ain't enough for these cow balls and this horse dick.' And in would come two strumpets to suck you off and slurp you down."

I grinned. "Yeah, but Saturday was my chill-out night."

"Okay. If you wanna call smoking weed and watching X-rated movies all night chillin' out."

"Yo, that was my dick-beatin' night. Word up."

"Talk about recreational therapy. Every time the springs of your bed begged for mercy or the back of your headboard slapped against your wall, I'd grab the remote to the stereo in my bedroom and blast the sounds of Chic's 'Le Freak,' Anita Ward's, 'Ring My Bell,' and—my all-time favorite—Parliament's 'If It Don't Fit Don't Force It.'"

"Yeah, those were the days," I said.

"Yep, they sure were. Hey, whatever happened to that old woman you were messing with?"

"Old woman?" I asked, tryna sound like he lost me out in space. "I don't remember knocking off no old woman."

"Boy, don't play dumb with me. You know who I'm talking about. The one that looked old enough to be our grandmother."

I laughed. "Nah, yo, I ain't the one."

"Yeah, right. Since you seem to have selective memory, I'll be happy to refresh it for you. I walked in on you eating her out on the kitchen table."

"Nah, money, that wasn't me," I said, struggling to keep a straight face. "I don't eat pussy."

"Hold up, I know you're not gonna sit here and try to deny it. I came home from class and walked in on you, then I blacked, remember?"

I remembered, but I didn't want him to know it. Shit. After I told you I ain't down with any extras, he turns around and pulls my card. Yeah, I ate her. A couple of times. It was strictly business. I damn sure wasn't gonna hit her off with no dough. Fuck that. I'd stroke her down a couple of times a week and eat her real good, and she'd let me sell my work out of her shop. Yo, that was back when I had the Hampton roads on lockdown—from Portsmouth, Hampton, and Newport News to Norfolk, Virginia Beach, and Chesapeake. So as long as she let me get my hustle off, I blessed her. Yo, on the real, I think that was the first time I saw B black.

"Yo, what the fuck you think you doing?!" he had snapped. "How the fuck you gonna fuck granny on my motherfucking kitchen table?" Then he snatched her dentures off the counter and threw them up against the wall. "Now get gummy bear and your sloppy-ass dick off my motherfucking table, or there'll be more than dick slinging going on in here."

Yo, that little nigga flipped. Word up. I don't think I ever heard him curse the way he did that day. I guess it was kinda foul to have her propped up on the table. But how did I know he was gonna come home early? He stood there and watched us for a minute before he said anything, then blacked as soon as I was about to slide up in her. And, for the record, she wasn't *that* old. She was like fifty-something. A'ight, a'ight, she was older, but she had some seasoned pussy. Check it, whoever said over fifty was over the hill was buggin', word up, 'cause granny could throw down.

"Yo, why you bring that up?" I asked. "You betta not mention that ep to anyone."

He laughed. "Well, for a couple pair of Air Maxes, I might be willing to forget."

"Yo, nobody'll believe you anyway," I said confidently.

"Oh yeah? I got your ass on videotape. So pay up or else."

"Yeah, a'ight. Don't make me throw your little ass in that ocean."

Brit laughed hard. "One thing's for sure: The way you ate her pussy led me to believe she had more snap, crackle, and pop than any bowl of cereal I would have eaten." He was laughing so hard, tears were in his eyes. "Mmm-mmm…got milk?"

Man, listen. He had me rollin'. Sometimes he says some real funny shit. He kinda reminds me of that evil-ass Indy with his quick wit 'n shit. It felt good as hell to just laugh and bug the hell out with someone who knows me better than I sometimes know myself.

After about another ten minutes of laughter, he wiped his eyes, then his posture and tone became serious. He said, "Well, I'm glad to hear you're gonna slow down. I worry about you."

Uh-oh. I knew he was about to get all clinical 'n shit on me. "Worry about me?"

"Yeah. I've always worried about the way you channel your anger toward women into sexual energy."

"Yo, I'm not angry with women. Have you ever heard me refer to them as *bitches* or *hoes* or any other degrading name?"

"No. But that doesn't mean you don't think it or feel it. Actions speak louder than words. You degrade them sexually."

"Yo, I love women, so how you figure?"

"Tee, you love sex, not women. You love the orgasmic pleasures they bring to the table. You see them as a means to satisfy your own needs."

Orgasmic pleasures. See what I mean? He's always analyzing shit. Who needs a therapist when I have him? "Well, isn't that the whole point of sex—satisfaction?"

"Yeah, but at what expense?" He stared at me for a second, then said, "I know what you need to change you."

I grinned. "Oh yeah? And, what's that?"

"Don't worry about it. When you feel it happening, you'll know what I'm talking about. One day, my brotha, it's gonna hit you when you least expect it." He smiled. "Tee, you're gonna be alright."

The way he said that made me wonder what he could have been talkin' about. But with him, you can't always tell 'cause sometimes he talks in riddles. I didn't press it but I would keep it in the back of my mind, like everything else he's said to me over the years. Yo, between you and me, a lotta the shit he's said to me in the years has been on point. It's like he can see shit before it happens. Sometimes I wonder if he has a little crystal ball in his pocket.

Brit got up from the sofa and said, "I'm going upstairs to take a shower. Cook us something to eat."

"Yo, I'm on vacation. You're supposed to be entertaining me."

He laughed. "Okay. Entertain yourself in the kitchen. And make sure you wash your hands first."

I picked my nose, then scratched my ass. "Hands clean," I said, holding them up in the air. "Now, what was that you said you wanted to eat?" We laughed, then he went upstairs and I went into the kitchen to entertain myself.

The first thing I thought about when I stepped off that plane three days ago was how good it was gonna be to take off this mask. Word up. The minute I walked through my boy's door, I embraced him with a strong-ass, brotherly, "I miss the hell outta ya" hug. Word up. Yo, all my life I've been frontin' like shit don't matter to me. But on the d.l., some things do, like my friendship with Brit. I guess over the years, I kinda took it for granted because I always expected him to be within arm's reach. But when he bounced, I realized just how important our friendship really is.

I'm cool with a lotta niggas, but that's on some cool-out, bullshit level. There's still a front goin' on. Hell, most niggas, that's all they do. We're afraid to show who we really are. Scared to be seen as vulnerable. Fuck that. If it weren't for my boy challenging me, I don't think I would have ever given myself a chance to get close with anyone. Yo, I know from experience that you can't let just anybody in your space. It's really fucked up that some niggas never even let themselves experience a true friendship, a real brother-hood. They're stuck on dissin' each other, playa-hatin' 'n shit, and just tryin' to outdo each other. They're all caught up in being fake. They think being honest and expressing their true feelings compromises their manhood. Yo, I was one of 'em.

See, niggas expect you to be hard if you wanna be down, and if you're not, you'll get stepped on. So you gotta watch your back 'cause there's a lotta snake-ass niggas out there who will do you in if they think you're weak. Niggas be thinkin' that if you show any emotion other than anger or aggression, you're weak. So if you sleep on a nigga, he's gonna get your ass. You gotta always be on point.

Sometimes niggas gotta front like they all hard 'n shit just to survive. They walk around mean-muggin', but deep inside they all fucked up and lonely. I know. That was me most of my life. That's how I had to be 'cause the streets raised me. There was no one in my life who genuinely cared enough to wanna know the child behind the mask. No one was invested in lookin' beyond the front. So I grew up hard and lonely. Yo, the streets mighta taught me how to survive, but they damn sure didn't teach me about friendship. I owe that to my boy.

And on the strength, I could tell Brit was glad I came. I sensed something was wrong even though he tried to play it off. When you're close to someone, you can tell when shit ain't right. When I saw him sitting out on his balcony just staring out into the ocean, I thought I saw him wipe tears away from his eyes.

"Yo, Cool, what's on your mind?" I asked. "You a'ight?"

"Nothing," he said. "Yeah, I'm fine. I'm just chillin'."

"C'mon, B, this is me you're talking to," I said. "You know I know better." But he insisted he was just chillin'. So I hit him with what he usually hits me with: "Listen, bro, when you're ready to talk, I'm here for you."

He smiled. "Thanks."

I made a fist, gave him a pound, then said, "Just remember, you don't always have to be strong for everyone else." I went back downstairs and turned on the stereo. I put in Queen Latifah's *Order in the Court* CD and blasted that piece "Black on Black Love." Yo, that sista knows how to take shit to another level. I really digs her style.

I guess about an hour later, B came down and was ready to talk. I was sittin' outside on the patio chillin' to the beats and reading my book. Basically, that's all I could do since he doesn't have television. Yo, I'm not a TV fanatic or anything, but I do like to watch *Jeopardy*. Now, that's my show. Hey, yo, don't sleep on my skills 'cause I kills 'em on that shit. Word up!

Anyway, money comes down and he tells me how his pops wants to see him 'n shit, but he's really not feelin' him. Yo, I could dig it. But then he handed me the letter to read and I kinda had a change of heart. All the years I've known B, he's never really talked about his pops. I know his moms, and he always talks about her. Yo, mom dukes is fly. And I know his sister and her family, but he's never mentioned his pops. I kinda thought the man was dead or something. So we went around and around with him saying he was sending the plane ticket back 'cause he didn't want anything to do with him and me tryna convince him to just go out there. Hell, what did he have to lose?

I said, "Check it. That's your pops. Go see that man. Hear what he has to say. Yo, at least you know who your pops is. I don't even know who mine is. At least you got a pops who has been tryna reach out to you. Okay, maybe he isn't who you want him to be. Maybe he hasn't been the way you think he shoulda been. Regardless, he's your pops. Don't turn your back on him."

"Well, I don't owe him jack."

I shook my head. "It's not about owing anyone anything. It's about you tryna resolve whatever has been troubling you. Maybe he was the man he was because that's all he knew. Maybe that's what he saw. You yourself have always said kids become what they see, right?"

He looked at me, in shock that I had flipped the script on him. He smirked. "You're right. But I'm not interested in trying to analyze him."

I stood up and leaned my back against the railing. "Yo, don't give me that shit. You love analyzing shit. I mean, there have been times when you hit me with some ole pyschological-thriller-type shit. Because that's where you go with it. And I dig that about you. All I'm sayin' is, maybe he is what he saw as a kid. I'm not sayin' it's right. But maybe that's just how it is. You know, B, the one thing I've always admired about you has been your ability to look deeper into people and situations. I have always been able to count on your insight. But I can see that following your own advice doesn't apply to you, huh?"

I could tell by the way he just stared at me that he was surprised that I could drop it on him like that. But, hey, I've listened to this brotha for years. I've watched him. Fuck that. I've studied him. And I've learned from him. Sometimes you gotta take what someone's given you and throw it back at 'em. Dig what I'm sayin'?

I said, "We've known each other for a long time and I got mad love for you. But I think it's really fucked up for you to blame him for you pushing him away. You never gave the man a chance. So how did he fail you? Hell, he made sure you wanted for nothing. You said he tried, right?"

"Yeah."

"Have you ever wondered what his struggles mighta been as a child and a man? If I could find out who my pops is, I'd wanna know. I'd wanna see him. Whether he's living right or is some fucked-up nigga, I'd wanna look him in the eyes to let him see how his absence in my life affected me. See, your father wasn't absent from your life because he wanted to be. He was absent because *you* wanted him to be."

Damn. That shit sounded pretty decent, huh? You damn straight. I looked my boy in the eyes and told him straight up to stop frontin' like there was some kinda catalog from which we can pick out our parents. Who they are is who they are. Fuck it. I know my moms was a drug addict. But she was still my moms. She was killed before I could ever find out what her struggles were. I never got a chance to understand her pain. Yo, I saw it. I felt it. But as a little boy, you don't know what it all means. But it's still with me. Maybe it wouldn't be if I knew. I don't wanna see B spend the rest of his life not knowing.

I handed him back the letter. He said he'd think about it before he made any decision either way, then he thanked me for listening. Hell, I shoulda been thanking him for all the times he gave me reality checks. We embraced, then spent the rest of the night laughing about old times and catching up on the day-to-day shit in our lives. We sat outside eating (baked fish, shrimp, and fruit salad) and drinking strawberry and pineapple smoothies and laughing until the sun greeted us. Yo, that was some beautiful shit.

Damn, time flies. Two days had turned into two weeks. Two weeks turned into a month, and I'm still parlayin' on white sandy beaches. Yo, check this shit out. This morning I went into Brit's room to see if he wanted to go down to the beach and chill 'n shit, and his little ass musta dipped out late last night or early this morning. He's hooked up with that little dime piece from Washington Heights—Lina's her name—and he's doin' it up lovely. At first, I thought he was bullshittin' me when he explained all those big-ass hickeys on his neck. Yo, he musta been slayin' her little ass, the way she sucked his neck all up. I was like, "Get the fuck outta here." But when she peeped him at the beach two weeks ago, he introduced us and, word is bond, her ass is fine as hell. He thinks she looks like Sade. Fuck that. She's a Salli Richardson clone. Word up. Yo, remember when she played in *Posse* and *A Low Down Dirty Shame*? Now that's a dime piece. Nah, fuck that! She's a half-ounce. A kilo. That's one bad-ass sista. And this little dime B's knockin' off is her look-alike.

I don't know how he does it, but he can go months without fuckin' and be cool about it. Then out the blue, he'll be on some rampage fuck-style shit. And he'll only dick down one type of woman. Fine. Fuck that. When I wanna fuck, I wanna fuck. When the lights are off, who cares how she looks? As long as her ass is clean, I'ma knock her back out. It's not like I'm tryna marry her ass or sport her around like she's my girl 'n shit. But not Brit, she's gotta be on point.

After I ate five scrambled eggs with cheese and a fruit salad, I yanked a quick nut while I showered, slipped on my red and white swim trunks and a pair of Miu Miu beach sandals, and threw on the Versaces to block out that bright-ass sun. Yo, you'd never know it was November the way the sun is beamin.' It's, like, eighty-nine degrees. The beach was definitely calling me. What's real slick is the fact that Brit is, like, ten minutes' walking distance from the beach. I can really see why he's big on this spot. I feels it, for real.

Yo, Sosua is divided into two separate villages that are separated by a bay. At the base of that bay is a sandy white beach more than half a mile long. Yo, it's real sweet. And the honeys? Man, listen, it's a feast out here.

I was kinda shocked to see so many Germans living around here. But Brit explained how a lot of them immigrated here when the Jewish refugees were being persecuted by the Nazis; eventually, many of them stayed on and made this spot their home. Once again, he impressed me. He's always studying up on shit.

I grabbed my Polo beach towel, my tanning oil, my book, and my Sony Discman. Can't go to a beach without beats. While walking through the village, I gave some young heads a few dollars, then out of nowhere, all these little kids came running up to me asking for spare change and shit. It was like there was some kinda silent alarm around my neck or something 'cause they were all around me. I hooked 'em up. I saw myself at their age in a lot of those young faces. Poverty is a real bitch.

When I finally made it down to the beach, I found a nice spot to lie out and catch the sun, near a wooden hut that sells fresh fruit, shrimp, and drinks. I took off my shirt, put on some sun block, then found my place in the book I was reading.

"Hello," a soft voice said.

I looked up and there stood this biscuit-brown sista with thick lips and hips in a skimpy two-piece. I knew from the gate she was from Brooklyn, with her thick accent and with all her shine on from her gold bangles and her nameplated gold earrings to her thick rope chain and her gold-capped tooth. She was a walking jewelry store.

"Hey, what's up?"

"Brit asked me to see if you wanna join us over there," she said, pointing to where Brit and two females were sitting. Brit stood up and gestured for me to come over.

I gave him the peace sign, then turned my sights back on the sexy treat in front of me. "Nah, baby. I'm cool. I'ma chill here."

She smiled. "Alright. But if you change your mind, we're right over there," she said, this time gesturing with her head. She turned around to walk back. *Damn, that ass is thick*, I thought.

"Hey, yo," I yelled.

She came back toward me. "Yessss?"

I licked my lips. "Yo, you got a name?"

"Carmen."

"You got a man?"

"Nope."

"I tell you what, why don't you come by my boy's spot later tonight and check me out."

She smiled. "Maybe."

"Yeah, a'ight."

An hour later, I finished my book and Brit came over with his things.

"Hey, what's that you were reading?" he asked.

"Oh, just this corny-ass book I picked up," I lied, then changed the subject. "Yo, where your peoples go?"

"They had to get back. But I understand you invited Carmen over to check you out. So I guess you've fallen prey to your addiction."

"Nah, man. I told you, I'ma chill. I'm doing the celibate thing for a minute."

He squinted his face up, stared at me for a second, then asked, "Tee, what's really going on? You didn't get hit off with an STD or something, did you?"

"Why would you ask me something like that?"

"I don't know. You've been acting real strange. You've been here for a month, and you haven't tried to get a nut off. That's not like you."

"And?"

"Well, I wanna know if you're alright. Did you get a hold of some rotten sex?"

I told him, "Hell no!" Yo, fuck that. I ain't no sucker. My dick don't hit no skins raw. So after ten minutes of probing, I finally told him. I told him about the flashbacks I'd had of my mother and how that shit had me really fucked up.

"Yo, I'm a'ight now. It just came outta nowhere," I said. "One thing's for sure: I ain't smokin' no more trees. Yo, that shit had me spooked, for real."

"You sure you're alright?"

"Yeah, I'm cool."

"Well, I'm glad that after all these years you've finally decided to leave the weed alone. Smoking that shit's no good for you anyway. After a while, it just starts tearing your body and mind down—"

"Yeah, I know," I said, cutting him off before he went into one of his long antidrug speeches. "I've smoked enough trees to last me a lifetime." Yeah, I've been getting bent since I was thirteen. But, I never laced my shit, so what's the big deal? It's not like I was snorting coke or shooting dope. I just felt like I needed to be smoked out to keep shit in perspective. It kept me calm. And it damn sure kept me from thinking 'bout my empty life.

Hell, after the shit I've been through, it's surprising that I haven't ended up strung out on drugs and shit. I found my moms dead. I don't know who the hell my father is. I had no other family members willing to step up to the plate and care for me. And, then, had to spend seven years of my life bouncing in and out of different foster homes. After the tenth one, I just jetted, deciding I could make it on my own. So I embraced the streets. I learned to hustle—shooting craps, stealing cars, selling drugs and, yeah, pumpin' this dick. I learned to do whatever I needed to survive. See, while cats like B were in school hittin' the books and tryna make something outta their lives, I was on the street corners stackin' chips and tryna live. But, you wanna know something? Even though I didn't give a fuck about school—'cause school didn't give a fuck about me—I still read books. I still wanted to learn.

On the real-for-real, I'd probably be dead by now if I hadn't gotten bagged at sixteen and sent to a youth facility for eighteen months. And even though I sat up in that piece and learned how to be a better hustler, I still got my G.E.D. With the help of two social workers, I got into Norfolk State.

We let silence blow in with the wind. Brit rubbed coconut tanning oil over his chest, legs, and arms, then lay back on his blanket. I stared out into the ocean. I took in the breeze and smiled as I watched all the fine ass that covered the beach. *Fuck that celibacy shit*, I thought. Hell, I'm on vacation and there's nothing wrong with a little bump-and-grind. I'm poppin' a nut in some island pussy before I leave this spot. There's just too much pussy in one place to not get a taste. I took off my shades, hid my book under my shirt, then went for a swim.

When I came back, Brit was sitting up, groovin' to the Mr. Fingers CD in the Discman. "How's the water?" he asked.

"Yo, it felt good. You should really learn to swim."

"One day." He stared at me for a minute, then said, "Tee, I wish there were something I could do to help you with your pain."

I was silent while I thought about it for a minute. "You already have," I said while drying myself off. "Just having you around to talk to does more than you'd ever know."

I don't think I'd ever be able to find the right words to explain to him how much his friendship has meant to me. I'm sure he knows that I'd cut my right hand off for him. After all, he's the only one who's always been in my corner. Yo, when I got knocked off on bullshit drug charges down in Maryland and got hit off with four years, this brotha handled my business matters—made sure I had what I needed and not once lifted any of my dough. I know 'cause I counted that shit when I got out. Yo, a nigga gotta be sure 'cause money can turn a worm into a snake. But not Brit. All three hundred and twenty-five Gs were stacked the way I left 'em. Plus, when the prosecutors and five-oh were pressin' him for info, he never folded. Yo, he was the only person I had to trust, and he didn't let me down. That level of loyalty I don't take lightly. Those four years on lockdown made me realize how important it is to have at least one person in this world you can rely on and trust. Yo, a lot of cats were up in that piece just rotting away, many of 'em with no outside support. No family. No friends. No hope. No future.

On the strength, I'm glad I stacked my dough and got outta the game when I did. With all these mandatory sentences and conspiracy laws, the feds would be tryna hang my ass. And jailin' ain't for me. When I finally got released from my cage and heard those gates snap shut behind me, I knew I'd never do another bid. Word up.

Brit handed me my Discman, then asked, "You keep in touch with any of our frat brothers?"

"Other than you, not really," I said. "I haven't seen any of the old heads in years. Things are different than when we pledged. Hell, B, you know how it was. We'd be on line for five to six weeks underground, then another ten to twelve weeks once we came out. Now, two to four weeks and you're in. There just seems to be a whole lot of frat and not many brothas."

"Yeah, I know what you mean. It really should be about the brotherhood."

"Yeah, but everyone has their reasons for pledging."

"Ain't that the truth," he said. "So why'd you pledge?"

I had never really given it much thought. "Why you ask?"

"No particular reason."

But I knew better. Anytime Brit asks you something out of the blue, there's a reason. Regardless, I answered his question.

"Many of the cats who pledged had a hidden agenda, whether it was for the step shows, the parties, the road trips, or the pussy. At first, I wanted to be down with that, but then I really got into it and wanted the brotherhood."

"Did you find it?" he asked.

"Yeah," I said, giving him a brotherly pound. "I found out the true meaning of friendship and brotherhood."

He smiled. "Ditto." He lay back on his blanket and closed his eyes. "I love you, bro."

"Hey, I love you, too. And, for the record, I've missed the hell outta ya."

I took in a deep breath, put my shades back on, stared at the ocean, then slowly exhaled. I smiled. Not only did I have someone I could be myself around, I had someone I could trust, I could discuss my fears with, someone I could share my deepest thoughts and feelings with without feeling any pressure to prove my manhood. I had someone I didn't have to be hard around or try to be cool around. I had a best friend. I had a soul brotha. It can't get no deeper than that. Word up!

9

CHYNA: **CHILDREN OF THE NIGHT**

THE PAST SIX WEEKS HAVE BEEN PURE HELL. Do you hear me? Pure h-e-double-l. I've been racking my brain trying to figure out what I ever did to deserve this level of disrespect and disobedience. The closer Miss Sarina gets to her eighteenth birthday, the worse she gets. Do you know she had the nerve to tell me, "You can't tell me what to do." Now, had I ever thought to say something like that to my parents when I was growing up, I would have been picking my teeth up off the floor. No one in my family tolerated back talk from a child. I wouldn't dare talk fresh to any adult. Back then, adults stood firm on the fact that children should be seen and not heard. But, for some reason, the kids today think it's okay to be disrespectful to adults, particularly their parents. I didn't raise any of my children to sass adults. My boys would never think to raise their voices to me. But Sarina? She's another story. She walks around here like she runs this house. She's up all hours of the night, wandering and rummaging through the house like she's lost her mind. And she has no regard for any-one or anything.

The other night, she actually had the audacity to throw a party on a school night. I woke up around three o'clock in the morning because I thought I smelled something burning. Well, it was Miss Sarina in the kitchen cooking up a storm. She was frying chicken and broiling six filet mignons. She had invited eight young men into my home, as if it were some kind of after-hours lounge. I had to wake Ryan up to have him put them out. He was furious.

"What the hell is going on in here?" he had yelled while he tied his bathrobe.

"I want all of you out of my damn house *now* or I'll have the cops arrest your asses!" The young men grabbed their coats and beers and ran out the door—with the exception of one who just strolled on out with a beer in one hand and two pieces of chicken in the other. Ryan snatched the drumsticks and beer out of his hands. "IHOP and the pub are down the street," he snapped, then slammed the door. Thank goodness none of them got indignant because it would have been a mess. I'm sure Ryan would have lost his cool on them. Then, to make matters worse, Sarina started yelling and screaming.

"You are always tryna spoil my fun. I can't do anything around here. What's the big deal? I was only having a couple of steaks with a few friends."

Sometimes I think she forgets who the mother is around here. I mean, she really thinks she's grown. Of course, that only applies when it's convenient for her. She comes and goes as she pleases, stays out two and three days at a time, doesn't tell me where she's at or who she's with or what she's doing, and has the nerve to say, "None of your business" when I ask her anything. But the minute she gets into any kind of trouble, I'm the first one she calls. Well, guess what? I am tired of bailing her behind out of trouble. I'm tired of her smart mouth and I'm tired of her disrespect of my rules. I had to finally break down and tell her father how she's been acting because I'm just plain old tired. So, for the last six weeks, he's finally gotten a taste of what it's like living with Miss Sarina.

Now he's ready to put a strap to her behind, but I won't allow it. I never spanked or hit our children when they were younger, so why start now? Although now I'm thinking maybe it wouldn't have been such a bad thing to spank her on her bottom a few times when she was younger. Maybe I wouldn't be having all these problems with her. Oh well, what good would it do at this point? She's almost eighteen. Besides, I never liked the idea of fathers spanking or hitting their daughters because it conditions them to think it's okay for the men in their lives to hit them. Well, Ryan has his own ideas about that.

Last week, he was fit to be tied when he saw her hanging on one of the corners in the southeast section of D.C., wearing a black tube top, army fatigue pants, a pair of black mittens cut off at the knuckles, and unlaced Timbs. Ryan swerved over into the left lane, made an illegal U-turn in the middle of the intersection, then pulled up at the corner. He opened the passenger side of his Navigator and told her to get in.

"No," she said. "Don't you see me with my friends?" Then she had the gall to turn her back on him.

"Girl, if you don't get your behind in this car —"

"I *said* no! Now, leave me alone."

Then, to add salt to the wound, one of her friends—a tall, lanky kid with dreads—walked over, leaned in toward the truck and said, "Hey, dig, Pops, she said no. So beat it." Then he slammed the door. The nerve of him.

Well, that didn't sit well with Ryan. He jumped out of the truck with an aluminum baseball bat in his hand, snatched Sarina by the back of her tube top, and threw her in the truck. "Try to jump out and I'm gonna break your damn legs," he threatened. Then he took off his jacket and tie, turned to her five male friends, and said, "Now, if any of you got a problem with me taking *my* daughter home, we can handle this."

"Nah, pops, do your thing," they said in unison. "We ain't got no beef with you." I guess they had a change of heart when they saw how big he was. I would too if some tall, black man with big arms and a wide chest came at me with a baseball bat.

"I didn't think so," he said in a deep, heavy voice that sounded like that of a man who would break every bone in your body if you got in his way.

I told him he was crazy. A baseball bat? He could have gotten hurt or killed. These teenagers today carry guns and would not hesitate to pull the trigger without blinking an eye. After it's all said and done, most of them express no remorse or guilt over it. I told him he shouldn't be going into rough neighborhoods and getting tough with the kids there. Southeast D.C. can be a little hard on someone who's not from the hood. Violence and danger affect all of us. But he made it very clear he'd do it again if he had to.

"Chyna, I'm not concerned about some snotty-nose kid carrying a gun. Especially when it involves my daughter. I don't like that crowd she's hanging out with. I smell nothing but trouble."

"Well, I don't like her friends either, Ryan, but we can't pick her friends. She's gonna see them regardless of what we say."

I had to admit Sarina's choice of friends has been an issue for me for some time, but I've always tried not to bad-mouth any of them. Whether I liked them or not, I just kept it to myself, because anyone I liked she stopped hanging with, and the ones I disliked she made it her business to spend the most time with. Ever since she was allowed to attend public school, her peer group had changed dramatically. Over the last two years, I think she's gone through several groups of friends, most of whom are high school dropouts, substance users, or kids who have had some kind of brush with the law. When I asked her why she no longer associated with the kids from our neighborhood or from the private school she attended, her excuses were, "They're boring …they're corny …they're too snobby." To her, *boring* and *corny* apply to those kids who are honor students, kids who are respectful or preparing to go away to Ivy League colleges.

"Oh yeah? Well, if she wants to hang out with deadbeats, that's on her," Ryan had said. "But the next time her behind gets into trouble, tell her to call her friends up. 'Cause if I gotta go down there to get her, I'm gonna whup the skin off her behind. I'm getting sick and tired of her foolishness. Running in and out of here like this is some Motel Six. I mean it, Chyna; if you don't get her behind under control, I'm gonna handle her fresh behind my way."

Sure, put it all on me. Hello! Doesn't he know I wouldn't have told him about this whole mess if I could get her under control? I would have kept on doing what I've been doing for the last five years; handling things on my own. Besides, why do I have to be the one to get her under control? Shouldn't it be a joint effort? I didn't bring her into this world by myself. I know that deep inside, Sarina's behavior is tearing him up. She's always been his little angel. His princess. But now that he's been home more over the last month, he's seeing her true colors. So I can understand his disappointment. *Well, get over it*, is what I wanted to say, but I kept my mouth closed.

At seven o'clock this morning, I was standing by the double glass doors in the kitchen staring at all the colorful autumn leaves and the purple, white, yellow, and orange mums, and purple and white Oriental cabbage that lined the walkway leading to the gazebo. I must have been deep in thought because I didn't hear Ryan walk in.

"Good morning," he mumbled. He was standing under the archway in his custom-tailored suit, with his briefcase in his left hand and the newspaper under his right arm. I suppose he was off to manage his businesses.

"Excuse me?"

He repeated himself, then asked, "What the devil has gotten into Sarina? I saw her yesterday leaving for school wearing a pair of cut-up jeans that showed all of her behind. I don't think the girl had on any drawers. The pants looked like they'd been through a shredder." He shook his head. "I told her behind to get upstairs and change, but she refused. And what's with this bald head and shaved eyebrows?"

"Ryan, she's just trying to make a statement. I don't even let that bother me anymore," I said, trying to dismiss her appearance as typical teenage rebellion. However, I was concerned when she'd told me she cut her hair off because she felt bugs crawling in it. I decided not to mention that to him. "I am more concerned with her following the house rules and graduating high school," I said. "I just want her to do what she's told and not be so disrespectful."

"Oh, she's making a statement, alright. Well, is she following the house rules?"

"No."

"Is she going to school?"

"No," I said as I massaged my forehead. My head throbbed along with the whistle of the kettle. I removed it from the stove's flame. Sarina has already missed twenty days of school and it's only October. Last year, she missed a total of eighty-seven days. "And I'm not paying for her to go to summer school again. If she doesn't earn enough credits to graduate this year, then she'll just have to repeat the year over."

He put his briefcase on the kitchen counter, then placed his glasses on top of the soft black leather. He poured himself a glass of orange juice, sat at the kitchen table, and shuffled through the mail while he spoke. "Summer school? You mean to tell me she had to go to summer school and you never mentioned it to me?"

Before I could say anything in my defense, his attitude changed immediately upon opening one of his credit card bills. "Who in the hell charged five thousand dollars on this card?!"

Uh-oh. I forgot to get the mail before he did. Once again, I'd planned to cover for his sweet little princess. This isn't the first time she's taken a credit card and charged up thousands of dollars' worth of stuff like some kind of maniac. Oh well, maybe it's about time he saw just what I've had to put up with for the last four years. It seems like, the minute Sarina hit thirteen, something in her brain clicked on or off and she started becoming opposi- tional. There must be some kind of hormonal secretion that turns some kids into terrors at that age, because before then she was every mother's dream. She was an honor student, respectful, polite, and would do anything you asked of her. But now, forget it.

I poured myself a cup of hot water for my herbal tea, then sat across from him at the table. "Well, I wasn't going to tell you. But since you opened the mail, there's no need to keep it from you," I said. "Sarina took the credit card and bought a few things without permission."

He looked up from the five-page bill and frowned at me. "She bought a few things without permission?" he repeated, then shifted his eyes back to the bill. "No, she stole, that's what she did. If you take something without permission, it's called stealing." He *tsked*. "Four hundred and twenty-five dollars for a pocketbook, nine hundred and ninety-five dollars for a man's watch, fifteen hundred dollars for a man's jacket, seven hundred dollars for a digital camera…ten pairs of shoes? Who in the world was she shopping for?" He answered before I could speak. "She has lost her damn mind, taking some hoodlum shopping at my expense."

"Well, I didn't want to make a big deal about it. She promised she would pay the bill."

"You didn't want to make a big deal about it? Five thousand dollars and you didn't want to make a big deal about it? Well, it *is* a big deal." Now he was completely worked up. "Chyna, she steals my credit card and makes thousands of dollars' worth of purchases and you don't want to make a big deal about it? And how the hell is she gonna pay the bill? With her looks? I don't believe you. Where is she?"

"I don't know," I said, then glanced up at the oval clock.

"What do you mean you don't know?"

"She didn't come home last night, that's what I mean."

"She didn't what?! Has she called?"

"Ryan, Sarina does what she wants. This is nothing new."

He slammed the bill down on the table. "She is not going to continue doing what she wants in this house. No seventeen-year-old daughter of mine is going to be staying out all night—not while living under this roof."

I just looked at him. Now, all of a sudden, he's ready to take charge and lay down the law. Trying to take a firm hand now, I think, is a little too late. I needed his firm hand a long time ago. But I didn't want to put all the blame on him, so I just let him rant. I mean, just the fact that he was taking time out of his busy schedule to talk to me about our daughter was a shock to me.

There have been a lot of things that I've kept from him or forgot to mention to him. I didn't think he cared either way. By the time he'd get home from work, whatever crisis I had to deal with was already resolved. So what would have been the point of going back over it? Most of the time, he made me feel like I was exaggerating things anyway, because Sarina would bat her eyes at him and put on her innocent, sweet little girl routine, which he'd eat up. And then he'd have the nerve to undermine me by letting her do or have what she wanted after I had already told her no. As far as he was concerned, she could do no wrong. If he only knew half of what she's been up to, he'd really go off. Well, I'm tired of covering for her. She won't listen to me; maybe he can get through to her.

"Is there anything else you haven't shared with me that you'd like to tell me before I go to work?" he asked in a sarcastic tone.

"No. Nothing that can't wait until you get home," I replied. I figured there was no need to tell him she'd stolen the keys to the convertible the other night and let God knows who drive it. She claims she accidentally hit a divider when she was driving backward on the BWI because she had missed her exit. Why would anyone do something so reckless and dangerous on an expressway?

I also figured there was no need to let him know I'd had to go down to the police station to get her because she was arrested for assaulting a girl in the mall. She said the girl disrespected her—"She was smiling at my man." I never knew a smile could be the cause of a "beat down," as she put it.

"I'll be home around seven," Ryan said. "And I hope Sarina's behind is home before I get here. I am not having this nonsense. I'm taking her car, I'm taking her name off all the credit cards, and I'm going down to the bank to withdraw money out of her account to pay for these charges. Then I'm removing the rest of her money and putting it in an account she can't get her hands on. And I want all of the PIN numbers to all the bank cards changed today."

No one told you to buy her a new car for her birthday or put her name on the credit cards anyway, I thought. Sarina made such a stink about getting a Lexus for her birthday that she actually threw a tantrum when he said, "No, I'll buy you a Jeep or a Beetle but you're not getting a Lexus." But she has always had her father wrapped around her little finger, so she badgered him to no end for weeks, calling and paging him nonstop until he gave in. Besides, she made it very clear: "I'm not going to school unless I have a new Lexus." So he broke down and bought it for her. And she's been hell on wheels ever since. The difference between him and me is that when I say no to the kids, they know I mean no.

Ryan walked out the double glass doors and went toward the garage. I have no idea why, since he was parked out front. But I was too preoccupied with my own issues to question him. A minute later, he walked back in the kitchen with steam coming from his ears. "What happened to the M3?" he asked, grabbing his head. "Tell me that child did not take that car without permission, then back into someone or something."

"Okay," I said. "I won't say it, but I didn't give her permission."

"Was anyone gonna tell me about this?" he shrieked. He slammed the door shut so hard that I thought the glass would shatter. "I'd like to know what the hell else has been going on around here that I know nothing about."

I kept my cool. I lightly tapped my fingernails on the glass-top table, then counted to ten before I said anything that would start an unnecessary argument; but inside I was screaming: *If you had paid more attention to your family the last four years, maybe you'd know what the hell has been going on!*

"Ryan, there's no need to yell," I said in between sips of tea. "I know I should have told you, but I thought I could have it fixed before you found out. The car is going to the shop this afternoon and should be done by the end of the week."

He stood in the middle of the kitchen and stared at me for a few seconds. He lowered his voice and spoke very slowly and deliberately. "The next time she takes something that doesn't belong to her, I want the cops called. If she punches another hole in a wall or damages any more of my damn property, I want her hauled out of here in handcuffs. You don't want me to put a strap to her, I won't. But I won't tolerate this criminal behavior in this house. If she wants to hang in the streets, fine. But when she comes through these doors, she had better leave the streets in the streets." He sighed heavily. "I gotta go. I'll address this later with her." Then he headed for the front door, angrily swinging his briefcase.

The police? I couldn't believe he would call the police on our baby. Sign complaints? How could he want to do that? Yes, she's an out-of-control pain in the behind, but I don't want police coming to my home. This is not the kind of neighborhood where police are summoned unless something tragic has happened. If we called the police on her, wouldn't that be a sign that we have failed as parents? Wouldn't calling the police be like saying we've given up? I can't imagine seeing my child hauled off in cuffs. The thought of turning her in made me dizzy.

I got up from the table and was starting to clean the kitchen when the phone rang. I ran water in the dishpan, added a few squirts of Palmolive, then answered. "Hello."

"What's up, lady?"

"Britton, boy, how are you?" I asked while washing the dishes. I tried to keep the phone steady between my ear and shoulder as we talked. "I've been thinking about you. Did you get the pictures I sent?"

"Yes, I got them. Thanks. Everyone looks great. I can't get over how the kids have grown."

"Yeah, pretty soon I'll be a free woman," I said with a sigh of relief. I meant that literally and figuratively. I've been feeling like a prisoner in my own home lately. I have to lock up everything and anything I don't want Sarina to get her hands on in the safe, I have to hide my pocketbook, and I can't trust her to stay in the house without bringing friends over without permission. I don't care how many times I tell her there's to be no company in the house when I'm not home and no boys in her bedroom, she does it anyway.

"Did I catch you at a bad time?"

"Not at all. I'm washing dishes and waiting for Sarina to get home. So how are you?" I asked.

"I'm doing good. And you? How are things going with you? I'm sorry I didn't get back to you sooner."

"Oh, that's alright. I know I'm in your thoughts," I said, looking up at the clock again. "Things are alright, I guess. ...No, things are a mess here. Sarina is really starting to wear my nerves thin. Brit, I'm telling you, if someone would have told me I would be going through this much trouble, I would have gotten my tubes tied after I had Kayin."

"Wow, she's really gotten worse, huh?"

"If you only knew," I said.

"I heard you say you were waiting for her to get home. Shouldn't she be off to school by now?"

"Yeah, if and when she goes. She left here yesterday around seven in the morning, and I haven't seen her since."

"Humph. Sounds like she's getting that 'I'm almost an adult' itch. Once teenagers get to that point it's really hard to rein them in," he said.

"Brit, I'm telling you, I don't know what I'm gonna do with her. I've been dealing with her nasty attitude for too long. I'm afraid that one of these days, she's going to say the wrong thing to me and I'm gonna go off on her. There's just so much verbal abuse a person can take."

"Chyna, just be patient. She'll come around. Once she turns eighteen and realizes life isn't as easy as she thought it would be, she'll change her tune. When she realizes no one is going to let her just live for free, she'll get it together."

"Well, I've tried to be patient with her. I've tried to be nice to her. I've tried to be understanding, and I've tried to turn the other cheek. But I'm telling you, my daughter is really starting to press her luck with me."

I dried my hands, then sat down at the table and gave him the abridged version of my conversation with Ryan and filled him in on what Sarina's been doing. Brit listened, then said he was concerned that her oppositional behavior seems to have become conduct disorder behavior now that she's stealing, fighting, lying, and skipping school. He suggested she see a psychiatrist, given her outbursts. I tried not to laugh, but he really sounded like a psychiatrist himself.

"Well, as much as I hate to admit it, I have to agree with Ryan," he said. "Sarina needs to learn that she can't go around stealing and damaging property. She has to be held accountable for her actions. Just because you're her parents doesn't mean you shouldn't report her for breaking the law. Whether it's done in your home or in the community, it's still breaking the law."

"Brit, I hear what you're saying, but I still don't like it. I don't want—"

"Chyna," he said, cutting me off. I dislike it when he does that. "Get over it. Calling the police doesn't mean you're a bad parent or a parent who has failed. It says you're a parent who needs help. It says you're a parent who has tried to do what's right but now needs some outside intervention. It's okay to be frustrated. What are you teaching her if you continue to let her get away with this? Do you understand that there are kids out there killing their parents for no real reason…just because?"

"Oh, Brit," I said with a nervous laugh. "Don't you think you're exaggerating? Sarina isn't dangerous."

"Maybe not intentionally. But given her level of anger and aggression, anything's possible. Do you think she's using drugs? I mean, dramatic changes in peer groups, appearance, and behavior can sometimes be warning signs."

Well, other than the time three years ago when I found eleven tiny Ziploc bags filled with what I thought was oregano in her bedroom, she hadn't left any evidence around. When I found those bags, I was shocked. *You can't get high off oregano, can you?* I had asked myself. I couldn't understand why she started yelling and screaming at me when I told her I threw the bags out. She was so irate that she started breaking things in her room. All over bags of dried leaves. I didn't think that kind of outburst was warranted. But once I learned it was reefer, I put her in a drug treatment program. She was thrown out after four days because she didn't want to be there and didn't think she had a problem. I never heard such bullshit. Of course she didn't want to be there or think she had a problem! How many teenagers actually want to be in any kind of treatment or see anything they do as a problem?

"No, I don't think so," I answered Brit. In fact, last week at the police station, I demanded she take a drug test before I'd take her home. The test came back negative. I continued, "I know she smokes cigarettes, and those Philly cigars, but I wouldn't put anything past her, considering the unsavory crowd she hangs with."

"They're called Phillies Blunts. And most kids buy them to roll and smoke weed in."

Now my blood pressure started to go up. "If that child has been smoking that mess again, there's no telling what else she's using."

"Chyna, maybe Sarina needs counseling. She really sounds depressed to me."

I sighed. "Been there, done that."

"Well, maybe you need to try it again," he said with concern in his voice. "Because it really sounds like she's a walking time bomb. I'm worried something is going to happen."

"You're telling me. But there's nothing I can do since she refuses to go. We've tried every type of counseling available—group, individual, anger management, family, you name it. Nothing has helped. She just gets worse."

"She needs help *now*," he urged. "Don't wait until she turns eighteen. It'll be too late. Maybe the courts can order her to cooperate with treatment."

In my heart, I knew what he was saying was right. I could sense there was something terribly wrong with my baby. Every time I look at her, I see darkness. When she looks at me it's with a vacant, cold stare. But as a mother, it's hard to accept that maybe there's something mentally wrong with your child. Sometimes we're blinded by our own children's pain.

Sarina had left the house on a Tuesday and didn't return until Friday morning. She had the nerve to walk through the door like it was just an ordinary day. No *Good morning, Hello,* or *How are you?* She strutted into the kitchen wearing a leopard-print vinyl dress and matching knee-high boots, with a matching scarf tied around a curly, brunette Afro wig. Her makeup looked like it was put on with black crayon. To top it all off she had a Black and Mild cigar dangling from her mouth. I just stared at her, then I thought about Indy's description of my poor child: "That girl looks like a porcelain

Homey the Clown with that bald head, those painted-on eyebrows, and that bad makeup job." I had to admit she really did look a mess. But I would never say that to her because I've always tried to allow my kids to express themselves. I encouraged self-expression and always tried to accept their individuality. Besides, I know that part of being a teenager is trying to develop your own identity. I've prayed she'd hurry up and decide who she's going to be and how she wants to look.

"Sarina, where have you been?" I asked. "Your father and I have been worried sick."

"The two of you make me wanna shit hot coals, the way you're always fuckin' tryna be in my business," she snapped while she took off her wig, opened the refrigerator, then stuck it in the vegetable bin.

I cringed. I couldn't believe Sarina was talking to me as if I were some girl off the street. And putting her wig in my refrigerator made me raise an eyebrow.

"Sarina, why in the world did you put your wig in the refrigerator?"

She sighed impatiently, rolled her eyes, then lit her cigar on the stove. "Duh, to keep it cool, why else?" I stared at her in disbelief, then decided not to question it any further; I'd remove it when she left the kitchen. Besides, I figured she did it to try to agitate me, so I changed the subject instead.

"Your father saw what you did to the car."

"Big deal," she said, taking two pulls off her cigar and going back into the refrigerator to pull out eggs and beef sausage to cook. "I don't care about his raggedy-ass BMW."

"Watch your mouth, young lady, and I've told you about going into the refrigerator without washing your hands," I said. I watched her prepare herself a hearty breakfast. She stays out for days, then comes in here like this is some twenty-four-hour diner. "I thought I asked you to come home by midnight," I said calmly, trying not to be confrontational.

She put her hand on her hip. "Yeah, and?"

I overlooked the attitude and continued. "This is the third time this month you broke your curfew. You're grounded this weekend."

"You're buggin', right?" she asked. "You are out of your mind if you think

I'm staying in this funky-ass house. You can cancel that. I have people to see and places to be this weekend."

Funky house? This girl has a gorgeous home with an in-ground Olympic-size heated pool, steam room, game room, and every imaginable electronic device created. She even has her own private living area with a private bath, and she calls this a funky house. She'd rather hang out at someone's nasty, unkempt bungalow than be here.

"Don't talk fresh, young lady," I said, still trying to remain calm, cool, and collected. "You're grounded and that's that. Now put that daggone cigar out and give me your car keys."

"Yeah, right," she said as she tossed her cigar in the dishwater. "I don't think so. It's my car and I'm not giving you jack." She put her food on a glass plate, poured herself some orange juice, then prepared to prance her rude behind upstairs. I got up from the table and again asked her to give me her keys, but she continued to talk fresh to me. Before I could stop myself, I lost my cool.

"Give me those damn keys," I snapped while I got up in her face.

"Get out of my face," she said, then shouldered me out of her way. "I'm not giving you shit."

I stumbled back a few steps, then grabbed her by the arm. "Well, I tell you what; you won't eat anything in this house. Wherever you were the past three days is where you should have eaten," I said, knocking her plate of food to the floor. The glass plate shattered as scrambled eggs and sausage hit the white ceramic tile.

"Get the fuck off me!" she yelled. She snatched her arm from my grip, then tossed her orange juice in my face. The glass smashed to the floor.

Slap! I had slapped her face. Her head swung to the right. *Slap!* Then to the left. "Don't you ever use that tone with me, young lady!" I said through clenched teeth. "I am your mother, not one of those hootchies in the street. Now give me those damn keys."

She stood there in shock for a minute, then said, "No! What you gonna do, slap me again? Go ahead. I'm not giving you shit." She stomped toward the spiral staircase, which led to the north side of the house. "If you *ever* hit me again," she yelled, running up the stairs, "I'm calling CPS on you."

The nerve of her to say she'd call Child Protective Services on me! No one is coming into my home to tell me how to raise my children. I've been a damn good parent, and if anyone has a problem with me slapping my child for throwing juice in my face and cursing at me, they can kiss where the sun don't shine. And if they do try to come up in here, I'll have a few choice things to say to them. These state agencies have been given a bit too much power, thinking they can tell good, law-abiding citizens how to discipline their children. I understand there's a thin line between discipline and abuse, and I agree no one should cross it. No child deserves to be abused by anyone. But these state workers bounce in and out of homes acting like they're experts on abuse. Well, I'd like to know this: If they know so much about abuse, why is it they remove some children from one abusive environment only to place them in one they fund? Why is it that many of them cover up their own negligence? Doesn't that make them just as guilty of "endangering the welfare of a minor" as abusive parents? Why is it that the children who truly need to be removed from abusive environments aren't always removed until it's in a body bag? Why is it that many of these experts seem uninterested in truly helping families and children who *really* need them the most? All these things that I learned in school and in life raced through my head as Sarina's threat echoed in my ears.

"Go right ahead!" I screamed at her closed door. "And I'll slap them too."

With orange juice dripping from my face and hair, I weighed my options. Either I jump on her back and snatch the keys out her hand or be creative without getting into a power struggle. I opted for the latter, then tried to think of what Indy would do in this situation. I went outside, popped the hood of her car, and removed the battery and distributor cap. *Let's see how far she gets now*, I thought. Then, to be on the safe side, I put the Club on the steering wheel.

10

CHYNA: WHAT'S COME OVER ME

LORD KNOWS I TRIED TO BE STRONG. For weeks, I tried to ignore the throbbing sensation between my legs. But it finally overwhelmed me. It was a throbbing that grew in the pit of my soul, then traveled through my body with such intensity that my whole body ached. Cold showers didn't help, hot and cold compresses didn't help. The Jacuzzi and steam room didn't help. Prayer didn't help. And neither did my conversation with Indy, not that I expected it to.

"Girl, your ass is just horny," she said, laughing. "You need to go out there and get you some. One good stickin' is what you need to knock the cobwebs outta that dusty pussy."

"Indy, my goodness. Do you have to say it like that?" I said, trying not to laugh myself. "You make it sound like a household chore."

"Well, after two years, it's gonna be a chore tryna get up in that. Whoever you get to handle the job is gonna have his work cut out tryna scratch that cat."

"Oh, no, girl. I couldn't. I'm not sleeping with some strange man. It's too dangerous out there for casual sex. In case you've forgotten, I'm still a married woman."

"Humph. In name only," she said sarcastically. "Well, if you want, I can send you a few dildos to hold you over."

"It wouldn't be the same," I said, trying to hide the fact that I'd already tried it. "I want…no, I need to feel the heat of a man I've built something with. I need to feel a connection."

She snickered. "Well, I guess the only heat you'll feel will be the steam from

that hot pussy. And the only connection you're gonna feel is a wet dream."
She was laughing so hard, I could tell she had tears in her eyes.

"Indy, this is not funny," I said, feigning feeling hurt. "I'm really having a
hard time with this. I've never had this kind of throbbing sensation. I thought
it would pass, but every night it just gets worse. Do you think I should go see
a doctor?"

She tried to pull herself together and sound serious. "Chyna, please. The
only thing a doctor is gonna do is write your ass a prescription for a stiff
dick." She paused a moment, then continued. "Girl, I really don't know how
you've managed this long. It would drive me crazy. I'd be bananas right
about now."

"All I know is, I'm one spasm away from losing my mind," I said. "I really
thought I could hold out, but this is too unbearable."

"I hear you, girl. Maintenance. That's what you need. There's only so much
a hand or finger can do, and you know dildos are only for those last-minute
tune-ups. What you need is a pussy overhaul, and the only suitable tool for
that kinda job is a dick attached to a maintenance man."

I laughed at what she said, but it wasn't a laughing matter to me. It's easy
for her to joke because she's single and can sleep with whomever she wants,
whenever she wants. Which is what she does. Yes, I needed some sexual
healing but not at the expense of compromising my values. I refused to
cheat on my husband. Regardless of our current situation, he was *still* my
husband, and I had vowed to be faithful. Just because he cheated on me
doesn't mean I should cheat on him. So an affair was out. Mechanical sex
wasn't really exciting for me, nor fulfilling. I've tried it and I've still felt
clogged up. It's a tease that doesn't completely please. Like Indy said, it's
okay for a tune-up but not for any heavy-duty work. So sex toys were out. I
had no other choice. As a woman, I needed to do what I needed to do in
order to maintain my sanity and to give my neglected womanhood the attention it was demanding.

So last night, I gave myself a manicure and pedicure, meditated in the steam
room for about an hour, drew myself a bath, and poured in my most expensive bath crystals. While I waited for the water to rise, I trimmed the hairs
around my privates, then stood naked in the vanity mirror. I examined the

front of my body, then turned around to get a glimpse of my backside. With the exception of wishing I had a wider nose and fuller lips, I was pleased with my findings. At thirty-six, with four kids, I don't have one stretch mark, no cellulite, and no unwanted inches. Although my hips and breasts are fuller than in my youth, they are firm and I'm still shapely. I smiled. Then I thought about how a few of my sons' friends would sometimes make flirtatious comments and give me lustful stares. My sons have always been proud of showing me off, but they're extremely overprotective of me, so they'd block an admirer from a mile away. Not that I was interested. There's no way I'd entertain the thought of becoming involved with any teenager. But I've noticed that a lot of young men today have no problem trying to rap to an older woman. What's most disturbing to me is the fact that many of these women have no problem becoming sexually involved with them. I heard through the neighborhood gossip mill that some country club member's wife is involved with her seventeen-year-old son's best friend. She's forty-three and he's sixteen. Then there was the time Jayson told me his friend's mother was sleeping with his sister's nineteen-year-old boyfriend. Now, that's downright trifling. The thought turns my stomach. Although the law says the age of consent is sixteen, I still see it as statutory rape.

Anyway, the only man I've ever wanted to notice me or admire me is my husband. The only man that has ever made me feel beautiful is my husband. These days, it seems like a lot has changed. But that didn't matter to me.

At the stroke of midnight, I pressed my ear against Ryan's door and heard the faint sound of moans coming from the TV. I bit my bottom lip, then patiently waited for the butterflies to settle in my stomach. I took a deep breath and gently knocked. Anxiety flooded me when I heard his footsteps across the carpet. As always, I had half hoped he was asleep or would just ignore my tapping. Being ignored would be better than being rejected.

He opened the door a crack and stared at me. "What's wrong?" he asked. His voice was deep and resonant.

I smiled, trying not to show my nervousness. "Nothing," I said. "I was hoping you'd have a moment to talk."

As he had many times before, he let the door fling open as he walked back toward his bed. My eyes focused on his nude backside, then down to the back of his muscular thighs and his heart-shaped calves. He was still built like a running back. My mind started to drift off to the first time I ever saw him nude, but my thoughts were disrupted when he spoke.

"So what's on your mind?" he asked. "What's Sarina up to now?"

"I'm not here to talk about Sarina tonight. I'm here for something else," I said coyly.

I breathed deeply, positioned myself in front of him at the foot of the bed, and untied my robe. I let it slide off my cream-colored shoulders and onto the floor. His eyes opened so wide I thought they'd pop out of his head.

"Woman, have you been drinking?" he asked.

"No, Ryan, I haven't been drinking," I said in a slow, soft voice. I walked around to the side of the bed, grabbed the remote off the nightstand, and turned the TV and VCR off. "You won't be needing this tonight."

"Chyna, do you know what you're doing?" he asked while trying to stop me from pulling the covers off him. I tugged three more times before he gave in. He tried to cover his excitement with his hand.

"Yes, Ryan," I said in a whisper. My breathing was slow and heavy. "I know exactly what I'm doing." I climbed on top of him, clamped the inner part of my thighs around his hips, then kissed him. His full lips felt so good against mine. "Make love to me," I whispered as I continued lightly kissing him. It had been so long since I felt him next to me. His mint-flavored tongue slowly found its way inside my mouth, and the minute his tongue touched mine, a flood of lust raced from the pit of my loins. I smiled away my embarrassment at the warm wetness that slid down my thighs and onto his stomach. He removed his hand from his erection and placed both hands around my waist. Then he ran his hands along the center of my back and moved them slowly along my hips and thighs. His hands were still strong. Still soft. I felt every part of my body melting like butter in his warm hands. I needed him, and his touch told me he needed me as well.

"Chyna, are you sure?" he asked between long, wet kisses. "Don't do it unless you're sure."

I reached down for his erection, lifted my hips, and after slow maneuvering, guided him inside me. I gasped. I leaned in toward him, held my breasts in my hands, then placed each nipple one at a time in his mouth. When his lips and tongue touched them, I sighed with pleasure. "I'm sure, Ryan. I'm more sure than I've ever been." And with every stroke, every kiss, and every orgasm, I knew Ryan was still the only man I could ever love.

It was 5:00 a.m. when I snuck out of Ryan's room. I left his bed partly out of embarrassment for what I'd done and partly due to his loud snoring. His snoring was more like a pig's mating call than anything else. I wanted to stay covered under the warmth of his hug, but he grunted and gurgled to no end— it became unbearable. *How in the world could anyone stand that noise?* I asked myself. I tried to remember if he snored or grunted like that when we shared a bed together, and I couldn't. But if he did, it surely wasn't something I missed.

I crept down to the kitchen to put on a pot of hot water. While I waited for the water to boil, I replayed my night with my husband in my mind. It was better than I ever imagined it would be. I was still shocked at myself for being so brazen, but it was worth it. I had made love to my husband. At first, it was slow and gentle, then I became aggressive. The lady in me stood back and let the beast out. I spoke in tongue. The words became rough and dirty, like a scene from *The Devil and Mrs. Jones*. I took what I needed from him and it felt good. I felt relaxed, relieved, and now I had the appetite of three men.

I warmed a big piece of bread pudding, topped it with vanilla ice cream, then sat at the kitchen table. *Men, can't live with them, can't live without them* came to mind as I waited for the whistle of the kettle. I smiled. Even though I had let space and time come between us, I still needed Ryan in my life. Even though I suspected him of cheating on me, I still wanted him. I know I need to confront him and I will. But I still want my marriage. Not that I'll ever forget what he did. Seeing him kiss another woman felt like someone biting down on my heart with razor-sharp teeth. That kind of pain you never forget. I knew I could forgive him, but would I ever be able to trust him again? I hope so, because without trust, no relationship can survive.

Ryan's voice startled me. "Oh, I didn't know you were down here. I heard something whistling."

I pulled my long braid over my shoulder and smiled. "It's just me," I said, then got up to take the kettle off the burner. "I came down for some tea."

He was wearing the green-and-white-striped pajama pants and matching robe I'd bought him four years ago. "Mind if I join you?"

"Not at all," I said as I watched him move around the kitchen. He poured himself a glass of milk and cut a piece of the pineapple-carrot upside-down cake I had made. He wiped the moist remains of cake from the knife with his fingers, then licked them.

Our eyes met as he sat down across from me. His dark brown eyes were warm. He smiled, then lowered his head. "Chyna, I'm sorry," he said in a whisper.

"Sorry for what, Ryan?"

He looked up at me. Although he tried to hold them back, I saw them. His eyes were filled with tears. "For what I did. I knew you saw me with her; but I never slept with her. I probably would have, but I didn't. We were together a couple of times, but we never slept together. Never," he said. "When I came home and saw you had moved my stuff out of our bedroom, I didn't say anything because I knew there wasn't anything I could say. I saw the hurt in your eyes. I never wanted to hurt you…"

I just kept staring into his eyes. His eyelashes were heavy. For the first time in years, I saw the gentleness of the man I fell in love with. I listened intently. His words flowed from his thick lips with sincerity.

"…But I know I did, and that hurt me more than anything. I've felt so guilty. If I didn't get caught, I probably would have slept with her, eventually. But seeing you standing there made reality hit like a ton of bricks. And the reality is, my life is with you. It always has been and always will be. No other woman could ever give me what you've given me. I've been ashamed for not being man enough to know that then. Chyna, I love you. You're not just my wife, you're my soul mate," he said as tears fell. "My life has been so empty without you. Whatever it takes, I want you back. I need you back."

My face was void of expression, but my heart raced. Then a little voice in my head reminded me of the fact that nearly 75 percent of married men or men involved in serious relationships cheat. The thought of my husband being one of those men in search of a "secret lover" made me want to slap his face; instead, I let my hand rest on top of his. Silence consumed us until I asked, "So why'd you do it?"

"I don't know," he said. "Stupidity… insecurity…curiosity."

I wasn't satisfied with his answer, so I let a myriad of reasons why men cheat stomp through my mind. Because women accept it? Well, this woman is not going to accept it. I am not going to stand for that "boys will be boys" concept. I would rather sleep alone than next to a cheater. Because men need other women to stroke their egos? Well, if I can't be the only woman to reassure his manhood, then I'm going to toss his cheating behind to the curb. Because men don't know how to set proper boundaries with the opposite sex? I'm not accepting the "it just happened" excuse; nothing happens unless you want it to. If a woman brushes up against you, bats her eyes, or smiles your way, that doesn't give you the green light to have a freak on the side. Of course, other reasons entered my mind, but I decided to let them sift through without dwelling on them.

"Is there anyone else you've kissed, danced with, or wanted to sleep with?" I asked.

"No one."

"So you're telling me you haven't been with anyone in the last two years?"

"Yes."

"Well, how do I know you won't try to stray again? How do I know you'll be man enough to turn down some other woman's advances?"

"Because you're the only woman in my heart and the only woman I want to share my bed with."

Between you and me, I wanted to believe him and I needed to trust him. But I had to be certain. Which is why I hired a private investigator to track his every move. And I will continue to have him watched until I'm convinced he's able to live by his words to love me and only me. If he isn't, I'll follow Indy's advice and "take him for everything he's worth." In the meantime, he will have to court me all over again. That's right, wine and dine me. Smother me with affection and attention. Send me flowers and balloons. Write me love poems. Make love to me in every position invented and then create new ones. Oh, yes, he'll have a lot of making up to do to get back in my good graces.

He reached down in the pocket of his robe and pulled out the diamond anklet he'd bought me for my birthday ten years ago. The one I thought I lost. "I think this belongs to you," he said. "I found it yesterday on the floor beside my bed."

I blushed. "Oh," I said, then walked over to him. He pushed his chair back from the table so I could place my left foot between his legs. "I guess it fell off when I was, um …"

Earlier that day, I took the spare key to his bedroom and snuck in. There was a faint scent of his Cigar Aficionado cologne still lingering in the air. I breathed in what was left, then looked around. He had cleaned up. The linens were stripped and all of his clothes were hung up. There were no wet towels laying around, and with the exception of the toilet seat being left up and the cap being off the toothpaste, the bathroom was clean. I hate it when he leaves the seat up. That was just one of his annoying habits that irked me. But it was *his* room.

When I opened the door to his walk-in closet, the smell of cedarwood greeted me. Everything was neatly in place. His shoes were lined up, with dress shoes on the right, casual shoes on the left, and sneakers and boots in the middle. I touched the collar of a few of his crisp white dress shirts and wondered when he found time to do all this cleaning. Then I wondered whom he had cleaned up for. "Uh-uh, he wouldn't be crazy enough to bring his floozy in my home," I'd said out loud. I'd heard stories of women finding their men in bed with other women, or vice versa. And Indy always had a story to tell as well. So anything was possible. Similar scenes from *The Young and the Restless* and *The Bold and the Beautiful* replayed in my mind. Before I let my imagination get the best of me, I prayed I was wrong, then quickly dismissed the thought. I sat on his bed, ran my hands across his pillow, then peeked inside the drawers of his nightstand. I relaxed, blowing the anxiety slowly out of my mouth, when nothing incriminating caught my eye. My mama always said, "Seek and ye shall find." Or, "Be careful what you look for, 'cause you just might find it." Well, while I was seeking, I was hoping I wouldn't find. And if I did, I didn't know what I'd do. But it would serve me right for snooping.

I grabbed his remote to his TV, turned it on, then pressed play on the VCR. Soft moans came through the speakers, the same kind I had heard many nights before. The same moans I heard when I'd press my ear to his door. Moans of pleasure. On the screen were two women in very compromising positions with four big, strong men. Each man found a place to bury his privates, and the women seemed greedy for more. I fast-forwarded. There were three women with one well-endowed man. The women explored one another with their tongues while the guy shared himself with a smile. Again, I fast-forwarded, this time a woman was on her knees savoring her man with her mouth. She swallowed all of him and not once gagged. I blushed. I had never seen a porno movie, nor had I ever done any of the things I had just witnessed. Some of the acts seemed painful yet pleasurable. My embarrassment at their naughty deeds was tempered by a tinge of jealousy as I watched the pleasure each scene brought its participants.

Now Ryan smiled. "Yeah, I guess it did fall off," he said with a wink. He made sure the lobster clasp was fastened tightly, then he rubbed his hands up my thigh to just below the crevice of my buttocks. "Did you find anything?" he asked, grinning.

"No," I answered. But he knew I was telling a small fib, because when I'd looked under his bed I found a handwritten note that read: Chyna, you are the essence of my total being. Within you lie the best moments of my life. I will always love you. Please find it in your heart to forgive me. After I read it, I laid it on his nightstand. Watching that X-rated movie had me so flustered that I left his room before putting it back where I found it. He had cleaned up his room because he knew I had been in there several times before snooping around.

I straddled my legs across him, then pulled his robe open until it fell off his broad shoulders. I licked the darkness of his shoulders and neck. His beautiful black skin glistened with the wet streaks of my tongue. The heat from his breath across my neck made me delirious. His hands rested in the small of my back, then gripped my rear tightly. I felt myself holding him. With my neck pressed against his, my heart beating along with his, my body pressed close to his, I could tell the heat from my womanhood had him aroused. This time, he lifted my hips up, pulled his erection out, then slipped himself deep in me. And with my lips flush against his ear, I whispered, "I love you, Ryan Joshua Littles."

His hands gripped me tighter as he whispered back, "I love you too, Chyna Saron Littles." I lifted my head from his shoulders, then kissed his lips hard and long. And then we cried. Together, we cried tears of lost time, of unspoken words. Together, we cried twenty years' worth of tears—tears of passion, tears of mistakes, tears of forgiveness. Together, we cried until the sun rose.

I I

INDERA: **TELL IT LIKE IT IS**

"YOU DID WHAT?!" I asked, not believing what I'd just heard.

"I slept with Ryan," she repeated. "Two weeks ago, I made love to my husband."

"Chyna, girl, your ass is outta control. So now what?"

"I don't know," she said in a depressed tone.

"You don't know? Girl, your ass is crazy. How the hell could you let him fuck you?"

"Do you have to use that word? You make it sound so dirty. Besides, he didn't do anything to me. I did it to him. And he was just as shocked."

"You don't sleep with the man for two years, for whatever reason, then you turn around and screw him. That shit makes no sense to me. If you're not happy with him, why fuck him?"

"Because I have needs too," she said with an attitude. "Maybe it's not him I'm unhappy with."

"So…did a good fuck bring you happiness?"

"Indy, please. Don't start, okay? Not today."

"Girl, you need to get a damn grip and figure out what the hell you're gonna do. Enough is enough. Both of you are ridiculous."

We were silent for a few seconds. I could tell I had hit a nerve because Chyna gets real quiet when she's trying to collect herself. It wouldn't be ladylike for Miss Priss to go off. I guess you think I was a little rough on her. Well, I'm sick of her sitting in that big-ass castle worrying herself over King Kong. She's too damn fly to be stressin' over some sorry-ass. An ugly one, no less.

She needs to get herself together and start doin' her. And I was too through to hear she let him stroke her cat after two years. She kicked his ass outta their bedroom, said she's unhappy in that marriage, then turns around and lets him knock her suga walls. Uh-huh. To be so smart, her ass is dumb as hell. And this shit about how he and that other woman "only kissed." C'mon, *Hillary*. Whether it's a kiss or a suck, if it's done with someone other than your spouse or mate, then it's cheating. Point-blank. I just had to let her have it. I told her I thought her ass was crazy for giving him the time of day. Either she's going to try to work through her marriage or stop complaining and get the fuck out of it.

I understand her kitty-kat was aching, but damn. She didn't have to let that beast soothe it. Okay, she was thirsting for a little maintenance. Two years? Then again, her ass needed a lot of maintenance, but she didn't have to give in. I just think she shoulda been a little stronger. Hell, use your hand, buy a vibrator, wrap a cucumber, sit on a hot dog, rub a few ice cubes between your legs—hell, I knew a girl who stuck a curling iron in her hot pussy—but don't go backward. If you don't feel like a man is treating you right, kick his ass to the curb, then keep on steppin'. But I guess Miss Prude put me in my place in a very nice way, didn't she?

"Indy, I don't care what you say, think, or feel about it. Ryan is still my husband. I have no intention of running out in the streets looking for a Mr. Goodbar. I think you do enough of that for the both of us."

Oh no, she didn't? Oh yes, she did. Miss Chyna got real spicy with me. I couldn't get a word in edgewise. She continued.

"Until you have a husband or even a man in your life, don't lecture me on things you know nothing about. Maybe I shouldn't have slept with him, but I did. So what? He's my husband. I've been with this man for over twenty years, so about the idea of letting another man touch me sexually is unthinkable right now. I needed one night of release. If it's a crime for me to use my husband for that, oh well. Everything is not always so cut-and-dried in relationships. And until you fall in love or find someone you're capable of loving, you'll never understand."

I was shocked at Miss Thing's spunk. It's amazing what a stiff dick will do.

"Well, excuse me," I said. "I didn't mean to set you off. I was just speaking my mind because I know how unhappy you've been. I just don't want to see you get hurt."

"Well, sometimes I need you to just listen and keep your comments to yourself. I love you dearly, but sometimes you're a bit too opinionated. Instead of putting all your energy into everybody else's business, why don't you try to focus more on getting your own business in order? Look, I gotta go. I have a lot of things to tend to today. I'll call you soon."

And before I could say another word, she gave me the dial tone. Homegirl had slammed the phone down in my damn ear. I yelled into the phone, "I still think your ass is crazy!" Of course, I called sista-girl back.

"Yes, Indy," she said with an attitude. She knew it was me, thanks to Caller ID.

"Are we still on for Saturday?" I asked.

"As long as you leave that attitude of yours in Brooklyn. If you start up, I'm sending you home."

"Oh, girl, please," I said. "What in the world would you do without me?"

Her tone lightened. "Miss you," she said. "Look, girl, I really gotta go. I'll see you on Saturday."

"And make me some of that blueberry crumpet," I said. Homegirl makes a killer blueberry crumb roll that's to die for, okay? "I want it nice and hot when I get there."

"Maybe."

"And, Chyna?"

"Yeah?"

"Does the kitty-kitty still need a little sticky-sticky with hubby's dicky-dicky?" I laughed. She didn't. *Click* is the only thing I heard. Meeeeeeooooooow!

Alrighty, then. Now, on to another matter. Let me tell you how I had to black on another triflin'-ass man. I'm sure some of you don't wanna hear another one of my man bashings. Too bad. Look, to keep it real with you, I know sometimes I can get beside myself. But, between you and me, I don't really like getting ugly with anyone. Before I let you know how I had to go into my trick bag on this fool, I do want to reiterate that when I vent my hostilities about men, it's not directed toward *all* men, because I do know that there are many responsible, loving, dependable, sharing, faithful, and committed men out there. Somewhere, someone is lucky enough to have such a man. My rage is based on my own experiences with them. Nothing more, nothing less.

Anyway, to get to the point, I would like someone to *please* tell me how the hell a man is gonna try to be fly rockin' dingy underwear? I don't care if you're makin' two beans or two hundred Gs, there is no excuse for any man to step out in raggedy-ass drawers. That is an automatic strike, okay? Now, don't get me wrong, it's okay to have a pair of raggedy underwear to lounge around in when you're home chillin'. Hell, I have a few pair of my own, but I don't step out in 'em. And I definitely don't rock 'em when I know I'm gonna drop 'em. So any man tryna bed down this sista needs to be correct from head to toe, from his outerwear to his underwear.

Now, you can say and think anything you want about me 'cause, like I told you before, I'ma do me, regardless. But there are two things I do not tolerate, and one is disrespect and the other is a dirty ass. Before I lay down with any man, he must wash his ass 'cause I'm not down with dick grit, musty armpits, or a stank bottom. Point-blank: I'm not havin' it, okay? That's why I had to go off on Stanley's nasty ass. Stanley and I met at the Cactus Café, a cute little Mexican spot over on West Third in the Village, about a month and a half ago.

Anyway, I tried to be nice to the brotha. But I gave him props a little too soon. On the surface, he seemed on point. Nice haircut, clean fingernails, chunky jewels, sweet ride, fly gear, heavy money clip, et cetera, et cetera. He's a nice-looking, brown-skinned brotha from Connecticut who works for American Express as an international accounts manager. So I'm thinking, maybe we can do this. Hell, he looked well groomed, was financially on point, and, of course, more than willing to spend his dough. And, for the record, he told me he wasn't married or involved with anyone. But, of course, my gut told me he was lying through his chipped tooth.

So after a delicious meal at Tavern on the Green, we get to our hotel suite and he starts tryna get his mack on. He's kissing my neck, squeezin' my Charmin-soft ass, and grindin' his hips into me nice and slow.

"Damn, baby, you taste and smell good," he said sounding real sexylike in a low, deep voice. "I've been waiting patiently and tonight"—kiss, kiss—"you're mine." More kisses.

I took his hand and slid it up my knit micromini dress. He rubbed the front of my crotchless black panties, then slipped his long fingers in my juicy fruit. "Mmmmm," I moaned.

He smiled. His chipped tooth gave him an added sexiness. "Damn, baby, you wet."

"You want this?" I asked.

"Yeah, baby," he said, breathing heavy in my ear and rubbing my clitty-clitty bang-bang.

I pulled his face to me, looked him in his gray eyes, then said in a soft whisper, "I want you to eat my pussy like it's the Last Supper." He pulled away from me, looked at me for a second as if what I said shocked him, then pulled my dress up. I walked over to the king-size bed, climbed up on all fours, then parted my ass cheeks open. "Guess who's coming to dinner?" I asked with a smile. See, I like it when a man eats my pussy from the back, okay?

Needless to say, he licked his way to my fat clit, rolling it in his mouth until it throbbed with pleasure, then he ate his wet buffet. "That's right," I said as I slammed my sweet hole in his face. "Suck this pussy. If you wanna stick it, you betta lick it good." He licked and slurped all the drippings from his pussy platter (that's right, finger-lickin' good), then he had the audacity to stand up with his dick hanging out of his Phat Farm jeans, and offer me his uncircumcised dick to snack on. Now, I like my dick a little meaty, but extra skin? Thanks but no thanks. Besides, five dinner dates and two eighteen-karat bangles aren't worthy of a dick suck, okay? But, to keep him happy, I gave him a greasy hand job. I oiled my hands up with a few drops of my secret love gel, then stroked his heavy Ball Park frank until it got nice and plump. But he started getting on my nerves when he kept tryna get me to suck him off. I tried to maintain my cool and be gracious.

"Look, don't be tryna force your dick in my damn face," I snapped. "You have one more time to hit me in the mouth with your shit and then I'm gonna do a Lorena Bobbitt on your ass."

"Oh, so it's like that, huh? I eat you, but I can't get no justice," he said with an attitude.

"If I'm gonna slob you, it's on my terms, okay? And tonight, the slurp shop is closed. Now, I'm gonna let you get your fuck on all night, and if you're a good boy," I said, throwing my legs up and showing him my tight asshole, "I'll let you get some of this chocolate puddin'." I rubbed my fingers across my hot furnace, then licked them. He grinned. I licked my lips. "Let's get in the shower so I can suck those big, hairy ox balls."

Yeah, he liked that. His dick got as hard as a roll of quarters. Men. Homeboy pulled off his clothes and headed for the bathroom. While he was in the shower waiting for me, I casually pulled his wallet out of his back pocket and scanned the contents. And guess what? I came across an insurance card with the family plan. Two kids and a wife, okay? Strike. Another lying, cheatin'-ass man. So you know Miss Indy was gonna do him dirty for lying, right? I made a mental note of all the vital info (his wife's name and date of birth), then headed for the bathroom to join him.

"Hey, baby," I said. "You ready for me?"

"Yeah, baby, I been ready."

Well, just as I'm getting ready to step in the shower with loverboy, I looked down, and what do I see? Suga Daddy's dingy drawers with the raggedy waistband lying in the middle of the bathroom floor. Now, I'm too through. But I keep my cool. I walk out of the bathroom.

"Hey, where you goin'?" he yelled. "I'm ready to put it on you."

Nasty motherfucker. I bet you are, I thought. *You shoulda put a clean pair of drawers on that nasty ass of yours.* "I forgot something," I yelled back. "Hold tight, baby. I'll be right there to give it to you nice and hot."

So I go into my Louis Vuitton satchel and pull out my "Indy Supply Case," which consists of latex gloves, tweezers, a vibrator, French ticklers, a variety of condoms, a dildo, anal beads, K-Y jelly, handcuffs, and a few other items you don't need to know about. I pulled on my gloves, went back into the bathroom, then picked up his drawers. I looked inside 'em real quick, then dropped 'em in the little white trash bag for later. I pulled off my gloves, then stuck my head behind the shower curtain. I smiled. He smiled. I smiled again, then turned the cold-water knob off. That's right, I scalded his ass.

"Ow, ow, ow, ow, ooooooooouch," he screamed. He was so loud, you woulda thought I threw acid on his ass. "Ooooooooooouch, what the fuck are you doin', bitch?" He ripped open the shower curtain, jumped out of the tub, then tried to grab me but slipped and busted his rusty ass.

"You fuckin' bitch, what the fuck is your problem?"

"You're the problem, you nasty motherfucker!" I yelled. "How the hell you gonna step out without wipin' your ass?"

"I'ma whup your ass, bitch, for burning me." He got up to come after me. But then he stopped when he saw me just standing there waiting for him to make his move. "Bitch, just get the fuck out before I really hurt your ass," he said, sounding like a wounded animal. "You're a real crazy bitch."

"Oh, I'ma get the fuck out, make no mistake," I yelled. "But the next time you wanna drop your drawers, make sure you wipe your ass first, you nasty bastard. And since the word *bitch* seems to be a favorite of yours, I'ma show you how a *real* bitch gets down, okay?"

"Fuck you, bitch!"

"No problem, Doo-Doo Brown." I grabbed my shit and quietly shut the door behind me. And this morning I went straight to FedEx and shipped a nice little care package to his wife. That's right, I sent her his nasty drawers with a little note attached: My darling, Here's a little something for putting up with all my shit. Love, Stanley Shit Stains

I still can't get over that. As fine as he was, he didn't know how to wipe his ass. The raggedy drawers were one thing, but shit stains? C'mon now. The only reason for not wiping your ass is if you're a quadriplegic, okay?! And his wife? What kinda woman would allow her man to step out with a dirty bottom? Doesn't that nasty bitch know her man is a reflection on her? If he ain't correct, she ain't correct.

I will say, he has really turned my stomach. I am not fucking with another man for a very long time. And I mean that shit. Oops, no pun intended.

Bright and early Saturday morning, I had my bags packed, my CD player loaded up with beats, and I was pulling out of my driveway headed for Maryland. Things in Manhattan were quiet this time of morning, so my ride to and through the Holland Tunnel was relatively smooth. As soon as I got out of the tunnel into Jersey City, I decided to pull into the Exxon to get gas. A tall, attractive Indian man came over to serve me.

When I let the window down, the November chill blew in his odor. I twisted my nose up. "Fill it up with premium," I said.

He stuck the nozzle in my tank, then asked, "Check oil?"

"Yes, please." I popped the hood, then watched him check the oil level. He came to the driver's side window to show me my oil was full. "Thanks," I said, trying to be cordial.

While the tank was filling, I decided to run inside to pick up a pack of Double-mint. Hell, I figured I might as well click-clack and pop my way to Chyna's. So I bought my gum, a Tastykake peach pie, and an Ocean Spray cranberry juice, then returned to my car. That's when I noticed a young brotha standing alongside a black seven series Beemer with Jersey tags, getting gas and talking on a cell phone. There were three other brothas in the car—one in the front passenger seat and the other two in the back. *Humph, another young brotha selling drugs. He probably just got finished picking up*, I thought. I paid the Indian man, then, just as I'm about to get back in my ride, I hear his deep voice.

"Aye, yo, shorty, come here," he said. *Aye, yo, shorty? Wrong move with me.* I started to ignore him and let the smoke from my tailpipe greet him, but I was feeling good, so I turned around to face him. His gear was on point, haircut crisp; he had all his shine on, and he was just too cool for his own breeches.

"Excuse you?"

"Yo, come here. Let me rap to you for a minute," he said.

"I don't think so. You wanna talk, you come to me." Who the hell did he think he was talking to? Talking about some "come here." I think not. So he comes beboppin' over to me like he's some pimp daddy or something. He was leaning so hard to one side that I thought he was a stroke victim.

"Yo, shorty, where you off to?" he asked. The gold fronts in his grill shined brighter than the sun in August.

I squinted, then rolled my eyes. When he stepped in my space, I knew I was gonna have to read him for getting a little too up close and personal. His breath smelled like weed. I jerked my head back.

"How old are you?"

"Twenty," he said proudly as he licked his thick lips.

"Well, let me tell you a few things, Mr. Twenty," I said. "First of all, don't 'yo' me or 'aye' me, I'm not one of your peers. Second of all, back up outta my grill," I demanded, pushing him back with my hand. "Third of all, my name ain't Stella, now step! If I wanna get my groove on, it won't be with some young buck."

He stared at me for a moment, then blacked. "Aye, yo, don't ever put your muthafuckin' hands on me. You got that, bitch?" He pointed a finger right at my face.

Believe it or not, I kept my cool. Had it been any other day, I would have pitched a sookie. Instead, I smiled my "I will fuck your ass up" smile, then said, "Boy, you betta get your young ass outta my face before I give you a firsthand experience of what the word *bitch* means." I started digging in my Louis Vuitton backpack when he decided to back away.

"Yeah, I got your boy, a'ight. I'll show you a young buck," he said, then unzipped his brown leather pants. "When I shove this young dick in your ass." He stood there swinging his dick. Eight in the morning, and this fool is off the hook.

Well, that was it. This "bitch" was livid, okay?! It's one thing to call me out my name, and it's another to disrespect me by pulling your fuckin' dick out. I felt my left eye narrow to a slit as my right eye popped open two sizes wide. I felt my teeth clench.

"Why, you low-down, dirty, disrespectful son-of-a-bitch," I snarled. "I'll snap that muthafucka off, you stinkin' bitch-ass nigga." I heard his boys calling for him.

"Yo, Born, c'mon, nigga. Leave that ho alone," the one on the passenger side yelled. "We don't need no heat right now."

Born? Well, he shoulda been born with some respect. But since he's *Born*, I'll give him a little taste of the *afterbirth*. Before his little nasty ass could get away, I pepper-sprayed him, then smacked the shit out of him.

"Take that, you nasty bastard!" I yelled. "You wanna play Big Willie nigga, then you betta know how to rumble with the sharks." I Maced him again. His boys jumped out of the car to help carry his gagging ass. And you know what? The whole time, that little dot-dot, green snot was standing right there and did nothing. Then he had the nerve to look at me like *I* was crazy.

"What the fuck you lookin' at, you musty bastard?" I snapped, then hopped in my car.

En route to the New Jersey Turnpike, I flipped open my cell phone and called the police. I gave them a clear description of that disrespectful asshole and his front-seat partner, as well as the make and model of the car they were driving. And for an added bonus, I gave them the license plate number. I had memorized it when I peeped to see where they were from. "You won't get your hustle on today," I said out loud, then flipped my phone shut. I always say, When you come for me, you betta bring it high or bring it low, 'cause if you don't, I will tallyho your ass, okay?!

Five hours later, and I was still another two miles from Fort Washington, one of the elite suburbs of Washington, D.C. After that long-ass drive, I was so happy to see the Welcome to Maryland sign, it's a damn shame. That Jersey Turnpike had worn me out. That is just one long-ass stretch of road. But with a little help from my girls Adriana Evans, Dionne Farris, Amber-sunshower, and Angie Stone, I was able to sing my way right to Ginger Crest Estates.

You betta work, I thought to myself as I pulled my car around Chyna's horseshoe driveway and parked behind Ryan's Navigator. Chyna's home appeared more lavish than I remembered. I've always loved a home that's located in a cul-de-sac; it just seems to make it that much more impressive. Chyna's seven-bedroom, three-car-garage house is nestled on four acres of neatly manicured lawn with a gorgeous pond and waterfall. What I like most about it is that it's laced with cathedral and vaulted ceilings, large sky-lights, floor-to-ceiling windows, and a magnificent view of the Potomac River. *Better Homes and Gardens*, eat your heart out.

Before getting out of my car, I checked myself in the visor mirror to make sure my hair and face were in place. There's nothing worse than tryna be fierce with sleep in the corners of your eyes or a booga hanging from your nose. And you know there are people who will hold a conversation with you and never mention that there's something hanging from your face. After I passed my spot check, I headed for the door. It opened before I could ring the bell. It was Ryan, wearing cutoff sweats and a hooded Howard sweatshirt. I glanced down at his strong legs.

"Well, I see you finally made it," he said, then reached out to give me a hand with my bags. "Damn, girl, you packed like you're staying for a month. How was the ride?"

I gave him a half-assed grin 'cause you know I can't stand him. But I always bite my tongue and stay pleasant 'cause he's never really said or done anything to me. Besides, Miss Alexis Carrington told me to keep my attitude in Brooklyn. To be honest, Ryan's done nothing but try to be nice to me. I think the only time I ever heard him say anything negative about me is when, about three years ago, I overheard him telling one of his golf partners, a very successful business owner who was interested in me, "Man, I wouldn't mess with her if I were you. Stay away from her. …Yeah, she's pretty, alright. But, I'm telling you, she's crazy, so whatever you do, admire her from afar." I almost went off on him, but basically, he was telling the truth. I am pretty, and I probably would have had to go into my trick bag on his partner, especially when I heard that his fourth wife had left him. If homeboy can't hold on to a woman, something must be wrong.

"Thanks," I said, handing him my garment bag and carry case. "The ride wasn't that bad. Where's Chyna?" I asked as I followed him into the house, through the Italian marble foyer, then up the double-wide staircase toward my room. I say "my room" because it's the only room I stay in when I visit. It has cream-colored walls with plush burgundy carpet, a queen-size sleigh bed, a private bath, and a fireplace. I love it.

"Chyna had to run out to the store. She should be pulling in any minute now. Here's your room," he said, opening the double French doors. "I'm going for my afternoon run, so just make yourself comfortable."

"I always do," I said.

I walked to the huge window and watched him jog his way down the long winding road. I thought about my conversation with Chyna and tried to figure out what it was about him that kept her with him. Over twenty years with the same man, humph. Why would anyone stay with someone who has cheated on them? I knew it wasn't for money because she wasn't a materialistic woman. I mean, yes, she has a gorgeous home, the finest china and crystal money can buy, and he spoils her with any material thing she wants. But none of those things really matter to her. For as long as I've known my girl, I've known the one thing she's always wanted is a man who'd love her forever. I wondered if there were such a thing as forever. Is true love really that powerful?

When I could no longer see Ryan, I unpacked my things, then flopped my body across the bed. "Aaaah," I sighed, then started to sift through my mind's Rolodex for any trace of memories of "forever." My frantic search came up with nothing. "Just what I thought: There's no such thing," I said aloud, then drifted off to a sound sleep.

It was 6:30 in the evening when I finally woke and made my way downstairs. Instead of going down the way I came up, I decided to take the spiral stairs at the far end of the hallway that lead down into the kitchen. The minute I approached the staircase, I smelled Chyna's shrimp gumbo. I knew she was busy stirring those pots New Orleans style. Although she was raised in Norfolk, Virginia, her roots ran deep in New Orleans.

"Girrrrl, you betta work it out," I said as I winded down and around the staircase into the kitchen.

"Well, well, well…the sleeping diva has finally risen," she said with a warm smile, then reached out to give me a sisterly embrace. "I checked in on you when I got in, but you were sleeping like a baby."

"Girl, that road wore me out. I knew I should have flown like I started to." I walked toward the countered aisle, then peeked in the three pots on the stainless-steel stove top. "Now, this is what I'm talkin' about," I said when I spotted the thick stew with jumbo shrimp.

"That hair is laid, girl," she said. "You look good."

I smiled. "Well, you know how I do," I said playfully. "Look who's talking? You are working them pants. Four kids," I said while checking out her thin waist and round hips, "and you still have the curves of death. Girl, please." I had to give it to her—sista-girl was fierce in her black hip huggers, black Lycra mock turtleneck, and spool-heeled slippers. Jennifer Lopez didn't have shit on her. And homegirl had a glow radiating beneath her beautiful, smooth skin. *The glow of a good fuck*, I almost said aloud but decided I had better keep it to myself.

"So where's Ryan and Sarina?" I asked. "The house is so quiet."

"Ryan had to go up to Silver Spring to handle some last-minute business with one of his funeral directors. And Sarina," she said, shaking her head, "her fresh behind *should* be upstairs hibernating in her room. She was suspended from school again, so she's grounded until she's able to go back."

"She's been stuck in the house, huh?"

"That's right. No car, no money, no telephone, and no company. So, in the meantime, she can blast her stereo, she can slam doors, and she can give all the attitude she wants, but she's not leaving this house." Chyna then shared with me all of Sarina's ill-mannered ways and how she was afraid she was going to really lose it with her.

"Humph," I said while shaking my head. "Well, it would serve her right if you jacked her up. You've given that girl the best of everything, and she doesn't appreciate anything. I really don't think I'd be as calm as you. I would have tossed her by now. There's one thing I can't stand and that's some disrespectful, fresh-mouthed child. One thing's for sure: Being a parent isn't an easy job and being a teenager today is even more difficult."

"Amen to that," she said, waving her hands in the air, then changing the subject. "So what's up with you? How are things down at the shop?"

"Girl, nothing. I've just been tryna keep peace. I've been working and tryna stay the hell out of trouble. Business is booming. Other than that, everything is everything."

"Do you have any plans for Thanksgiving?" she asked as she started setting the table with ivory Lenox plates and matching flatware. "If not, you know you're welcome to come here. Ryan's parents and three of his brothers and their families are coming up. And the boys will be home."

"Ooooh," I said playfully. "I'd love to see them three fine, strapping young men. As soon as they hit thirty, I'm gonna saddle 'em up and ride 'em until the sun sets, then rises again." We laughed. "No, seriously, I'd love to spend Thanksgiving with you, but I'm planning to go down to see Brit."

"Now, that should be fun. Speaking of Brit, I spoke with him last week. He promised he'd come home for Sarina's birthday party and Jayson's graduation party," she said, then glanced at her Rolex. "Girl, I don't know about you, but I'm ready to eat."

"Well, let's grub."

After a magnificent meal of corn bread and gumbo over white rice, we cleaned up our dishes, then went down into the steam room to sweat off our gluttony. She talked about her desire to make changes in her life but not being sure exactly what she wanted to do. She told me how Ryan has been spending more time around the house and how she has decided to work things out with him. I could hear her love for him in her tone. When she said I'd never understand her situation until I found love, she was never more right. I just listened.

For the rest of the night, we laughed and reminisced over times shared. We sat in the middle of her thick carpeted floor with our slippers off and curlers in our hair, flipping through old photo albums, listening to oldies by Marvin Gaye, Aretha Franklin, the Supremes, the Stylistics, the Emotions, Enchantment, the Unifics, the Brighter Side of Darkness, and others. We ate blueberry brumpet, sipped champagne, and enjoyed sisterhood until two in the morning.

"Girl, it's time for bed. We have to be up for church bright and early," she said.

I choked on my drink. "Church? Girl, I can't do church," I snapped while trying to wipe my mouth. Okay, I'm not religious, but I say my prayers daily before I go to sleep and as soon as I get up. I don't have to go to church to be spiritual. Besides, I have my own special relationship with the Lord.

"Yes, church," she said, doing the Negress neckroll. "You can and will do church tomorrow. A little spiritual cleansing and healing never hurt anyone. Besides, the family that prays together, stays together."

Church? The last time I stepped foot in her church, I almost tossed the place up. That was my third visit. Each time I had gone with her, I had heard and seen some things that made my skin crawl. I can't stand fake Christians. The treachery and thievery disgust me. I felt like something was suffocating me, so I got up and walked out before I went off. I swore I'd never set foot in that place again.

But at 7:00 a.m. Chyna was tapping on the door for me to "rise and shine." Of course, I ignored her. "I'm up," I yelled with my eyes shut tight. A few seconds later, she was in my face like a drill sergeant.

"Wake up, sleepyhead," she coaxed, pulling the burgundy comforter off me. "The service starts at eleven, and I want to get there before it gets crowded. So get up. I'm making breakfast before we go." Brightness flooded the room the minute she drew back the drapes.

I opened one eye, then raised one eyebrow. "Miss Thing, can I please catch another forty winks?"

"No," she said, then went on to explain how today's service was a special program. There were going to be several visiting ministers, and the bishop was expected to attend. Then she springs on me that church will be an all-day affair, with lunch being served before the afternoon service. She indicated the program was going to focus on bringing the community, the church, and the family together as one.

As soon as we turned left onto the cobblestone road leading up to the church, my stomach twisted in knots and I broke out in a light sweat. *I'm not sure why I'm flooded with so much anxiety*, I said to myself. *It's only church. What could possibly happen?* I pulled out my compact and checked myself in the mirror. I lightly patted the sweat from around my arched brows, the bridge of my nose, and my upper lip with a white hanky. Ryan shifted his eyes when I caught him staring at me in the rearview mirror.

"You alright back there?" he asked.

I nodded.

The church was located up on a hill and was a beautiful brick building with brilliant stained-glass windows. It was 10:00 a.m. and the parking lot was already filled with impressive luxury and sports cars. Anyway, we stepped into this gorgeous house of worship and were handed our programs, then seated by a very handsome usher wearing a black suit and cheap shoes. I glanced over at Chyna and Ryan, then smiled to myself. I had to admit, Ryan looked sharp in his navy Hugo Boss suit with matching shirt and tie. Chyna, as always, was the picture of elegance. Her mink wrap was draped over her shoulders, and she wore a navy Armani dress with matching soft leather pumps and handbag. For added effect, girlfriend accessorized with a diamond and pearl choker and matching teardrop earrings. *You betta work, girl*, I thought, giving her a mental finger snap, then I looked around and noticed that many of the women were dressed in their finest and most of them had set their outfits off with some type of hat: pillbox, feathered, wide brimmed, veiled, unveiled—you name it, they wore it. It was clear this place of worship was a big fashion show for some. And then there were those who came as they were. Which is how it should be. Come as you are, isn't that what they say? I lowered my eyes down to my green Gucci leather-and-beaded pumps, scanned up and down my designer pantyhose for any snags, then ran my French-manicured hands along the sides of my Gucci beaded scoop-neck dress. I smiled, then rubbed the front of my matching handbag. I was confident I would *work* the runway when it was time to put a little sumthin'-sumthin' in the collection plate.

When Chyna slammed the truck door shut, I knew homegirl was too through. I've never seen so much steam coming from her ears.

"Girl, I don't believe you," Chyna said, shaking her head. "I have never been so humiliated in all my life. How could you turn the church upside-down like that? Couldn't you, for once, just keep that darn mouth of yours shut?"

"Girrrl, look, I tried. Lord knows I tried," I said, trying to plead my case. "But something just came over me. You know I would never do anything to embarrass you, not intentionally anyway. But I just had to give testimony."

She flipped down her visor, then spoke while looking at me in the mirror. "Testimony? My goodness, Indy, try mudslinging. Did you have to call Sister Craft 'Sista Knottyhead'? Did you have to refer to Deacon Brown as 'Miss Thing' and his wife as 'Sista Big-Face,' then call the organist 'Brotha Butterfingers'? And how could you take Brother West's money, then announce to the congregation that he gave you 'hush money'? I told you this was going to be a special service and that there would be many visiting ministers, including the bishop. And what do you do? You get up and air out everybody's dirty laundry."

She slammed up her visor, then turned around to face me. "Well, do you have no shame? Do you feel the least bit of guilt for what you did?"

"Nope."

"Come on, Chyna," Ryan interrupted, trying to hold back his laughter. "Don't you think you're being a little too hard on her?"

She cut her eyes at him. "Ryan, I don't believe you're actually sticking up for her after the way she embarrassed us today."

"She didn't embarrass me," he said. "She only spoke the truth. Besides, somebody needed to come shake them up." He looked at me in the rearview mirror, then winked.

I was surprised that Ryan found it amusing. Although, when he saw me get up, I heard him whisper to Chyna, "What in the world is she getting ready to do?" He didn't like going to that church anyway "because many of the members are phony hypocrites." And, like I said, I tried to just sit and keep my mouth shut.

I sat tight-lipped all morning, but by the afternoon, something came over me. I'm not sure if it was the Holy Spirit or the devil's pitchfork, but before I knew it, I had jumped up from my seat, walked toward the altar, snatched Sister Parkerson's microphone from her hand, and then it was time to shake, rattle, and roll.

"Good afternoon," I said to the congregation.

"Good afternoon," echoed back.

"My heart is heavy," I continued.

"Take your time," someone said.

"But I feel there are a few things I gotta say. I can't leave here without giving testimony."

"Amen! Alright now!"

I turned to Sister Parkerson. "Girrrl, you tore the place up with that song, 'My Soul Has Been Anchored.'" She smiled. I heard a few "amen"s, then I continued. "I wish there were many more souls anchored in here today because, if there were, I wouldn't be standing here. You see, I came here searching for the Word this morning," I said, turning to face the six ministers, then the congregation.

"Amen!"

"But I feel like I've been dancing with the devil!" I snapped. Well, the place shook with shock. Heads lowered, mouths swung open, bodies shrank back, eyes popped. And then I lit the place up. That's right, I read them hypocrites from A to Z, then upside-down from one, two, and three.

I started with Reverend Stimley. I let them know just what he meant by 'Love thy neighbor,' "'Cause you've been loving Sista Marshall, ain't that right?" I asked with a sidelong glance at him. "Tell 'em how I accidentally walked in on the two of you upstairs in that little study this morning before the service. Now, maybe I had no business up there. And maybe I shouldna been snooping around, but I was and I saw. The good ole reverend might be a man of the cloth by day, but he's a freak in the sheets at night. Ain't that right, Sista Marshall?" I hissed while pointing over at her. "Let's tell 'em how thy greasy lips found comfort around thy reverend's rod."

The congregation gasped. The reverend looked like he saw a ghost, and Sista Greasy Lips ran out of the church with her husband screaming behind her, "Why you dirty, heathenish whore!"

Then I turned around to the organist. I smiled. "Boy, you know you can make some music," I said. "You're something else on that organ. I love the way your fingers just melt like butter, slipping and sliding over those keys. Well, let's tell 'em how your fingers slip and slide across the collection plates, then into your wallet. Ain't that right, Brotha Butterfingers? Tell 'em how you like to steal from the church."

Then I started in on Sister Craft. "And you, Sister Craft, or should I say Sista Knottyhead. How dare you sit in back of me and talk about Sister Briner and her twin coming to church wearing dirty dresses and backward wigs, smelling like liquor, when it looks like you just rolled out of bed without putting a comb through that head of yours. If the Niglet Twins want to party all night, then come to church on Sunday, it ain't nobody's business if they do."

And then I noticed Deacon Brown, with his big boulder head, sitting with his big-faced wife. He came into my shop over the summer in drag, and, of course, Alexi gave me the scoop on him being married and in the closet. Now, I wouldn't have gotten him, but when he was in my shop he tried to come for me, then finger-snap me. I started to beat his ass but smiled it off instead. But I warned him I'd get him. And you know when I say, "I'm gonna get you," that's what I mean.

"And you, Deacon Brown, don't try to act like you don't know me, Miss Thing!" I accused. His face turned to stone. "Sista Big Face, did you know your husband comes to New York and becomes a chick with a dick? Tell 'em how you like the Brooklyn thugs. If it ain't rough, it ain't right. Ain't that right, Deacon Bubblin' Brown Suga?" His mouth dropped open. "Don't gag, girl." I snapped my fingers at him this time. "Pick your face up."

"Oh, and, Brother West, don't worry," I said, watching him sweat bullets. "I put the thousand-dollar check you wrote me outside this morning in the collection plate. I won't be needing your hush money since your wife confronted me in the women's room. One thing I won't do is lie for no one, especially no cheatin' a— I mean, cheatin'-behind man."

His wife saw him hand me something outside this morning, so when she saw me go into the bathroom, she came in behind me, introduced herself, then asked me what her husband had given me. I told her. Then she wanted to know, Why? So I told her how he was nervous that "I might tell you he ate me out like banana split." Well, dumb-ass didn't understand. So I asked her to come outside so I could break it down to her. There's no way I was gonna talk dirty in a house of worship.

"Basically," I said. "Your husband likes banana-flavored pussy."

"Excuse me?" she asked, still confused.

"Look, he stuck a banana in my pussy, then ate me out."

"No, there must be some kind of mistake," she said with conviction. "My husband would never put his mouth down there. And he would never cheat on me."

"Well, dear, never say never," I warned. "There is no mistake. Your husband may not put his mouth down on yours, but he put it on mine. Next time, try using a banana," I said, then walked back into the church and took my seat next to Chyna and Ryan. She jumped in her Lexus and sped off in tears.

Anyway, by the time I finished pulling everyone's card, I had emptied out half the church because no one knew who else I might have dirt on and no one wanted to take a chance on me blowin' their spot up. I handed Sister Parkerson her microphone, excused myself, then strutted down the aisle and out the door. The ones who lived right and did right stayed and finished praising the Word. My thing is if you're gonna be a Christian, then live like a Christian. If you're gonna preach the Word, then you need to live by the Word. Simple as that.

12

BRITTON: **WHAT'S GOIN' ON**

THE PAST MONTH WITH TEE AROUND HERE HAS BEEN GREAT. We've laughed and talked about everything under the sun, and it's made me realize just how important our friendship is. However, his extended stay has also helped me realize we could never, ever be roommates again. I'm happy he's here, I've enjoyed his company, and I've missed him but, I tell you, I can't wait to see him go. Don't get me wrong, I love him as much as any man can love a brother, but I can't get with his ways. It's almost like being back at college. He's a slob. Okay, maybe he's not a slob; he just doesn't clean up after himself the way I like things cleaned. And I'm getting tired of seeing him walk around here in his boxers scratching and pulling at himself. Damn! Where is *it* going? And ever since he hooked up with Lina's girl Carmen, it's been nonstop sex. Every other day, homegirl is knocking on my damn door for an extra dose of his love. She's practically moved in. I've warned him twice to make sure he puts something underneath her when he's doing his thang. He and his messy screw have messed up three of my good sheets. It's a good thing I have my mattress covered; I can only imagine what that would look like.

Nonetheless, I have to admit, the last month has been very fulfilling for me, both mentally and physically. Lina and I have been like two octopuses entangled in lust ever since that night on the beach. Since then, we've spent several nights making love in that same spot. But, above all things, we're able to be honest with each other about our intentions. Neither one of us is interested in having a serious relationship. She aspires to become an actress and intends to go to California to pursue a few auditions. And I enjoy the freedom that goes along with being single. We've enjoyed each other's company and the sex has been great, but there's no desire for anything beyond a friendship. We've promised to keep in touch and spend time with each other whenever she's in D.R. or when I'm in the Big Apple. So, as with so many other good things in life, our whirlwind romance is coming to an end.

"Brit," she said, then kissed me on the lips, "I am really going to miss you. These past four weeks have really been great."

I stroked her hair, then let my hand lightly rub the side of her face. She kissed the inside of my hand. "I'm going to miss you, too," I said. "A part of me wishes you didn't have to go."

I wasn't sure if I said that because I really meant it or because it seemed like the right thing to say. Yes, I liked her. But on the other hand, she was starting to get on my nerves. She's clingy and too emotionally needy for my liking. A few times, after the loving was done, I wanted to wake her up in the middle of the night to put her out. But where was she going when home was hundreds of miles away?

There's nothing wrong with being emotional and wanting to be up underneath someone, but I like being lovey-dovey only when I'm feeling it. I don't like to feel smothered. I'm affectionate and I like romance, when I'm feeling it. Luckily, this month, I'm feeling it. Unfortunately, that changes with the weather. A part of me feels bad because she's really a nice girl, and I don't want to give her mixed messages. That's the worst thing anyone can do to a person. But I'd warned her how I am because I don't believe in misleading anyone.

She smiled. "Thanks."

"For what?"

"For restoring my faith in me," she said. "Spending this time with you has helped me realize that I can't be afraid to take chances. I've got to do for me, live for me, and love for me. I can't sit around daydreaming about what-ifs. I've got to try to make things happen for me."

I wrapped my arms around her and kissed her lightly on her forehead, then her lips. "I hope we both find whatever it is we're looking for in life," I said. "I want you to know, this last month has meant a lot to me. You just make sure you keep in touch with me."

"No doubt. You my peoples, boy," she said, then pressed her softness close against my rising nature. Her voice was soft and sexy. "Brit, you are such a beautiful person. You're different than any man I've ever known. I really believe we could be good for each other."

I smiled, but I wasn't sure if I truly believed we would be good for each other. I had gotten used to having her around, which I liked. Sometimes I liked waking up to her soft body lying next to me. I liked the way her body felt under mine and on top of mine. I liked the way her lips felt against mine. I liked rubbing her back and her feet. I *loved* kissing her pretty toes. I liked taking showers and baths with her. I liked the way she ran her fingers through my braids and twirled the curly hairs on my chest. And when I shifted into freak mode, I liked the way her hands and her mouth brought my limp manhood to life. I also liked the smell and taste of her excited womanhood. But none of these things made me think or feel we would be good for each other for the long term.

I grabbed her by the hand, then led her into the bedroom. We sat on the bed. "Lina, you're a very beautiful, articulate, talented, exciting, and sexy woman. I'm sure one day, someone will come into your life and make you very happy."

"Someone already has," she said, then kissed me on the cheek. Her tongue found its way in my ear. "How about giving it to me good one more night?" she asked in a seductive whisper.

I lay back on the bed and looked down at the bulge in my shorts. "If you want it," I said, "take it. Tonight, you can have it any way you want."

And without another word said, she removed her clothes, pulled my shorts off, spread my legs open, then took me in her mouth. One inch at a time, she brought me to the point of a sexual explosion, then stopped just long enough to leave me hanging on for more. She teased me with her mouth and tongue with so much passion and intensity that I literally thought I was gonna lose my mind. Then, without missing a beat, she shifted her body, straddled my face, and lowered her sweetness. While she took me deep in her mouth, I let out a deep moan, let my toes stretch open, then curl under tightly. And just when the heat within me was beginning to erupt, her wet love melted in my mouth like a peppermint patty until I drifted to a place called ecstasy.

At 7:00 a.m., the phone rang. Before I could open my eyes or reach over to answer it, Lina had picked it up. Wrong move. No one answers my damn phone unless we're cool like that or unless I tell you to. She knew damn well no one would be calling her here. But instead of snatching the receiver from her hand, then throwing her nude behind out of my house, I decided not to trip since it wasn't anything big, until I heard how homegirl was talking to the person on the other end of the line.

"Don't worry about who this is. Who's this? ...Look, don't talk slick, bitch, 'cause I ain't the one ...Hold on." She tossed the phone over her shoulder, then headed for the bathroom. "It's for you," she said with an attitude.

I wanted to scream on her, *Well, no shit! It's my phone, after all. Who else would anyone be calling for this time of morning?* But I bit my tongue. "Hello."

"Brit, boy, who the hell was that answering the phone like she's runnin' shit? And did she just call me a bitch?" It was Indy and she was heated. "You betta teach your houseguest some phone manners, or I'll get with her when I get there."

I jumped up. "When you get here?! Where are you?"

"That's right," she said over the hustle and bustle of people and departure and arrival announcements in the background. "I'm at the airport. My flight will be there around eleven-thirty. Now, who's the Spanish chick with the thick accent?"

"Lina."

"So where is this Lina from? And why haven't you mentioned her to me?"

"She's from uptown. And stop asking so many questions."

"Is she staying there with you?"

Lina had come back into the bedroom with a towel around her body and another around her hair. She cut her eyes over at me, then headed back to the bathroom. "No," I said.

"Good," she said. "Then get that imitation Rosie Perez outta your bed and outta your house 'cause I want you all to myself when I get there. If not, I'm gonna give her a lesson on phone etiquette."

"Indy, don't come here starting no shit," I pleaded in a whisper. "This is not the place for any of that rah-rah shit. If you come here starting up, I'm gonna throw your ass out. I'll handle it."

"Well, you betta."

"I mean it, Indy," I warned. "Do not start."

"Oh, boy, shut up," she said playfully, then laughed. "I'm not thinking about her dick-whipped ass. Actually, I find it quite amusing that Miss Rice and Beans got a little jealous."

I propped a pillow in back of me and leaned against it. "She did not," I said, then shifted the phone to my other ear. "We're just friends."

"Mmm-hmm."

"And why'd you say she's dick-whipped?"

"You gave it to her real good, didn't you?" she asked, trying to hold back her snicker.

I laughed.

"I rest my case," she said. "You know how some women can get after a dose of good dick. Especially if she's not used to getting any. And if you're pumpin' that dick to her the way I know you can, if she's not strung, she'll be strung, trust me."

Indy then kindly reminded me of Sonji, a thick-hipped, brown-skinned sista from Richmond who was a freshman at William and Mary College in Colonial Williamsburg. We met at a Sigma Gamma Rho party in 1984. Truthfully, I really wasn't interested in her or anyone else for that matter since I was still trying to recover from my one-year breakup with—or should I say my escape from—my crackhead wife. But she was persistent and very cute—Jada Pinkett cute. From the moment I walked through the door with my frat brothers, she was on mine, hard. She liked what she saw and went after it. I've always liked that in a woman, so I gave in. But after a couple of months, that long-distance fling across the Hampton Roads Bridge became a drag for me, so I told her I wanted to end it. Well, instead of just going on with her life, she made my life a living hell. She slashed my car tires, spray painted the word *asshole* in big black letters across the hood of my brand-new red Mustang, then took it a step further by making a big scene in front of my apartment complex, screaming obscenities and yelling that I raped her. After two weeks of interviews and interrogations by the authorities, it was concluded that she made up the whole story. Needless to say, I vowed to never sleep with another young girl.

Then, in '85, there was Alicia, another thick-hipped girl who worked as a telemarketer. We met at a local Norfolk club called The Big Apple. We dated for about nine months, and in the beginning, I thought she was the one for me. She was attractive, well spoken, supportive, understanding, and compassionate. In addition, she was a good cook, kept a clean house, and knew how to throw down in the bedroom. But then she wanted me to spend all of my time with her. If she didn't go to work, she expected me not to go to class. If she didn't like something or someone, she expected me not to either. If she said, "Jump," she expected me to say, "How high?" Then she started getting possessive, saying things like, "You're mine.....Don't ever try to leave me 'cause if I can't have you, nobody will." And she meant it. When I returned from one of my many weekend excursions with Indy, I walked into what looked like the work of a narcotics task force. Crazy-Horse broke into my house and slashed up everything—from the furnishings to clothes and shoes. She stabbed my waterbed, cut up the curtains, broke all my dishes, slashed family pictures and paintings, smashed my five-foot-long, walled saltwater tank, and killed my eleven-hundred-dollar parrot. Why in the world would anyone kill a helpless parrot? "Because that fucking bird yelled out 'cuckoo-cuckoo.'" Well, her ass *was* cuckoo. Not only did she destroy my things, she fucked up all of Tee's stuff as well. That was the first time he and I fought. He was mad as hell and I couldn't blame him. But I damn sure wasn't gonna take an ass whupping. So we just banged it out. Anyway, she cost us over twenty thousand dollars' worth of damage. Not only did I sign complaints against her ass, I had a high-tech security system installed and vowed never to date anyone I met in a bar or club.

In '90, there was Luanda. I was a graduate student at NYU and she was an aspiring artist who spent most of her time painting portraits in Central

Park. We first met in Washington Square Park. While I was sitting on a bench studying for an exam, she walked over and asked me if she could do a portrait of me, free of charge. I agreed and two hours later she had finished her masterpiece. I was impressed. She was six feet tall, model thin, and very attractive. Keep in mind, I'm only five-eight. So we were like Mutt and Jeff. Nevertheless, we dated for about six months. At first things were great. But once I got to know her, I realized she was a bit bizarre and too kinky for my liking. She had this thing for reptiles. Her apartment was filled with lizards, iguanas, and snakes. She even had pictures of them all over her walls. Every time I went to her place, I felt like I was walking into a jungle. But that was the least of my concerns. What really bugged me out was the fact that she liked to let her snakes slither over her body while she was naked, and that any time we made love she'd want to hump on my butt first. She said it intensified her orgasms. I tried to be open-minded and just go with the flow but when she started pissing on me to get her rocks off, that's when I knew this chick was a nut. So when I told her I wanted to end our relationship, she slapped me, then threw one of her pythons in my lap. I jumped up and ran out of her apartment, screaming for my life. I avoided Snake Woman like the plague and swore I'd never date another artist, anyone taller than me, or anyone with a strange name.

Unfortunately, however, there were three others who were either born crazy or just went off the deep end. I thought about all of them for a while as Indy chatted, then closed my eyes and prayed Lina wouldn't become another fatal attraction. That was the last thing I needed.

"Well, Indy, I think you might be wrong this time," I said. "We're friends. She has no reason to trip."

"We'll see," she said. "Oooh, I gotta go; my flight is boarding. I'll see you soon."

"Hey, Indy, wait a minute. I forgot to—"

She had hung up. "Tell you Tee was here," I finished saying into the receiver.

Well, I guess she'll find out when she gets here. Tee and Indy under the same roof, this should be interesting. One thing's for sure: I knew I had better speak to Lina about her attitude toward Indy. If Indy said something to agitate her, I want to know about it. I know she can be rude from time to time. If Lina is gonna be here when Indy arrives, I can't have the two of them getting into a confrontation. Indy's ass gets crazy, and once she gets going, there's no calming her. Homegirl has been known to toss a house up.

When Lina came out of the bathroom, she was fully dressed and had major attitude. She started shoving her things in her duffel bag.

"Excuse me," I said. "Is there something wrong?"

"Nah, everything's peace," she said without looking at me. "We cool."

"So where you going so early?"

"I'm heading back to my grandmother's," she said while throwing her cosmetics in her carry case.

"I thought you said you were leaving this afternoon."

She sighed. "Well, I've changed my mind. I want to get on the road early so I can be there when my family gets there."

I remembered she'd told me her mother, her two sisters, three aunts, and several cousins were flying in to spend Thanksgiving with her grandmother. But that still didn't explain her abrupt change in attitude.

I got out of the bed, walked toward her, then turned her around to face me. "Hold up, what's the problem? Did I do or say something to offend you?"

"Not at all," she said as if I asked a dumb question. "Don't sweat it. It's cool."

"Don't sweat what?" I asked. I was trying to keep my cool, but she was starting to annoy me. "If everything is so damn cool, then what's up with the attitude change?"

"Because I don't appreciate being disrespected or lied to."

I looked at her, confused, then scratched the side of my head. "Disrespected? Lied to? How were you disrespected or lied to?"

"I don't appreciate you having another female calling here while I'm here. That shit ain't cool, especially when I'm laying up in your bed. I thought you said you were on some solo shit?"

I shook my head, then twisted my face up. "Wait a minute. First of all, I haven't lied to you about anything. I am solo. I've been up front with you from day one. Second of all, that other female happens to be my good friend. Third of all, you had no business answering my phone, and fourth, I'm not your man, so why you tripping?"

"Well, the way she interrogated me, she acted like she was more than a friend," she said with her hand on her hip. She said Indy had asked, "Who's this answering my man's phone?"

"So how come you never mentioned her?"

I felt my tension level rising two notches and my nose flaring but I didn't want to argue with this girl over something that was as petty as a simple phone call. A call she had no business picking up. I thought we were both clear on the fact that this thing we had going was just a fling. Nothing serious, only something to do until she went back to New York. Besides, she has a woman back at home.

I took a deep breath, then sat back on the bed. "Look," I said, "I don't want to argue. As a matter of fact, this is nothing to argue about. Indy is like a sister to me. Not that I owe you an explanation. I think you're cool. I've enjoyed your company, and I really don't want to waste what's left of our time together arguing over something stupid."

I stared at her for a minute, then felt this urge to hold her. I don't know what that was all about, but I knew I didn't want her leaving here on bad terms. So I bit my tongue. Not to mention, I wanted some more of what she gave me the night before and earlier in the morning. She was just too damn sexy; I didn't want her to go until we sweated one last time. Then she could go on her merry way. Plus, I wasn't sure when the next time I'd have sex with anyone would be, so I wanted to feast while the lust in my loins was still plentiful. Even though I wouldn't sweat it if nothing kicked off, I was confident she'd be a willing participant if I made the first move.

She glanced down at my semi-awake sex, then tried to keep from smiling. I covered myself with her wet towel when she came back over to the bed and sat next to me.

"You're right," she said, slipping her arm through mine. "You don't answer to me. We're just friends. I don't know why I started tripping. Can you forgive me?" she asked, then batted her eyelashes like a schoolgirl with a crush.

"Well, I guess I can forgive you," I said as if my feelings were really hurt, then smiled. "Just don't let it happen again."

She kissed me on the cheek, licked my neck, then rubbed the inner part of my thigh. She knew that was a sensitive spot for me. Just like I said, she was a willing participant. So it was on.

I kissed her neck, sucked on her earlobe, then whispered, "How about giving it to me real good, one more time?"

She smiled, reached under the towel, and rubbed the head of my now fully awake sex. "If you want it, take it," she said.

I drew her into a deep, tongue-probing kiss while removing her clothes. I savored her Dial-fresh body with my tongue and fingers until her middle dripped with a lusty, hot juice. Today, I would take her to the place she took me last night. With slow, deep thrusts and long passionate kisses, I transported her to a world of untouched treasures. With fast, long strokes, I took her over the hills of passion and through the lilies of romance. With heavy moans and inescapable excitement, I filled her nature with the fruit of erotic desires. And, then, in a whisper, I heard the words "I love you" roll off her lips.

When Tee and I arrived down at the beach, Indy was already becoming acquainted with the natives—or should I say they were becoming acquainted with her. There were five or six island men of various ages standing around her like she was some type of beach goddess. Another young man walked over, handed her a drink in a coconut, then attempted to impress her with his island charm. Even the native children ran through the sand to get her attention. I felt warm inside seeing her with the kids. In a motherly fashion, she hugged them and kissed them on their foreheads. Her popularity impressed me. It was like she wore a magnet that drew people near. I swear, you would have thought she was a celebrity, the way people were entranced by the phenomenon known as Indera.

Actually, she's been this island goddess ever since she came down to the beach Saturday wearing a white crochet jumper with a V-line in front that plunged below her navel and a cutout in the rear that revealed the small of her back. I tell you, this girl has a body on her that can make a blind man look twice. Most of these island boys were buzzing around her like a bee to honey. But what really turned them out was when she flicked on my Sony boom box and cranked up an impromptu beach party the way we used to do on the sands of Virginia Beach and a few times down at Belmar in Jersey.

"You ready to turn this place out, boy?" she asked me as she popped in her *Garage Classics Volume 1* tape. "'Cause I got some moves for your ass." She laughed, then hit play.

"Come on, now," I said while the rhythm of "Give Yourself to Me" hit the airwaves. "You know I'm outta touch." I shifted myself on my white beach towel, then swayed a little. But I tried to maintain my composure. I didn't really want to cut up out here, but she kept hitting me with one beat after another. "Time Marches On," "Seven Ways," "Stand in Line," "Love Is the Message," "Don't Make Me Wait," "Dr. Love," "A Little Bit of Jazz," "Looking for a Lover." The beats just kept coming at me. When "Go Bang" hit me, I finally jumped up.

"Alright, now!" She finger-popped as she jumped up and down, then shook and twirled her behind around. "Don't start no shit, Brit," she warned when I started giving the rhythm back to her. "See…now, I'm gonna eat that ass up. …Ooooh, you shitted on me with that move," she yelled when I dropped down, then kicked one leg up between her legs.

By this time we had a slowly growing audience that seemed quite entertained by our fast rhythms in the hot white sand. There's one thing I know: I don't care where you are in the world, if you throw on house or club music, you are bound to be approached by or draw the attention of other heads who are either from, or familiar with, the tri-state area. Which is what we did. But Indy had a little too much energy for me. She started high kicking like she was a majorette in the Hampton marching band, then started her backbends and ballet spins. I couldn't keep up with homegirl, so I sat back down.

"Oh, no, you won't sit your tired ass down," she said while she dropped, kicked, and spun around. "Boy, get your ass up." She yanked me back up, then started her tribal mating call. It's when you roll your tongue to make these high-pitched jungle sounds. Well, before I could get myself together to work her over, one brother came behind her and started dancing. He clearly had some Northern club training. She turned to face him. "Alright, now, you betta work," she said as she two-stepped toward him, hopping, twisting, and kicking. Then another brother, then another, and then another. Indy was sand-wiched in the middle of four bare-chested, chiseled men in swimming trunks. That nice behind and little waist of hers just shook, twisted, and rolled.

"Alright! Bring it high, or bring it low!" she challenged them while she spun around, went through muscled, hairy legs while turning to give them all equal attention. The beach heated up, and Indy's captive audience went wild when she found her way over to the six-foot umbrella pole that stands erect in the middle of the beach and started swinging from it. When Indy said it was going to be a "classic club" weekend, that's what she meant. So with the help of Sylvia Striplin, Chaka Khan, Grace Jones, Inner Life, First Choice, Loose Joints, Double Exposure, Colonel Abrams, Sylvester, and many other legendary artists, Indy came to the D.R. and left a lasting impression.

Anyway, I have to admit it: Indy did look good as hell in her orange two-piece. Her cinnamon brown skin glistened with a reddish tint under the sun's tropic rays, and her almond-shaped, hazel eyes had a sparkle I hadn't seen in years. She waved and smiled at islanders as if she had just won a beauty pageant. Tee and I watched her glide across the white sand, graceful and poised like a model who works a runway. I smiled. Tee just stared.

"Yo, she needs to go somewhere and sit her fast ass down," he said while rubbing coconut tanning oil on his arms and chest. "Bouncin' her ass 'n shit all up in them niggas' faces."

I laughed. "What, you jealous?"

"Jealous? C'mon, B, you know betta than that. I'm just sayin'. She came here to chill with us, and she's spent more time with these niggas."

"Excuse you," I said, then shook my head. "She came here to chill with me. She didn't even know you were here."

"Well, *I am*. And her little ass should be over here."

I chuckled softly. *Yep, your ass is jealous.* "Where you going?" I asked when he got up to walk toward her.

"I'm going to cool her hot ass off," he said.

"Tee, I wouldn't do it if I were you." He kept on walking.

For the past five days, I've held my breath wondering when Tee was going to say or do something to set Indy off. Surprisingly, the two of them have been extremely cordial to each other. But it's only a matter of time, especially since they haven't really spoken to each other since their little squabble over a month ago. See, there's no rhyme or reason with Indy. If you keep your distance from her when she's pissed, she cools off and may not say anything else to you about it. But the minute you do something else to set her off, she's gonna jump all over you for that and everything else she didn't get you for. It's just easier to let her go off on you right then and there and be done with it instead of letting her stew, because when her father's West Indian temper flares in her, she is a walking stick of dynamite. And when I saw Tee pick her up and throw her in the water, I knew it was on. One thing you don't do is mess up Miss Indy's hairdo.

Now, I'm not sure if Indy spun around three times or what; all I know is she turned into Wonder Woman right before my eyes. She chased Tee around the beach, jumping over tanning bodies, beach chairs, sandcastles, and anything else that was in her way. I never knew homegirl could run so fast. Onlookers were laughing while ten or more kids thought it was a game and joined in on the chase. I'm not sure if Tee slowed down or if Indy just had the speed of a track star, but she caught up to him, jumped on his back, then tackled him down on the hot sand. The kids who were enjoying this wrestling match encircled them and chanted, "Get him! Get him! Get him!"

Then they jumped on him. I heard Indy yelling out orders, then they all grabbed a hold of Tee and lifted him up by his legs, arms, and feet while Indy gripped him under his arms and directed her little troops. They charged toward the water, then *splash!* They threw him in. But the funny part was that when he went in, so did Indy. How? That remains a mystery. But when she came up and started walking toward the beach, she was topless. Homegirl had lost her bikini top. If you could have seen the eyes of the men popping out their heads. Even some women did double-takes. I thought everyone was just admiring my sista-friend's beautiful breasts with their Hershey Kiss nipples, but when I was able to get a clearer view, I saw that her pierced nipples were the attraction. There were a whole lotta tongues wagging. Homegirl strutted toward me topless in a shoestring-thin bikini bottom. "Indy," I said. "Your top is missing."

"I know," she said calmly. "Eighty dollars lost in that big-ass ocean. That damn Tee makes me sick. Now I have sand 'n shit all in my hair, all in the crack of my ass." She brushed herself off, then tried to fix her hair. Tee was walking toward us with what looked like the rest of her bathing suit.

He smiled as he looked down at her breasts. She covered them. "Here, I found your top." He smirked, handing it to her. "Now, what do I get in return?"

"A break from an ass whippin'," she said, snatching her top out of his hand. "I'm gonna get your ass. When you least expect it," she assured him, "I'm gonna get you." She put her top back on, then dug in her backpack for her compact. "You're lucky I don't have my mirror with me," she said once she realized she'd left it at the house. She patted her head with her hands and tried to smooth out her wrap. "I can tell my wig is wrecked, thanks to your ass."

He laughed. "Yeah, that mop is a mess, but you still look good," he said, trying to smooth things over. "I'm sorry. I just couldn't resist throwin' you in."

I looked at her again and laughed. "Tee, c'mon now, you know damn well she looks like a scraggly-ass sea witch." We laughed, but she didn't.

She glowered at him. "Boy, get the fuck away from me," she said, then slapped him in the back of his head. She slapped him again.

"Ooow, girl," he said while trying to rub away the sting from her heavy hand.

"I couldn't help myself," she said sarcastically, then tried to slap him upside the head again. "You make me sick, you fuckin' musclehead. Just be glad there are kids out here, else I'd really hurt you for fuckin' up my wig piece."

"What I tell you about your mouth?" he asked, trying to pop her on the lips. "And what do kids being out here have to do with anything?"

She grabbed his hand and twisted it. "Don't even think it," she warned, then answered his question. "Boy, don't you think they see enough violence on TV? Why should I expose them to seeing you get your ass beat on this beach?"

Tee covered his head with his hands while Indy tried to box his head. "Brit, help me out here," he pleaded.

"I'm not in this," I said. "You got yourself in it, you'll get yourself out of it. I told you not to do it."

While Indy and Tee argued back and forth over who would or wouldn't do what to the other, a very attractive, young-looking woman walked toward us pulling a caramel-colored boy with copper-tinted curly hair by the hand. He was one of the children who had helped Indy throw Tee in the water. Indy and Tee stopped arguing and I smiled as they approached us.

"Excuse me, we have something for the *señora*," the woman said, then pushed the little boy in front of us. "Go ahead," she instructed.

The little boy, with his hands behind his back and his head down, seemed nervous and had tears in his big, brown eyes. He looked back at the woman, then held out his hand. "Señora, I bring dis to you," he said while handing Indy a beautiful gold locket on a thin diamond-cut chain. I'd seen that same locket many times before.

"Oh my God!" Indy exclaimed, suddenly touching her bare neck. "My locket! Thank you," she said, then hugged and kissed the boy. "Thank you."

"I don't raise my brothers to take nothing they don't earn," the woman said proudly in a thick accent. "He wanted to keep, but I no let him."

Indy took the little boy's hands and rubbed them with hers. "What's your name?" she asked.

"Pedro," he said.

"That's a nice name. My name is Indy, and these are my friends, Brit and Tee," she said, pointing to us, respectively.

"Hey, little man," Tee said, holding his hand out for the young boy to give him five.

"Hi," I said, then threw my hand up in a wave.

"Pedro, how old are you?" Indy asked.

"Eleven."

"Eleven? Wow, you're a big boy. Are you in school?"

He shook his head no.

She looked puzzled. "Your parents don't make you go to school?" she asked, looking up at the young woman.

"*Señora*," she said in a low, trembling voice. "Our parents are dead."

I glanced at Tee, then returned my attention to Indy. It seemed like everything in her softened at once. "Oh, I'm sorry," she said.

The young woman explained how their parents were killed in a hurricane seven years ago, leaving her to care for her three brothers at the tender age of sixteen. But thanks to extended family and friends in the village, she and her brothers were able to stay together and remain in the family's home. What was most distressing was when she said Pedro and his brothers couldn't attend school regularly because she couldn't afford to buy their uniforms. She said attendance was mandatory until sixth grade, but Pedro and his brothers would have to work to help support the family.

As a school psychologist, I'm disturbed by the number of kids here who can't obtain an education beyond the sixth grade because poverty and limited educational resources prevent them from excelling academically. Basic supplies such as paper and pencils have to be provided by teachers and parents, and textbooks and other supplies are scarce. I've compared the D.R.'s school system with that of the United States and found dismaying similarities. Although the U.S. provides free education and all the basic supplies and makes attendance mandatory through age sixteen, teachers and administrators invested in ensuring that everyone receives a quality education are still few and far between; many of our youth in urban areas still function on or below a sixth-grade level; and educational resources and parental support are still limited.

"Pedro, what do you want to be when you grow up?" Indy asked.

His face lit up with a big, bright smile. "A doctor," he said. "I want to help the sick and the poor and all my people."

"Then a doctor you should be," she said with a smile. "You hold on to that dream, okay?" He nodded. "Don't let anyone take your dreams away from you. You can be anything you want to be as long as you believe." Indy turned to his sister. "Excuse me, what is your name?" she asked.

"Isabella," she answered.

"Well, Isabella, I want to commend you for raising your brothers with values." She reached into her backpack, pulled out seven crisp one-hundred-dollar bills, then handed them to her. "I want you to take this and buy Pedro and his brothers their uniforms and school supplies."

"No, *señora*, I no take your money," she said with pride.

"Please," Indy insisted. "I'm not giving it to you. It's a reward," she said, then rubbed the front of the locket. She opened it and stared at the picture of a beautiful brown skinned woman with thick, black shoulder-length hair who had the features and grace of an African queen. Indy's mother, a statuesque woman of Nigerian and British descent, was from royal bloodlines and had insisted that Indy have the finest of everything. From extravagant vacations and expensive shopping sprees to the best private schooling money could buy, nothing was too good for her baby.

"This locket belonged to my mother," Indy said while holding it in her hand. "She died when I was eight."

"How?" Pedro asked.

Indy took a minute to collect her thoughts, then began telling the little boy her story. It was the first time I ever heard my friend tell a stranger how her mother had passed. Chyna and I were the only two people she ever talked to about it. Her mother's death struck like lightning. It was quick and unexpected. They had just returned from a weekend trip in the Bahamas when her mother collapsed in their kitchen. For weeks, she had been struggling with severe headaches and blurred vision, but she had dismissed these symptoms as stress-related. But this time it was different. Her headache was skull-splitting, followed by intense nausea.

"Mommy! Mommy! What's wrong, Mommy?" Indy yelled hysterically. As Indy rested her mother's limp body against her small frame, her mother's speech was slurred as she instructed Indy to take her locket from around her neck. While Indy held the locket, her mother kissed her delicate hands, then in a fluttery whisper said, "I love you, my precious baby." Silence and darkness surrounded her. There was no pulse, no breathing, no movement. At forty years old, Nandi Fleet died of an aneurysm in the arms of her only child. Tee had his head down and I tried my best to hold back tears. Although Indy had told her story with emotion, she shed no tears, but you heard them in her voice.

"Please," she said, forcing the money in the young woman's hand. "This is my way of thanking you for giving me something back worth more than all the money in the world. Let Pedro have his dream."

She gave in when she saw Indy wasn't going to take no for an answer. *"Gracias."*

"*Muchas gracias, señora,*" Pedro said, then hugged Indy. Indy hugged him back, then stood up to embrace his sister. We watched in silence as the young woman walked away holding the future of a young black male in her hands.

"Indy, that was real sweet of you," I said.

She smiled her pretty smile and said, "Well, isn't that what Thanksgiving is all about? I was just giving a little thanks."

"Yeah, Indy, that was mad love right there," Tee said. "I really dig what you did for little man and his family."

She glared at him. "Well, meathead," she said, "you just ought to. After all, it *was* your money I gave 'em." Indy and I laughed at Tee's expression. "And I'm still gonna get your ass." She slapped him upside the head again.

"Ooow," he yelped, covering up his head. "Yo, B, help a brotha out," he begged, then jumped up and ran out toward the water.

13

DAMASCUS: DON'T DENY

MAN, LISTEN. REALITY HIT REAL HARD the minute our plane flew over the Elizabeth seaport preparing to land at Newark International Airport. Everything just seemed so different—people's attitudes, their postures, the sense of urgency. Who knows? Maybe I'm just buggin'. But one thing's for sure: After spending over a month surrounded by beautiful beaches and constant sunshine, coming back to Jersey to face this cold-ass weather is depressing as hell. Who in their right mind would wanna leave eighty-five-degree weather for this cold-ass place? And this congestion and dirty-ass air is enough to make me wanna pack up my shit and head back.

Yo, the whole three hours on that flight, Indy's ass practically ignored me. Around Brit, her ass was sweet as pie. He could say or do anything, and she'd be grinnin' and cheesin' all up in his face. But the minute I said anything she didn't like, she'd jump all over me. Hell, he called her a scraggly-ass sea witch, and I'm the one she slapped. And then she turned around and gave my money away. A few dollars woulda been cool, but seven hundred! Damn, that was a bit excessive. Don't get me wrong, I'm down for helping those less fortunate, especially kids, but I like to do it on my terms. The way Indy did it was real foul. Yo, she just straight up did me dirty. Hell, I'm the one who should be heated, but it's all good. I'm not takin' much more of her mood swings, though. One minute we cool 'n shit, then the next minute she's cold as ice toward me.

For example, when we got down to the baggage claim, Indy stood next to me and started up her shit right away as we waited for our luggage to roll out of the chute.

"When you gonna pay me the money for fuckin' up my hair and breakin' my damn nail?" she demanded.

I looked at her ass like she was real crazy, then snapped. "You own a damn hair and nail salon! What I look like giving you money for something you can get done for free? That shit makes no sense to me."

"Well, that's beside the point," she said, totally dismissing the fact that it was a stupid-ass request. "If I had to pay for it, it would cost me over a hundred beans. Regardless of whether I paid or not, it's the principle of the thing."

"You know what, Indy? You're sounding real stupid right now."

"So what you sayin'? You're not gonna cough up the cash?" she asked with her hands on her hips.

"Basically," I said, then walked around to the other side of the carousel. Her eyes followed.

While the bags dumped out on the revolving ramp, some cat with a fucked-up grill and turned-over Timbs was tryna sweet-talk her, but she was in no mood. I knew a brotha who looked like he chewed on concrete was gonna get it. Dig, this rotten, razor-toothed cat even had the nerve to crack a smile. Yo, this nigga's grill was wrecked.

"Hey, pretty, how you doin'?" he asked.

She looked him up and down. "Get the fuck away from me," she barked, then turned her back on him.

"Damn, sista, there's no need to get nasty. I was just tryna give you a compliment," he tried to explain before walking away. Between me and you, I'm glad he stepped without talking slick 'cause I didn't wanna have to bust his snotbox open. But Indy holds her own—very well.

"Well, try giving your breath a mint. Betta yet, how about giving your dentist some business, you dusty bastard," she snapped as she reached for one of her Louis Vuitton cruiser bags. All the bags were coming down so fast, she missed her other three.

"Tee, do me a favor, grab those bags for me?" she yelled over, then added, "Please."

I grabbed my one bag, let her three go by, blew her a kiss, then stepped. What the hell did I look like, her bellhop?

When I finally got home, my spot was an icebox. The thermostat gauge was below fifty degrees. "It's cold as fuck!" I yelled, then flipped the heat on and jacked the controls up to eighty. I kept my gloves, hat, and coat on while I unpacked my things and waited for the heat to thaw the place out. I sat on the edge of my bed and listened to the thirty messages on my answering machine.

"Hey, Tee, this is Crystal. I thought you might be back by now. I've called twice already. Listen, I really wanna see you. My man's gonna be outta town all next week. Give me a call. Maybe we can spend a few nights together." She left three more messages.

"Hi, baby, it's April. I'm feenin' for some of that big, black...well, you know the rest. Call me A.S.A.P."

"What's up, sexy? This is Amy. It's Friday, ten p.m. Give me a call when you get in. I need a taste of that chocolate."

"Tee, this is Bridget. I'm still waiting for my rematch. Call me when you're ready for round three. And this time, I'm on top."

"Tee, this is Trisha. That was real fucked up how you threw me outta your house. Well, you won't *ever* get any more of this pussy."

I laughed at that shit. "Who the fuck cares? I already fucked your loose ass every which way, so your ass is old news," I said aloud, then fast-forwarded through the other booty calls.

"Tee, this is Lourdes. Where the hell are you? You've missed eight shows already. Time is money and money is time. We have fifteen shows out in California. We're leaving on December eighth for two weeks. Now, get your ass in gear and give me a call."

Shit, I knew I was gonna have to hear it from her ass. Yo, she's one of the chicks who own Daddy Long Strokes. I know her ass has been blackin' since I've been off the set. Fuck it. Damn, the eighth is two days away. I betta call her ass, soon.

After a few minutes, I decided to call April. Hell, as cold as it was, I needed a warm April to thaw out this bone.

She picked up on the first ring. "Hello."

"Aye, yo, baby," I said, real low and sexy.

"Hi, baby," she said, pleased to hear from me. "It's about time. I thought you ditched a sista."

"Nah, baby. I've been outta town. So, you still feenin'?"

"Mmm-hmm, you know that. I'll be right over," she said, then paused. "And tonight I want it real rough."

"Bet."

I removed my coat, hat, and gloves, then peeked out the window and stared at the fresh blanket of snow that covered the ground. I smiled at the big flakes of snow that fell fast and hard from darkness. *There's nothing like fuckin' a freak in a winter wonderland*, I thought as I headed for the shower.

Thirty minutes later, April was at my door rocking blue Timbs, blue cords, and a chunky Phat Farm sweater. She smiled, brushed the snow off, then gave me a wet hug. I stopped her before she could take off her blue three-quarter-length shearling and matching hat.

"Dig, baby," I said. "Tonight we're gonna roll in the snow."

She twisted her face up. "You buggin', right? You see all that snow? It's cold as hell out there."

"Yeah, I see it. And you see *all* this?" I asked, pulling my dick out of my long johns. "I wanna fuck in the snow." I handed her three large, thick wool blankets while I grabbed a bag of ten Sternos and a rolled-up piece of indoor/outdoor carpet. She followed as I walked out onto the patio. I opened the huge awning over the sliding glass doors, shoveled the patio area clean, unrolled the green carpet, then laid all three blankets over it. She stood there looking at me like I had lost my mind. It was a cold thirty degrees, but I knew once I stuck this dick in her, we'd both warm up like spring.

"Yo, go inside, take those clothes off, put on the gray thermals on my bed, grab the matches off the counter, and bring out the two blankets and pillows on the dining room table."

"You know, the crotch is cut out in these pants I'm wearing," she said with a smile. "Never mind."

When she came back out, I was lying under one of the wool blankets rubbing my balls. She shook open the other two blankets, spread them over me, jumped under the covers, then helped me light the Sternos around us.

"Oooh!" she shivered. "It's too damn cold out here."

I grinned while I pulled at my dick. "Once you suck on this wood log, you'll warm up."

She smiled, buried her head under the blankets, shifted her body so I could play with her pussy, then took me in her mouth. She sucked and licked until her lips stretched, then gagged when the head of my dick closed up her airway.

"Relax, girl," I said while I slapped her ass. Gurgling noises came from her throat as she covered eight inches of my dick with her mouth. "C'mon, baby, three more inches to go….Yeah, that's right. Just like that."

I rubbed and fingered her shaved pussy until she dripped a hot, sticky juice. The world around us mighta been cold, but the heat from her mouth and wet pussy could melt an iceberg. So with three pairs of wool socks on, two pairs of thermals, and a stiff, heavy dick, I slid all this "big, black…well, you know the rest" up in her while she humped her hungry pussy round and round, up and down, and side to side. She was purring, "Oh, yes! …oh, yes!" Doggie-style, I straddled her, locked my thighs around her hips, slapped and smacked her ass, then gave her a one-horse *sleigh* ride, fucking in our winter wonderland until she screamed my name at the top of her lungs.

At 6:00 a.m. Friday morning, the phone rang just as I was about to slide up into Tasha's bony ass. She came over the night before to get a dose of this dick boppin' around in a little Santa hat talking about "'Tis the season to be jolly!" So after an hour of sweaty sex, we fell asleep. I figured instead of throwing her ass out in the wee hours of the morning, I'd just let her sleep it off, then tap that ass again when we woke up. I let the phone ring three more times before sliding my dick in her. She gasped. I answered the phone.

"Yeah?"

"Yo, nigga, what's up? This is Hammer. Yo, where you been? You dipped outta Miami so quick, niggas been tryna track your ass. We didn't know what happened to you."

"Yeah," I grunted as I deep stroked. "Yo, I bounced down to my peoples for a minute. I needed to get away."

"I can dig it. Check it, you know Lourdes and Ramona have been flippin' 'cause you just bounced without saying anything."

"Yo, I don't answer to them. Fuck 'em," I said over Tasha's moans and yells of pleasure.

"Yo, nigga, what the hell is that?" he laughed. "Aaah, shit. Don't tell me you bonin' some chick while we speak?" He burst out laughing. "That's my nigga!"

I was thrusting so hard into Tasha's soppy pussy, I dropped the phone. I threw her right leg up over my shoulder, wrapped her left leg around my waist, then reached over to retrieve the phone. "Yo, you still there?"

"Yeah, I'm here. So I guess you're not doin' this Cali tour?"

"Nah," I grunted. "I'ma sit this one out."

"I feel you. Damn, nigga, slow down," he said in response to Tasha's screams about "pain that feels so good." He was still laughing. "It sounds like you're tryna tear somethin' up. Yo, get one off for me. I'll get up with you."

"Bet," I said, then let the receiver hit the floor. I bent her legs all the way back over her head until her feet touched the headboard, then shoveled my dick in and out of her. She screamed and begged, moaned and groaned, until I pulled out, snatched my rubber off, then slapped my dick between her stretched pink lips. While I rubbed my dick back and forth over her wet hole, I whispered, "'Tis the season for a jolly good fuck," then let the eggnog from my nuts spurt and splatter on her stomach, on her tits, under her chin, and in her eye.

Here it is, two days before Christmas, and people are running around like chickens with their heads cut off. They act like it just snuck up on them without notice. Hell, I don't understand why everyone's so pressed when the malls have been advertising the Christmas season since October. But everywhere I go, people are arguing and fighting over shit like parking spaces and who took the last toy off the shelf or out of someone's cart. Then they're cursin' and shit at the cashiers because the lines are too long. It seems like even the most festive person in the world would be ready to dig into you if you tried to disrupt their shopping. Yo, that madness is on them.

Instead of being out in all that craziness, I decided to just chill today. It's too damn cold to be out beefin' with some crazy, last-minute shopper. I figured I'd check on Indy's mean ass to see what was up with her. Half the time, I don't know why I even bother. She picked up on the fifth ring.

"Hello."

"What's up, Indy? We still beefin' or what?"

"Boy," she snarled. "What do you want?"

"Yo, I just called to see what's up with you."

She let out an annoyed sigh. "It's eight o'clock in the morning. I'm sleeping, that's what's up."

"Aye, yo, why the hell you so hard on me?"

"'Cause you get on my damn nerves."

I smiled. "Can't we just get along?"

"Hell no," she snapped. "Ain't shit peace until you pay for fuckin' up my damn hair."

"Girl, will you knock it off," I said, then changed the subject. "Yo, what you doin'?"

"I'm playin' with my fuckin' pussy. What else would I be doin' in bed this time of morning? Tee, don't make me go off on you, okay?! I'm in bed. I'm tired."

I smiled, trying to imagine what she had on. "Yo, meet me on the moon," I said while I rubbed the head of my dick. "I don't know why you keep frontin.'"

"What the hell are you talking about now?"

"You know you want me just as much as I want you."

"Boy, lick my ass." *Click.* I burst out laughing. Yo, she's just funny as hell to me.

After I hung up, I made myself two cheese and spinach omelettes, some turkey bacon, grits, and three slices of wheat toast. When I'd finished getting my grub on, I popped a nut while I showered, wrapped a towel around me, then went down to the basement to lift a few sets. I figured I'd work on my upper body—chest, back, shoulders, and arms—today and my lower tomorrow. The whole time at Brit's, I just lounged. Hell, as long as I'm still on the market, I gotta keep my *thang* tight. I worked out nice and hard until my heart raced and my body dripped with sweat.

After about an hour, I showered again, threw on an old pair of NSU sweats, and headed back down to the basement to shoot a few games of pool and check out that flick *The Jackal* with Bruce Willis and Richard Gere. Just as I was about to rack the balls up, the phone rang.

"Hello."

"What's up, boy?" I smiled when I heard his voice. It was Brit. "Thanks for calling to let me know you made it back okay."

"Yo, man, I apologize. You know how I am sometimes…"

"Yeah, real inconsiderate," he said. "I was worried about your ass."

"A'ight, you right. I shoulda hit you as soon as I touched down," I agreed, then went on to something else before he could go into one of his lectures. "Yo, when you gonna check out your pops?"

"I don't know." He sighed. "It's an open ticket, so I might go after Christmas. I'd rather wait until spring 'cause it's cold as hell over there right now. I'll have to buy all new winter clothes. Everything's there in the attic."

"Oh, yeah. That's right." I had forgotten. When Brit decided to jet, I offered to keep his things here instead of him paying for storage. Yo, it was the least I could do since he had sold me his townhouse for practically nothing.

I pressed pause on the VCR, then sat on the arm of the sofa. "Yo, don't put it off too long."

"Yeah, I know. I might as well just get it over and done with," he said reluctantly. "Anyway, I just called to make sure you were home safe and sound. I hear the weather is brutal up there."

"Word up. It's almost as cold as Indy's evil ass," I said, laughing. "Tell you one thing: I wish I was still parlayin' in the sun."

"Yeah, it was good having you here. But I'm glad your nasty ass is gone."

I laughed. "Yo, I wasn't that bad."

"Humph, tell that to my bedsprings. For someone who was just gonna chill out, you put more miles on that mattress in one month than anyone could in a lifetime. I thought you were gonna kill that poor girl, the way she screamed and yelled."

Yeah, I tried to tear Carmen's insides out. Not to be mean or anything, but to let her know she shouldn't talk shit unless she's sure she can really back it up. She was talkin' so much smack about what she was gonna do to me and how I couldn't handle her that I just had to put it on her rough. I hate it when a woman tries to talk that slick shit: "Boy, you can't handle none of this. ...I'll fuck your brains out. ...I'll suck your dick so good you'll think your head caved in. ...I'll rock your world. ...You ain't ready for this. ...You can't hang." But that's just what Carmen did. When I finished with her ass, she walked like she had been riding a horse bareback for months. Hell, my thing is, put your money where your mouth is. Show and prove. Don't talk about it, be about it.

"Let's just say she wrote a bigger check than she could cash."

He laughed. "Boy, I don't know about you."

"So what's up with your peoples?"

"I guess she's back in the city. She called me last week saying she was going out to California soon."

"Word? Yo, that honey is really big on you, boy."

"Nah," he said, dismissing the possibility. "She's just real cool people. Listen, I gotta go. Oh, Amira and my mother said hello. And my mother said to make sure you come see her the next time you're in the neighborhood. What are you doing for the holidays? 'Cause my mom wants you to come over for dinner. She's cooking all of our favorites. It's too bad I can't be there."

"Nothing," I said, staring down at the veins in my feet. "I'm just chillin'. Tell your mom I'll take a rain check, and tell Amira I said what's up."

"Well, if you can make it, she'd love to see you."

I changed the subject. "Yo, have a safe trip. And make sure you give me a call to let me know how things went."

"Yeah, if I can remember," he said sarcastically. "You know how I am sometimes."

"Yeah, a'ight."

I fell back onto the sofa with my legs dangling over the armrest, then let silence come between us. My mind drifted back to the Linden Boulevard projects. I was, like, four. The building might have been rundown with trash and liquor bottles everywhere; darkened stairwells might have been the spot for drug deals, assaults and sex; and the smell of piss and unbathed bodies might have greeted you when you stepped on or off the elevator. There might even have been roaches all over the place and leaking pipes or dirty clothes scattered around, or dirty dishes overflowing in the sink. There might have been gambling, drinking, and smoking going on or the sounds of fucking and sucking in the bathroom or bedroom. So what if my mother would disappear for days at a time? Whatever the circumstances, apartment 11F was home.

Throughout the year, there may not have been food in the cabinets or meat in the freezer, and I may have had to wander the streets late at night, looking for something to eat. But, you betta believe every Christmas, AnnaMae Miles would have that little four-room apartment cleaned and she'd be in that kitchen singing "This Little Light of Mine" and "Amazing Grace" while washing collard greens and cleaning chicken. There'd be the smell of a fresh turkey basting in the oven, and she'd make sweet potato and apple pies and bake a big chocolate cake. And she'd let me lick the bowls. I'd sit at our little kitchen table with the mismatched chairs and watch my moms dance around the tiny kitchen. Then I'd ask, "Mommy, how come you cook so much food?" And she'd say, "Because we celebrate Thanksgiving and Christmas together. It's so we can share with family and friends." We'd have a little Christmas tree that sat on top of a milk crate covered by a red blanket. We'd decorate it with strings of popcorn, candy canes, and all the little ornaments we'd make out of construction paper and cotton balls. Moms would say, "Baby, that looks so pretty. It's the prettiest tree ever." She'd kiss me on my little forehead, then say, "Santa's bringing you a special surprise." And in the morning, I'd wake up bright and early to a tree surrounded by gifts. We mighta been poor and my moms mighta been a fiend, but she always made sure her little boy had a Christmas and that my four older brothers, who were in prison, had care packages filled with fixings from home.

"Yo, Tee, you still there?"

"Yeah, I'm here," I said, trying to keep my thoughts in check.

"Happy holidays to you," he said with a sound of good cheer. "I love you, bro."

"I love you too, man. Be safe." We hung up.

I thought about what he said, then frowned. Happy holidays. What's so happy about them? It's not like I have any family to share it with. My moms and three out of my five brothers, none of whom I knew, are dead. The other two might as well be dead since they're somewhere shooting dope through their veins. So the holidays, although they're no longer sad, damn sure aren't happy. My only family and real friend is Brit, and he's not around. So why bother being festive? After all, sharing the joyous holiday spirit is reserved for family and friends. I was reminded of that many years ago.

"Merry Christmas, Mr. James! Merry Christmas, Mrs. James!" I shouted while I ran through the house. "Wow, that's a pretty tree! Ooooh, look at all the gifts Santa brought us. Can I open them, please, please?"

"Merry Christmas to you too," Mrs. James said.

"Young man, settle down," Mr. James said in a heavy voice. "Those gifts are for our family. Now go on back to your room until we call you."

"Oh, please, Mr. James," I begged. "Can I open just one? I'm gonna burst waiting to see what Santa brought me. Pleeease, can I?"

"Honey," Mrs. James interrupted, then smiled nervously. "Why don't you run on back to your room. I'll bring you some warm milk and cookies, okay?"

"Okay," I said with a big smile. "But you won't forget to come get me, will you?"

"Of course not, sweetheart. Now run along."

I skipped back up the stairs to my little room with the cot and waited as patiently as any eight-year-old could to be called on to open all the beautiful gifts in the bright and colorful wrapping paper. I stood on my tippy toes and stared out the tiny glass window and counted the big snowflakes, one by one, as they fell toward the snow-covered ground. And then I asked Santa a special favor: "Santa Claus, please don't forget to give my mommy a present too. Amen!"

I said my ABC's, then counted to one hundred. I waited and waited and waited for what seemed like forever to see my new toys. But when I heard laughter and "Ooohs" and "Thank-yous" and the rustling of paper and the sounds of new toys, I couldn't wait any longer. I ran out of my room and down the stairs into the living room, where Mr. and Mrs. James were opening gifts with their three children.

"Did you call me yet?"

"No!" Mr. James yelled harshly. "Now get back in your room."

"But you promised you wouldn't forget me," I said sadly, watching the other kids tear open their presents. "Can I please see what Santa brought me?"

Mr. James stood up, then slapped me down with the back of his hand. "Don't backtalk me," he yelled. "Santa didn't bring you nothing."

"But Santa promised he would bring me something really nice. He promised," I said, crying and holding my bruised face. "My mommy said Christmas is for family and friends."

"Well, your momma ain't here, and you ain't nobody. Now get back in your room." His eyes turned to ice and his voice was cruel.

I ran up to my cold, lonely room and cried myself to sleep singing "This

Little Light of Mine." And for three Christmases after that, Santa brought me nothing. Other than the soft hands and warm mouth of Mrs. James in the middle of the night, Santa didn't bring me shit 'cause I wasn't family. 'Cause I didn't have family. 'Cause I was *nobody*.

14

CHYNA: **VOICES INSIDE MY HEAD**

WOULD YOU LIKE TO KNOW HOW RYAN AND I SPENT OUR CHRISTMAS EVE? In the ER with Sarina's drunk behind. That's right. My child's blood alcohol level was so high that another drink would have probably put her in a coma or, worse, killed her. We had to drive an hour and a half to Baltimore Medical Center, then we spent another seven hours waiting for her to be released to us. In the meantime, we sat in a triage room watching Sarina drift in and out of consciousness. The room smelled like she'd swum in a pool of liquor.

"Will you just look at this child," Ryan said, shaking his head. "What the devil is wrong with her? And what in the world was she doing down here?"

"Ryan, I'm just glad she's alive," I said while rubbing the side of her face, then holding her limp hand. "We'll worry about the details later." He stood beside me and rubbed my back.

"Me, too." He sighed, trying to keep his composure.

Ryan had spent the last three weeks driving up and down the streets of D.C. looking for her and asking people if they might have seen her. The answer was always, no. Not knowing any of her friends or where she hung out made his search all the more difficult. Sarina has taken off many times before, but never had she been gone this long. After we filled out our twentieth missing person's report, one of Maryland's finest had the audacity to comment, "She keeps running away, so why even bother? She's almost eighteen, so why don't you just cut your losses?"

"Because she's our *daughter!*" Ryan had snapped.

There's nothing more frightening than worrying yourself sick over the possibility of never seeing your child again or getting a call that something tragic has happened. I prayed she wouldn't become another face on a milk carton. It's dangerous out here. Kids today think they can take care of themselves, that they can handle any kind of situation. Well, they can't. The world is filled with predators. Kids are being kidnapped, raped, and killed every day.

"Mommy?" Sarina said, trying to keep her bloodshot eyes open against the room's bright white lights. Her speech was slow and slurred. "Daddy, I don't feel good. I think I'm gonna throw up." Her eyes were glassy, her lips were chapped, and she had a white paste in the corners of her mouth.

"I know, baby," he said, kissing her forehead. "We're just glad you're alright. Your mother and I have been worried sick."

"I'm sorry," she said while tears ran down her face. "I just wanna go home."

Now, I don't care if they were the tears of a drunk or not. The fact that they were her tears and the fact that she wanted to go home was all I needed to soothe my heart. While Ryan sat with her, I went out to the nurse's station to speak to the doctor.

"Excuse me," I said to the attractive, young, freckle-faced nurse sitting behind the desk. "Can I speak to the doctor in charge?"

"I'm the charge nurse. How can I help you?" she asked.

"I'd like to know when Sarina Littles can be released?"

"Well," she said with concern in her tone. "We'd like to run a few more tests and keep her under observation for a few more hours. Then, once she's fully alert, we'd like to have our crisis social worker speak with her."

"Is there something else going on that we should be concerned with?" I asked with anxiety swelling in my heart.

She rubbed the side of my arm. "Mrs. Littles, I think you should ask your husband to come out here." I walked over to get Ryan, who was sitting beside Sarina, holding her hand, and informed him of my conversation with the nurse. He kissed Sarina's hand, then followed me back to the nurse's station.

"Nurse, what seems to be the problem?" he asked. "My wife said you want our daughter to be screened."

"That's correct, Mr. Littles," she said, then paused, trying to find the right words. "There's no other way to tell you this but to just say it. We believe your daughter was trying to commit suicide."

I grabbed Ryan. "Oh my God!"

"There must be some kind of mistake," Ryan said, holding me tight in his arms. "My daughter would never kill herself. You know how kids are. Sometimes they say and do things for attention."

"I'm sorry," she said, attempting to console us. "But your daughter was found walking in the middle of oncoming traffic, and when the paramedics brought her in, they reported she kept mumbling, 'I just want to die…Let me die.'"

Ryan and I stood there in shock, trying to absorb the thought that our child would want to kill herself. *Suicide?* How could I not know? I've worked with families in crisis. I know the statistics—each year, more than five-thousand young people from ages fifteen to twenty-four take their own lives. I should have been able to be more objective. I should have been able to see the signs. Maybe if I would have paid more attention to her, I could have prevented this.

"Mr. Littles," the nurse continued. "Suicide is never a cry for attention. It's a cry for help. Many parents believe suicide attempts or threats are just attention-seeking acts. I'll admit, there are some kids who make threats as a means of manipulation. However, you need to understand that *many* adolescents who commit suicide have previously threatened to do so. Therefore, *all* threats should be taken seriously."

"Sarina has never threatened or made any attempts to hurt herself in the past," I said, trying to convince myself this woman didn't know what she was talking about. "I mean, we've had our problems but nothing we couldn't handle as a family."

"Mr. and Mrs. Littles, maybe your daughter doesn't really want to die. Maybe your daughter is just looking for a temporary means of escape from reality. Whatever the case, she is definitely crying out for help. Excuse me for one minute," she said, then walked over to a tall, clean-shaven, brown-skinned man. While they spoke, Ryan and I tried to figure out what we had done wrong as parents. He started blaming himself for working too much and not spending enough time at home with her. I tried my best to reassure him, but what can you possibly say to someone who speaks the truth? I kept silent, but underneath I blamed myself as well. In a lot of ways, I placed a great deal of pressure on her to do well. And I probably subconsciously compared her to her brothers and expected her to be as good as them academically, if not better.

As a professional, it's always easier to assess and identify someone else's crises objectively because you have no emotional involvement. But, as a parent, I don't care how many degrees you have or how much theoretical or practical training you have, when it's your own crisis, you become blinded by emotion.

"Excuse me, Mr. and Mrs. Littles, this is Dr. Grady. He's one of our psychiatrists."

"How are you, Dr. Grady?" Ryan said, shaking his hand. I smiled, then shook his hand too.

"Fine, thanks," he said in a smooth, silky voice. "Follow me so we can talk in private." We followed him into a small sitting area with four chairs and a desk. "Your daughter refused to speak with the social worker, so I met with her. She denies wanting to harm herself in any way."

"Thank God!" Ryan sighed out. I closed my eyes and silently thanked God as well.

"Let me ask you," he said while flipping through his case notes. "Is there a history of suicide or depression on either side of the family?"

"Not at all," Ryan answered. I thought about the question for a moment, then shook my head.

"What changes in her behavior have you noticed?"

"Well," I said. "The past four years, Sarina's mood and behavior have been up and down. One minute she is quiet and seems withdrawn, the next minute she's having angry outbursts, and other times she's bouncing around like she ate a bowl of sugar. And she's always changing her look from one extreme to the next."

"I see," he said, rubbing his narrow chin.

"Doc, what do you think could be the problem?" Ryan asked. "Why do you think she's acting out like this? I mean, it's not like we abuse her."

"Mr. and Mrs. Littles, as you know, adolescence is a time of change, crisis, pressure, and a tendency to react impulsively. On top of biological and chemical changes that can occur in the body, young people tend to feel burdened with anxiety about parents' expectations, peer acceptance, intellectual abilities, physical appearance, and even identity issues. To be honest with you, I'm not sure what's going on with your daughter. She was very guarded with me and unwilling to answer most of my questions. It sounds like your daughter has an underlying mood disorder, but clearly I'd recommend you get her a psychiatric evaluation in order to get a better diagnostic impression and to rule out the need for medication. I'd also recommend individual counseling as soon as possible."

Ryan grabbed my hand, then lowered his head. "We love our daughter," he said, trying to hold back tears. "Whatever help she needs, we'll get it for her."

"Good," he said. "Then let's get your daughter signed out so you can get her home where she belongs."

"Thank you, Dr. Grady," Ryan said, then stood up to shake his hand. I did the same, then we walked down the corridor to sign our daughter out. She was up, pacing the floor.

"Well, do you think we can blow this rathole?" she asked with an attitude when she saw us coming toward her. "I'm getting real tired of *these* people all in my damn face. I wanna get out of here before one of these maniacs tries to kill me. They're standing around gawking at me like I'm some circus freak." She did look a little outlandish standing there wearing a chinchilla coat with a platinum Cleopatra wig, a black wool miniskirt with black tights, and a pair of black high-heeled gladiator sandals with leather bands that tied up to her thigh.

Ryan and I stared at each other, then wrapped our arms around her. "We love you, baby," we said, then took turns kissing her face. She still reeked of alcohol.

"Alright already," she said as she broke free from our bear hug and readjusted her wig. "If you love me, then get me outta this joint." The three of us walked arm in arm down the corridor, through the ER glass doors, and to our car. *Whatever it takes*, I thought, *we will help her find the strength to face her future optimistically.*

I should have known the past three weeks were too good to be true. Sarina was good as gold. She was being respectful coming in on time, and eating dinner with Ryan and me. She even cleaned up after herself. But the minute she heard her charges for assaulting that girl in the mall were being dismissed, she went right back to being nasty. After spending all morning and all afternoon in court, the prosecutor finally came out to tell us the charges were being dropped because the girl's family didn't want to pursue it any further. Before we could get out of the courthouse, Sarina got into a verbal confrontation with a girl who had to be no more than eighteen over some boy. The scene became out of control when Sarina yelled out, "Suck my dick, bitch!" and then the girl screamed back, "*You* suck my dick, bitch!" I was never so mortified. Since when did girls start sucking each other's dicks? It took me a minute to figure out what they meant. The officers had to escort Sarina out of the courthouse.

"Fuck that bitch!" she yelled as the two officers dragged her. "Don't pop shit, bitch, let's just do it."

"Knock it off," a tall, burly, white officer ordered. "Or I'm gonna haul your ass downstairs."

Sarina settled down until they let her go. "Bite me," she snapped. "I don't have to listen to you." Before the officer could come after her, our attorney stepped in front of him to speak with him while Ryan snatched Sarina by the arm and yanked her forward.

"We'll handle this, officer," he said, now dragging Sarina himself. "Let's go. And if you say another word, I'm gonna knock your teeth down your throat." Needless to say, she rolled her eyes and sucked her teeth, but she kept her mouth shut.

Clearly, Ryan and I were happy to hear the charges were being dropped because no parent wants their child to have a juvenile record. But when you have a child who has no respect for authority, shouldn't there be some level of accountability? I'm sure if an adult had turned the courthouse out like that, he or she would have been taken into custody.

I was saddened to see the number of young adults waiting to go before the judge for crimes committed in the community, at home, and in school. Kids break the law, and who gets punished? The parents. We miss time from work to spend all day—and in some cases, several days—in court, and then we're responsible for paying for an attorney to get them out of trouble. If we're not at work, how do you expect our bills to get paid? What about those parents who are in jeopardy of losing their jobs? What about the kids who just don't care? Sarina's lawyer cost us twenty-five hundred dollars, and she had the nerve to say, "Oh well." Oh well? Well, what would happen if we said *oh well* the next time she got in trouble? We'd be summoned into court to be chastised and threatened by some judge.

I am livid! I have been on hold with this insurance company for the last twenty minutes waiting for someone to assist me. And this stupid recording keeps coming on stating: "Thank you for calling Behavioral Health and Managed Systems. All of our representatives are currently busy helping others. Please remain on the line and someone will be right with you. ...If this is an emergency, please press one." Well, I've pressed one twice already and I'm still waiting. If this were a crisis, it wouldn't be by the time someone finally gets to me.

At last I heard, "Thank you for calling Behavioral Health. This is Priscilla, how may I help you?"

"Yes, good afternoon..."

"Good afternoon."

"My name is Mrs. Chyna Littles, and I have a seventeen-year-old daughter who needs a psychiatric evaluation and outpatient treatment. I'd like to check to see what our mental health benefits are."

"Okay, may I have your policy and group number and the name the policy is under?" she asked in a very pleasant and professional tone. I gave her the information she requested. "Please hold," she said, then placed me on hold for another three minutes. "Hello, Mrs. Littles?"

"Yes?" I responded calmly.

"I'm sorry, all of our systems are down at the moment, so I'm unable to access your benefits information."

"*Whaaat?!*" I snapped. "You mean to tell me, after I've spent over twenty minutes waiting for someone to help me, all the computers are down? What kind of operation are you people running?"

"I'm sorry, Mrs. Littles. I understand your frustrations, but if you'd call back…"

I pulled the phone away from my ear for a second in disbelief. Call back? "What did you say your name was?"

"My name is Priscilla Grahams," she said with what I'm sure was a "customer satisfaction" smile.

"Well, Priscilla Grahams," I said, pausing to take a deep breath. "When your computers are up and running again, I expect *you* to call *me* back. I am not going to wait on hold for another twenty minutes."

I tried to keep my cool and remain professional, but when she started explaining it wasn't their policy to call policyholders back to inform them when their system was up, I thought I would snatch her through the phone line. I rested my elbow on the kitchen table, then let my forehead rest in the heel of my palm.

"Listen here, Priscilla," I barked. "Your insurance company makes a lot of money off of my husband and his business associates. Now, if I don't get a return call from you when those damn computers are back on-line, not only will I make sure my husband pulls all of his business from your company, I will make sure you are no longer a representative there. Am I making myself clear?"

"Very," she said in a quite dry yet professional tone. "Thank you for calling Behavioral Health and Managed Systems."

"No, thank you," I said. "I look forward to hearing from you. Have a good day." I hung up. *The nerve of her,* I thought, then decided to start dinner while I waited for her to call back. I looked up at the clock. It was 3:30 p.m.

At 4:45, the phone rang. "Hello."

"Hello, Mrs. Littles?"

"Yes."

"This is Priscilla Grahams with Behavioral Health. I have that information you requested."

"I'm listening," I said.

"You have a lifetime maximum of twenty-five thousand dollars for inpatient benefits and are covered at one hundred percent for twenty outpatient visits as long as you stay in network. Out-of-network services will be covered at twenty-five percent. And I have a list of network psychiatrists who should be able to help you with your evaluation."

"Hold on, let me get a pen," I said, then wrote down the twelve names. "Thank you for your help."

"Thank you for calling Behavioral Health, and if we can be of further assistance, please don't hesitate to call."

"Trust me, I won't. As a matter of fact, I'll make sure I ask to speak with you," I said sarcastically, then hung up. She really thinks I plan on spending another day on hold?

Out of the twelve psychiatrists, only three were adolescent psychiatrists. And out of those three, only one spoke English clearly enough for me to understand that his next available appointment wasn't for another six weeks. I slammed the phone down, snatched the phone book out of the pantry closet, and flipped through the Yellow Pages until I got to the listing for mental health/counseling services. A big picture with two parents and a child with her arms folded and her back toward them caught my attention. It read: If this is you, we can help. I called.

"Thank you for calling The Center for Helping Families. How can I help you?" a male voice asked.

"Yes, I'd like to set up a counseling appointment for my seventeen-year-old daughter. I'd like for it to be individual *and* family counseling." I had decided that whatever was going on with our child was a problem that affected us as a family and therefore needed to be addressed as a family.

"Okay," he said in a very friendly tone. "I need to get some background information. Can I have your name and the name of your child?" I told him. "Okay, can you tell me what problems you and your family are having?" I told him that. "Okay, is there any mental illness in your family?"

"No."

"Mrs. Littles, is your daughter willing to cooperate in counseling?"

"Not really," I said. "But she needs it."

"Oh, I'm sorry," he said. "Unless your daughter is willing to cooperate, we won't be able to take your referral."

My blood pressure hit the roof. "What?! How in the hell are you helping families if you're turning them away? I'm telling you, my daughter needs help, whether she wants to cooperate or not. We need help. Now, I want a damn appointment and I want one today."

"Mrs. Littles," he said apologetically, "I didn't mean to upset you. How's Wednesday at three o'clock?"

"That will be fine," I said in a more friendly tone. "I'll see you then." I placed the phone back in its cradle. I didn't hear Sarina coming down the stairs. She startled me when she spoke. She was standing with her hands on her hips, wearing a zebra print catsuit with a matching scarf wrapped around her bald head, black Converse sneakers, and a pair of black Catwoman glasses.

"I hope you don't think I'm going to some goofy-looking shrink."

"Yes, I think we need someone to help us understand what's going on with you."

She laughed hysterically. "And you think some quack doctor is going to be able to help you with that? Please. If you believe that then *you* need to see one," she said while going into the refrigerator to pour herself a glass of lemonade. "I can tell you why I do what I do. Because I feel like it. Because you're always treating me like I can't take care of myself. Because you're always trying to keep me locked up in this prison camp. Just because you're lonely and miserable doesn't mean I am."

"Sarina, sweetheart," I said, trying to not let her get the best of me. "Is that what you think? I'm lonely and miserable and I have nothing else better to do with my life besides worrying about my daughter?"

She rolled her eyes, then slammed her glass on the counter. "'Sarina, Sweetheart,'" she mocked, then her tone became crass. "Bow-wow. You sit around in this house with your high-pro glow thinking you're all this and that," she said. "But we both know you're jealous that I have a life and you don't."

"Alright, Sarina," Ryan said as he walked into the room. "That's enough. There's no need for you to talk to your mother like that."

"Oh, yeah, take her side," she snapped. "I guess you're out to get me too.

I should have known you were in on this with her. Both of you are trying to destroy me."

Ryan gave me a confused look, then directed his attention back to her. "In on what? Out to get you how? Sarina, what in the world are you talking about?"

"I'm talking about both of you trying to ruin my life," she said while staring at me. "I'm sick of you being all up in my business."

Ryan set his briefcase on the floor, then took off his suit jacket. "Listen here, young lady," he said in a very calm yet direct tone. "Your mother and I are not going to let you just run the streets. If you want to be treated like an adult, then you need to act like one. Since you don't want to go to school, then you need to get a full-time job and pay for room and board and your own meals. As long as you pay your way around here, your mother and I won't question your comings and goings; but as long as you are living at my expense, you have no business. Do I make myself clear?"

She rolled her eyes. "Whatever!" she snapped, then went upstairs.

Ryan washed his hands, removed his tie, then came over to massage my shoulders. "You feel real tense," he said, then kissed me on the top of my head. I rolled my head around to help unkink my stress. He leaned over, then whispered in my ear, "What in the world did that child have on?"

I shook my head. "Another Sarina creation," I said.

"And, what's a high-pro glow?"

I shrugged my shoulders. "I think she was referring to me as a dog with a shiny coat."

"Were you able to get her a psychiatric appointment?" he asked, as if her outfit and comment made it that much more urgent.

"No, they're all booked," I said, then informed him of my phone conversations. "But I was finally able to schedule an intake appointment for counseling on Wednesday."

He shook his head. "That's a damn shame. Kids have too many rights. When you and I were growing up, we did what we were told or else."

"Yeah, times have changed. Now kids are telling their parents what to do and how to do it or else."

Wednesday at 2:20, there was no sign of Sarina. I called her school and was told by the attendance officer that she hadn't been there. Instead of sitting around waiting, Ryan and I decided to keep the appointment. If for nothing else, we needed hope that things can get better.

When we got there, we signed in and waited to be called. Sitting across from us was a white couple with their three preteen boys, who were running around the place, horseplaying, and tearing out pages of women in the *Sports Illustrated* swimsuit edition. The parents sat there reading their magazines, oblivious to the havoc their children were causing. On the other side of us sat a woman with her young daughter. When the woman asked her to stop twirling her chewing gum with her fingers, the girl said, "No!" When the woman slapped her hands down from the child's mouth, the girl slapped her back, ran from her, then stuck her tongue out at her. I shifted in my seat, gave Ryan one of those looks, then picked up the *Cosmopolitan* off the wood coffee table.

"Mr. and Mrs. Littles," called a white middle-aged woman, adorned with twenty tarnished silver bangles and silver rings on each finger. She had big red hair and was wearing a white sweatshirt with a big rainbow on the front and matching earrings. "Thanks for waiting," she said, extending her hand. "My name is Katalina Bergenstick. I'll be working with you and your daughter. Speaking of your daughter, where is the little darling?"

Now, I'm not one to talk about anyone but this woman reminded me of Rainbow Brite. And this time, Ryan gave *me* one of those looks. "Oh, Sarina wasn't home in time for the appointment," I said. "So my husband and I decided to come without her."

We followed her into a spacious office with rainbow-painted walls and a large fish tank filled with colorful tropical fish. In one corner of the room, she had a round table covered with stuffed animals and Barbie dolls. On another side of the room, she had an easel and paints. Over the door there was a sign that read Happiness is on the other side of the rainbow. On another wall a sign read Life is full of colors…a rainbow awaits you.

She sat behind her desk, then turned on an orange strobe light. "Please have a seat," she said while she read her referral sheet. "Let's see, your daughter is seventeen, and you've been having problems since she was thirteen." She closed her eyes for a minute. "I'm feeling a lot of warm, positive energy. I think we'll do well together."

Humph, I thought. There's no way I could see Sarina sitting in here with this woman. Still, I wanted to give her the benefit of the doubt. But when she started giving us her clinical advice, I decided that perhaps *she* needs treatment. She told us we shouldn't punish Sarina if she doesn't go to school. If she wants to go to the mall or to a party, we should let her because her failing is her punishment. She told us if Sarina wants to punch holes in her walls or destroy her furniture, let her. If she wants to leave dirty dishes in her room, let her. It's her room. Basically, she was saying we should let her do whatever she wants.

"Excuse me," Ryan said. "Do you have someone who is qualified to work with African American adolescents?"

She smiled. "Why, of course, Mr. Littles. We all have received culture sensitivity training," she said, as if that made her an expert. "Adolescents are adolescents regardless of their color. Some may like rice and beans while others may like fried chicken and collard greens, but it doesn't change the fact that they're still adolescents struggling with the same developmental issues."

Ryan and I gave each other that look again, then got up from our seats. "Thank you for your time," Ryan said. "But we're going to the other side of the rainbow." Before she could open her mouth, we were out the door.

The past week, I have cried more tears than I ever thought humanly possible. Never in a million years did I think that my child, the child I spent twelve hours in labor with and almost died giving birth to, would ever raise her hand to me. Ever! I've heard about kids beating and terrorizing their parents, but I never thought I'd have firsthand experience. I've done nothing but try to be a good parent. I've tried never to raise my hand to my children. I've never called them names. I've never raised my voice to them. I've tried time-outs, positive reinforcement, and simply ignoring their behavior. I've tried global praising, I-praising, and you-praising. And if there are one hundred ways to love your children, I'm certain I've loved them at least sixty-eight of those ways. Most important, I've tried to respect their privacy. But Sarina crossed the line this time. One, by raising her hand to me and, two, by having sex in my home. I've never been more hurt in my life.

"What in the hell is going on in here?!" I'd yelled when I'd walked into her bedroom and found her in bed on her knees with some broad-shouldered boy who was humping her like a dog in heat while she had her face buried between the legs of the same girl she had cursed out in court. They all jumped. "Get the hell out of my house, or I'll call the cops."

The thick-armed, hairy-chested boy jumped out of her, then tried to cover his large man parts. The girl scurried out from Sarina's lip-lock, then raced around trying to find her clothes.

"Get the fuck outta my room!" Sarina yelled. "You have no business in my fuckin' room."

"I most certainly will not," I snapped while I grabbed things off her dresser and threw them at her bed guests. "This is my fucking house, and I want you disrespectful kids out of here, *now!* You have ten seconds to get out of here, or I'm going to smash your heads," I warned, swinging a metal crowbar I found on Sarina's floor. "No one disrespects my house. No one, do you hear me?! And don't you dare climb out that window. I expect you to walk downstairs and walk out my front door and never step foot in here again, you got that?"

"Fuck you, bitch!" Sarina yelled, then charged at me. "I'm sick of you." She came at me swinging like a wild animal. Instead of knocking her in the head with the crowbar, I dropped it and tried to grab her hands. That's when she punched me in my eye and then in my mouth. Before I knew it, I was on the floor, rolling around with my nude daughter who was screaming, "I'll kill you, bitch, before I let you hurt me."

"Sarina!" I yelled as she dug her nails in my face and pulled my hair. "What is wrong with you? I'm your mother!"

"You're not my fucking mother! I *hate* you…you *white* bitch!" That's when I really lost it.

The fact that she hit me didn't hurt as much as her words. They stabbed me in my heart. They pierced my soul. I've spent my entire life trying to validate myself as a black woman. I married a beautiful black man thinking that would validate my blackness. I thought having a beautiful black daughter would validate my blackness. But it hasn't. No matter what I've done, I'm still seen as a white woman trying to be black. I was raised in a home where being black was dirty because "white was right." For twelve years of my life, I didn't know who I was because being white didn't feel right to me. I didn't want to just speak French in the home. I didn't want to just associate with blonde-haired and blue-eyed or green-eyed beings; that's what you were expected to do if you wished to remain a part of the Devereaux household. Most of my family has devoted their lives to "passing" as white in order to access better opportunities and more wealth. I've never denied my French ancestry. How can I? It's a part of me. It's the result of the era when it was common practice for mothers to arrange marriages for their beautiful Creole daughters to wealthy Frenchmen or Spaniards. So my family structure has always been woven with threads of prejudice and racist attitudes. Anyone marrying or associating with anyone with one-fifth or more African blood was disowned. How could they be ashamed of their rich heritage and their beautiful blackness? Well, I couldn't. I wanted to be smothered in blackness. I wanted to be a part of the many beautiful shades of our beautiful blackness. Because I've always known it was right. Because I realized I am a beautiful black woman. It's one thing to be ridiculed by peers and society based on the color of your skin, but when it comes from within your own family, your own race, it hurts the most.

Before I knew what came over me, I had flipped Sarina off of me, dragged her across the carpet while she kicked and screamed obscenities, then I let go. I'm not sure when her friends left the house, and I didn't care. I slammed her door shut and locked it from the inside.

"You say I'm not your mother? You hate me?" I shrieked. "Well, since you want to fight me like I'm some girl on the streets, this *white bitch* is gonna whup your bare, disrespectful ass," I snapped. She stood there in shock, just long enough for me to tuck my braid down in my shirt, then she realized there was nothing but air and space between us. "Bring it on," I said, then commenced to sling her behind from one side of the room to the other. "You punch me in my eye, bust me in my lip, and scratch my neck and face up and think you're gonna walk out of here without an ass-beating? You are sadly mistaken," I warned as I kept slapping and punching her. "Don't you *ever* raise your hands to me, *ever!*" *Slap!* "I gave birth to you." *Slap! Slap!* "And I almost lost my life." *Slap!* "Your ass belongs to me, and I will bury you before I ever let you raise your damn hands to me."

"No!" she yelled. "I'm sorry—"

"Sorry, hell!" I screamed while I snatched an extension cord from out of its plug, then wrapped it around my hand and I whipped her with it. "You don't want to go to school?" *Slash!* "You don't want counseling?" *Slash!* "You want out of this prison camp?" *Slash!* "You want to do what you want?" *Slash!* "You want to run the streets?" *Slash!* "Well, when you turn eighteen"— *slash!*— "you can leave this house and you can do whatever you want." *Slash!* "But until then"—*Slash!*—"you are staying here where you belong." *Slash!* "This is your home!" *Slash!*

My child screamed and yelled and begged. But it didn't matter. Why should I show her any mercy? For four years, she'd had none for me. "I have warned you." *Slash!* "I have begged you." *Slash!* "I have bribed you." *Slash!* "I have compromised myself for you." *Slash!* "And you have continued to disrespect me. I *am* your mother! We *are* your family." *Slash!* "I love you, and this hurts me more than it will ever hurt you!" *Slash!* "But if you ever raise your hand to me again, it will be on your deathbed!" *Slash!*

"Chyna, *no!*" Ryan yelled as he kicked open the door, then grabbed me. Sarina was huddled in a corner, crying and screaming with rug burns and welts all over her body. I dropped the extension cord and walked toward the door hanging off its hinges.

"*Now*, you can call Child Protective Services," I said. I picked up her phone and threw it at her.

15

BRITTON: LOVE BEGINS AT HOME

I AM GLAD THE HOLIDAYS ARE OVER. This was the first time I didn't spend them with my family and it was a lonely feeling. The cards were nice, the phone calls were nice, and the gifts were nice. But those thoughtful gestures weren't enough for me. I needed to be home. Truthfully, I wanted them here with me and when I saw the pictures of my eight beautiful nieces—Ashley, Noelle, Brittany, Nicole, Milira, Taylor, Kayla, and Paris—pictures of my pregnant sister and my brother-in-law, pictures of my mother and stepfather, it was the first time I really felt left out, and it wasn't a fun feeling. While I flipped through each snapshot, I felt a sadness stirring inside me until I came across pictures of Tee having Christmas dinner with everyone. Seeing him there replaced my frown with a smile. He wasn't alone for the holidays. He was with family and in a home filled with love, and that's all that mattered. Here I was, moping around feeling lonely because I wasn't with my family by choice, and there are many people like Tee who really don't have a choice because they don't have a family to share anything with. Because they don't have a family to love or be loved by. I had to get on my knees and give thanks for my blessings.

What really threw me over the edge was the care package Indy had sent filled with gifts. I was overwhelmed. She never ceases to amaze me with all the thoughtful things she does for me. Everything—from the six pairs of sneakers and Tag Heuer watch to the IQUITTOS cologne and silk bathrobe—was wonderful. But the book *Sacred Bond: Black Men and Their Mothers* by Keith Michael Brown was the greatest gift of all. In all my life, I never thought the most priceless gift I would ever receive would be a book. Yes, I know reading is fundamental. But when you're given a book that can move your spirit, a book that can evoke nostalgia with the turn of each page, it does something magical to your heart. It becomes a powerful vehicle that allows you to emote in ways you never knew possible. *Sacred Bond* did just that. It was because of that emotional uprising that I was able to make the decision to go to Germany to put closure on my nonexistent relationship with my father. The first step was calling him to inform him of my travel plans.

"Hello, is this the Landers residence?" I asked nervously.

"Yes," a young man said with a hint of a German accent. "Who's calling?"

"This is Britton Landers—"

"Britton, how are you? This is Wilson Landers. So that would make us brothers," he announced, as if I should be excited. "I've heard a lot about you."

"That's nice," I said, emotionless. "Well, is our father in?"

"No, I'm sorry. He's in the hospital having tests done. He should be home in a couple of days. If you'd like, I can give you the number where he is."

"That won't be necessary," I said. "Just let him know I will be flying in on Wednesday."

"That's great news, Brit," he said. "I have been anxious to finally meet you. I'm sure this will lift Dad's spirits. He'll enjoy having you stay with us."

"Oh, I won't be staying with you," I said coolly. "I'll be staying at the Penta International."

"Oh, I see," he said, sounding disappointed. "Well, he'll enjoy seeing you and spending time with you. What time should we be at the airport to pick you up?"

"Thanks, but don't worry about it. I've made arrangements. I'll call when I arrive."

"Well, I guess we'll see you when you get here. Brit, this visit means more than you'll ever know."

"Excuse me, Wilson," I said, trying not to sound too rude. "But I'd appreciate it if you called me Britton. Only close friends and family call me Brit."

"Oh, I see. Well, Britton, have a safe flight. I'll make sure Dad gets the message." The only thing left between us was the dial tone.

I hoped he'd gotten the hint that I had no interest in getting to know him or his family. I didn't want to give any false impression of wanting to embrace him as a brother. I intended to see my father to give him a chance to say whatever he felt he needed to say, then I was out of there. Nothing more, nothing less.

I walked out on my balcony, leaned on the railing, then closed my eyes and prayed I wouldn't get out there and curse that man out on his deathbed. After I thanked God again for blessing me with a wonderful mother, I went back into the bedroom, opened the closet, and pulled out the old family albums. I carried ten over to the bed then and sat down. The phone rang as I opened a wooden photo album with the words Our Family inscribed on the front. "Hello."

"Brit, boy, why haven't you called me? I've been calling you all week." It was my sister.

"Because I spoke with you last week and the week before that and the week before that. And I didn't feel like hearing your shit this week," I said. "Now, what do you want?"

"See, Mom?" she said. She had our mother on three-way. "I told you he has a nasty attitude."

"Hi, baby," my mother said.

"Hi, Mom," I said, smiling. "Amira, you make me sick. You always trying to get somebody in trouble."

"Oh, boy, be quiet," she said, joining me in laughter. "When are you going to see Dad? He's in the hospital again."

"I know," I said while turning the pages of the photo album. "I spoke with *your* brother Wilson."

"Oh, I'm glad you finally called," my mother said. "How'd your conversation go?"

My sister didn't let me answer. "So, when are you going out there?" Amira asked again. "And, for the record, he's *your* brother too."

"Yeah, whatever," I said, then gave them the *Reader's Digest* version of my conversation with Wilson. Of course, Amira thought I was extremely rude to him and couldn't understand why I would waste money staying in a hotel. My mother was just glad to hear I was finally going.

"Look, Amira, be glad I'm going. I have no desire to stay in their home," I said, then changed the subject. "Hey, Amira."

"What?"

"You sure was ugly," I said, looking at a picture of her crying.

"What are you talking about, boy?"

"I'm going through pictures of us growing up. And I'm looking at some of your snotty-nosed baby pictures." I laughed. "You kept a snotty nose, huh, booga bear?"

"I know you not talking, Dumbo," she said. "I've got pictures of you when you were all ears. See, Mom, I told you he took your photo albums. Didn't I? That's why you wet the bed, pissy face."

"That's why you don't take a bath, stinky butt," I said.

"That's why you don't brush your teeth, sewer breath."

"And that's why you have crotch rot," I snapped back.

"Britton," Mom said, cutting in, "I've been looking all over for my albums. Here I am blaming your sister, and you had them all along. Boy, what I tell you about going in my things, and what I tell ya'll about name-calling? I see both of you still need the strap." We laughed.

"That's right, Mom, you tell him."

"Mom, I didn't take them from you. I borrowed them from Amira, who stole them from you. You know how she's always in your stuff. Now, how you like that, booga bear?" I said jokingly.

"You're such a tattletale," she teased. "And as soon as Mom hangs up, I'm gonna get you." We all laughed because that's just what she used to do. If I got her in trouble she'd give me that "I'm gonna get you" look, then plan her attack. If she got yelled at or punished, she'd twist my arm, or grab a big chunk of skin and pinch me until I screamed, or wring my ears until they turned red, or give me a wedgy, or tickle me to get my mother to think we were playing, and then she'd sock it to me. But if she got a whupping, she'd knock me off my bike, or stick her foot out to trip me, or slam my fingers in the car door "by accident."

Amira and I went back and forth name-calling and teasing each other until we laughed so hard our sides hurt and tears were falling from our eyes.

"You two are too much," Mom said, still laughing. "Look, you two, I gotta get going. Jay and I are going into the city for dinner. Britton, baby, your mother misses you and wants you home."

"I know, Mom," I said with a smile. "I miss you too. Give Mr. Jay a hug for me."

"Hey, what about me?" Amira asked, feeling left out. "Don't you miss me and want me home?"

"Yes, baby, I miss you too," Mom said. "But the way you and your army eat, you'll eat me into the poorhouse." We laughed once more. "Have a safe trip, sweetheart. And call me the minute you get back."

"I will," I said, then kissed her through the phone. She did the same and hung up. "Amira, you still there?"

"Yeah. But I'm gonna get off this phone too. I need to lie down so Wil can rub my feet and my back. I'll be glad when I have this baby. This pregnancy is my worst."

"Rub your feet and back? Now, that's love," I said. "'Cause I've seen what the bottom of your feet look like."

"Kiss my behind, boy," she said playfully. "Oh, before I forget, Noelle got the money you sent. That was really sweet of you. She sent a card thanking you."

"Hey, that's what uncles are for. How's she doing down at Spelman anyway?"

"She's doing good, actually. I just hope she keeps up with her grades. We don't hear from her much now that she's hooked up with some boy who goes to Morehouse. And she just had to go after some light-skinned, green-eyed boy with all this pretty hair. I told her about running behind them pretty boys. Whatever she does, she just better not bring me home no babies. 'Cause I ain't raising nobody else's kids." I laughed, but she didn't. "Look, I gotta go. Have a safe trip, and please try to give your brothers a chance to get to know you. And don't be mean to Daddy."

"Yeah, yeah, yeah." We said our "I love yous" and hung up.

Give your brothers a chance to get to know you. And don't be mean to Daddy, I repeated in my head. "Yeah, right," I said aloud, then returned my attention to the photo albums.

Tuesday afternoon. I was at Puerto Plata International Airport preparing to board Flight 56 to Frankfurt, Germany. From there, I had to catch a connecting flight to Nuremberg. With all the chaos going on in the airport,

I was glad I took precautions to ensure these fools wouldn't lose my luggage by packing everything in two carry-ons. The only things I was concerned with were being able to adjust to the six-hour time difference and not getting airsick. I can fly three or four hours in the friendly skies, but anything beyond that brings on terrible nausea. After I found my seat in first class, I popped two Dramamine tablets, then wondered why anyone would pay sixty-two hundred dollars for a first-class ticket when coach was only seven hundred. *Because I'm worth it, and he knew I wouldn't come if he hadn't*, I answered with a smile, then looked around to see who else was worth it. Of course, I was the only man of color in the "privileged" section. The plane was filled mostly with Germans or other Europeans returning to their respective homelands. I put on my headphones, turned on my Walkman, and prepared for takeoff.

Forty minutes after departure, my groove to Jomanda's "It Ain't No Big Thing" was disrupted by our blue-eyed, tanned Ken and Barbie flight attendants taking orders.

"Cocktails, *weinen und aperitifs und deutschem Bier*?" Ken asked the Italian couple across from me, while flashing his pearly whites. "Cocktails, *weinen, spirituosen, kaffee oder tee*?" Barbie asked me while modeling her cosmetically engineered breasts.

"*Nien habla deutschem*," I said, mixing German with Spanish while removing the left earplug from my ear. "But I'll have orange juice, please."

"Coming right up," she said while filling my glass with ice. She handed me my drink, smiled and said, "*Wir heißen sie herzlich willkommen an bord.*"

"*Danke*," I said with a smile before she could translate in English. I put my earplug back in, turned the music off, then stared out the window into dark clouds. The sound of my mother's voice played in my mind. It was the day she announced to my father that we were going home.

"Brandon," she said. "I'm leaving you."

"What are you talking about? Leaving me? This is your home," he protested.

"No, Brandon, this is a house. And I'm leaving this house, and I'm leaving you."

"You're what?" he asked, still confused.

"You heard me the first time," she said in a calm, soft voice. "I said, I'm leaving you."

"Leaving me to go where? Without me, you have nothing. You have no money, no job, no skills, and no education. You're nothing without me," he said with a harsh laugh. "But if you wanna go, *you* can go. But the kids stay here. The only things you'll take out of here are the clothes on your back."

"Brandon," she said, still calm. "Being with you has made me nothing because I let you control me. You're right, I don't have a job or an education, but I'm a survivor and I have enough sense to know how to make it without you." There was a slight pause, then a sigh. "I have no problem leaving here with the clothes on my back, but I *am* taking my kids with me and there's nothing you can do to stop me."

"You wanna go, bitch?!" he snapped. "Go! Take *your son* with you, but Amira stays. I'd like to see how your simple ass manages without money to feed and clothe him. What kind of life do you think you'll have? If you walk out that door, you're never getting back in. You'll be on the streets, do you hear me, bitch?!"

"First of all, Brandon, this is not about the kids. Let's be real. We both know you don't want them. This is just another way for you to try to control me. The difference this time is that I'm not going for it." For years, he'd kept her isolated and alienated. He didn't allow her to work or be independent. He didn't allow her to have friends unless he approved of them. If he did approve, they were allowed in the house only when he was home. She couldn't leave the house without his permission, and when she did, she had better return within a certain time period. He wouldn't allow her to make her own decisions or to have a life outside their nicely decorated and immaculate home. In sum, he held her hostage emotionally, mentally, and physically for fifteen years of her life, and now she wanted her freedom at any cost. "Second of all, Brandon, when I walk out that door, I have no intentions of walking back in. I would rather be on the streets than under the same roof with you."

"Why, you dirty bitch!" he screamed at the top of his lungs. "I've given you everything, and now you turn around and give me your ass to kiss. Don't you know I will kill your fucking ass before I let you leave this house?"

"So be it, then," she said, and I imagined her trying to hide her fear. "Because I'm leaving you, and I'm taking *my* babies with me. End of discussion. If that means I have to die in the process, then let the games begin because I've reached my limit with you." She took a deep breath, then exhaled slowly, as if she needed time to gather her thoughts. "You're right, you've given me every material thing possible in between the years of aggravation and beatings. But not enough of either can change what I've never felt. You can't buy love, and you surely can't beat it into me. I'd rather live in a cardboard box or a tin can than spend another day of my life being beaten and abused. Truth-fully," she said, "the sight of you makes me sick."

She shocked him and herself with her brazenness. In the past, she'd never dared to stand up to him. She'd do whatever he said in order to avoid his violent wrath. But this time, she was prepared to stand her ground.

"You fucking bitch!" he bellowed. *Slap! Slap!* Then there was silence. My sister and I stood behind the closed door with our ears pressed tightly against it, desperate to hear what wasn't being said yet afraid to see what we'd seen so many times before. My sister grabbed my hand tightly and closed her eyes like she knew what was about to happen. Our hearts raced to keep up with our fear. Then the silence was broken.

"Vera, what are you doing? Put that away before you hurt yourself. Baby, let's talk this over," he pleaded.

"Baby?!" she screeched. "What happened to dirty bitch this and fucking bitch that? Now it's baby? Fuck *you!* I got your baby, you no-good son of a bitch." *Boom! Boom! Boom!*

I opened the door, and before my sister could scream, "Noooo, Mommy," he had fallen to the floor. My sister's screaming and the sight of my father's blood froze me in my place. My mother had shot him three times, once in the arm he'd raised to hit her with many times before and once in each leg he used to walk over her with. In a trancelike state, she walked toward him, stepped over him, then pointed the barrel of her shiny silver .22 in his face.

"I should kill you," she said in a cold, dry tone. For the first time in her life, she felt powerful, watching fear etch his face and sweat drip from his pores. "But that would be too easy. I want you to live with this for the rest of your life."

"Vera, I...I'm—"

"Sorry? Don't be," she said as she walked down the hallway and stood in front of the large mirror hanging in the foyer. She paused long enough to look into her purse for her makeup case. "Be careful," she snapped while covering the bruises on her face with foundation. "Because the next time you try putting your hands on me or even letting the thought cross your mind, it *will* be your last." Her voice was steady and low. "No man," she pointed out while putting on her lipstick and talking at him through the mirror, "will ever put his hands on me, again. *Ever!*"

My mother directed my sister and me to help her take our packed suitcases to his car and for us to stay in the car. When my sister and I walked past him, a part of me felt his pain and wanted to reach out to him, but the other part of me was glad to see him feel pain the way my mother had. Tears welled in my eyes when he looked at Amira and said, "Daddy loves you." He looked right through me as if I were invisible. His eyes showed no emotion toward me. They were vacant and cold.

"I hope you bleed to death!" I yelled, running toward the door and out of his life.

"And for the record, Brandon," my mother said as she removed her house keys from her key ring, "I'm far from broke. What do you think I've been doing with the weekly allowances you've given me over the last fifteen years? Saving for a rainy day. And you might want to check the bank withdrawals and cash advances I got today. Don't worry, I only took what I've earned for putting up with you. Come on, Amira and Britton. We have a plane to catch. We're going home." She set the phone down next to him so he could call for medical help, tossed her keys in his lap, then walked out with fifteen thousand dollars from her "rainy day" savings account and another eleven thousand dollars from cash advances and withdrawals, never looking back.

At 6:00 a.m. Wednesday, the captain announced that we were a half-hour from Frankfurt and that the weather was a wet, bone-chilling thirty degrees. The night before, I'd tossed and turned trying to escape the emotional storm stirring within me. I was able to finally sleep when the wind slowed its pace, even though the storm's downpour soaked my heart.

After eating breakfast—a tropical fruit salad, crêpes topped with strawberries, blueberries, and a light syrup, and two glasses of orange juice—I washed my face with my herbal face wash, brushed my teeth, checked to make sure I had my connecting flight information and ticket, then waited for our landing. In a matter of hours, I'd be face-to-face with the man I've wanted nothing to do with. I'd be walking back into the life of a man who left a lasting impression in the mind of a six-year-old boy.

The large airport was impressive. It reminded me of being in a United Nations building with all its national and international flags hanging. Over the loudspeaker, announcements of arriving and departing flights were spoken in many different languages. I was able to distinguish French from Italian and Russian from Spanish but I clearly understood only the English.

Trying to kill some time before my next flight, I window-shopped for a while, but then the cravings, the urges, to really shop got the best of me. So I went into a Davidoff store, tried on a few things, then decided to buy a three-quarter-length brown leather jacket with mink lining, a pair of brown wool pants, a matching turtleneck sweater, and a pair of brown leather riding boots. Thirty-six hundred dollars later, I was in line waiting to charge it to my Amex. *I'll worry about how I'm gonna pay this later,* I thought. *I'll be hungry and homeless later; but, for now, I'm gonna be fly as hell,* I rationalized.

While I waited for my charge approval, my heart began to race when I thought I heard the voice of someone from my past. *It couldn't be,* I thought. *Not here. No, my mind is playing tricks on me,* I reasoned. *He wouldn't be here in Germany.* But then I heard the laugh. It was the same thick, heavy laugh I'd heard on so many nights, long ago. It was a laugh I'd never forget.

"This whole trip has got me spooked," I mumbled to myself. I signed my name on the dotted line, grabbed my bags, then turned toward the door. Our eyes met. They were the same light brown eyes that stared into mine on so many nights, long ago. And then I heard his name.

"Bryce, sweetheart," a strikingly beautiful woman said in a soft, sweet voice. "What do you think about this one?" she asked, holding up a navy blue suit jacket. He answered her but kept his eyes locked on mine.

"Excuse me," he said in his smooth, silky voice. "Is your name Britton?"

I forced a smile. "Hello, Bryce. It's been a long time."

"Oh my God!" he said, smiling and walking toward me. He grabbed me in a tight bear hug, then kissed me on the neck. "I can't believe it. Britton! How's the family? Honey, come here. You won't believe who this is."

"Yes, I would," she said. Her thin, red lips parted in a smile as bright as sunshine. "You announced it loud enough for the whole airport to hear." She extended her slim, neatly manicured hand to shake mine. Her pear-shaped diamond ring seemed too big for her delicate fingers. "Hello, Britton. I've heard so much about you over the years. I'm glad we finally get a chance to meet."

"Brit, this is my wife, Chanelle," he said while still hugging me.

"Hi," I said, trying to mask my uneasiness. An eerie feeling surrounded me.

"I feel like I've known you for years," she said. "You're even more handsome in person than in Bryce's pictures."

"Oh, you're too kind," I said, trying not to blush.

"Brit, I have to say, you haven't changed a bit," Bryce said, then grinned. "You still got it goin' on. What, you're about thirty-four now?"

"Close, I'm thirty-five. And at forty-one, you haven't changed much yourself." With the exception of being about thirty pounds heavier, having a hint of gray hair scattered in his thick, neatly trimmed mustache and beard, and having a slightly receding hairline, he still looked pretty much the same. He still had that smooth brown skin, that thick wavy hair, those thick eyebrows, and big, brown puppy-dog eyes.

"So what brings you to Frankfurt? Where are you staying?" he asked, finally letting go of me. His wife took her place beside him, then put her arm through his. "Don't tell me you've moved here? The last I heard, you were living in the Dominican."

"I'm still there," I said, then gave him the "none of your damn business" version of why I was there. I told him I'd be in Nuremberg and only planned on being in Frankfurt briefly. He indicated his wife and sons were going to England to spend a week with her sister and family. I gave him a brief update on my family, and he did the same. He told me he and his wife met while he was stationed in Japan and have been married for sixteen years. Although he retired from the army three years ago after twenty years—he now teaches chemistry at American High School—his wife still had five more years left in the service. They've been stationed in Frankfurt for the last eighteen months and have three sons: ages twelve, nine, and six.

"Well, it sounds like you're doing very well for yourself," I said, checking my watch for the time. "Oh, I need to get going so I can check in. My flight boards in forty minutes."

"Britton, please keep in touch," Chanelle said while giving me a hug. "It was nice meeting you." She turned to her husband. "Honey, I'm going back over to check on the kids. Maybe you and Britton can spend a few days together while the kids and I are gone? I'm sure the two of you have a lot of catching up to do."

Thanks but no thanks, I said to myself. *I don't think so.* "Thanks," I said, trying to avoid his stare. "Maybe next time. I need to get back as soon as possible. It was nice meeting you too. Well, Bryce, it was nice seeing you," I lied. I quickly grabbed my things and headed out of the store.

"Hold up," he said, then gave his wife a kiss. "Let me help you with your bags."

"That won't be necessary," I said, keeping up my New York stride to gate 58. He caught up with me and grabbed my arm.

"Brit, I haven't seen you in years. At least let me walk you to your gate." I slowed my pace, and we shared some small talk while we walked through the terminal. He wanted to know about D.R., then invited himself for a visit.

"Well, here's my stop," I said, biting my bottom lip. "Thanks."

"Here, let me give you my address and phone number." He pulled a pen out of the flap of his front pocket, then wrote the info on the inside cover of a matchbook. "I'd like to hear from you before you leave," he said while his eyes remained focused on mine. "I don't want another twenty-three years to go by without us talking." He smiled, then gave me another one of his bear hugs. He was still strong. I halfheartedly returned his embrace, then let go. "I hope you enjoy your stay."

"Take care, Bryce. I'll be in touch." This time I avoided his eyes. I stuck the matchbook in my coat pocket, then headed toward the security check and through the metal detectors. I could feel his eyes still on me but I refused to acknowledge them. I refused to think about what those eyes meant to me. *I can deal with only one thing at a time*, I thought to myself. *Right now, I have a plane to catch.*

At 10:15, my flight landed in Nuremberg. I was exhausted. My body was still on Dominican time. *It's 4:15 in the morning and I should be home sound asleep*, I said to myself while I yawned. I stepped out into the cold morning air and let its sharp chill cut into me as I waited for the next cab to pull up. When a white Benz taxi-cab pulled up alongside me, the heat and smell from its leather interior greeted me as I hopped in. "The Penta International, please." The foreign driver sped out of the airport and headed west toward my destination.

The minute I checked in and got to my room on the eighth floor, I jumped in the shower, hung up my clothes, then lost myself in the queen-size bed, between crisp white sheets. As soon as my head hit the goose down pillow, I fell into a deep sleep. Three hours later, I was awakened by an annoying chiming sound. It was the phone. "Hello," I said, still drunk with sleep.

"Why aren't you at Daddy's?" It was Amira.

"Damn, girl, you're worse than having a wife," I said. "Can't I go away in peace?"

"Hell no. You can run, but you can't hide," she said with a chuckle. "I just wanted to make sure you got in okay. I was going to leave a message at the front desk, but the operator rang through anyway. I just wanted to let you know that I love you and that I'm glad you're there. That's all. Now, give yourself a hug from me to you and go back to sleep."

"I love you too." I smiled. "Thanks for calling." We gave each other kisses, then hung up. I sat up, gave myself a big hug, then flopped back down. *Well, there's no sense in dragging this out any longer than necessary*, I thought. I picked up the phone and dialed his number.

"Hello," a male answered.

"Hi, may I speak to Mr. Landers? This is Britton."

"Hello, Britton. It's Wilson. Are you all checked in at your hotel?"

"Yes," I said, trying to sound more pleasant than I did the last time we spoke. "I was hoping I could get directions to your house."

"Are you driving?" he asked while coughing in my ear. "Excuse me."

"No," I said. "I'm going to have a taxi bring me over." He immediately insisted that it would be easier if he came to pick me up. After a minute of being resistant, I gave in and told him I'd be down in the lobby around five o'clock. He indicated he'd pull up to the door and would be driving a silver S500 2000 Benz. *Humph…another Benz owner, I thought.*

"Great," he said, sounding pleased. "I'll see you then." Again, the only thing we had in common was the dial tone.

At five sharp, Wilson was already outside waiting when I arrived downstairs. I spotted his silver Benz outside the lobby door. He got out when he saw me coming through the automated glass doors. It was like seeing a ghost. From his mocha-colored complexion to the small freckles across the bridge of his nose, from his reddish-brown hair to his tall, stocky build, he was the spitting image of my father. *I'm glad I look like my mother,* I thought as he came around his car to greet me. He too had that flat, round Landers mole on the left side of his face. He smiled, then extended his hand. I shook it firmly.

"Britton, it's really good to finally meet you," he said, embracing me as if I were a long, lost kid. "I've waited for this day for a very long time. I'm glad you made it."

"Thanks," was the only thing I could say. I didn't return his embrace, nor did I share his enthusiasm. I was just there to tie up loose ends in my life. When he opened the car door, I melted into the soft leather seat, then stared out the passenger side window.

During the ride and with his small talk, it was clear he and I had nothing in common. He played football; I ran track. He dated mostly white women; I *never* would. He studied electrical engineering; I studied psychology. He grew up with my father; I didn't. He didn't experience his mother being beaten; I did. As far as I was concerned, there was nothing else to talk about. So for the rest of the ride, I stared out the window into the dreary, cold world while he drove. My thoughts were interrupted when the sounds of Grace Jones's "Feel Up" pumped out of his factory-installed system. He turned up the volume, then bounced to the beat doing ninety. When ABC's "One Better World" came on, I smiled. *Not that many people are up on them,* I thought to myself. *Those white boys are hot to death. Well, maybe we have something in common, after all.*

Their house was a two-story brick building with a cobblestone driveway and walkway. Wilson parked, then led me into their neatly furnished home. When we walked into the house, the smell of sauerkraut and German coffee greeted us. A husky woman wearing a nurse uniform was sitting in the living room watching the news. In her thick accent, she informed us she had just finished bathing and changing our father and that he was in the back room resting. I followed Wilson into the dining room, through the kitchen, then down a narrow hallway to a door. He knocked.

"Come in," a hoarse voice said in almost a whisper. Wilson opened the door.

"Dad, I have a surprise for you," he said, stepping out of the way for my father to see me. Wilson had told me on the way over he hadn't let my father know I was coming. He wanted it to be a surprise; besides, he didn't want to tell him I was coming and then have me not show up. I understood, since that is something I would do.

"Britton?" he asked, trying to raise himself up from his bed to get a better view.

"Yes," I said, walking toward him. "It's me." He didn't look like the man I remembered seeing in my nightmares or in pictures. He wasn't the same tall, stocky man who flipped up the dinner table or dumped pots of food in the middle of the floor when he disliked the meal being served. He didn't sound like the same man with the deep, heavy voice and piercing brown eyes who cursed my mother and called her degrading names. He wasn't the same heavy-handed, thick-knuckled man who beat my mother's face in until her eyes swelled shut or the man who was responsible for the busted lips and broken jaws. He wasn't the same vicious man who wrapped a cord around my mother's neck until she was unconscious, then threw her into a wall or the same big-footed man who kicked her across the floor, then stomped on her ribs. He seemed nothing like the same mean-spirited man who dragged my mother out of the tub by her hair, then beat her until she bled, like the father responsible for the splattered blood of my mother. The man I saw wasn't the same man I hoped would "bleed to death." He was old and frail. His voice was soft. His face was kind. His eyes were sad. His hands trembled.

On one wall of his room, there were pictures of Amira and me, from kindergarten through high school and beyond—every year of our lives to the present. There were graduation pictures from my senior year, cap and gown pictures of me at NSU and NYU, pictures of my wedding. He had my whole life on his wall. On the opposite wall, there were pictures of his current family. And over his bed hung a sixteen-by-twenty portrait of him sitting and with his two sons standing on either side of him. They looked proud. I smiled, then returned my attention to him.

"I'll leave the two of you alone," Wilson said. He walked over to our father, lifted him up from his reclining position on his bed, then propped two pillows in back of him. After he kissed him on his forehead, he headed for the door. "Britton, can I bring you anything to eat or drink?"

"No," I said without taking my eyes off the man sitting up on his deathbed. "Thanks."

"Dad, how about you?"

"Maybe later, son," he said in his hoarse whisper. "Thanks." When I finally turned around to acknowledge Wilson, he stared at me, then smiled. He indicated he'd be upstairs if we needed anything and closed the door. We were alone.

"Please," he said, gesturing for me to sit in the plaid chair beside his bed. "Come sit. I'm so glad you came." He stared at me for a moment. "It's so good seeing you after all these years." He spoke slowly as if he were trying to carefully choose his words. "I should have never let so much time and space come between us. I'm sorry."

"Well, you did," I said, staring him in the eyes. My tone was nonthreatening. "And nothing can change that. So what do you want from me, now?"

He turned his head, became quiet for a moment, then turned back to me. "I want to know what I did to push you away from me. Britton, I've made many mistakes in my life. Some really didn't matter to me. But for the mistakes that truly have mattered, I've had to live with that pain for the last thirty years of my life. I don't want—"

"Why'd you beat on my mother?" I asked, cutting him off. "Why don't I remember you ever hugging me or holding me or saying you loved me? Why?"

"Guilt," he said in a low whisper. His head hung low.

"Guilt? Guilt from what? Are you saying you never wanted me?"

"No, Britton," he said, looking at me. "I was happy your mother was pregnant with you. It was the way in which you were conceived that hurt me. My guilt prevented me from bonding with you. And I'm sorry." I just stared at him with one eyebrow raised. When he married my mother, she was eighteen and he was thirty-three. They had known each other for only a few months when he proposed to her. He was in his fourteenth year in the Marine Corps and was preparing to leave for Okinawa, and he just had to take "that pretty young thang" with him. So off she went, against the wishes of her strict religious parents. Although he was in love and obsessively smitten with her beauty, he knew she had no emotional attachment to him and that she married him as a way to travel and explore the world. Knowing this only fueled his insecurities, but he had hoped that in time she would grow to love him. Because she was young and naive, she was friendly toward other men, but he interpreted that as flirtation and would become enraged. She got her first taste of his jealousy when he smacked her face and busted her lip for smiling at a man who simply said hello. Anytime another man looked at her, he'd become extremely jealous and would blame her for them looking at her. He'd tell her it was her fault that other men found her attractive.

Because he was afraid of losing her, he thought if he intimidated her and kept her isolated from family and friends, she'd become emotionally closer to him. When that didn't work, he decided having children would bond them. Fortunately, my mother loved children and wanted them as well, but for different reasons. She had hoped that having a baby would keep him from accusing her of infidelity and keep him from beating her. In any case, after two miscarriages, one stillborn baby and five years of marriage, she conceived Amira. After the birth of their "little miracle," things seemed to be going well. He was relieved that my mother wanted to make their marriage work. She was a wonderful wife and mother. He showered her with gifts and even allowed her to go out with the baby. Unfortunately, things went downhill once they were stationed in Germany. My mother was twenty-five by then, and with motherhood, her girlish innocence had blossomed into refined womanhood. She wanted more out of life than just being a housewife but he wouldn't allow that. He wanted her all to himself.

To keep her in line, he initially would use military tactics he learned throughout his marine training to inflict physical pain without causing bruises. Gradually, they became beatings that left marks. But he still feared she'd run out on him with another man, so he thought another baby would keep her busy. He thought the more babies she had, the less likely she would be to leave him. But this time, although she loved children and wanted more, having another baby right away wasn't what she wanted. She wanted to make her own decisions and be independent. In a word, she wanted control over her own life. The one thing she thought she had control over was her body and her right to deny him sexual intimacy. But when he beat her, gagged her, ripped her panties off, then forced his manhood into her, she knew that that belief was just a figment of her imagination. It wasn't until her fourth month and three beatings later that she found out she was pregnant. I was conceived as a result of my mother being beaten and raped. And my birth was a constant reminder of his need to control her.

"I've never been more sorry about anything in my entire life. I loved your mother, and I just wanted her to love me," he said, trying to contain his emotions. "I didn't want her to be another woman who walked out of my life." I could tell he wanted to explain how his mother had walked out on him and his four brothers and how he resented his father for not doing something to stop her. He wanted to share his story of how his first wife also walked out on him. I cut the saga of his life short.

"Listen," I said sternly. "I don't give two shits and a duck's fuck what your life was like as a child. That's an issue you should have resolved long before you got involved with my mother and before you started having kids. But because you didn't, I had to suffer. I had to watch you beat the shit out of my mother. I had to rock myself to sleep every night listening to you yell and scream at her and call her degrading and filthy names. Every night, I prayed that someone would help her because I was too young and too helpless to do anything. I'm just glad she was finally strong enough to stand up to you and leave you. If she hadn't, you would have killed her. So if you think telling me about your past is going to make me see things any differently, you're wrong. The only thing I see is a weak, insecure man. A man who inflicted his insecurities on his wife and children. I see a man who treated my mother like shit. No one deserves to be beaten or treated like dirt. And no child should have to witness that level of violence or cruelty. If you feel beat up by the world and unhappy, you *don't* come home and take it out on your family."

"Britton," he said as he raised a trembling hand to wipe his eyes. "You're right. It took your mother leaving me and never coming back for me to realize I needed help. I did get help and I was able to understand my own pain. I was able to learn how I inflicted my pain on your mother. I'm sorry I wasn't able to be a better husband and father. You have every right to hate me."

I stood up and stared at the picture over his bed, then walked over to the wall covered with pictures of my mother with my sister and me. I ran my fingers along the frames trying to remember the events going on in each one. With my back toward him, I spoke while I studied each picture.

"You know, I don't hate you. Hating you would take too much negative energy to generate and, truthfully, you're not worth the effort. My mother didn't raise me to hate you. She never even bad-mouthed you. She never spoke about any of the abuse or torture. When we left California, she left that part of her life behind. She always encouraged me to love you, and she always pointed out good qualities in you. I know my mother loves you in her own way. She understands you. Regardless of what you put her through, she never took it out on us. So I could never hate you. I just don't like you. I never have and I never will. But I do thank you for teaching me how a real man shouldn't behave. Because of the scars you left, you've taught me to never raise my hand to a woman. You've taught me to never bring children into this world until I've addressed my own issues because I would never want my children to be scarred by my pain and suffering."

I walked over to his bed, then sat beside him. I held his wrinkled hand and stared at him. I felt nothing. I wasn't sure what I expected to feel; but whatever it was supposed to be, it just wasn't there.

"Britton, I am proud to see the man you've become," he said with tears running down his face, clinging to the sides of his chin, and finally dropping onto his gray robe. "I just wanted to be able to tell you I love you before I closed my eyes." He squeezed my hand. "I love you, Britton."

I hugged him. "You can call me son," I whispered. I hugged him tighter. "I love you, son," he said, then sobbed. I just let him cry. There was nothing else that needed to be said. I knew that when it was time for him to go to his final resting place, I wasn't the one he'd have to answer to.

16

BRITTON: THE RAPE OF MY SOUL

AFTER SEEING MY FATHER, I spent four days in my hotel room sorting through my emotional baggage. I wanted to release the flood of tears welling up inside me, but I couldn't. Something wouldn't let me. So my spirits became drowned in my emotions. It was a process that forced me to deal with terrible memories I thought could be buried deep down and erased from my mind forever. I thought by repressing these demons, I would be free from them. I thought by being strong for everyone else, I could forget about my own fragility. I thought I could go through life pretending I was un-touched by the ugly scars that had formed over deep emotional wounds. I've spent most of my life putting Band-Aids over them in order to hide the feelings that haunted me and tried to control me. As a result, it has been difficult for me to trust or allow anyone to really get close to me. It just seemed safer to emotionally isolate myself from others. It made life much easier for me to not feel. I wouldn't be vulnerable. I'd be in control of whom I let in my life and to what degree. This way, it wouldn't hurt if someone did something to me.

But this trip to Germany has made me realize that I can't keep running and hiding from the past. No matter how fast I run or where I run, it always has a way of finding me. I know if I ever expect to heal, I can't keep putting Band-Aids on this pain. If I ever want to move on with my life, I can't let it haunt me, ever again.

I got on my knees and prayed. I prayed for the strength to fight these demons. I prayed for emotional freedom and inner peace. And then I prayed for all the children who are forced to endure the cruelties of this world. I prayed for Chyna, Indy, and Damascus and for all the men and women in this world who still carry the hurt and pain of their childhoods. After I finished my prayers, I stood up, stared at myself in the mirror for a few seconds, then returned to my emotional baggage. This time, I was ready to sweep my pain out of my heart and my life, for good. I pulled out my past, shook off the dust, then dialed the number of its owner.

"Hello, can I speak to Bryce?" I asked, still staring at myself in the mirror.

"Hey," he said pleased to hear from me. "I was hoping you'd call. Are you still in Germany?"

"Yeah, I'm still here. But I'm outta this piece tomorrow. That's why I'm calling. I was hoping I could see you before I leave."

"That would be great. When do you want to get together?"

"I'm flying into Frankfurt today," I said while pulling and twisting at my braids. "My flight gets in around one-thirty this afternoon."

"Great. I'll be there to pick you up—"

"No. There's no need to pick me up because I won't be staying with you. I'm staying at the Kempinski Hotel." I walked over to the huge window and stared out into the thick mist that hung in the air, then looked up into the gloomy gray sky.

"Brit, you don't have to stay in a hotel when I have more than enough room here for you."

"No, Bryce," I said between deep breaths. "I prefer it this way. I would rather we talk in my hotel room."

"Alright," he said, sounding confused. "But if you change your mind, the offer still stands."

"Thanks. I'll call you when I get in."

"I'll be waiting."

After we hung up, I packed my things and took a forty-minute shower. I stepped under the showerhead, leaned my head back, closed my eyes, then let the warm, heavy stream beat against my body. I let my thoughts drift.

"Mommy, do you think I'm pretty?" I asked.

"Oh, sweetheart," she said in her motherly tone, then hugged me. "You're Mommy's handsome little man."

"Well, how come people call me 'pretty boy'?"

"Because you were a pretty baby. You see these pictures?" she asked, pulling out a photo album of baby photos. The cover read Britton's First Years. Inside there were pictures of a red-faced baby with big, brown eyes; thick, long lashes; and thick, curly hair. "Everyone just thought you were the prettiest little boy they'd ever seen." Her tone was proud. "And because of all that pretty hair, those pretty eyes, and that big beautiful smile, you were just a pretty baby."

"Well, I don't want to be pretty!" I screamed. "I don't want pretty hair or pretty eyes. I don't want to be handsome either. I want to be ugly!"

I ran upstairs, hid under my bed, and cried myself to sleep. And every night, I prayed: *Dear God, please make me ugly.* And when he didn't, I grew to hate myself.

Frankfurt was hidden in a fog as thick as my thoughts when we landed. I walked through the airport not hearing or seeing anyone. I felt as though I were suspended in air, detached from the present because my past was my present. I don't remember how or when I got to the hotel or when I called Bryce, but when I stepped out of my fog, he was there.

"Brit," he said as he walked in and removed his wet leather trench and hat. I hung his coat in the closet and laid his hat on the dresser. "I'm glad you called me because I really wanted to talk to you."

"Oh yeah?" I asked, contemplating how I would say what needed to be said. "About what?" I fell onto the burgundy sofa with my back resting on its arm while he sat in the burgundy wing chair across from me. The only thing between us was the octagon-shaped glass table that sat in the middle of the floor.

"Yeah, my mom told me you were a school psychologist," he said, then rested his right ankle on his left knee. He placed his right hand just above his ankle. "So I was hoping I could talk to you about Bryson." Bryson was his six-year-old.

"Alright," I said, shifting my eyes from his eyes to his black Bally loafer. "What's up?"

"Well, I think there's something wrong with him. He likes putting on his mother's makeup and wearing her high heels." I just stared and listened.

"And?" I asked.

"Well, that's not normal."

"Really?" I said, trying to let him get his point across before I lit his ass up.

"I'm not raising my boys to be sissies. He's not a little girl. He's a boy, and I want him to act like one. Chanelle thinks it's cute, but I don't."

"Just because he likes wearing your wife's clothes doesn't necessarily mean he's going to be a sissy," I said, trying to keep my composure and not get clinical on him. "Did you know that there are some heterosexual men who like wearing women's clothing, for whatever reasons? Maybe that isn't normal, but who are we to decide what's normal? Anyway, maybe it's a phase. Maybe it's just a period of exploration. But if not, so what? He's still your son, and he still needs you to love him, unconditionally."

"I do love him. But I don't want him acting like a girl or turning *funny.*"

I felt tension mounting inside me. "Well, what do you and your family do or say when he does this?"

"Chanelle gives him a hug and lets him prance around in her things. I beat his behind and yell at him. His brothers tease him and call him names."

"Is that so? Well, if you think beating on him is going to make him act more like a boy or calling him names or teasing him is going to make him tougher, it won't. The only thing it's going to do is make him insecure. It will make him withdraw into emotional isolation, which can become potentially dangerous. Kids who retreat emotionally tend to become self-destructive. They are at increased risk of self-mutilation, self-medication, and/or committing suicide."

He shifted in his chair, then placed his foot back on the carpet. I stared at him until he averted his eyes. I stared until the silence got the best of him. "Let me tell you a story of a woman who left her abusive husband and moved into her sister's home with her two children," I said. "This woman had a quiet and shy six-year-old son who stayed up under her until her twelve-year-old nephew took him under his wing. Do you know this story?" I asked calmly.

He shook his head, then nervously shifted back in his seat. And so the story began.

"The woman's nephew befriended the little boy and began referring to him as his little brother. He taught this little boy how to play basketball, football, and how to fish. He even promised to protect him. Everyone trusted the twelve-year-old with this little boy because he would be a good role model. The little boy trusted him because he looked up to him. He idolized him. Do you remember this story now?" I asked while my eyes cut into him. He shook his head. "Well, I do. I remember it as if it were yesterday. I remember the first time that little boy was robbed of his innocence. He was nine years old. He was raped by the one person he trusted and looked up to. A fifteen-year-old boy taught this little boy how to feel helpless. He taught him what it was like to be victimized."

"Brit," he said quietly and uneasily. "Can we change the subject?"

I got up, locked the dead bolt, put the chain on the door, then sat back down. "Oh, no, brother," I snapped. "We will talk about this because while you've moved on with your life, I've had to live with this story. I've had to walk around with this story for over twenty years. So you will sit and you will listen because if you don't, I will make this public knowledge. Do you understand what I'm saying?" He nodded, then put his head down. "No, Bryce, you need to look at me when I tell you this. I want you to look me in my eye and listen to and hear what I'm saying."

"Look," he said angrily. "Why the fuck are you bringing all this up? We were kids. It happened a long time ago. Can't you just forget about it?"

"No, I can't forget about it like you did," I said. "*You* fucked my life up and you want me to just forget about it?! Wrong answer. I want you to know what it's been like for me. So don't fucking interrupt me because the next time you do, I don't know if I can be responsible for what might happen in here." I stood up. We were silent while I paced the floor. Then I walked over to him and leaned over the back of his chair to speak in a low, chilling tone directly in his ear. I continued while he sat stone still.

"I still remember the first time you penetrated me. I can still remember the feeling of your warm fluid being ejaculated into my rectum. I cried, thinking you had peed in me. But then you gave me my first lesson in Sex Theory 101. You told me not to cry because it was *cum* and cum was how men made babies. So you know what I did? I obsessed over the fear that you, a fifteen-year-old man, had impregnated me. Why do you think I stopped riding bikes or climbing trees or doing all the other things little nine-year-old boys should be doing? I stopped doing those things because I didn't want to hurt *the baby*. I fucking walked around thinking I was going to have a baby until my mother told me, 'Little boys can't have babies. Men can only make babies with women.' And when she asked me why I had asked, 'I don't know' was the only thing I could say."

For three years, I was manipulated and coerced into thinking that this act of indecency was my fault because I wanted it, that if I wasn't "so pretty" and hadn't been "a dick tease," he wouldn't have to "give it" to me. Picture that! I wanted a fifteen-year-old booty bandit twice my size pumping his fat dick in me whenever he wanted to get his nut off. What the hell does a nine-year-old know about dick-teasing? And every time I cried, he'd say, "Stop acting like a little girl. You know you like it." Yeah, right. The pain was always excruciating, as if he were ripping me at the seams. But he knew enough to use a lot of Vaseline and to take his time until he had all of himself in me. He told me to stop acting like a girl, yet he kissed and licked on me and treated me as if I were one because I was "pretty."

For three years, I just let him have his way with me. Anytime he got the opportunity to get me alone, I knew what would come next: He'd pull his penis out, scoop two fingers of Vaseline in his hands, stroke it until it swelled with excitement, then instruct me to "Drop them drawers and bend over." Other times, he'd grind on top of me, then stick his tongue in my mouth until he came. But he preferred forcing himself inside of me. He preferred the grip of a young boy's rectum. Accidentally, I learned that if I moved my hips, instead of lying still, it didn't hurt as much and he'd spill his seed quicker. So each time he mounted me like a pony, I'd swing my hips fast and hard like a galloping wild horse. And each time he finished, I cried. But he reassured me it was okay. In my heart, I knew it wasn't. It didn't feel right. I was afraid of him, but I liked being around him. I disliked what he was doing to me, but I liked getting his attention. I was confused and scared, but I wouldn't tell. Besides, who'd believe me? He paid attention to me. I was his "little man" and he loved me, so the secret was kept. And every time he crawled on top of me and pushed himself in and out of me, he stabbed at my soul. Every time he ejaculated inside of me, he tainted my spirit.

"Britton," he said, shamefaced. "I was young. I didn't know what I—"

"Bullshit!" I snapped in his ear, then lowered my tone. "You knew *exactly* what you were doing. Until you turned nineteen and went into the service, you knew exactly what the hell you were doing. So please don't give me that. And I'll bet you, to this day, you still know what to do, isn't that right, Bryce?" I blew in his ear to make him uncomfortable. He moved his ear away.

"I'm sorry, Brit," he said, turning around to look up at me. Our lips were close enough to touch. The room was thick with chills from the past. Again, I stared straight in his eyes until he lowered his head. "I am truly sorry. I've always had nothing but love for you. I never meant to hurt you."

"I know," I said, then moved away from his chair. "We never *really* mean to hurt the ones we love, do we? Well, after you left for the army, I was relieved you were gone. But I was sad. I missed you. Guilt and shame were like an annoying fly constantly nagging at me. I looked up to you, Bryce. And you betrayed me. You took advantage of me. You intimidated and bullied me. And that hurt because I trusted you.

"So I grew angry and started acting out. I blamed my mother for having to work two jobs and go to school and for leaving me alone with you. I blamed my father for not being around to protect me or even love me. When I had no one else to blame, I blamed the world for being what it was—mean and lonely. And when no one noticed my agony or even bothered to pay attention to what I wasn't saying, I started running away as a means to escape. But guess what, Bryce? No matter how fast I ran or where I ran to, the stinging and burning pain that ran up my spine and pierced my insides every time you penetrated me was *always* with me."

He got up from his chair, walked over to me, and embraced me. His eyes were heavy with tears, but none fell. I stood still. I didn't acknowledge his guilt or his touch.

"I'm so sorry, Britton. Please know, I'm so sorry. My life was—"

"Bryce," I said with my eyes closed and my arms down at my sides. "I don't care what your life was like. It doesn't matter to me. That's your struggle, not mine. I just needed you to know how my life was affected by you. I needed to give you the guilt I've carried all these years because I've realized it wasn't my fault. It was *never* my fault. This guilt belongs to you. It's your baggage, not mine."

"I'm so sorry."

"There's no use being sorry now. Just be aware," I said. I felt the warm droplets of his tears hit against my neck. "You have a little boy who needs you to be supportive. He needs you to nurture him and guide him. Not call him names. Names hurt. He needs you to protect him or at least prepare him for how to deal with the bullies of the world who prey on younger, more vulnerable kids. He needs to know he has an emotionally safe, healthy, and supportive environment where he's loved without reservations."

He let go of me, wiped his eyes, then walked toward the door. I followed behind him.

"Take care," I said while unlatching and unlocking the door, then handing him his coat and hat. This time, I gave him a hug. I whispered in his ear: "The next time you open your mouth to ridicule or put down your son, remember the story of the six-year-old boy."

I opened the door, stared at him until he lowered his head, then followed him out the door. I stood outside and watched him walk down the hall and onto the elevator. When the elevator doors closed, I went back into my hotel suite and gently closed the door behind me. And for the first time in my life, I felt the shackles of guilt and shame snap open. Finally, I was free to move on without painful demons haunting me. It was like a ton of bricks had been lifted off my shoulders. "Thank you," I whispered. Then, without warning, an ocean of tears fell from my eyes. I thanked God I never dealt with my victimization by becoming sexually assaultive. I cried and cried, thanking God that I, unlike so many other victims of abuse, didn't act out inappropriately by becoming abusive toward someone more vulnerable than me. I cried, thanking God that I didn't turn my rage outward and become aggressive or develop antisocial behaviors or abuse drugs to numb my pain. I cried and cried until I sobbed for every child who is sexually abused or victimized. I cried for the pain of every survivor. I cried and cried until I rinsed away all of my pain. I cried until I was able to find the bridge between freedom and peace…by letting go.

17

INDERA: **FLASHBACK**

OVER THE LAST WEEK, I'VE BEEN FLOODED WITH BEAUTIFUL GIFTS AND FLOWERS. My mother and I share our birthday next week and those closest to me know this is the hardest time of the year for me. Every year, until my mother's death, we spent that day as if we were celebrating New Year's. She'd always say, "The New Year isn't the first of January. It's the eighth of February." Together, we'd go off on one of our extravagant excursions—Greece, France, Belgium, London, Spain, or Egypt—and we'd shop in the finest boutiques and eat in the most exquisite restaurants. She'd have matching outfits made for us in the finest cloths, and we'd celebrate our bond as mother and daughter for weeks. Because I was "Mommy's little princess."

I used to cry heavy tears because of the emptiness I've felt since her death; but now I'm all cried out. I know she's in a safer place. I know her heart and soul are safe. I know her spirit lives inside of me and that makes this loneliness bearable. That gives me the strength to keep on keepin' on. Tomorrow, I'll put a thick blanket of fresh flowers over her snow-covered grave. She loved fresh flowers. With the change of every season and with every birthday and every Mother's Day, I make sure she is covered with the most beautiful flowers.

Britton, Chyna, and Tee have all called me daily and several of our sorors have come by to visit. Yes, my mother and I belonged to the same sorority. I pledged at her alma mater, Spelman College, and sometimes it hurts me that I didn't graduate from there. But, with all the gossip, I couldn't. Thanks to a no-good man, I didn't.

I was seventeen when I traveled to Atlanta in pursuit of my dreams, leaving behind friendships and the comforts of my prestigious boarding school. But I quickly embarked on new adventures, new friendships, and became popular. By the end of my freshman year, I was working circles around the brothers in the growing metropolitan mecca. In my sophomore year, I was chosen "Miss Morehouse." Oh, yes! This fly girl was all that. And although I flirted with the brothers, I wasn't humping 'em. But one decided to take my love without permission. One decided to violate me and allow his boys to join in. I was nineteen when it happened. I was a victim of date rape, acquaintance rape, or whatever nice term they give it these days. Bottom line: I was raped.

I had gone out on several dates with a man four years older than me. He wanted romance. I wanted a good time. We had nice conversations and spent quiet moments together, but I ended it when he started pressing me for sex. I told him I wasn't feelin' him like that, and I thought he was cool with it. Then, one night, he invited me to his lavish house under the pretense of cooking me dinner, then going to the movies. It was my birthday. Instead, he slipped barbiturates in my drink while I went to the bathroom. That nasty, bitch-ass nigga drugged me, stripped me of my clothes, then took my pussy without permission. Then he invited his two friends, who were waiting in his bedroom, to join the fun. So he and his coward-ass boys ran a dirty train on me. They gang-raped and sodomized me. They disrespected me. They violated me. They stole a piece of my soul, and there was nothing I could do.

Next thing I knew, it was all over the campus that I had fucked three men. Apparently, one of the guys attended a nearby school and had painted their dirty deed out, advertising me as a willing train ride. So the gossip spread. Thanks to him, I was made out to be a real trick. Fortunately, after a few months, the other guy confided in one of his friends about what really happened. Somehow, his friend's girlfriend (one of my sorors) found out and told me. Even after learning the truth, I still beat myself up with blame, believing that it was my fault for going to his house. It was my fault for being up front with him. If I hadn't hurt his feelings, it wouldn't have happened. But it did. And it wasn't my fault. And I didn't deserve it. *No one* deserves to be raped.

I didn't want to go to the police. For what? To be probed and interrogated like some lab animal? Besides, I had already scrubbed off and douched out the evidence. I knew of girls who reported their rapes and were persecuted in court while perpetrators sat there with smug looks on their faces. They'd get off scot-free or with probation. I wasn't going through that.

So I kept it silent. Out of embarrassment and guilt, I closed the windows to my soul and held on to the pain. The only thing I was sure of was this: Since he'd wanted to play, he'd have to pay. I held on to the anger until I was able to leave him with a reminder of what he did to me. He took this pussy by force? Then he'd have to suffer the consequences. He'd have to live by the choices he made. This time, it would be on my terms.

After two months of leading him to believe things were peace between us, I finally called him up and told him I wanted to spend the night with him. I told him in low, dirty moans how much I wanted to give him my pussy. He took the bait. So with two bottles of champagne and a bag of vengeance, I went to his place. This time, I served the drinks. And each time I'd returned with another drink, I'd remove another piece of my clothing. I played this little game until his words slurred. While I stood in front of him wearing a red teddy and a pair of matching fuck-me pumps, I charmed him into his bedroom and teased him until I had him wrapped around my finger. I stripped him of his clothes. I grabbed and pulled at his dick until he begged for this pussy. Then I removed my tampon, stood up on his bed, squatted over his face, and lowered my pussy onto his lips. It was time for his just reward.

I pumped my pussy in his mouth while he jerked off. I pumped and pumped until he nutted himself to sleep. Then, in the middle of the night, I quietly snuck out of his bed and scrubbed my body and cried in his shower for an hour. While he snored his way to hell, I dressed and dusted off anything I touched in his house. I put on rubber gloves and wiped my presence away. Then I tiptoed to his kitchen and pulled out from my travel case a recipe given to me by a soror. She was from the woods of Alabama and knew many of her great-grandmother's and grandmother's secret potions. I pulled out one of his five-gallon pots, poured in a jar of piss, added my girlfriend's powdered substance, then slowly poured in Alaga syrup. The thicker the syrup, the better the stick. I waited until it boiled and thickened. I stirred and cried until it was ready. When it was, I carefully poured it into a metal bucket. I tiptoed back into his bedroom, flipped on his light switch, and stood at the foot of his bed. I stared at his nude body, then woke him up. I wanted him to see me. I wanted him to look in my eyes the way he looked in mine when he violated me. I smiled, then slung my bucket of potash all over him. It scalded and stuck between his legs, on his stomach and his chest. I stared him in the eye as the sticky substance burned into his flesh. His screams echoed throughout his home. But no one heard them. He lived out in the woods.

I grabbed my things, silently closed his bedroom door, and walked out, leaving him in agony. Maybe he'd never see my pain, but he'd always feel it. Although mental wounds take longer to heal and overcome, I wanted him to feel the pain he caused me. I wanted his wounds to leave scars to remind him of how he forced me to suffer the indignity of rape.

As for the guy who made up the lie and stirred the rumors, several years later, he died suddenly after a few hits of crack. Warning: Drugs…they *can* kill. Especially when they're cut with a little strychnine.

On the eve of my mother's and my birthday, as I've done every birthday before, I went down to my basement, sat in front of my mother's baby-grand piano, and played her favorite songs: "Amazing Grace," "I Won't Complain," "His Eye Is on the Sparrow," and "Bridge over Troubled Water." I sang my heart out in tribute and in loving memory of a woman who always made me feel like the most beautiful and most special person in the world. It's times like this when I miss her the most. I miss her encouragement, her embrace, and her love. Sometimes I can still hear her soft motherly voice. Her tone was always warm and soothing.

"Indy, baby, no matter what you do in life, do your best, be your best, and never let anyone stand in your way. …Remain determined, stay strong, and whatever you do, *never* rely on a man, do you hear me, baby girl?" I'd look into her beautiful face and shyly respond, "Yes, Momma." Yes, as hard as it may be to believe, there was a time when I was shy. There was a time when

I had a warm, caring heart. But with life experiences, so many things change.

"Indy, as a woman, you must be financially and socially independent, and, baby, *always* keep your head up, be proud, and never be ashamed of your blackness."

I'd smile and listen intently to her motherly advice. "Never completely trust a man with your heart and always keep one eye open." I'd gaze into her brown eyes in search of what was hidden in her soul. But she'd never let me in. She was a proud woman.

She was a woman who held her head up high in the face of adversity, and not once did she ever complain or shed a tear. She'd turn her head from my father's womanizing ways and never concerned herself with his sexual appetite or his business activities. Oh, yes, Robinson Fleet was an extremely handsome man of West Indian descent. Make no mistake, the Casanova loved spending his time slinging his dick in as many woman as he could. And she afforded him plenty of space to "sow his wild oats" and run his "business" as long as he maintained her lavish lifestyle. Although he was a very shrewd and well-connected businessman who ran a lucrative so-called "pharmaceutical company," she'd say, "Indy, if a man wants to play, you make him pay."

It wasn't until years later that I truly understood what she meant. When I received my inheritance I realized that *everything* was in her name. The summer home in Grenada, the brownstone, the safety deposit boxes, the stocks, and the insurance policies. When she died, everything became mine. Though she left my father only one dollar in her will, she left behind a million dollars' worth of hurt and pain. She'd never let me see it, but I felt it the day I cried out for my father's help and he was nowhere to be found. I saw it the day my beautiful mother died in my arms. That look of unforgivable despair was all over her face when she knew she'd close her eyes forever and never again see the only man she'd ever loved. I saw my mother die of a broken heart.

I know that in many ways I'm a lot like my mother. I'm determined, self-confident, educated and ambitious. But in other ways we are totally opposite. She loved a man so much that it blinded her. It stifled her growth as a woman. She didn't know how to let go or to move on because her heavy heart weighed her down. I believe that with her words of wisdom, she was trying to shape and mold me, at a very young age, to be better than she could ever be. I'm convinced my mother wanted me to be strong enough to love myself first. She wanted me to define who I would be as a woman. She wanted me to demand respect. As much as I love her, as much as I miss her, a part of me is angry at her for allowing a man to hurt her.

Oh, Lord, I wish she were still alive. Tomorrow, I'll be thirty-seven years old, and there are so many things I'd like to know. I'd like to know why she stayed with a man who cheated on her regularly throughout their ten-year marriage. I'd like to know why she married a man who was intimidated by her social grace. I'd like to know why she stayed with a man who was emotionally neglectful. I'd like to know how a woman who held a doctoral degree in education, who was a renowned author of children's books and sat on the board of many foundations, condoned her husband's behavior of importing and exporting drugs throughout the country. Most importantly, I'd like to know why she didn't demand that he respect her as a woman and as his wife. Didn't she deserve it?

Today is the one day out of the year I always dread. My birthday. It's the one day when I have to be reminded of how unkind the world can be. It's the day on which I can expect to hear from my confused-ass father. But the sad thing is, a part of me looks forward to hearing his voice. As neglectful as he was as a parent, a part of me still loves him. I guess that's one of the reasons why I haven't done anything to him, even if I won't forgive him. The minute the phone rang this morning, I knew it was him.

"Happy birthday, Indera," he said in his thick accent.

"Hello, Father," I answered nonchalantly. "How are you?"

"Fine, sweetheart. Did you get the money I sent?"

"Yes. Thanks. But you really didn't have to."

"Indy, you're my daughter. How could I not send you something for your birthday?" I rubbed the front of my mother's locket, then closed my eyes. The last time I cursed my father I was fourteen years old, but today I felt it coming. He's never let a birthday go by without sending me extravagant gifts and large sums of money. But that's only one day out of the year. What about the other three hundred and sixty-four days? It's as if I don't even exist the remainder of the year. For years, I'd send him birthday cards and Father's Day cards and he wouldn't even acknowledge them, so I stopped acknowledging him. Shortly after my mother's death, he shipped me back to my elite boarding school and basically abandoned me because he had no paternal investment in me. He provided for me financially but neglected to call or visit. I felt like I had a father only on holidays and birthdays.

"Did you ever think that maybe it's not your money or the expensive gifts I want from you?"

"Indy, sweetheart—"

"No, don't 'sweetheart' me," I snapped while I pulled a picture of him out of my wallet. "Do you know the last time you told me you loved me?"

"Indy, you know I love you—"

"I don't know shit. I am thirty-seven fuckin' years old, and the only thing I know is that the last time I heard you say you loved me was when I was seven fuckin' years old. Buying me fuckin' gifts and sending money doesn't mean shit to me. The only thing I've ever wanted from you was your love. Not your fuckin' drug money."

"Indy, I do love you. Come to Grenada for a while."

"Are you still with your wife?" I asked with an attitude while staring at myself in the floor-length mirror. I blinked my eyes real hard. I was almost eleven when he finally introduced me to her. He had been married to her for two years and was raising her two dark-skinned, knotty-headed daughters. After almost three years of not seeing him, he had the nerve to show up at my school to "bring me home." He had the nerve to tell me he had a "wonderful surprise" for me. When I walked into *my* mother's home, he introduced this intruder as my *new* mother. I burst into tears. How could he think anyone could ever replace my mother? I had hoped he was bringing me home because he wanted me and needed me in his life. I allowed my fantasy of being loved and cared for by him seduce me into agreeing to return to the place my mother and I called home. Despite his absence in my life, I still loved him. Despite the fact that I had gradually found a sense of family within the confines of my lavish boarding school, I still wanted him to love me. Despite the fact that I excelled in my studies and flourished in dance and piano, emptiness dampened my soul. Loneliness became my best friend.

I needed desperately to relive my mother's existence, but, instead, there stood Grace, a thick, yellow-skinned woman with blonde hair, big red lips, and a wide nose. At first, she tried very hard to appear genuinely nice and concerned about me. But through her Coke-bottle lenses, her wiggly, brown eyes revealed a story of a woman who had been a victim of a cruel, lonely life. Her voice was raspy and cold. As time marched on, I landed a three-year part in *Mommie Dearest*, starring the wicked albino stepmother from hell.

"Yes," he said solemnly.

"Then I guess you and I have nothing else to talk about." He knew my answer would be no. As far as I'm concerned, he chose that cockeyed bitch and her two crispy critters over me, and I will never forgive him for that. He'd rather spend his life wiping her ass than trying to have a relationship with his only child. The last time I saw him was a week after my twenty-fifth birthday. He was returning to Grenada and taking his wife with him. So I refuse to see him until he leaves her.

"Indera, sweetheart," he said, sounding dejected. "Grace isn't the same woman she was back—"

"Well, of course she's not," I said sarcastically. "The bitch doesn't have any arms."

He became silent for a moment. "I'm just hoping that one day you can find forgiveness in your heart," he pleaded in a whisper. "I don't want to see you eaten away by bitterness."

While I stood gazing in the mirror, I blinked my eyes three more times. Suddenly I was twelve again. I woke up in the middle of the night because my period came on for the first time while I was asleep. Instead of Grace explaining the menstrual process to me, she smeared my face with my blood-stained underwear, then rubbed them across my mouth as a lesson for not wearing a pad. From that moment on, I learned to sleep with one eye open and to keep my mouth closed.

I blinked my eyes again. Now I was standing butt-naked with my arms extended straight in the air. I was forced to stand in that position for hours, and every time I lowered or moved my arms, a razor strap came down against my back and slashed into my skin. Being beaten by that bitch with anything she had in her hand, or waking in the middle of the night to ice water being tossed on me because I didn't scrub the toilets right, or having to scrub floors and walls with a toothbrush before I was allowed to eat didn't hurt as much as her words. She broke my spirit with her words, "You think you're cute, don't you? You ugly, little spoiled bitch…you dumb, dirty, little whore…you worthless piece of shit." They sliced into my spirit with fierceness. Hiding in my closet or under my bed couldn't block out her hate for me or shelter me from her vicious attacks. Every day, for three years, I had to listen to that cruel, beady-eyed bitch degrade me.

She broke my spirit when she turned her head and closed her eyes and ears to the sounds that came from my room every time her forty-five-year-old brother crept into my bed. But of course she would. As long as he was in my room, her daughters were safe from him. They'd no longer have to be subjected to his perversions. But, fuck my safety.

After Grace's beatings, he would play a game with me: He'd rub and tickle my body and between my legs to make me laugh. He said he'd make me laugh my hurt away because I was "a special little girl." Gradually, he showed me that if I took my panties off and let him tickle me with his tongue, it would make me "feel real good." And every time he finished his play, he'd leave a crisp fifty-dollar bill. He promised to stop the beatings as long as I let him in my room. As long as I let him suck my young budding breasts and lick my tender, underdeveloped vagina, he'd keep me safe from her. So I let him suck and lick my beatings away and each time he wanted to explore my pussy with his fingers and, eventually, with his dick, I'd make him pay. Because Momma had said, "If a man wants to play, you make him pay." When I cried for my father's help, he was nowhere around. Why should he be? Momma had forewarned, "Never rely on a man," hadn't she?

"Bitter?" I said into the phone as I rubbed the small scar on the back of my neck. I closed my eyes tight. The sizzle of a cigarette searing my skin played fresh in my mind. The smell of singed hair suffocated my nostrils. That bitch used the back of my neck for an ashtray. Please tell me how anyone could have so much hate for a child?

"I have a right to be bitter," I barked. "But make no mistake, it's not something I will let eat away at me. Yes, I hold on to it. It's my way of ensuring I never let anyone hurt me or disrespect me or neglect me again. It's my way of making sure no one ever physically abuses me again. It's my way of making sure no one ever walks over me. I will always be good to those who are good to me. But no one is ever gonna do something to me and get the fuck away with it. After today, I'd like to bury you and these memories, so please don't ever call me again." I hung up.

Although I disconnected his call, my thoughts lingered on my childhood. "Indy, *no!*" my father yelled as he rushed toward me and grabbed my blood-stained wrist. "You'll kill her." When his precious wife threw a bedpan of piss and shit on me because I refused to clean up after her sick father, something inside of me snapped. That was the last straw for me. I was fourteen years old, and I had endured her insanity for three whole years. I had slashed her chest and arms up with a butcher knife and I was getting ready to stab her when my father ran in.

"Fuck her and fuck you," I screamed hysterically. "Get the fuck off of me. Don't you touch me! Where the fuck were you when I needed you to save me from this crazy bitch? Where were you when I needed you to love me? To protect me? To be my father? Where were you when my mother needed you? But you rush in here to save this fuckin' cockeyed psycho from me."

"Indy, sweetheart, I'm sorry. I didn't know. I would never intentionally let anyone hurt you. Please know I really didn't know. Please forgive me."

"Forgive you?! I will never forgive you. If you had paid attention to me instead of running the fuckin' streets, you woulda known. But the streets and all of your whores are more important than me."

"Listen, baby, I—"

"Just shut up. There's no need to fuckin' explain. You never wanted me. You never loved me, and you'll never be able to hurt me again. I promise you," I yelled, "That bloody bitch will pay for what the fuck she's done to me! I swear on my momma's grave. She will pay." I dropped the bloody butcher knife, walked over to his bleeding wife, and kicked the shit out of her. "This one's for my mother, bitch!" Then I picked up the phone to dial 911. "Yes, I'd like to report an end to my abuse," I sighed out with tears in my eyes, as

I looked over at my father holding and consoling his wife, "and an end to my neglect. I'm at 1583 East Seventh Street." I washed my hands, opened the front door, then waited patiently for the approaching sirens.

Needless to say, my father quickly shipped me back to boarding school. My words hadn't made a dent. I saw him only when I had to return home to testify. After six months of court hearings, that bitch was sentenced to four years' probation for endangering the welfare of a minor. Please. The lawyers had the nerve to paint *her* out to be the victim. That bitch tortured me and that's all she got. Oh, and counseling for her "extensive psychiatric issues." It took thousands of dollars for them to figure out the bitch was crazy. Give me a fuckin' break. Anyone who tortures or abuses a child deserves more than fuckin' probation.

I waited ten more years before I got her ass. I waited until they thought all was forgotten, and then she received her punishment for tormenting me. I made sure she'd never raise her hands to another child. She'd never get a chance to destroy another vulnerable child's innocence. You see, one good thing about going to an elite boarding school is that you befriend wealthy girls with well-connected families. So, over the years, I learned to plug into those connections because you never know when you might need something. Anyway, I made one call and *voilà!* Somehow, the bitch's arms were pulled out of their sockets, then chopped the fuck off. Now, I know you might think I'm vicious, but I'm not. Do you really think I would come up with such a savage way to torture someone who abused me?

And that's not all. I turned her stinkin' brother in too. He was sentenced to ten years in prison for sexual assault, criminal sexual contact, lewdness, and endangering the welfare of a minor. Well, I'm sorry, ten years wasn't sufficient for me. That fuckin' tree jumper shattered the soul of an innocent young girl. But what goes around comes around. He was brutally gang-raped and beaten in prison. So now he walks around with his asshole ripped open. He'll have to spend the rest of his life with a monkey butt. Every time he laughs or coughs, his asshole will collapse. Isn't that a shame? Too fuckin' bad. The only thing I was ever guilty of was hoping my father could love me enough to fill the hole in my heart caused by the loss of my mother; but instead,

I became a victim of hate and cruelty. So I don't want to hear shit about being bitter. Unless you've walked in my shoes and endured the pain I was forced to endure, unless you know what it's like to spend three years of your life sleeping with your fuckin' eyes open, unless you have a tilted uterus because a grown-ass man liked stuffing his big dick in little girls, don't open your mouth to say shit to me about forgiveness. An eye for an eye, a tooth for a tooth.

Every day, a child is being beaten, tortured, or killed by a caregiver. Please, tell me why? Well, I will never stand by and let anyone abuse a child. I will never turn my head or close my eyes and ears to the pain of a child. I'm sorry I just can't. I won't. And anyone who does…well, let's just say your day is coming too.

18

CHYNA: **BITTERSWEET**

THE PAST TWO MONTHS HAVE BEEN EMOTIONALLY DRAINING for everyone. The whole incident with Sarina opened up a chapter of my past I spent most of my life trying to forget— my life back in New Orleans. Sadly, I've been guilty of trying to disown my past and parts of my family history. I really thought I could go through life acting as if that part of me never existed. But it does and knowing my daughter has been affected by it reminds me of that. If I had been honest from the beginning about my family history, maybe I could have prevented all of this. Sarina would have gotten the proper help she needed a long time ago.

Two weeks after the beating incident with Sarina, she began to emotionally deteriorate. She gradually became withdrawn, noncommunicative, and unconcerned about her hygiene, or appearance. She stopped bathing and changing her clothes. That was bad enough, but when I walked in her bedroom and found her hiding naked under her desk screaming, "They're trying to kill me!" my life in New Orleans flashed before my eyes. I knew then something was terribly wrong. We had to have an ambulance come out to the house to transport her to the E.R. She yelled at, kicked and bit anyone who tried to touch her. It took two EMTs and four police officers to restrain her. After going over insurance information and filling out forms, it took one and a half hours before we were seen by a triage nurse. I'm sure it would have taken longer if Sarina hadn't started cursing and shrieking at the top of her lungs, "I can't stand this fucking shit! What the fuck are these sick bitches staring at!" She made such a scene that security immediately escorted us to one of the padded rooms for the mentally distressed. Finally, after waiting another three hours for the psychiatrist, she was screened and determined to be in need of inpatient treatment. The sad thing is, there were no adolescent psychiatric beds available in the state. We spent almost twenty-one hours waiting for a bed to open. My mind raced with questions. On the one hand, we were relieved to have some kind of diagnosis for our daughter; but on the other hand, it was hard to digest. I don't think any parent wants to hear that their child has an emotional or mental illness.

"Mr. and Mrs. Littles," the short doctor said in his thick Indian accent, "your daughter has symptomology indicative of a manic-depressive episode with psychotic features." He explained how her decreased need for sleep, her dramatic mannerisms and flamboyant style, her reckless and impulsive behaviors, and her racing thoughts were symptoms associated with the disorder. Her physical aggression and delusional thinking comprised the psychotic dimensions of the illness. All of this information was too overwhelming for Ryan and me to absorb at once.

"So what you're really saying is, our daughter is dangerous?" Ryan asked, holding his head in his hands.

"No, what I'm saying is, until we can get your daughter stabilized via medication, she does continue to present a threat to herself and others." The doctor spoke in a reserved tone while glancing over at me. "Given the family history, I'd also like a further evaluation to rule out a schizo-affective disorder."

"Schizo? What are you saying, doc? You think my daughter's crazy?" Ryan asked defensively.

"I don't like the term *crazy*," the doctor said as he removed his round glasses. "Your daughter could have a brain disease that causes a severe disorganization of thought and feeling. But I'd like to do further tests to rule it out. With adolescents, it's hard to tell exactly what's going on because many of the behaviors they exhibit can mimic more than one disorder. I believe, many times, adolescents are misdiagnosed. I would like to be sure of what's affecting Sarina so that we can prescribe the proper medications."

Ryan closed his eyes and shook his head in disbelief. He was truly confused. I grabbed his hand, glanced over at the doctor, then lowered my head. Ryan patted my hands with his, then got up from his chair and walked over to the huge bay window, where he stood staring out for a few moments.

He turned toward the doctor. "How? Why?" Ryan asked, searching for any sign of error on his face.

"Well," the doctor said, rubbing his chin. "There is mounting scientific evidence that suggests some people who develop mood disorders may have a genetic or hereditary predisposition toward it. And, just like mood disorders, schizophrenia and other psychotic disorders tend to run in families."

"Then there's some kind of mistake," Ryan said, looking hopefully over at me. "Neither of us has any mental illnesses in our families."

I shifted my eyes, then turned my head. The severity of Sarina's episode had compelled me to break down finally and confide my past to the doctor hours earlier. But I still hadn't mustered the courage to tell my husband. How could I tell him he was married to a woman who had a family history of psychiatric illness? How could I tell him I watched my grandmother mentally deteriorate until she was placed in a psychiatric institution? How could I tell him my own mother killed herself? What would he think of me?

"Um, Ryan," I said, trying not to let guilt overwhelm me. "I think we need to talk." I stared at the doctor with pleading eyes, silently thanking him for having opened the door to this inevitable conversation. "Dr. Zahar, can you excuse us for a moment?"

"Sure," he said, looking over at Ryan, then turning his attention to me. He smiled and nodded. "I'll leave the two of you in here while I do my rounds." He got up from his desk, then quietly closed the door behind him.

"Chyna, what's wrong?" Ryan asked while he took my hands and held them in his. "You look like you're on the verge of tears."

"Ryan, all of this is my fault."

"What do you mean?" he asked, staring me into my eyes.

"I haven't been honest with you about my family history. I never told anyone until this morning...when Dr. Zahar kept asking me..." I kissed him on his lips, then lowered my head. I couldn't look at him while I spoke. "Ryan, out of shame and embarrassment, I've been denying the mental health history of my family. Now I realize that not being completely honest has prevented Sarina from receiving the proper help. A lot of her opposition could have been better understood if I had just shared with everyone the fact that manic depression and schizophrenia run in my family."

I'm not sure why I became so emotional, but before I knew it, I had burst into tears. Ryan got up from his seat and placed his arms around me.

"My grandmother was a paranoid schizophrenic," I continued between deep breaths and heavy tears. "The reason I was sent to live with my aunt Chanty in Norfolk was because she was committed to a psychiatric hospital, where she stayed until she died." Ryan thought I moved to Norfolk because my grandmother died of cancer. But the truth is, she was severely mentally ill. She ran out of the house in the nude with a butcher knife, chasing her husband. When he tripped and fell, she stabbed him repeatedly in his neck and chest while yelling, "You killed my baby! You killed my baby! The prophet has come and you must die." The whole neighborhood watched as she was dragged away by the cops, laughing hysterically at the sight of her husband's blood on her hands. Two days later, my bags were packed and I was sent to live with Chantille, who decided it was best no one knew the truth because "folk will talk." So the truth and the secrets stayed within the family.

For the first twelve years of my life, I thought my grandmother and grand-father were my parents. I had spent those years in a glass bubble, sheltered from life because "we will be assassinated if you go outside." The curtains and windows were never opened, and the doors were always dead-bolted with eight locks. I watched my grandmother walk around the house mumbling and having conversations with herself and, sometimes, hiding under the kitchen table. She wore white gloves and face masks because "the air burns my face and hands." I saw her burn candles, chant, and pace around with voodoo dolls. I saw her bite into the necks of chickens for their blood. I watched her go into fits of rage, slashing the air with butcher knives because "the darkies" were after her. I had to live in a house of darkness, void of emotion and affection, where the atmosphere was thick with utter fear and bitterness. It wasn't until my move to my aunt's that the threads of our family secrets were unraveled. My grandmother, Lucretia, was married to a man who spent his time drinking scotch and staring at young girls. Together, they spent their lives belittling and berating each other for their past indiscretions. He was her third husband.

At age fourteen, she was married to a young, wealthy, French-Indian businessman as part of an arrangement. From this union, there were two daughters, Amelia and Chantille. However, her heart belonged to her nineteen-year-old lover and distant cousin, Pierre, with whom she continued liaisons while her husband was away on business trips. When he found her in bed with her young lover, he shot him in the back of the head as she lay under him, then he turned the gun on himself. It turned out, she and Pierre had conceived twin daughters, Sierra and Celine, whom she secretly gave birth to, then gave away to a distant relative. They were never spoken of or seen again. Unfortunately, my grandmother never recovered emotionally or mentally from the loss of her lover and her husband, and as a result, she self-medicated her guilt and shame with tranquilizers and vodka.

At twenty-one, Lucretia's second marriage was to Felippe Cousteau, and of this union, three more daughters were born, Cypress, Felicianna, and Emily. However, after twelve years of marriage, her newfound happiness ended in tragedy when her firstborn was killed. Felippe ran Amelia over with his car because she had eloped with and gotten pregnant by a dark-skinned man. "No coons are welcome in this family," he yelled in French out the window of his car as he drove forward and backward over her body, twice. She was eight months' pregnant. Incidentally, he committed suicide by tying a rope around his neck, then jumping off the roof of their house.

Eight years later, Lucretia married her third husband, Emerson Devereaux. But again, she was eventually faced with tragedy. Her youngest daughter, Emily, by this time a twenty-year-old, blue-eyed, blonde-haired manic-depressive, secretly gave birth to a daughter in her bedroom, then killed herself two hours later. She took to her grave the shame of having a four-year sexual relationship with her stepfather. Emily was my mother and Emerson was my father.

Between sobs, I confided all this to Ryan. When I was done, I didn't dare look in his eyes. But Ryan was immediately supportive. "Chyna, sweetheart," he said, hugging me, then lifting my chin. "What happened in your family is not your fault. Every family has their share of secrets."

"I know," I muttered, trying to catch my breath. "But secrets can tear a family apart."

"The important thing is, Sarina's going to get the help she needs now," he coaxed in an effort to alleviate the guilt that was written all over my face. "Everything is going to be alright."

"Ryan, I truly hope so," I said while he wiped my tears with his hands. "Because I chose to be dishonest, our daughter has suffered. Because I withheld important family history, our child has been deprived of appropriate intervention. Because of my denial, I almost beat our child to death—just because I didn't want to accept the possibility that maybe she had the family disease. I hoped and prayed she was just confrontational and not mentally ill."

The whole ordeal made me realize how important it is for people to be completely honest with one another about their family backgrounds. I have learned that parents have a responsibility to share pertinent medical histories when seeking help for their children. How can we expect our children to be honest when we can't be?

Three weeks ago, Sarina was released from the hospital, and she's in much better spirits. Although she still has that feisty edge, she's not as impulsive and she's much calmer and more open with Ryan and me. The doctors indicated her prognosis is good as long as she takes her prescribed medications and continues in individual therapy. We are extremely hopeful that she will be able to lead a healthy and productive life.

For the first time, Sarina and I have been able to talk about her anger and resentment toward me. I never knew she felt neglected by me. Even though I was always there for her, she still felt as if my attention and energy were focused on her three brothers. She knew I loved her, but she still felt I favored them over her because of their fair skin. Our family sessions gave her the opportunity to vent her pent-up anger. As her mother, I needed to hear her pain. And I knew I needed her to understand my history if I was ever going to build a stronger relationship with her. If I wanted us to heal, I needed to be honest.

"Sarina, sweetheart," I said, "I just assumed you wouldn't have to struggle with identity issues because there would be no question as to who you were based on your skin tone. I assumed you would grow up being proud of the color of your skin because I was. You were born my beautiful black daughter. And I knew you would grow into a beautiful black woman, strong and self-assured. Subconsciously, you were who I wanted to be."

"But I never felt beautiful," Sarina replied. "No matter how many times you said I was, I never felt it. I would see you and my brothers and wonder where I fit in. I wanted to be light-skinned with light eyes and straight hair too. I wanted to be you. Anytime my friends saw you, they'd question if you were my real mother or they'd want to know your race. Anytime they saw my brothers, they'd say, 'You don't look *anything* like them.' I never took that as a compliment. It felt like an insult, and that hurt me."

"I'm so sorry, Sarina," I said sincerely but calmly, trying my best not to get emotional. "I never meant to make you feel unsupported or abandoned. I always thought I was being attentive to your emotional needs. But now I see that I let my own racial insecurities prevent me from accepting the possibility that you would experience more negative feelings about your identity than your brothers."

"I felt rejected by you because of all the extra attention you gave them. I felt like you rejected me because I was dark-skinned."

The truth of the matter is, I did focus more on her brothers. Not because I favored them, but because I didn't want them going through life feeling the way I did. I didn't want them to be confused about who they were like I was. I felt I needed to ensure they would develop into strong men who were proud of their black heritage. I didn't want them to be ridiculed by peers the way I was. And, if they were, I wanted them to be able to handle the cruel remarks. I didn't want their souls to be dampened by sadness and insecurities because they couldn't feel connected to any ethnic group.

In New Orleans, I was like everyone else in my school. Light or white. But in Norfolk, I was different. I was fascinated by the many different shades of beautiful, black skin people were born with, the many different hair textures. I felt like an outsider. Most of my peers disliked me because of my fair skin, green eyes, and long hair. I was called "pale face" and referred to as the "white girl look-alike" by the darker-skinned girls. The brown-skinned girls would snicker and roll their eyes when I walked by. The light-skinned girls acted extremely snotty and uppity. I didn't want to be a part of that "I'm better than you because I'm light-skinned" clique. So I spent my junior high school years feeling alienated and, eventually, began to despise the color of my skin.

"Aunt Chanty, why are people so mean?" I used to ask with tears in my eyes.

"Honey, wherever you go, whatever you do, you will run into people who are filled with prejudices and hatred. And it will hurt. But don't let ignorant remarks make you ashamed of who you are."

"But that's the problem. I don't know who I am or who I'm supposed to be. Back home, I was expected to act white and be white. Here, I want to be black, but I don't know how."

"I know, baby, I know," my aunt said while she held me in her arms and gently rocked me. She understood my pain and felt my sorrow because she too grew up feeling alienated and isolated by her family and peers. She knew what it was like to be an outsider and the victim of cruel insults. Her stepfather, Felippe, favored her sister over her because she was born a shade darker than her fair-skinned, almost-white sister. And he blamed Chanty for Amelia's elopement with a black man because "she wouldn't have run off with some darkie if you didn't look so black and ugly." He beat her with his words and his fists until he took his own life. And not once did her mother, my grandmother, defend her, protect her, or make an attempt to rescue her from his verbal and physical abuse, all due to the color of her skin.

"I too felt confused at your age. Growing up in that house, most of us were."

"What was wrong with them accepting that they were black? Why was it so important for them to be anything other than black?"

"Baby, I wish I knew. I guess it stems from our history of being conditioned to think white is right and the lighter you are, the brighter life's opportunities. We were always supposed to be *better than* because of our lineage."

"Well, that's ridiculous."

"I know. But that's how it was. That's how it still is. But it doesn't have to be that way. Just follow your heart. That's why I left New Orleans and that sick, twisted thinking behind. That's a part of my past I never want to encounter again. I don't want my children growing up the way I did or feeling the way you do. Chyna, as light as you and I are, we are still black. It's a part of our roots. It's in our veins. No one can take that from you. And you don't have to ever prove your blackness to anyone."

"But, Aunt Chanty, I do. And I will always have to because of the color of my skin, the color of my eyes, and the texture of my hair."

"Chyna," she said sternly, "you listen to me and you listen good. You *are* black and you *are* beautiful. Hair, eyes, or skin color doesn't change that." She kissed me on my forehead, wiped my tears, and told me to never forget how beautiful I was. But in my eyes, I was ugly and I wanted desperately to look, act, and be black. The darker the better.

I saw black as beautiful. It didn't matter to me that the boys chased me with lust because I was "exotic." It didn't matter to me that I had the highest G.P.A. in the school. The only thing that mattered was being accepted by my peers as black. And when the darkest, the most beautiful, blackest boy made love to me, the only thing that mattered was my desire to have all of his blackness inside of me. At fourteen, I had hoped the juice from his dark berry would make me black as night. I had hoped having his babies would validate and solidify my blackness. With each pregnancy, I prayed for beautiful babies with rich dark skin. But I continued to feel hopelessly empty until I had Sarina. She represented and confirmed my blackness. Her birth made me feel black and beautiful.

"Sarina, sweetheart," I said as I embraced her. "I love you. And I am proud to be your mother. Skin color, eye color, and hair texture can never change that. You are my beautiful baby. You *are* black and beautiful. I am black and beautiful. And every shade of our blackness is beautiful. So, sweetheart, don't be ashamed of your beauty because I'm no longer ashamed of mine."

"I love you too, Mom." Hearing those three words from my daughter was music to my ears. With the fall of our tears, I felt real hope bloom that, as a family, we would be able to heal and that Sarina and I, as mother and daughter, would move forward in our relationship.

19

INDERA: **THE BIG PAYBACK**

"GOOD MORNING, WEAVES AND WONDERS. How may I help you?"

"Yes, I'd like to schedule an appointment for Tuesday with Alexi," a young woman said.

"I'm sorry. Alexi is no longer with us."

"What?" she snapped. "Well, how can I find her? I need my weave done for the Players' Ski Feast."

"I really don't know," I said. "But if you'd like, I can schedule you with another one of my weave technicians."

"Oh, no. Can't nobody work a weave like Alexi. Thanks but no thanks." *Click.*

Well, alrighty then, you bald-headed ho, I thought. *I guess you'll be going to the Ski Feast with a raggedy-ass weave, looking skied the fuck out.*

Anyway, for the past three months, it's been like this—nonstop calls from Alexi's customers. Oh, you didn't know either? Yes, I let Miss Thing know her services were no longer needed. In layman's terms, I fired her ass. Of course, when she went, so did her customers. Well, like I said, I don't care how many coins you bring in this shop, no one is gonna talk slick and think it's all good. Now, for the sake of business, I was gonna just let her slide for a minute, but when I stepped up in this piece and saw her in *my* office, sitting in *my* chair with her big-ass feet propped up on *my* desk, using *my* phone talking shit about me, that was the last straw. I just quietly stood in the doorway, listening to her conversation.

"Please. I don't know when Miss Indy is coming back and I don't care. She walks in and out of here like she's the fucking queen of England. …Mmm-hmm…I know. But, I'm not the one, see. …Oh, please, I'll do a switchblade sammie on her ass… That's right… Ooooh, now you tryna be *fieeeeerce*, girl. Please. I'll slice and dice that fish right on up. Catch it! She can try it on my time, if she wants, but you know I am not the one. …Chile, listen, that bitch can't even do hair, okay? And she's tryna give fever. Humph. Well, she's lucky I didn't stomp her ass a few months ago when she tried to get fierce. …Uh-huh, I wish she would… Mmm-hmm… Get caught? Chile, please. I've been milking this cow for months. The bitch has more money than she knows what to do with. …I'm too slick. …Don't worry. Well, lovey, *ciao!* Kiss, kiss." *Click.*

So not only was she talking shit, but the bitch was stealing from me. You know she had it coming. 'Cause there's one thing I can't stand and that's some thievin'-ass transvestite, okay? I tiptoed over to her workstation, took off my jewelry, laced my Nikes up real tight, pulled a stocking cap over my hair, then sat in her chair. I was glad the shop was dark and everyone was gone. *I'm gonna give you a nice royal greeting*, I thought as I waited for her.

"Aaah!" she screamed when she walked out of my office and over to her workstation. "Who's that?"

"It's the fucking queen of England," I snapped as I jumped out of her chair and flicked the lights on. Her face was cracked. "What the fuck were you doing in my office, peasant?!"

"I was—"

"Uh-uh," I said while I opened a big jar of Vaseline and smeared a glob of it over my face and neck. "So you thought you could steal from me and not get caught? Oh, no, bitch. It's about to get real ugly up in here."

"Fuck it then," she snapped. "It's about time you get a real down-home ass beating," she said while she took off her earrings, kicked off her shoes, then charged at me.

I took my fighting stance and it was on. We were both ducking, dodging, and blocking jabs and punches. Homegirl swung a right hook that landed on the left side of my head, and then she followed that with a left hook to the right side. "Take that, bitch. I'm gonna fuck your ass up." *Punch!*

"Oh yeah, you big bitch? Don't talk about it, be about it," I said, then decided it was time to whup her ass. But Miss Thing punched me in the jaw. Wrong move, okay? She came at me with a right swing; I ducked, then hit her in her ribs with a one-two punch. She buckled but then, somehow, knocked the shit out of me. My lip swelled. That's when I went off. I went into my *Kung-Fu, Get Christy Love,* Coffy Brown moves. I kicked her in her chest, kneed her in her nuts, then slung her ass from one side of the shop to the other. We tossed this motherfucker up, okay?!

"You wanna talk shit, bitch, and think I'm gonna let some chick with a dick beat *my* ass in my shop? *I think not!*" I yelled as I swung her into one of the large wall mirrors. I threw her ass into walls, then started yelling and screaming for help and throwing shit around the shop like she was tryna kill me. Miss Honey was a big bitch and I knew it was gonna take a lot of work to bring her down. But the bigger they are, the harder they fall.

"Get the fuck off me, you crazy bitch!" she yelled, then bit me until I let go of her. Her eyes got real big and she started talking like some possessed demon. "I'm gonna fuck you up real good," she snarled in a deep, manly voice with blood around her mouth. And this time when she came at me, she had a box cutter in her hand. "You stinkin' bitch!"

When she slashed my arm, I snapped and everything else became a blur. All I know is, minutes later, I was being hauled off in handcuffs and she was being rushed to the ER. See, I couldn't let that fifty-foot bitch beat my ass. When she pulled out that cutter on me, did she really think I was gonna let her get her shit off? Well, it backfired on her ass. Every time she looks in the mirror, she'll see her permanent happy face and think of me. That's right. Since she-male was feelin' a little slicey-dicey, I cut that bitch from ear to ear with her own work. Since she wanted to attack me like an Amazon warrior, I gave her sixty-seven stitches of permanent battle carvings across her face and forehead. You wanna talk shit, you talk shit. But don't step up in my face. And if you're gonna pull a weapon out, you either use it or lose it. Lord knows, if the police hadn't come in when they did and pulled me off of her, I would have killed her.

To make matters worse, I'm charged with aggravated assault and possession of a weapon. Can you believe that shit? She came at me, and I'm the one charged for protecting myself! I've never heard such crazy shit in my life. And these stinkin' pig-ass cops had the nerve to tell me I should have called them instead of taking matters into my own hands. Yeah, okay. In the meantime, I woulda been cut the fuck up. So we'll just go to court. I'm not pressed. I got one powerhouse lawyer who will work circles in the court-room. And if he can't, I'll just have to go into my trick bag. 'Cause I've got a lot of dirt on a few of our fine D.A.'s and a few judges. It's nothing personal. It's all about being politically correct, okay?

Anyway, between you and me, last month I called my peoples from the Boogie-Down (the Bronx, that is) and made sure Miss Finger-Snapping Alexi was taken care of. That's right. Like I told you before, I am very well connected, okay? So don't ever think you're gonna steal from me and be able to brag about it. Oh, I know you didn't think me cutting her was gonna be it. Please. The face-cutting was her punishment for pulling her cutter on me. The only way that bitch will *ever* be able to stitch another weave or work a pair of shears is with her teeth. She won't be finger-snappin' or stealin' from anyone else 'cause I made sure all ten of that bitch's fingers were cut off at the knuckles. *Now, finger-snap that*, I thought when I got the call that the mission was complete. Let's see how fierce Miss Knuckles is now. And if she ever opens her mouth to talk slick again, I'm gonna see to it that her tongue is cut the fuck out, too.

Yeah, this cow has a real nice surprise for anyone else who thinks they're gonna milk me.

For three weeks now, I've had this strange feeling that someone has been following me. It's bad enough that someone has been calling the shop and hanging up. But to be stalking me? Now, that's a bit much.

At first, someone was calling on my private line, breathing heavy and shit, then hanging up on me. So I shut 'em down by changing the number. Now someone is tryin' it on the business line.

"Hello. Weaves and Wonders."

"Indera," a deep, muffled voice said. "You better watch your back."

"And you betta watch yours," I said while I rubbed polish remover over my silver-painted fingernails.

"I'm gonna get you, you crazy bitch!"

"Don't talk about it, be about it," I snapped, then slammed down the phone. I called my homegirl down at the phone company and gave her the scoop. I'm gonna have that ass tracked the fuck down. The minute that number is traced, it's on. Please, motherfuckers can't spook me. Whatever's gonna happen will just have to happen. But it's not like I'm gonna be sleepin' on it. Hell, I know I've shitted on a lot of heads; so it's only natural someone would want to turn the tables. But what these bitches betta recognize is that I can give it and I can take it. So whatever goes around will just have to come around. Point-blank.

20

CHYNA:
IF MY SISTER'S IN TROUBLE SO AM I

ALL DAY I HAD AN EERIE FEELING THAT SOMETHING WASN'T RIGHT, but I just couldn't put my finger on it. By the time I finally drifted off to sleep, the uneasiness had settled in the pit of my stomach. When the phone rang at 1:00 a.m., I knew something was terribly wrong. It seems like the phone always has a distinct ring when tragedy is near. When I answered, I thought I had fallen into a dark hole. I heard the voice, but it seemed to fade in and out with the echoes of the screams in my head.

"Hello, this is Detective Procter from the NYPD. May I speak to Mrs. Chyna Littles?" the deep voice asked.

I sat up in my bed and turned the lamp on. "Speaking," I said as my heart pounded in my chest. "This is Chyna Littles."

"Mrs. Littles," he said with authority, "I'm sorry for calling so late. But there's been an accident. You've been identified as an emergency contact for Indera—"

"Oh my God," I gasped. "What happened?"

"I'm sorry to have to tell you this over the phone, but Ms. Fleet's been shot."

"*Noooooooooo!*" I yelled with the rapid fall of tears. "Oh, dear God, please tell me it isn't so. There must be some kind of mistake."

"I'm sorry. I wish there were."

"*Nooooooooo!* Oh, dear God, *nooooo!*"

I was so hysterical when Ryan ran into the bedroom that he had to take the phone to find out who was on the other end. He spoke to the detective and got all the information. Indera had been rushed to Columbia Presbyterian Hospital. She had been shot and was listed in critical condition. Shot? In critical condition? I couldn't believe it. I refused to believe it. Ryan tried to console me, but I just screamed and cried uncontrollably. I needed to be on the next plane. I needed to be by my sister's side. Ryan made the necessary flight arrangements while I tried to pull myself together. I just couldn't. I prayed I'd get there in time. Before...oh my God! *Brit. Someone's got to call Brit*, my mind cried. But Ryan was already on the phone with him.

BRITTON:

My mind raced with questions when I got the call from Ryan. *Who? Why?* There was no time for tears. I needed to get off this island. Even if I had to swim or hop a ride on a dolphin, I needed to be there with my homegirl. The only thing that mattered was helping Indy get through this. Whatever it took, for however long, I was gonna be by my friend's side. I only hoped she would still...I couldn't think the worst. "Please, God," I begged. "Let my homegirl pull through this. Don't let me get there too late." *Oh, shit, she's there in that hospital alone in critical condition., Tee. Call Tee.* I picked up the phone but couldn't remember the number. I couldn't think. My mind was too consumed with worry.

CHYNA:

By the time I finally arrived at the hospital, I was sick with worry and my eyes were swollen and red. The minute I stepped off the elevator, I spotted Tee. He was talking to a short, stocky man.

"Mr. Miles," the man said while putting on his thick round glasses and flipping through his pocket-sized notepad. "We're doing our best to track down her assailant, but currently we have no leads. Is there any reason why you think someone would want to shoot her?"

"How the hell would I know what crazy shit goes through people's minds?" Tee snapped. "This fuckin' world is full of crazy-ass...look, I just want whoever did this to her found. I don't care what the cost. I want them found."

The man nodded. "We'll do our best."

When Tee spotted me, he excused himself away from the detective, then greeted me with a worried smile. The kind of smile that tells you everything isn't alright. His eyes were red.

"Tee," I said as we embraced. "Where's Indy? How is she?" He looked away, then lowered his head and closed his eyes. "Oh my God…"

"Indy's in a coma," he said as he wiped a tear from his eye.

"Coma?" I repeated. "Oh dear Lord. How? Why?" He indicated she had severe swelling of the brain due to being beaten in the head with a blunt object. Why would anyone be so cruel? Yes, she's done some unkind things to people, but she's never tried to kill anyone. She's never intentionally gone out of her way to hurt anyone.

Tee gave me another hug. "They had to do emergency surgery," he said in a whisper. "So she's still in critical condition." He explained that the police found her unconscious at her shop. Somehow, her silent alarm was triggered, which prompted them to respond. There didn't appear to be any signs of forced entry or a struggle. Indy had been shot three times—twice in the chest and once in the abdomen. The bullets to her chest had just missed her heart, she had a ruptured spleen and both of her lungs had collapsed.

"Take me to her," I said as I tried to hold back tears. We embraced again, then headed toward her room. As soon as I walked into her room, a flood of tears fell from my eyes. I couldn't believe what I saw. Indy was hooked up to a respirator and heart monitor. There were I.V. tubes running through her arm and her head was bandaged in white gauze. Her face was swollen. She looked to be in tremendous pain. I grabbed her hand and just cried.

"Do you know when Britton will be here?" I asked Tee with my back to him.

"I'm not sure," Tee answered, handing me a tissue. "He was having trouble getting a flight."

BRITTON:

Seeing Indy lying in that hospital bed hit really hard. If there were anything I could have done to be in her place I would have done it. But there wasn't, and that tore me up inside. It took three days for her vitals to improve. Although she was in stable condition, she still wasn't out of the woods. She was still in a coma, and as long as she was there was the possibility of brain damage. A part of me wanted to be angry. But with whom? I didn't want to mentally exhaust myself being angry at some faceless fool. I just wanted my Indy back.

"You alright, Tee?" I asked, watching him pace the floor, then stare out of the eleventh-story window. "Why don't you go home and get some rest. You look exhausted."

"I can't," he said in between deep breaths. "I'm not leaving this hospital until I know she's alright."

"Tee, Brit's right," Chyna said. "You have to get some rest. At least for a couple of hours."

"I said I'm not leaving," he snapped. And he didn't.

"Brit," Chyna said. "Do you think Indy knows we're here?"

"I'm sure she does," I said while I rubbed her face, then kissed her on the forehead. "Indy knows everything."

Although we smiled, our hearts were filled with pain. I've always believed what goes around comes around. Even though Indy may have never pulled the trigger of a gun to hurt anyone, she carried around a heart loaded with vengeance. She would bitterly aim at anyone who had hurt her. But, in the end, we all have a price to pay for what we do to others. Regardless of how we justify our actions, somewhere down the line it comes back to haunt us. Still in all, it didn't seem fair. The only thing any of us could do was pray and that is what we did. Every chance we got, we prayed for our beautiful friend. We hummed her favorite songs. We relived times we shared with her. We did anything we could to generate enough positive, healing energy to revive her spirit. If nothing else, we had the power of prayer and love on our side.

CHYNA:

Britton and I each took shifts staying at the hospital while the other rested at a nearby hotel. Tee never left. He had the nurses put another bed in Indy's room. He wanted to make sure he was there when she opened her eyes. He just sat in a chair next to her bed, holding her lifeless hand while he spoke to her. Every day he bought her fresh white roses. No matter how bleak the situation seemed, we held on to hope.

My goodness, news travels. I made three calls to a few sorority sisters who live in the area, and within hours, Indera's hospital room was filled with beautiful bouquets, plants, balloon arrangements, and telegrams from across the country. I knew she was well known, but I truly had no idea to what extent. Within two days, she had over eighty visitors. I think Britton and Tee were just as touched and overwhelmed as I was. But what really touched us was when a young girl walked in.

"Excuse me," Britton asked the young girl standing in the doorway with tears in her eyes. "Are you lost?" She shook her head as she walked toward Indy's bed. "Are you looking for someone?"

"No, I found her," she said as she scooted around Tee. "Excuse me, mister." Tee turned around to Brit and me with a puzzled look on his face. When Tee moved out of her way, she rubbed Indy's hand, then asked Tee to pick her up so she could kiss her on her forehead. Tee lifted her up by the waist so she could plant gentle kisses, the kind of kisses a little girl gives to someone she's close to.

"Excuse me, sweetheart," I said while staring over at Tee, then Britton. "Are you sure you're in the right place?"

"I'm not 'sweetheart,'" she said very articulately. "My name is Ayana."

Britton and Tee looked at me. Britton smirked. "Oh, I'm sorry," I said. "Well, Ayana, how old are you?"

"I'm six," she said proudly with her little hand on her hip. Her fingernails were painted pink. "And I wish they'd hurry up."

"Who?" I asked.

"Them," she said, pointing in back of us. And in marched a small army of twenty girls ranging in age from six to sixteen, carrying flowers, teddy bears, homemade cards, and banners that read: We LOVE you! your little Sorors. Little Sorors? I smiled when I realized who they were. They were there to see their mentor, their drill instructor, and teacher. Many of them had lost their mothers to death, drugs, or prison, but these victims of circumstance had a chance for a brighter future thanks to people like Indy. They were there to see one of the few adults in their lives whom they trusted and who gave them a chance to be children. Indy sponsored this group of young ladies.

She taught them dance and piano for free, and she sent them away for the summer to Camp Safe Haven, a private camp she operates in upstate New York. She is their mentor, their role model, their friend.

BRITTON:

I tried so hard not to fall apart. But when those beautiful young girls came into Indy's room, made a semicircle around her bed, held hands, then said a silent prayer, I knew it was only a matter of time before I released a flood of tears. When little Ayana spoke, she shook all of our hearts.

"Miss Indy," she said in her gentle voice, "please don't leave us. What will we do without you? We wrote a poem called 'What Do We Do?' I hope you like it." She opened her little pink backpack and pulled out a little green notebook. When she found her page, she cleared her throat, looked around the room, then began:

What do we do when we're deprived of childhood years,
When we're denied comfort when filled with fears?
What do we do when we're longing for a motherly smile or a gentle touch,
When we're lacking the love we need so much?

What do we do when we're forced to do things beyond control,
When loneliness begins to eat our souls?
What do we do when we want to cry but don't know how,
When we're told to wait when we want it now?

What do we do when we're pushed aside,
When pain feels like a knife inside?

Miss Indy, what do we do?
We come to you.
You make us feel loved and special.
Miss Indy, you are our guardian angel.

You give us hope,
And we don't know what we'd do without you.
Miss Indy, don't leave us.
We love you.

When she finished, she tore the poem out of her notebook, neatly folded it, then laid the white paper across Indy's chest. "Please, don't leave us," she whispered. And, after a powerful prayer asking for strength to love our enemies and to pray for those who persecute us, we hugged and cried and found comfort in the love we all shared for Indy.

21

INDERA:
DON'T LET THE SUN COME DOWN ON ME

*S*omeone, *please get these bricks off my chest. I can't breathe. It hurts. Oh, please stop this pain. What happened? Oh my God! I've been shot. That fool really pulled the trigger. Where am I? Why are all these people here? Why is everyone crying? Oh, Lord, please don't tell me…Am I dead, or am I dying? Whether it's heaven or hell, Lord, please…not yet. My hair and face are a mess. Please stop all that crying and screaming. I can't take it. Please.*

Oh, no…Who brought all my babies here? Get them out of here. I don't want them seeing me like this. Please, babies, don't cry. Oh, God please…Please, not yet. I need to give my girls one last heart-to-heart. I need to tell them not to hold on to their anger. To learn to let go. I want them to know that there are responsible and caring adults who will love them and protect them. I need to let them know it's okay. Everything's gonna be alright. Please, God, please watch over these sweet, innocent girls. Help them with their pain. Please let them know it's not their fault. Please protect them from the vultures of the world who prey on children. Oh, Lord… Please wipe their tears. Get them out of here. My precious babies….Hold your heads up, always be proud of who you are, and never let anyone tell you you're nothing. You are someone. You are special. Please, Lord, don't let anyone steal any more of their dreams. Please don't let anyone else rob them of their chances for happiness. Children deserve a chance. Please give them a chance to live safe and be loved. Oh, not yet please…don't let any more children suffer from the ills of…that's right, get them out of here. They've suffered enough loss in their lives. I love you all. Please know I'll always be your guardian angel.

Oh, Britton, please don't cry. Please. It's gonna be alright. Oh, Lord, I don't think I'm gonna make it. I feel myself slipping. I'm slowly slipping. Please, not yet. I forgot to tell Britton what a good friend he's been to me. I need him to know that out of all the men who have come in and out of my life, he has always been there for me. He has always been the one person I can count on. He's always the first to call and the last to leave my side. Through the most difficult times in my life, he gave me encouragement and helped me be stronger. Through the good times and the bad, he's always been there without judgment, without questions, and without conditions. I need him to know that he was the one who restored my faith that there really are good men out there. I love the man that you are and the man you'll always be. I love you, Britton. Please don't cry. Thanks for always being what every friend should be. Thank you for always loving me.

Chyna, please, girl. Your makeup. Please don't cry. Oh, Chyna...please, girl, please. It'll be okay, I promise. God, please let it be alright. Thank goodness Ryan is here with her. Ryan? Thank God she has someone special in her life to love. Chyna, I'm so happy for you. Please! I need to let my sister know how much she has meant to me. I need her to know how much I appreciate her. I need her to know how precious her friendship is to me. I need her to know how her smile and pep talks always made a difference in my day. There were times she gave when no one else did. She's always stuck with me through thick and thin. I want her to know how lucky I've been to have a sister as wonderful as her. I need her to know how much I love her. Chyna, girl...my soror, my bestest friend, my sister in heart and soul. Thank you for always lending me your shoulder to lean on and your ear to bend. The special times we've shared will remain in my heart and mind forever. You'll always be a part of my life. A part of my spirit. I love you. Please don't cry.

Oh, God, please...not yet. Please don't let me slip into darkness. Please don't take me. Not yet. Please give me a chance to tell Tee how proud I am of him. I need to let him know how much I admire his strength. I need to let him know that I believe in him. I need to let him know that I understand...Please...not yet. Oh, my heart is getting weaker. Everything is fading. ...Oh, Lord, please not yet. Please, Tee... don't...please don't cry. I didn't know. I'll meet you on the moon. I'm not sure what we'll do when we get there, but I'll be there. Please know I've always wished I could ease your pain. I never tried because I figured only you knew what you needed to get through it. But I understand. Just know I've always wanted to be there for you.

Oh, Lord, please help my friends. Please wipe away their tears. Let them know it's gonna be okay. Please let it be okay…I wis… oh, Lord…I still have work to do. I still have business to tend to. Please, not yet. …I'm slipping. …Everything is fading. …It's getting darker. …Oh, Lord, please don't let the sun come down on me.

22

DAMASCUS: **THE ONLY ONE FOR ME**

Yo, I AM THE HAPPIEST MAN ALIVE. I finally feel like my life has purpose, and that shit feels good as hell. Seeing Indy unconscious hit me hard. I was at the hospital every day. I couldn't eat or sleep. My only focus was her. I prayed every day, something I haven't done since I was eight years old. But I asked God—no, I begged him. I promised him if he answered my prayers, I'd change my life. I'd live right and do right. And when Indy finally opened her eyes, the first thing she said was, "Oh, boy, please. Did you think I was gonna let a few bullets keep a bitch like me down? With a little cosmetic surgery, I'll be as fierce as ever." Instead of laughing, I cried. I never thought I, T-Bone the pussy bandit, would ever cry over a woman. But I did. I cried and cried and cried until my eyes swelled up and snot dripped from my nose. And I didn't give a fuck who saw. The only thing that mattered to me was knowing Indy was gonna be alright.

I knew then she was the only woman for me. I've been with a lot of women, but they were just blank faces. None of the pussy I've spanked has ever satisfied me. That's why I'd jerk my dick afterward. And the only face I would see was Indy's. She's always turned me the fuck on. I thought it was just sexual, but it runs much deeper. She stimulates me mentally and emotionally. I've never loved anyone in my life. Why should I? I never felt loved by anyone. When Britton said he knew just what I needed to change me, I wasn't sure what he meant then, but I'm more sure than ever now. I know what I need and who I need.

So last week I invited Indy over for dinner to lay my cards on the table.

Yeah, I cooked. Hold up, don't trip. Yo, my skills are up, don't sleep on the kid. I just never had anyone worthwhile to burn for. The table was set and the candles were lit. I served stuffed Cornish hens, fresh string beans, and whipped sweet potatoes. For dessert, we had a slammin' strawberry cheesecake. Nah, yo, I ain't even gonna front. I bought that at that little spot Veniero's over in the city. While we sipped the bottle of Cristal Indy brought with her, I handed her the keys to my heart.

"Yo, Indy, isn't there anything you want out of life that you don't already have?"

She placed her elbows on the white tablecloth, then picked up her flute. "I haven't really given it any thought," she said in between sips of champagne. "I've traveled the world, I'm financially stable, and I pretty much have everything I want. What about you?"

"I want Thanksgiving and Christmas dinners and a big-ass Christmas tree flooded with gifts," I said, staring at her. I smiled. "And I want you to be the mother of my kids." I thought she was going to choke on her drink. She set the champagne flute back on the table.

"Boy, you are so crazy," she said, trying to laugh it off, then twisted her face up when I didn't crack a smile. "You're joking, right?"

"Indy, don't you ever feel like there's something missing in your life?"

She shifted her eyes away from mine. "Not really. I can't miss something I've never had."

"Well, I can."

"And what's that?" she asked, taking another sip from her flute.

Our eyes met again. This time, I shifted mine and took a deep breath. For the first time in my life, I decided to be honest with myself. I lowered my voice. "Love," I said. "Everything else I have, had, or can go out and get, but I don't know what it's like to have love. I'd rather have love than all the chips I've stacked. I'd rather know I have someone in my corner than ride around in a fresh whip. I don't want to keep walking around with this loneliness. Life ain't shit without someone to share it with."

She rubbed my hand. "Tee, I love you," she said in a soft voice. "You do know that, right?"

"I'm not talking platonic love. I'm talking something much deeper. I never knew what love felt like until now," I said. I tried not to choke up, but I couldn't help myself. The tears came before I could check 'em at the gate. "I love you, Indy, and I'm in love with you. I've always loved you, but I didn't know it. I know it now. Seeing you in that hospital made me realize that. The thought of losing you overwhelmed me. Girl, I don't know what I'd do without you. I'm crazy about you. I want a chance to love you and be loved by you. I want you to have the key to my heart."

"Damn, that's deep," she said as she wiped my face with her hand. "Wow, that's really sweet, Tee. I never knew you felt like that."

"Well, you've never asked, and you've never given me a chance."

"I always thought you were just out to do you by any means necessary. I figured you just wanted some pussy."

"Check this out. I've knocked off over a hundred and sixty women tryna fill a void in my life. But you can't fill an empty heart with empty sex." I grabbed her hand, then kissed her palm. "I want more than just pussy from you. I want a life with you. What you see on the outside of a person isn't always what they are on the inside. You of all people should know that."

"You're right," she said in her sweet, sexy-ass voice. "I guess I misread you. And like they say, never judge a book by its cover."

"Indy, whether you want to admit it or not, I know you want the same things I want. I know you want someone to love you just as much as I do. I'm here for you, baby. I'm that someone to love you. I promise you, I won't let you down."

Yo, fuck that hard shit. Even brothas like me, who seem a little rough around the edges, are capable of loving. We just need someone to take a chance on us, to be patient with us, and to not give up on us. Brothas like me need someone who's gonna be committed to our struggles. Indy's a true soldier. She's been my motivation to get my shit together. I know she's the type of woman who's not gonna take bullshit from a brotha, and I like that. I know she's grounded and can hold her own. And as crazy as her ass is, I know she's good for me. I've studied her and I know what she wants in a man. I know what she needs in a man, and I'm ready to give it to her. Yo, I got my shit together. There's no more hustling, no more stripping, no more frontin'. I'm ready to commit myself to her, exclusively. Word up. From this day forward, I'm ready to step up and be the man she needs.

23

INDERA:
LOVE IS STRONGER THAN PRIDE

FOR THE FIRST TIME IN MY LIFE, I'M AFRAID. I'm afraid of the wonderful feeling stirring inside my heart. I'm afraid of opening up my heart and letting him in. I'm afraid of sharing my love. A love I never knew existed. This is all new for me. And, yes, Miss Indy is afraid. Okay, okay. I'll admit I've always been big on Tee. And, yes, I was shocked to hear how he really feels about me. But in many ways, he reminds me of my father. That's why I've always been hard on him. It was safer that way. It allowed me to keep a wall up between us, and to avoid any feelings beyond friendship that I might have considered. I don't want to end up like my mother. I don't want to close my eyes with a broken heart. I never imagined he'd lay his heart on the line like that. I never imagined he'd cry his heart out in front of me. I wanted so bad to lick his tears away, but I couldn't. Not yet. I need to be sure.

"If you want this sweet pussy," I'd said, "It's gonna cost you. First, respect. I want it. I demand it. And I deserve it. You will respect me as a woman. You will respect my strengths. You will respect my right to say no. You will respect your commitment to love me and only me. Second, trust. If there's no trust between us, then there can be no *us*."

"You got that," he said while trying to kiss me. I turned my head.

"I mean it. If you cheat on me, before I kick you to the curb, I'm gonna do a Chain-Saw Suzie on your ass." He laughed but I was serious. "I mean it, boy. If you try to get slick on me, I'm gonna kick your fuckin' chest in."

"Yeah, a'ight."

"I'm not playin' with you," I said, poking him in his head with my finger. "There will be no stripping, no chat rooms, no cybersex. You can look at other women, but if I catch you staring too hard or looking too long, I'm gonna Mace your ass, then claw hatchet your eyes out."

"Girl, go 'head with that," he said, still trying to kiss me. I pushed his lips away with my index finger, then stood up.

"Try it on my time, if you want, Damascus."

"Yo, that strippin' shit is dead. I'm not down with that chat room, cyber-sex shit, so that's out. And the *only* woman I need to look at or want to look at is you."

"Mmm-hmm," I said with my lips pursed and an eyebrow raised. "We'll see."

"What else?" he asked while walking over to me, then wrapping his thick arms around my neck.

"You say you want me, then you're gonna have to wait for me. There will be no suckin' or fuckin'," I said as I waved my fingers in his face, "until you put a rock on my hand. I'm not givin' away any of this sweet pussy milk until you buy the cow."

He looked at me for a moment, then smiled. "Damn, girl, no sex? Yo, you really pushin' it. I wanna test-drive that ass before I keep it," he said. He removed his arms from around my neck, then palmed my ass with his big hands. I slapped his hands off of me and stared him *down*. He got the hint.

"No diamond, no wedding… no pussy."

"Damn. A'ight. You got that. I don't know how, but you got that. Anything else?"

"Let me see," I said while I pondered for a moment. "Nah, I guess that's it for now. But I'll let you know when there's more."

"I'm sure you will," he said with a sigh, then he grabbed my hands and pulled me into him. "Dance with me."

"Dance with you? I don't hear any music," I said, pressing my body into his. The heat from his body made me melt like the candles on his table.

"Tonight, we're gonna make our own music." He started humming Luther Vandross's "Forever, For Always, For Love" in my ear. I let my crotch rest against his thigh. We smiled, then I rested my head on his chiseled chest. We did a nice, slow bump-and-grind until I felt my pussy trying to grab at his dick.

"So you gonna be mine or what?" he asked as his hands traveled along the small of my back, then over my ass, where they stayed.

"I'll think about it."

"Yeah, a'ight," he said while taking my right hand and placing it along the side of his inner thigh. "Hold on to this while you think about it."

His dick was hard. And his nasty ass didn't have on any underwear under those nylon pants. Did I feel the goods? You know that! Now, I'm not telling you nothing else about it. 'Cause I know how some women are. If I tell you how long and heavy it was, you'll be scheming on how you can get some. Not that I'll be mad at ya, 'cause I once knew a woman who'd sleep with somebody else's guy without blinking an eye. But she's changed her ways. Just know, if you do press and he goes for it, then you can have him—after I toss a bucket of potash on his ass! As you know, there's one thing I can't stand…well, you already know what that is.

"Don't think this is gonna make me change my mind," I said, stroking up and down over the length of his love stick. "I'm not givin' you shit."

"A'ight, I heard you. …Damn, girl," he said with his eyes closed. "Hmmm, damn, girl."

"You like that, Big Daddy?" I said while I talked real dirty in his ear. There's no need to spell it out since you already know how I like to get down. "You want this wet pussy?"

"Hmmm, damn, what you think?" he said in between moans and groans, while trying to keep his knees steady. That's right, I was yankin' and pullin', teasin' and rubbin', squeezin' and kneadin' every inch of him over his thin sweatpants. And, for the first time, I let his lips touch mine. They were soft and sweet. When his tongue touched mine, my extra-absorbent pantyliner caught my waterfall. Thank goodness, 'cause it woulda been a wet mess. I'll tell you this much: When I give up this love funk, the only thing this love snatch is gonna be able to grip again is a tennis ball. It won't be Calgon I'll need to take me away. It'll be a big-ass bag of Epsom salts.

I smiled, then squeezed the head of his juicy dick until the front of his pants leaked a puddle of love juice. When he kissed me and grunted, when his leg shook and the head of his dick swelled, I knew he was ready to pop that love nut. I smiled again, then bit his bottom lip real hard while I let go of his dick.

"Ooooouch!" he yelled while he placed his hand over his lip and tried to collect himself before he nutted all over the front of his pants. "Damn, girl. Why the hell you bite me?"

"That's for fuckin' up my damn hair," I said, then slapped him upside his head.

"Oooow!" He rubbed his head. "Damn. You know how long ago that was?" he snapped, then looked down at the large wet stain on his pant leg. "That's real fucked up."

"I told you I was gonna get you, now didn't I?"

"Yeah, a'ight. You got that," he said with a grin while pulling off his T-shirt and removing his wet pants. He looked down at his shiny, black dick. "So you gonna finish the job or what?"

"Nope," I said while I stared his smooth, chocolate body down. My pussy twitched. I took a deep breath and licked my lips. He stood in front of me butt-naked, looking scrumptious as hell. Girl, a sexy, chiseled Power Ranger. A Mandingo warrior. That's what he is.

"Oh, I see I'm gonna have to snatch your little ass up." He grabbed my hands again, then pulled me toward him.

I smiled. "Humph. We'll see." He pulled me closer into his rock-hard nude body then continued humming his song.

"So where you from?" he asked real low and sexy in my ear.

I smiled. "Brooklyn. And if you stick your tongue in my ear, I will slap the shit out of you." He pulled away from me for a moment; we smiled then pressed our bodies back together.

"Hmmm…that's nice," he answered. Then whispered in my ear: "Indy, I've been waiting all my life for you. I'm not gonna let you get away, ever. I wanna spend the rest of my life with you. Till death do us part, I wanna be the only man you'll ever need."

We kissed. Long, slow, passionate kisses. I closed my eyes while I swirled my tongue around his, until we met on the moon. We kissed and grinded until our bodies became one. We kissed until the gates of my heart opened. Between you and me, I'm gonna take it real slow and see where this thing leads us. "Thank you," I whispered, then felt tears of joy run down my face. Perhaps there'll be a forever, after all.

24

BRITTON: NEW BEGINNING

WITH THE TICK OF THE CLOCK AND THE CHANGE OF SEASONS, Father Time and Mother Nature danced in a whirlwind of surprises. One thing that holds true: never say never. Tee and Indy are engaged. Shocked? Well, that's an understatement. When they flew down here to share their news, I really thought it was some kind of joke. But the way they were hugging and kissing told me this was real. And seeing that big-ass rock he put on her hand put the icing on the cake. Her ring is the size of a boulder. He said, "The size of that ring is only a small measure of my love for her. Yo, B, I've finally bagged her, and I'm gonna spend the rest of my life expressing the depths of my love. This love here, boy, is forever." I smiled.

Of course, this wedding is going to be one of the most talked about social events in history. When Indy asked me to give her away, I burst out in tears. Who would have ever thought Indy and Tee would find true love right under their noses? Well, as the saying goes, there's a lid for every pot. Trust me, Indy is keeping a tight lid on hers. That poor Tee. Ooooh-wee. He really has his hands full. Then again, so does she. But they're happy; and that's all that really matters.

And check this out. There's been no sex. Indy made it very clear, "He's not even gonna smell this pussy until our wedding night. And then I'm gonna break his back." To tell you the truth, Tee doesn't know I peeped that book he was reading in D.R., *Bringing the Black Woman to Sexual Ecstasy*. I guess he knew he had better tighten his game up; 'cause, you know, if he's not on point, she's gonna blow his spot up. I laughed real hard. Seeing those two sex-crazed creatures with that glow of love is worth more than all the gold in the world.

Indy has decided to sell Weaves and Wonders. She wants to devote her time to teaching dance and piano and to spend more time at Nandi's Refuge, a crisis shelter she created three years ago for the victims of physical and sexual abuse. Her funding? The money her father has sent her over the years and private funds from "connections." She even sent for Pedro and his family to move to the States. "I wanna make sure Pedro is given the chance to pursue his dreams." That's my girl!

Unfortunately, they haven't found the person who shot her. But she said she's not worried about it right now. "Oh, trust me, he'll be found. But for now, I'm just gonna put it in prayer." Prayer? Now, this was coming from a woman who'd never turn the other cheek. But my gut told me she knew. 'Cause Miss Indy knows *everything*. I smiled. "I'm just happy to be alive," she said. We hugged. I was happy too.

And get this, Tee finished writing a book on his life and the struggles of being a young black man and has landed a contract with a major publishing company. Tee, a famous author? Picture that. Now, that makes me proud. Knowing where he's been in life, knowing what his struggles have been, and knowing the man he's become brings joy to my heart. So be on the lookout for the next best-seller: *The Young Brotha Behind the Mask* by Damascus Miles.

Chyna and Ryan are planning to renew their wedding vows next Valentine's Day. They've weathered twenty-three years together, and their love for each other is stronger than ever. In the midst of their family crisis, they found strength in each other and in prayer. The funny thing is Ryan wants another baby. But Chyna...well, she made it very clear that her days of changing diapers are over. "I've raised my children, and now, as Indy would say, 'I'm gonna do me.' I'm no longer gonna be knocked up or locked up. I'm taking control of my life." And that's exactly what Miss Chyna's doing. She's a big-time executive director of Soul Quests, a day treatment program that specializes in identity crisis issues faced by adolescents. She developed this clinical treatment program that will offer family, individual, and group therapy, art therapy, and crisis intervention in hope of helping children deal with racist attitudes among peers and within families. She believes that through self-love, self-pride, and respect, she can create a racial consciousness that will provide these kids with the necessary tools and resources to survive in a multicultural world. With counseling, mentoring, and cultural activities, she intends to help our youth develop positive self-images and increase their feelings of self-worth. She wants them to be proud of who they are, she wants them to love who they are, and, most important, to respect who they are. Next month, I'm flying home to hear her speak to the National Honor Society's School of Social Work Department at Howard University. You go, girl!

And me? Well, let's see. The biggest surprise was Lina showing up at my door. We hadn't seen each other since last November, and I hadn't spoken to her in over two months. She had been on my mind for weeks; so seeing her pretty smile brightened my day. Between you and me, I really missed her. But this time, she was different. Her breasts and face were fuller.

"Girl, where have you been?" I asked, giving her a big hug and kissing her on the cheek. "I've been worried about you."

"I've been around," she said nonchalantly, still embracing me. "I've missed you."

"So why haven't I heard from you? I thought you would have at least returned my calls."

She stared at me for a minute and smiled. "I've been meaning to call, but things have been really hectic for me."

"Too hectic to return a call?" I said with an attitude. "I can dig it. So what brings you to my door now? Did you forget something the last time you were here?"

"No, Brit," she said, walking toward the door, then waving for someone to come in. "I've been back and forth to the hospital for the past two months."

"The hospital?" I asked with concern. I tried to stay calm. The last thing I wanted to hear was that she had some kind of disease that I needed to get checked for. Because the truth of the matter is, I had been sick for three months; I was constantly nauseous, always throwing up, and always tired. No matter how much sleep I got, it never seemed like enough. It felt like the flu without the fever. But for the last two months, I've been back to normal. Healthy and strong. "What was wrong with you?"

When she opened the door, her girl Carmen walked in with a huge straw woven basket with crisp white blankets. "Hello, Brit," she said with a smile as she handed the basket to Lina. "It's good seeing you."

"It's good seeing you too," I said while I stared at the basket. *I know she didn't come way out here for a picnic*, I thought.

"Lina, I'll be out in the car." She looked at me again, smiled, then walked out the door.

"Are you going to tell me why you were in the hospital, or do I have to play a guessing game with you?"

"Brit," she said while pulling back the white blankets. "This is why I was in the hospital."

"Lina, I don't appreciate you coming to my house with this foolishness," I said, peeking into the basket and seeing two red-faced babies with thick, curly hair. I laughed. "Okay, good one. Now whose babies are they?"

She smiled, then kissed me on the cheek. "Britton, I'd like to introduce you to Amir and Amar, *your sons*." I fainted. I literally fell to the floor, hard. Sons? Not son. Sons. Lina had twins. I had twins!

When I finally came to, I still had a hard time believing her. I was insistent she was playing a joke on me. Even after she told me to do the math, I figured she could have been pregnant before she was with me. "Brit, besides you, the only person I was sleeping with was a woman." She said she got pregnant in October. We had sex in October, lots of it. Unprotected sex. The boys were born on July 18. It's now September. These calculations assured me I could possibly be the father. But my skepticism was finally put to rest when she picked up Amir, placed him in my left arm, then picked up Amar and placed him in my right arm. They both have little round, flat moles. Amar has one on his left cheek; Amir has his on the left side of his jaw. It's the Landers trademark. There was no denying it: I was their father. Father? Kids? Not one, but two. Can you believe this? My sister has another girl, and I wind up with two sons. Life is truly full of surprises. The only thing I could do was kiss her. With one son in each arm, I kissed Lina with warm, gentle kisses. Kisses of thank you. Kisses full of promise.

Now, I'm not sure what this means for Lina and me. I mean, I do have feelings for her; after all, she is the mother of my children. Wow... *my children!*

I like that. Slowly, the door to my heart opened. The chain lock was still on, but the door was open. Maybe, instead of "Love Don't Live Here Anymore," I'll try "I'm in Love Under New Management."

My father passed away last week, at the age of seventy-eight, from prostate cancer. I didn't go to the funeral, but I sent flowers. I had already buried him in my heart and mind when I boarded that plane to return here. Now more than ever, though, I'm glad I made that trip. I'm glad I was able to see the changes he made in his life and to bring closure to my own sense of loss. A part of me really felt sorry for him. But I know that there's no time for feeling sorry. It's too late. We all have to live with the choices we make in life and I've made the choice to move forward. That trip to Germany gave me the courage to move on and to learn to be who *I* need to be instead of who others wanted me to be. Regardless of what my perceptions of him might have been, regardless of what I may or may not have felt for him, the reality is he was still my father. That's something I can never change.

I've also spoken to Bryce several times and, since that night at the hotel, he's been having nightmares. We've talked for hours—actually, I've just listened. But there's nothing I can do for him. He has to work his issues out on his own. I've encouraged him to seek counseling. I told him that I didn't harbor any ill feelings toward him and that I really hoped he found peace. Because I have. The important thing is, I've learned acceptance. And I've learned to let go.

"Hello, Mom," I said.

"Hi, sweetheart," my mother said in her loving tone. "I was just telling Amira I hadn't heard from you. How's my number one son doing?"

"I'm sitting on top of the world, Mom," I said with excitement in my voice. It was torture trying to keep from telling her about my sons. But I decided I wanted it to be a surprise. I couldn't wait to see everyone's face when I walked through the door with Amar and Amir in my arms. "I'm coming home."

"Oh, baby. I'm so happy to hear that. Thank goodness. I've missed you. How long are you staying?"

"Mom, I've missed you too. Your son is coming home to stay. I'm finally able to move on with my life. I love you, Mom."

"I love you too, sweetheart." I heard the sound of tears in her voice. "Now, you hurry up home."

"Oh, I'll be home. And this time, I'm coming home without the weight of everyone else's baggage on my shoulders."

Making that call gave me a wonderful feeling because as long as I held on to the past, I was never able to see the future. But now my future is clear. I'm a parent. I'm not sure what mistakes I'll make and I'm scared to death. But one thing's for sure: I don't want to make the ones my father made. I want to live by example. I want my sons to be proud of me, not only as their father, but as a man. I want them to know the difference between manliness and manhood. I want them to know it's okay to show emotion. I want my sons to respect and love women and for women to feel safe when they're with them. I want them to respect adults and authority. I want them to understand that there are rules in life that we all are expected to follow, even when we don't agree; and they need to know there are consequences when we don't. I want them to love and respect children. I want them to understand that children *need* to feel safe. But, most important, I want them to respect themselves.

I will do my best to love them unconditionally. I will pledge my commitment to being a supportive, responsible, and loving parent. I will try to provide them a safe, healthy, and nurturing environment—mentally, physically, emotionally, and spiritually. I will make it my business to be a part of the PTA. I will see to it that my sons are properly educated at home *and* in school. If not, heads will roll. I will challenge teachers, principals, and school districts, if necessary. I will hold everyone accountable, including myself. I will always do my best to hear what they're *not* saying. And I will look to Indy, Tee, Chyna, *and* Ryan for support. I will look to my family for guidance. And I will turn to the church for spiritual guidance. I will become the most annoying parent in the neighborhood.

Children *need* adults to hear what they are not saying. They need for us to not turn our backs on them or throw our hands up in disgust. They need for us to not give up on them. Our children need and want to feel loved, wanted, and needed—unconditionally—by responsible, caring adults. Children need to know that they won't be victimized by the adults they believe they can trust. Is that too much to ask for?

25

CHYNA: VISIONS

WHEN I SAID, "EVERYTHING MUST CHANGE," I wasn't sure what would actually change. But the last year has been filled with changes. So if you're an outsider looking in, this time you'll see a woman who has made dramatic changes in her life. First, I've learned to be happy with me. It's taken me many years to get to this point. But I've finally made it. Last week, I turned thirty-seven, and Ryan threw me the biggest surprise party ever. What a surprise it was! My three sons were there. Jayson is planning to attend graduate school at NYU and announced his engagement to a beautiful girl. And she's a soror! Ryan Jr. is being stationed at an army base in New Jersey. And, interestingly, my son Kayin has been dating Britton's niece Noelle. It really is a small world.

Sarina? Well, she turned eighteen in August, and, as promised, I threw her her own huge party. But I didn't pack her bags. How could I? She's still my feisty baby girl. She didn't graduate with her class, but she went to night school and earned her G.E.D. I'm still just as proud as if she had received her high school diploma. She still achieved a goal. She's even thinking about going to college, close to home, of course. She wants to eventually become a fashion designer. Finally, she has the strength to face her future optimistically.

Indera and Tee came to my party too. My soror, my best friend, my soul sister...finally, she has a man of her own. And she's happy. And Britton, the man of the hour, waltzed in fashionably late with diaper bags and bottles. I think everyone burst into tears. Mr. I'm Never Having Kids is the proud father of two adorable sons. The love of a father is truly a powerful thing.

His "paramour," as he likes to call Lina, is in California auditioning for a movie. If she gets the part, he's going off to be with her. "Hell, why should I work? If she makes it big, she can bring home the bacon. I'll sit home, shop, and be Mr. Mom." We laughed. Yes, my dear friend is finally home.

But the biggest surprise of all was that everyone was staying for the whole week. My home was going to be filled with lots of love from family. My family. They were all going to attend my first speaking engagement on "The Adolescent Crisis." "And, you betta work them over," Indy said with a finger snap.

I was a nervous wreck when I reached the podium to address the seventy-five National Honor Society inductees and the hundred and twenty guests. But when I looked down in the front row and saw the smiling faces of my loved ones, it was lights…camera…action.

"Good evening," I began. "Many people might say adolescents have emerged as a particularly hard-to-reach population. To some extent, that may be true. Many of them have been hardened by social ills that have forced them to survive by any means necessary. A lot of who and what they are is not always by choice or by nature, but by force. So when you look into the kaleidoscope of the adolescent's life, remember that everything isn't always what it seems. We all know everything that glitters isn't always gold. Many of our youth are prisoners of guilt, hurt, shame, mistrust, rejection, and an array of other emotions. Many are misguided, mistreated, and definitely misunderstood.

"So if tonight's topic—The Adolescent Crisis: Preparing for Battle in the Field of Social Work—sounds like preparing for some kind of war, you're right, it is. I see Howard University as your boot camp and your professors as your commanding officers. It is the formal classroom training and your experiences through your fieldwork placements that prepare you for your professional roles as social workers.

"As we march into the twenty-first century, we need social workers who are armed and ready for battle. The ammunition needed to help you along the way consists of your ability to listen to others with understanding and purpose; your ability to engage clients in efforts to resolve their problems and to gain trust; your ability to create innovative solutions to clients' needs, and your ability to discuss sensitive emotional subjects supportively and without being threatening. You *must* be able to respond supportively to emotion-laden or crisis situations.

"Your arsenal must be filled with the abilities to speak and write clearly, to teach others, and to serve as role models. These are essential weapons. You must be able to provide concrete services, to facilitate environmental supports for clients, and to help people deal with social issues and conflicts.

"Indeed, you must be prepared to fight many battles in society. Because as long as there are adolescents who are being pushed through the educational system without the basic skills to become successful, as long as there are adolescents who are being thrown out of schools because they are behaviorally challenging, then it's a battle against the educational system as well.

"As long as there are adolescents carrying guns into schools, killing their parents, assaulting and killing one another, destroying and defacing property, committing rape, sodomy, and other sexual assaults, then it's a battle against crime and juvenile delinquency.

"As long as there are faces of missing children on milk cartons, as long as there are adolescents living under boardwalks, sleeping on subways, in abandoned houses, cars, and roach-infested motel rooms, then it's a battle against homelessness and runaway youth.

"As long as there are adolescents who can't receive adequate psychiatric or substance abuse treatment because insurance companies dictate and determine what level of intervention, if any, they're eligible for, then it's a battle against managed care.

"As long as there are adolescents who are abusing drugs, practicing unsafe sex, prostituting, cutting, burning, and killing themselves to ease pain, then it's a battle against self-destruction.

"As long as we have time-clock statistics indicating that every ten seconds a child is being abused, as long as the U.S. Department of Health and Human Services has reports that say, 'In 1997, among forty-three states, there were 440,944 victims of neglect; 197,557 victims of physical abuse; 49,338 victims of psychological abuse or neglect; 18,894 victims of medical neglect; 98,339 victims of sexual abuse; and 103,576 victims of unknown and other atrocities,' then it's a battle against child abuse. No, actually, this is a *war.*

"There are many other battles we as parents and professionals must be prepared to fight: poverty, racism, sexism. The list goes on. But one thing we must be clear on is the blinding truth that an increasing number of our youth are children of incarcerated adults, substance-abusing and mentally ill adults, and adults dying of AIDS. There are many harsh realities that we must be prepared to face and try to understand. Many of our youth sell drugs, prostitute themselves, and commit other crimes in exchange for food, housing, and clothing. Many of our youth run away from or abuse drugs to numb the traumas of physical, sexual, and emotional abuse and/or to forget feelings of abandonment and neglect. We must eradicate these feelings.

"In closing, I'd like to note that as long as social service agencies are being slapped with budget cuts and, far too often, being forced to put Band-Aids on emotional, mental, and social wounds that never completely heal, there will *always* be battles to fight.

"I wish you all the best in your educational and professional pursuits. And whatever battle you choose to fight, I look forward to seeing you in the trenches."

With the roar of applause ringing in my ears and a standing ovation, I smiled and took my seat beside my loved ones. Oh, yes…everything *must* change!

ABOUT THE AUTHOR

Dywane D. Birch, a graduate of Norfolk State University and Hunter College, is the author of *From My Soul to Yours*, *When Loving You is Wrong*, and *Beneath the Bruises*. He is also a contributing author to the compelling compilation, *Breaking The Cycle* (2005), edited by Zane—a collection of short stories on domestic violence, which won the 2006 NAACP Image Award for outstanding literary fiction; and a contributing author to the anthology *Fantasy* (2007), a collection of erotica short stories. He has a master's degree in psychology, and is a clinically certified forensic counselor.

A former director of an adolescent crisis shelter, he continues to work with adolescents and adult offenders. He currently speaks at local colleges on the issue of domestic violence while working on his fifth novel and a collection of poetry. He divides his free time between New Jersey and Maryland.

You may email the author at bshatteredsouls@cs.com

SNEAK PREVIEW! EXCERPT FROM

From My Soul to Yours

BY DYWANE D. BIRCH

COMING 2008 FROM STREBOR BOOKS

I

INDERA:
MY WHOLE LIFE HAS CHANGED

Hello there. I'm baaaaaaack! Live. Direct. And in your damn face! Well, don't just stand there with my door open. Come on in and take a load off your feet. Oh my God! It's good to see so many familiar faces. Did you miss me? Of course you did. Well, Chile. Fasten your seatbelts 'cause Miss Indy is in the house and I definitely have some dirt to dish. But before we get started, I would like to thank those of you who kept me in your thoughts and prayers during that whole shooting ordeal. And to all the brothas who showed me mad love. Thank you. Maybe I was a little too hard on some of you the last time we were together. Please accept my apology. Even if you wanted to slide that dick up in my...What? Don't try 'n front. It was inevitable for you to want some of this sweet sticky molasses. I ain't mad at ya, though. Now, don't get too happy 'cause I still can't stand lying, cheating-ass men. But as long as you stay in your lane: everything's peace.

But make no mistake. If there were more women out here—like me—who let you know from the gate that cheating on wifey isn't cute, perhaps you'd think twice before creeping. And the same thing goes for you cheating women. 'Cause your grimy asses are no different. Some of you trick-ass hoes have fucked over some really nice men. But that's neither here nor there for me 'cause I have more important things to be concerned about. What you do behind your closed doors and on your mattress is your business. I am only concerned about what I am doing. And the one thing I am *not* doing is sleeping with somebody else's man. Been there, done that.

Yes ladies, you are finally safe from the likes of me disrupting your homes and dogging your cheating-ass men.

Now, with all that said, sit back and kick off your shoes 'cause Miss Indy is about to get this party started, cause you know a party ain't a party until I run all through it. So, let's just do the damn thing!

Well, let me see. Where do I want to begin? Hmmm. Now, I know some of you are just dying to see what I've been up to. Inquiring minds just wanna know, huh? Well, first things first. Britton is back in the States. I'm not sure for how long though. Right now he's in California, running behind that psycho Latin love of his. I can't understand for the life of me why he is still with her. He says because she's the mother of his sons. Please. The only thing that Burrito did was spread open her legs to deliver them. Miss Goya—Oh, excuse me, Lina—is too damn busy with chasing stardom and licking pussies that she can't be bothered being a mother to her sons. Now back in my day, I would just slap her ass for playing him out. I never liked her from day one but he has told me on several occasions to just mind my business. So that's what I'm doing. I just keep my mouth shut. Surprising huh? Trust me. A few times I really wanted to sling her across the floor. But I keep things peace out of respect for Britton.

Sometimes I just don't understand him. I mean. It's not like he doesn't know that that heifer is sleeping around on him. After all, he walked in on her. Ooops! Don't let him know I told you that. He'd kill me.

Well, if his sons didn't look so remarkably like him, I'd wonder if they were his. But I guess, since she likes rubbing clits instead of riding dicks, there's no room for denying he's their father. Not that I have a problem with her being with other women 'cause, as some of you know, I had my share of the other side back in college. And let me tell you, it was good while it lasted. But to rub it in Brit's face is a bit too much. And I don't like it one bit. Well, like he said, it's none of my damn business. So, moving on.

Anyway, despite that piece of news, he's happy being a father to his beautiful twins. My godsons are so darn adorable I can't stand it. And spoiled rotten. I just love watching Britton's eyes light up every time they call out "Daddy."

Now, Miss Chyna? She is still the picture of elegance. And she is finally doing her. Ever since her first speaking engagement at Howard University, homegirl has been traveling around the country addressing the plight of adolescents. Ole glamour girl's calendar of events for her own children has been replaced with speaking engagements and tours.

Between traveling and running Soul Quests, she is making major power moves. I just love seeing this take-charge side of her. All of her kids are grown and on their own for the most part, with the exception of wild-ass Sarina. That's another story.

And I'm not going to waste my time with the details. All I'll say is, that girl just constantly keeps shit stirred up. I hate to talk about anyone's child, but she is crazier than a bedbug in heat. But that's their baby.

Outside of that drama, Chyna is enjoying life with her husband, Ryan. While their sons Jayson and Ryan Jr. are managing their four funeral homes, they're vacationing along the Slovenian Coast. I never thought I'd admit having an ounce of admiration for Ryan Sr. but times have changed. He truly loves my soror and keeping the flame in their marriage burning seems to be his only focus. All in the name of love. That's a beautiful thing. Now, their youngest son, Kayin, is finishing up his last year at Morehouse and planning to attend law school next fall. And word has it he and Britton's niece, the one that goes to Spelman...Oh, I can't think of that child's name right now. But, supposedly they are head over heels for each other. Hmm. Young love.

How sweet. If you ask me, they both sound whipped. But, you didn't hear that from me.

Okay. Moving on to my Damascus. Oh excuse me—I mean Tee. Well, he's a bonafide celebrity. You'll have to excuse me if I flip back and forth, calling him Damascus to Tee. It changes depending on my mood. Anyway, as you know he gave up that stripping scene and replaced it with putting pen to paper. His book *The Young Brotha Behind The Mask* has hit the best-sellers list. He's sold over four hundred-thousand copies of his book, and the sales are still flowing. *ChaChing!* He's just blowing up all over the place. And in between radio and talk show interviews, he's mentoring a group of teenage boys in a youth detention center and working on his next book. Oh, and get this. He even transferred his Norfolk State credits to John Jay College and completed his degree in Criminal Justice. Seeing him go across that stage to get his degree brought tears to my eyes. And you know I laced him lovely, don't you? I sure did. With a 2000 Range Rover and a Cartier. I'm just so proud of him.

Of course he still has a flock of salivating women tryna bed him down. You should see how some of these trick-ass women bat their eyes and flirt with him. It is sickening. Humph. Most of them know him with his thong on from his stripping days. And then there are those who know him with nothing on from his fucking days—and let me tell you, I never realized just how many females he had banged his dick in until *after* we got together. I knew he was a pussy fiend, but damn! Wherever we go in the tri-state, there's usually one chick who's either lusted him, sucked him or he's sleighed. Talk 'bout a male whore. Geesh! He swears most of his conquests were strictly tea bagging him (sucking his nuts) or piping him out, aka sucking his dick dry. Humph. Whatever.

Fortunately, I don't go to many of his book signings for the sake of keeping peace. I mean. It is so unnecessary the way some of these trollops just throw themselves at him. He kindly dismisses them with an autograph. I stare them down. Although, there was one time when I had to pull this sista to the side and forewarn her that she was pressing up on my man. I tried to be ladylike about it when I approached her in the bathroom.

"Excuse me." I had said. "I don't appreciate you trying to brush your titties up against my man."

Well, homegirl tried to get ghetto on me talking 'bout "so." *So?* Now it's one thing to step to someone's man when you don't know his woman's there, and it's another to do it right in her face. Particularly in mine, okay? That is grounds for an ass beating. Don't you think? So when she went to click her heels toward the door, I snatched the back of what I thought was her hair. Miss Thing yanked her big head around to face me, then snapped, "You don't know who you're fucking with, bitch."

"Really?" I responded, slapping her face with her ponytail. "Then I suggest we get better acquainted." Before she could open her mouth to say another word, I had slung her into the bathroom stall and jacked her up against the wall. I dug my nails in her throat. "Listen up, bitch. I don't fight over a man. So if you want him, you can have him. But don't ever think you're gonna disrespect me and do it in my face." I let her go. She tried to catch her breath, holding her neck. "Do I make myself clear?"

"Very," she said, glowering at me, heaving in and out. I slapped her again with her nasty-ass wig piece, then tossed it in the toilet. Bald-headed ho. She had the game fucked up, okay. Like I said. I will not fight over any man. But I'll be damned if some dick-thirsty bitch will quench her thirst at my expense.

So as you can see, I'm still the same old Indy. Still wreckin' and checkin' shit. Other than that, what's up with me? Well, you know how I do. I'm just flowin' and makin' things happen. The last time we were together, there was some discussion around me selling Weaves and Wonders. Well, I decided against it. As a matter of fact, I opened up another salon in Jersey and I'm looking at a potential spot in Connecticut. Shit. I'm a businesswoman. Okay? And trust me. This time, there is no room for anyone to steal from me. Not that I want to rehash old memories, but the last bitch who kept swiping a few dollars from the register ended up with her fingers cut off. So if anyone else is crazy enough to try it on my time, then they'll catch it too.

Speaking of catching it, that whole court ordeal with Alexi was a trip. Of course I was ordered to pay all of her medical bills for slashing her face up and I'm financially responsible for any therapy sessions she might need. That was the handiwork of my high-powered attorney. And let me tell you, she needs every bit of it.

'Cause Miss Finger-snapping, fly-guy Alexi looks a mess. Humph. She'd been better off if she had of kept the tribal gashes and slashes I gave her instead of that raggedy graft job her no-frills plastic surgeon gave her. The child looks like a circus ho, okay.

In any case, the charges of attempted murder and aggravated assault against me were dropped since it was deemed in self-defense. However, I was ordered to attend anger-management counseling—like *I* really needed it. Humph. Fine with me. But I betcha she'll think twice before pulling another cutter out. Oh, my bad. The only cutting she'll ever do *now* is with her teeth.

Chile, you should have seen that fifty-foot bitch coming into court waving her nubs in the air—being all dramatic 'n shit—tryna accuse me of being responsible for her fingers being chopped off. Do you know that she-man tried to sue me for permanent damages? Oh please. The bitch had no evidence and no witnesses, so she looked like a damn crazy-ass, fingerless fool. And then he—oops, I mean she—had the nerve to try to attack me in the waiting area when I finger-snapped her and whispered—as she walked by, "You betta work, Miss Knuckles."

Anyway, as I was saying before I got sidetracked—there's always gonna be a need for the bald and knotty-headed, hairy-faced, crusty-footed sistas to have a place to go. So why not keep 'em coming to Weaves and Wonders, right? After all, we do offer the best service around. And now with my new line-up of Dominican and African sistas on board, "Weaves and Wonders" is wrapping, weaving and braiding the hell outta heads.

I'm also still very involved in Nandi's Refuge. The crisis shelter I created—in honor of my beloved mother—almost five years ago to meet the needs of victims of sexual and physical abuse. Quiet as it's kept, my heart goes out to all of the kids who enter those doors. And I make it my business to ensure they feel safe and nurtured for the time they are with us. Yes, as hard as it may be for you to believe, I do have a heart. I'm just not wearing it on my sleeve for all to see.

Anyway, whether it's in one of my salons or at the shelter, I expect nothing but professionalism from my staff. And when it's not, all hell breaks loose. Girl, I had to go off on my shelter director when I heard Miss Thing hollering and screaming at some of the girls for not following instructions. I almost said, "Bitch, you betta check yourself, hollering at my girls like that." Instead, I waited for her to finish her tangent, then invited her into *her* office for a little supervision.

"Girlfriend, are you sucking on paint chips?" I politely asked. I figured if she were neurologically impaired from lead poisoning then I might be willing to get her the proper help she needed. When she denied it, I fired her ass. I don't know where the hell she *thought* she was, but Nandi's wasn't where she needed to be.

Many of my kids come to Nandi's to get away from the verbal abuse that goes along with whatever physical and/or sexual abuse they've been exposed to. So why the hell would I allow them to be yelled and screamed at. That chick had the mission statement fucked up, okay. So now I have the task of tryna fill the position. And let me tell you. You should see some of the whack jobs that come stumbling in for an interview. Humph. I wouldn't trust 'em with a dead hamster. So, as you can see, I am a very busy woman these days.

I know, I know. You wanna know if Tee and I got married. We did. *After* he signed a prenuptial agreement and an affidavit forfeiting any claim to any of my business ventures I made before or during our marriage. Of course he hemmed and hawed about not wanting my money. Which I'm sure is and was true. But I am no damn fool, okay. Love doesn't have shit to do with protecting my financial interest. And no man—husband or not—is going to enjoy what he didn't bring into this relationship. Make no mistake.

See. Tee will never know just how much I am worth. The only money he'll know about is the money *we* accumulate together. That's where so many people go wrong. They get so involved with someone and all of a sudden everything they've worked for becomes their partner's. Wrong answer. What you bring into a relationship is what you leave with. Especially when you're rocking a portfolio like mine.

And then there was the issue of where we'd live. He didn't want to live in Brooklyn—although he has agreed to until our home is built—and I refused to live in his brothel of a townhouse in Jersey. Because we both know, he had more tricks in and out of that den for whores than I care to know about. And, before I'd even go up in that spot, I demanded he get rid of every piece of furniture he might have been able to screw on. Of course, that just about emptied out the house. Which was fine by me. Oh, let's not forget the boxes and boxes of women's phone numbers I personally burned in the fireplace, along with his little black, booty-call book. "You won't be needing this," I snapped as I tossed it in the flames. He just smiled.

Well of course, smart-ass Tee wanted me to toss out all of the expensive trinkets I've collected over the years from no-good, lying-ass men. Now you know Miss Indy was not having that. We must have argued for three weeks before I decided to give in. So I tossed everything. I sure did. Right into storage and into a safety deposit box. Okay? Give away diamonds and minks? I think not. He must have lost his damn mind. But, as long as he *thinks* everything has been disposed of, he's happy. And I'm all about keeping my man happy. That's right. My man. Not yours. Mine.

Excuse me? Did I just hear someone say something slick? Didn't I have to read a few of you the last time we were together? Must I go there again? Oh. I thought so. Just because I'm a married woman now, don't think I still won't black on your ass. Please. Don't take me there. I'm tryna be a gracious hostess. But, if you force my hand, I'm gonna have to bring it to you. So please. Let's get along.

Anyway, after six months of house hunting and arguing over locations, we've settled on having our house built in the Fort Lee area of Jersey. Of course he didn't think it was necessary to live in a gated-community. But we've compromised. I get the gated community and he gets to have his game room. Who would have thought deciding on where to live would turn into such a big ordeal?

I still don't understand why we can't stay here. Humph. But since he wants to move, our home is gonna cost him every dime he makes on his book deals and then some.

Wait a minute. Stop the press. Before I go any further, I think we better clear the air about a few things. Now what was this mess I heard about some of you not liking me? Well, let me fill you in on a little something: Whether you like me or not doesn't make me or break me. Okay? I was fly then, and I'm fly as hell now. So don't hate the playa, hate the damn game. And this mess about me being no different than any other ho because I slept around with your man? Bitch, please.

The difference was and still is that I slept with your man to break him down. Not because I needed *or* wanted his sorry ass. Somebody needed to let him know that cheating on your dumb ass was going to have consequences. And like I told you back then, it was all about money, sex, and control. I'd run his pockets—not that I needed *his* change—then send his tired ass home to you. And make no mistake, as most of you know, a broke man was a no-can stroke man. Believe that.

Now, don't roll your eyes at me. It's not my fault your men loved trying to suck the guts out of this hot pussy. And since you wanted to go there, just remember every time you're kissing him you taste me on his lips. So, if I was a ho, I damn sure wasn't a broke one. Now flip open *your* checkbook and let's see what type of currency you working with. Another thing. If you don't like me so damn much, why the hell are you here all up in my business tryna see what I've been up to? Humph. Just what I thought: Nosey ass.

What? That's why someone shot my ass up, is that what you said? Now, let me tell you one damn thing. Yeah, I got shot. And? As you can see a bullet didn't keep a sista like me down. I'm still keepin' it movin'. So what's your point? I wasn't pressed when he pulled the trigger—well, actually, I was but I didn't let him know it. Shit. Even though I was *not* ready to die, I didn't beg his ass to spare my life, either. Please. I beg no one for nothing. So I took it like a soldier. Could you? Humph. I didn't think so.

Anyway, I guess pulling that trigger made him feel powerful. The poor thing couldn't handle having his card pulled, exposing him for the weakling he is. It's my understanding that his wife left him shortly after I put him on blast for all to see. Shit! If you ask me, he should have been relieved that I blew his cover. I mean. I just can't imagine him being happy living a double life the way he was. It was time for him to face the music and get it all out in the open so he could dance the dance—if you know what I mean. Oh well, the truth hurts. And so does a damn bullet to the chest, okay? But I'm still standing. And that's all that really matters, wouldn't you say so?

Anyway, he's out and about for the moment. But, you mark my words. It's just a matter of time before he's clipped and bagged. It's been almost three years and the police still haven't been able to track his ass but my "connections" have. Well, they *did* have him under watch up until the last four months. Homeboy is missing in action as we speak. And of course, I'm not the least bit happy about it. How the hell he dipped out is beyond me. But, like they always say: you can run, but you can't hide. So in the meantime, I'm having him hunted down like the rabid dog he is.

Excuse me? Oh, you want to know what I have in mind for him? Well, you tell me. What do you think should happen to a man who came up in my shop, shooting me, then beating me in my head with a blunt object? Hmm. Let's see. How about something really creative, something to let him know he fucked with the wrong one. Well, whatever I decide, you best believe he'll wish he never tried to come for me. Trust.

Again, as many of you know, Miss Indy is…well, let's just say I know someone, who knows someone, who knows someone who can take care of *whatever* needs to get handled. Don't get it twisted. It's just too bad he did. But for now, he can live a little. But the minute he's found, it's a wrap! I'm gonna give him his just reward for trying to leave me for dead. Believe that! So as you see, he's sloppy with his.

If he were really on point he would have sealed his mission with a bullet to my head. Now don't you worry yourself about whom I'm referring to, just know it ain't over by a long shot. And if some of you keep trying to come for me, I'm gonna have something for your ass too. Okay?

So as I was saying before I was rudely sidetracked, I am now Mrs. Indera Fleet-Miles and my wedding was the most talked-about social event for weeks…

Oh yes. My honeymoon. Well, let me just say we might have been in Europe for four glorious weeks but we spent the first eight days locked up in our suite like two wild animals, feasting on each other's lust. And believe you me; I threw this love gravy on him. Hell, mama had to go into her trick bag and show him a few things. Okay? There was no way I was letting him think he put a spanking on me without showing him how I like to really get down. But afterward, chile, listen. All I can say is, thank goodness for yoga and meditation exercises; otherwise, I'd be checking in for a pussy implant.